THE
THEORY
OF SECOND
BEST

J. BENGTSSON

The Theory of Second Best
Copyright © 2017 J. BENGTSSON

Published in the United States.
Edited by Dorothy E. Zemach.
Proofread by Chiara Hughes.
Book design by DJ Rogers.
Cover design by JustWrite Design

Printed in the United States.

ISBN-13: 978-1542354721
ISBN-10: 1542354722

DEDICATION

To my incredibly funny family! You guys are always making me laugh…and inspiring ideas for my books.

My husband, Ben

My children, Chris, Matt, and Lily

My parents, Les and Janet Wheeler

My in-laws, Maud, Erica, and Bengt Bengtsson

My brothers, Michael Wheeler and Eric Wheeler

My sisters (in-law) Michelle Wheeler and Angela Wheeler.

My nieces and nephews, Zach, Alyssa, Austin,

Adam, Gabriella, and Amelia

In economics, the theory of second best roughly refers to the idea that if the optimal choice is not available, it's possible to change some variables and make things work with the second best option. Well, that's me: Kyle McKallister, little brother to probably the most famous rockstar in the world. I've lived my life in the shadows of excellence and made a career out of being a step behind. You know, like the athlete who crosses the finish line milliseconds after the victor. Or the runner-up in a beauty pageant who stands there smiling as the winner accepts her crown.

In the words of the great Ricky Bobby, "If you ain't first, you're last." I don't subscribe to that way of thinking. In fact, I've always been okay with a second place finish. Not everyone is destined for greatness.

CHAPTER ONE

KYLE

My Brother's Keeper

"You want me to have Travis send her back?" I asked my brother Jake, as we headed to the dressing room after his show. Two hours of performing under the glaring lights had taken its toll on him. His shoulders were slumped, and his normally determined gait was heavy with exertion. Sweat clung to strands of his hair before giving way to the weight and dripping in a steady stream to the floor below. I purposefully kept my distance, knowing that Jake occasionally took pleasure in shaking his head and showering me in a fountain of his perspiration. Although I doubted I needed to worry tonight. By the looks of him, his state of mind was anything but playful.

"I don't know. She's hot, I guess," Jake replied, shrugging noncommittally, as he sponged his flushed face with a towel.

"You guess? Dude, you have warped standards."

"She just… she looks really clingy, and I seriously don't have the energy tonight."

"The energy for what? Sex?"

"For anything. I just want to sleep."

Jake had been doing a lot of that lately. Nothing seemed to really interest him anymore… not even an unbelievably hot chick. Covering up my growing concern, I opted to reply to my distracted brother with an insulting joke.

"I'm sorry. How small did you say your chode was again?"

Jake cracked a slight smile. Finally! Shit! It was taking more and more to coax one of those out of him. I had to resort to dick jokes… not that I had a problem with that.

"Anyway, I'll pass," he replied.

"Oh, good. More for me."

"Have at it."

"I will, don't you worry."

"Awesome," Jake responded sarcastically. "I'm happy for you."

"Yep. And this time, I won't have to settle for sloppy seconds," I smirked.

"Eww… god!" Jake complained, his face scrunched up in disgust. "That's just wrong on so many levels."

"Dude, what can I say? After you, they're begging me for it," I said as a smug dig.

Jake's response was a swift punch to my arm. The blow wasn't that hard, but I'd be lying if I said it didn't hurt. I wanted to rub the area to soothe the ache, but I couldn't let my brother know what a goddamn wimp I really was. Jake and I were about the same height, 6'1, both on the slim side of the body spectrum, but Jake made an effort to work out and look good. After all, it was his job to be hot up on the stage, and over the years he'd filled out nicely.

I, on the other hand, was like one of those gangly guys who'd gone through an unexpected growth spurt in a very short period of time and whose body hadn't quite caught up yet. I suppose I could put more effort into my physique, but working out really wasn't my thing. Sure, I'd lift a weight or two if the mood struck, but getting ripped was not in my vocabulary. It wasn't like I was trying to impress anyone.

There was nothing extraordinary about me, nor did I particularly care to be noteworthy. I was happy living my carefree, Bohemian lifestyle. Although referring to myself as *Bohemian* might have been a stretch; that implied I was actively trying to be hip or edgy, when in reality, I was just lazy.

Most days I simply rolled out of bed and was ready to go. Low maintenance – that was me. And since I wasn't genetically predisposed to growing a thick, full beard, the sporadic patches of whiskers on my face were generally left to fester for weeks before I got around to shaving. It was pretty much the same deal with my hair. The best way I could describe it was that it just hung there past my ears in an unruly mess.

"Don't you have to pack, or something?" Jake asked, pulling his sweaty shirt off and throwing it to the ground.

"Yeah, I'll get around to it at some point."

"You realize you're leaving tomorrow morning, right?"

"I know, hence the reason I'll get around to it *at some point*," I replied with a shrug.

"Whatever," Jake responded, looking pissed.

Oh, great! It was going to be one of those days. Recently there had been a lot of 'those' days. I studied him as he ran a towel through his sodden hair. He seemed burdened and preoccupied. Over the last couple of weeks, I'd noticed a change in his overall demeanor. Aside from the sleeping thing, my brother had been exceedingly moody. It's not like I wasn't used to Jake's particular brand of irritability, but his current behavior was unsettling, to say the least. With me set to fly back to the States the next morning, Jake would be alone with his thoughts; and that, in turn, filled me with excessive amounts of anxiety. Nothing good had ever come from Jake thinking too much.

Damn. Why did I have to leave now? Competing on *Marooned*, the popular survivalist reality show, was something I had been looking forward to since I'd been cast a few months back. After all, I almost never did anything on my own, and I figured a national television program was as good a place to start as any. That being said, I wouldn't hesitate to give it up if Jake really needed me. And I was starting to get the impression that he would struggle in my absence.

"Maybe I should postpone the trip," I blurted out.

He looked at me in surprise. "Why?"

"I don't know. I'm thinking this whole reality TV thing was a mistake."

"Since when? It's all you've talked about for three months now."

"I know, but I'll probably just embarrass myself. Maybe I'll stay on tour with you. Who wants to be a C-list celebrity anyway?"

Jake didn't immediately respond, and I assumed he wasn't going to. He was busy wiping down his guitar. Finally, though, he lifted his head and said, "I'll be fine… if that's what you're worried about."

"It's not," I lied.

Jake exhaled loudly. "I'm not suicidal. Jesus, K."

"I didn't say you were."

"Yeah, but you were thinking it."

He was right. I was thinking that. Could he blame me? It's not like he was unfamiliar with the word. Living with him all these years had been a roller coaster of ups and downs. For the most part, I found people to be fairly black and white, but Jake was more like fifty shades of gray… and not the good kind.

"So you're fine, then?"

"That's what I said," he replied passively.

"Jake, I…"

"Dude, I'm in pain, that's all. Just drop it."

"Your knee?"

He glared at me like I was breaking some unstated agreement. Jake always made the rules… and typically, I was in no position to refuse.

"What else?" He shrugged.

"You need to get it fixed."

"Duh."

"So then why don't you?" I pressed.

"With what time?"

"Make the time. Your fans aren't going to split if you take a few months off."

Jake was laying his guitar carefully in its case. When he finally looked back up, his eyes were dulled in somber resignation. "I know. I will… after the tour."

I nodded. *Yeah, sure you will.*

The room got quiet. The pained expression on Jake's face actually hurt me. I was acutely connected to his moods.

It had been this way for years and was the reason why I worked so damn hard to keep his environment upbeat. We could talk and joke all day long about the stupidest shit, but when it came to discussing things that troubled him, Jake was fiercely guarded. Sometimes I wondered how his head didn't just explode from all the years of built up pressure.

"I think you should go on the show," he replied, his voice void of emotion.

"You do?"

"I do."

"I don't know," I hesitated. "I'm just…"

"Kyle…" Jake interrupted, his impatience boiling over.

"Dude. I'm having second thoughts, okay?"

"Because of me?"

"Not because of you."

Jake huffed as he shook his head. I didn't know why I bothered lying to him. He always saw right through me.

"Okay, maybe a little bit because of you," I confessed. "I mean, you have to admit, you've been kind of a shithead lately."

"All the more reason to leave," Jake mumbled, frowning.

"I was kidding. Don't be so sensitive."

He grimaced and turned away. "I want you to go. It'll be fun."

I eyed him skeptically.

"Uugghh!" Jake made a weird throaty growl before picking up his sweaty shirt and throwing it at me.

I ducked just in time.

"I hate when you do that," he complained.

"What did I do?"

"You act like I can't manage my life without help," Jake replied, shaking his head. "But we both know I'm the fucking king of coping."

I raised my eyebrows at him. That was certainly the understatement of the century. I wanted to ask him if he ever got tired of just *coping*, but of course I knew such a question would never be answered. As close as we were, there were lines that were not to be crossed. I knew those limits, and the fact that I didn't push them was most likely the only reason he kept me around.

"And besides, if I needed a babysitter, I certainly wouldn't hire you for the job. I'd get myself a hot Swedish nanny." Typical Jake – always trying to redirect the discussion away from anything real.

I laughed anyway. "Okay. Fine. I'll do the show."

"Thank god."

My brother picked up his phone and turned away from me. I stood there staring at him. Without even looking up, Jake said flippantly, "You can leave now."

I scoffed.

"What?" He glanced up.

"Don't pull that *star* bullshit on me."

"I wasn't," Jake mumbled. "I just really want you to go."

Well, fuck you too. I didn't budge – not because I was making a stand for my self-worth, but because I refused to let him win.

"Seriously? You have nothing better to do than annoy me?"

I shrugged. "Not really."

Refusing to engage me, he replied with edge in his voice, "Fine. Stay. I really don't give a shit."

"Cool." I pulled my phone out and leaned against the door.

Finding a game to play, I was halfway through it when I heard Jake groan, "Really, Kyle?"

His glare was icy.

"What? You said I could stay."

I realized I was being annoying, but with Jake, my motto had always been *There's no such thing as bad attention.* I just wanted to make him feel something, no matter how negatively it reflected on me.

"I seriously can't wait to watch you crash and burn on national television," he huffed.

"It's going to be a train wreck," I conceded.

Jake looked up from his phone with an honest-to-god actual smile on his face. *Score!*

"Of epic proportions," he agreed. "It'll be awesome."

"I really hope I don't let you down."

"Oh, you won't. When it comes to making an ass of yourself, you never let me down."

We both laughed at that.

"Chances are I'll get voted out of the game pretty quickly anyway."

"Nah. You kill at swimming. Your team will need your mad skills in the water."

"Something tells me once my teammates find out you're my brother, they won't give a crap about any of that. They'll assume I'm a millionaire and kick my ass off the island."

"So don't tell them then."

"Well, I don't plan to, but you know me and secrets."

Jake laughed. "Oh, shit. Yeah, you're screwed."

I nodded. "And even if I manage to keep my mouth shut, strategic thinking has never been my strong suit."

"Uh-huh. That's for sure. You can't even pack your bags."

"Why are you so obsessed with that? Jesus. It's not like I need all that much stuff. I get one outfit for the entire show, and I already know what it's going to be."

Jake whipped his head around in alarm. "You're not going to wear that stupid t-shirt and the short shorts, are you?"

Of course I wasn't, but Jake didn't need to know that. I grinned and shrugged like it was already a done deal.

"Oh, my god, Kyle," he whined. "Do you have to be such a dipshit?"

"Hey, you said you couldn't wait to see me make an ass of myself, so there you go. You're welcome. Besides, you don't even know which t-shirt I was talking about," I teased, although we both knew which one he was referring to — my current favorite, a t-shirt with a beaver holding onto a log with the caption *Are you looking at my wood?*

Jake rolled his eyes. "The beaver one."

"Seriously? You don't like that one?"

"You know I don't."

"You have to admit it's funny."

"For a ten-year-old boy, maybe, yeah."

I grinned. "Okay, if you don't like the beaver t-shirt, what about the one with the bucks on it?"

"Nooo," Jake laughed. "That one's even worse."

I shook my head emphatically. I thought that one was hysterical. I didn't know what Jake had against it. What's better than two bucks checking out a doe and stating, *I'd hit that?*

"Can't you just try to be normal for once?" Jake asked, looking way less wary and annoyed.

I hesitated like I was pondering the seriousness of his request. "I… I guess I could try."

Jake grinned. "Get out. I have to take a shower. And go pack, you idiot!"

Wandering into the green room, I plopped down on the couch. I was in no hurry to pack my bags. Honestly, I was never in a hurry. Playing second fiddle to my handsome, successful, talented older brother meant there were zero expectations on me. And contrary to what people might think, I frickin' loved it! I'd made a pretty goddamn good living out of doing jack shit. My job mainly consisted of following Jake around all the time, which I would do whether I was getting paid to or not. Hell, I had been shadowing him my whole life. Why stop now that he was rich and famous?

Even as a toddler, I'd idolized Jake, and I'd shamelessly followed him around like an attention-seeking puppy. I'd taken hero worship of my big brother to a whole new level. Jake was the golden boy – charming, handsome, and talented. Everyone loved him. I was none of those things; and yet, for whatever reason, having no labels to call my own rarely bothered me. Somehow my worth had become tangled in his splendor. I basked in his glory, never striving for any of my own.

Although there were only eleven months separating us in age, Jake was the mature and composed brother and I was the hyperactive mess. If there was trouble to be had, I made damn sure I found it. I hadn't been a malicious kid, just a dumb one. The reckless choices I'd made never resulted in anything more than a few days of house arrest implemented by my irritated parents… that is, until that day. Flashes of it filled my senses with dread.

No. I never went there. My mind wouldn't allow it. I shook off the memory and sealed it back up where it belonged – far away from the life I lived today.

Refocusing on happier times, I remembered what a poser I'd been. Whatever Jake did, I copied… until it came to music. There was no competing with him in that regard. Don't get me wrong – I tried. I really did. And I guess I could be considered a decent guitarist by everyday standards; but I had never been up against average. When you grow up in the same household as a prodigy, even the smallest of accomplishments seems mundane in comparison. And it was clear from a very young age that Jake was truly gifted. Obviously, when the musical fairy was sprinkling her talent dust, she bequeathed Jake with a double dose. And I, of course, got none.

From my spot on the couch, I scanned the gathering of people in search of the hot chick from earlier. Had she made it past security? Sometimes the guys would let the smokin' ones slip by just for the viewing pleasure of our beauty-deprived roadies. And, bless their hearts, some of those hotties even occasionally went slumming, hooking up with a roadie when they couldn't nail down one of the more desirable members of the tour.

Yeah, there was definitely a hook-up hierarchy on the road. It started on the low end of the spectrum, with the sweaty, overweight truck drivers; moved up a step to the dentally challenged roadies, followed in equal parts by the more 'put-together' tech guys, managers, and security guards; and then on to the highly visible, and coveted, band members. Those guys got probably ninety percent of the booty to be had on any given night, leaving the others to fight for the leftovers.

Jake, of course, was the holy grail of hook-ups. It was, after all, his show. But given that he was so damn picky and cranky most of the time, getting into his pants was like winning the lottery. And who was there to pick up the pieces when the rock god didn't magically appear to whisk them away into a life of riches? That's right. Me. The consolation prize. See, just before the ninety percent trickled down to the band mates, they filtered through me.

That was the truly awesome part of my life: I got to share in the spoils. I didn't have to *be* a rock star to live the life of one. Hell, I was more into the lifestyle than Jake was. All I had to do was mention my last name, and boom – instant respect. Well, maybe *respect* was too strong a word. It was more like instant curiosity.

Really, the only obstacle with these singularly fixated ladies was getting the focus off Jake and onto me. First I had to get past all the annoying questions about Jake and then all the nauseating begging to go back and meet him. Once the desperate women understood that their chances with Jake were nil to none, I started looking a whole lot more appealing… certainly not ideal, but better than nothing.

I yawned and glanced around the green room. The crowd inside had almost doubled. I didn't recognize anyone; but then, why would I? These were people lucky enough to get backstage passes: VIPs, contest winners, people with connections… and, of course, hot chicks. Tonight's group milled around excitedly, waiting for Jake and the other band members to make their appearance. My brother was not done performing yet, and this was clearly his least favorite part of the night. He wasn't good at interacting with strangers on a social level. At times it was almost painful to watch. But there were reasons behind his awkwardness, reasons that had shaped his personality and pushed him inside his own head. Jake's life, for all its riches and awards, had not been an easy one. The kidnapping had turned his life upside down. I doubted anyone outside our family really understood what it took for him to stand in front of those people every night and make them feel welcome.

Once this group cleared out, the room would fill up once more with our crew, who would devour the buffet like starving tomcats. Jake was usually gone by then, slipping out and retreating to the quiet of the tour bus. Sometimes I stayed and hung with the guys, but more often than not I took my exit when Jake took his. My place was, and always would be, beside my brother.

CHAPTER TWO

KENZIE

My Mother's Daughter

Rain! Always rain.

My hand swiped over the foggy glass, heavy condensation trapped inside its panes, as I attempted to get a better idea of what I was dealing with… a steady spattering of rain or a torrential downpour? Did it really matter anyway? It wasn't like a ray of sunshine would be poking out from behind those dark clouds anytime soon. I wrinkled my nose at the offending smell radiating off the windowsill. Mildew was growing around the corners of the window, eating away at the wooden frame. The moist environment in which I lived was a breeding ground for the fungus. No matter how diligently I scrubbed and bleached, the black, moldy dots were always lurking, just waiting for the minute I turned away so they could creep back into their cozy spot by the window.

"Sunny California, my ass," I complained.

Growing up in the shade of the Coastal Redwood Forest, my tiny town in Northern California saw three times the rainfall that other parts of the state did. It felt like I'd been damp and cold the vast majority of my life. And although I lived a few miles from the ocean, there were no beach days for me. Even if the sun occasionally made an appearance out from behind the gray, heavy fog, not only was the sea-water freezing cold but the waves and riptides were unruly and dangerous. It always brought a knowing smile to my face every time a Hollywood movie made California out to be one big sunny beach resort. That wasn't the place where I lived. Not even close.

I stubbornly strapped on my big-city stilettos. I'd already been forced to change my planned outfit, the yellow sundress – it was summer, after all – to accommodate the downpour, but I wasn't budging on the shoes. My slim, straight khaki pants and flowing white top needed something to dress it up, and rubber boots just weren't going to cut it. I couldn't help but worry that my pointy toed pumps, although a fairly modest four inches, were way too ambitious for a girl like me. I was more the jeans and t-shirt type of woman, who preferred the comfort of flats to the sexy of stilettos. Maybe if I had someone to dress nice for… but as it was now, I could wear a burlap sack with Birkenstocks and no one would care.

Leaving the gloomy window behind, I plopped back down at my vanity and evaluated myself in the mirror. My naturally straight hair was now styled in big, bouncy curls that flowed down my back, and my makeup was spot-on after I'd taken the extra step of going online and studying the trends before applying. I nodded my approval as I went through my mental list. Hair? Check. Make-up? Check. Outfit? Meh. Kick-ass female? Check. Yep, I was sufficiently impressed with myself today, and that didn't happen too often. Normally I kept my preening in front of the mirror to a minimum because, really, on a day-to-day basis, there wasn't much to admire; but today – damn, I was feeling good. Maybe there would be a single guy out there who'd want to buy a little of what I was selling. Hold up! That didn't sound right, did it? I needed to cool it with the self-important inner chatter. Besides, a guy now would not be good timing, what with me leaving in a month. *That's funny, Kenzie.* I actually laughed at the mirror. As if I'd be finding me a man any time soon. Suddenly I wasn't feeling so full of myself. I stuck my tongue out at my reflection and then got up and grabbed my purse.

My heels made an annoying clicking sound through the kitchen, signaling to all in the house that I was indeed moving through it. My father, who'd been sitting at the table on his computer, looked up from his screen and stared.

"Mackenzie?" he asked in surprise, as if my beauty transformation was so stunning he no longer recognized me.

"Who else would I be?" I replied, slightly offended.

"I'm just... wow, you look so pretty," he said, appearing genuinely gobsmacked.

Again irritation spread through me. Sure, I didn't dress up often, but he didn't have to act like I'd started out as a warthog. Looking 'pretty' was my little sister Caroline's job. Mine was forty hours a week managing a rental business with untold amounts of unpaid overtime, followed by household chores and helping my younger siblings with all their insignificant teenage problems.

"Are you sure you want to wear those shoes? It's raining outside."

"I'm aware, Dad, but I can't wear rain boots to a television interview," I snapped. I didn't know why I was being so testy with him, but certainly the last person I wanted fashion advice from was a guy who'd worn the same basic outfit of Levis and plaid shirts for the last twenty years.

My dad put his hands up and made the face he always gave me when he thought I was being unreasonable.

"And besides, if you'd allowed them to come here to the house to interview me, I wouldn't have to go out in the rain."

"Look around, Mackenzie. Would you really want them coming here?"

Even though I didn't need to, I still took that look around and my resolve faded. No, I definitely didn't want the cameras in here. This was a house that was bought and furnished by a man… and not by just any man, but by a man with no style. Nothing in our home matched; everything had once been broken and then repaired back to an even shabbier replica of its prior dingy self. The carpet had not been replaced in all the time we'd lived here, and if I had to guess, it had probably graced these floors for longer than I'd been alive. None of us were certain what color it had actually started out as, but now it was decidedly a chocolate brown shade. And worse still, my dad's idea of home décor was displaying his children's school artwork on the walls with a single thumbtack. Over the years the flimsy paper had folded inward, and the original masterpiece could only be seen by smoothing it out against the wall.

"Hey," he said, interrupting my thoughts. "Relax. Everything will be okay."

He knew me well. I was scared. My shoulders drooped. Being the center of attention had never been my thing, and the idea of having someone interview me about my life sent shock waves of fear blasting through me. Granted, only viewers of our local county news station would see the interview, but still, for me, it was a huge deal. What was I going to say? I led the world's most boring life. In

25

fact, that's how I'd made it onto *Marooned* in the first place: I sent in a video of myself basically documenting my dull, small town girl existence and somehow that caught their eye. I was convinced that the fact that I'd never ventured further than three hundred miles in any direction from my hometown in all my life was what sealed the deal. I would be their token 'fish out of water' contestant.

And now here I was about to embark on the adventure of a lifetime. Thirty-nine days on a deserted island, living off the land, scrounging for my own food, and surviving with just the clothes on my back. There would be no bathrooms, stifling heat, and cameras in my face 24/7. Damn, that sounded awful. I mean really, just… yuck!

The truth was, I was far from an adventurous person. The only reason I'd applied in the first place was because the money I could potentially win on the reality show far outweighed the misery I was about to endure. That cash would not only provide for my family and secure their future, but it would be just the push I needed to finally make my stand and escape this monotonous life.

I looked up to find my dad still staring right at me with that surprised look in his eyes.

"What?" I asked impatiently.

"I never really noticed how much you look like your mother until today."

A lump instantly formed in my throat, and I fought the urge to cry.

"You're so much like her. Do you know that?"

"I know," I whispered my response. "You tell me all the time."

"But I never really saw the uncanny physical resemblance until today."

The far-off, pained look in his eye softened my resolve. I walked over and hugged him. "You still miss her so much."

"You don't just get over the love of your life, Mackenzie."

"No, I don't suppose you do."

We stayed quiet for a moment, remembering the woman we both loved.

"I know you're going to argue, but I'm just putting it out there again. You need to start dating."

"No one can replace her."

"I'm not saying replace. I'm saying move on. It's been sixteen years, Dad. Someday we'll all be grown and out of the house, and then you'll be alone."

"You'll never leave." My little brother Cooper burst into the room in order to make his thoughtless observation. I glared at him, bristling at his suggestion that I'd be an old maid living at home with Dad for the rest of my life. He flashed me his signature cocky smile as he ran his fingers through his brown overgrown hair. Cooper was in dire need of a haircut, and at that moment I wouldn't have minded shaving it clean off his head for him.

"Well, theoretically, Coop, I could find a guy and get married and have a family of my own."

"Yeah, I guess, theoretically," he shrugged, grabbing a snack from the cupboard.

I didn't know what I'd been hoping for, but it certainly wasn't such an apathetic reply. But then what could I expect from Cooper? He was the world's most self-absorbed sixteen-year old.

"You looking for a date?" He asked our father. "My English teacher, Miss Marshall, is single, and she's sort of hot if you like them old."

"Miss Marshall's in her early forties," Dad chuckled. "I'd hardly call that old."

Cooper shrugged again. "Whatever floats your boat, Pops."

Dad looked like he wanted to argue, but there was no winning with Cooper. He didn't have enough going on inside that brain of his to have a decent debate. "Anyway, let me know. I'll hook you up."

"Wow, so tempting. Where's your other half?"

Dad was referring to Cooper's twin brother, Colton. The two were identical in every way and never far from each other. When they were babies, the only way to tell them apart was by tying a length of colored yarn to their ankles. To this day I'm not sure if we switched them around a few times in the beginning.

"Locked in the shed," Cooper replied, matter of factly. He graced us with his third noncommittal shrug of the day.

Both Dad and I gaped at him.

"Is there a reason he's locked in the shed?" I asked, still unclear if I needed to be worried or not.

"Yep."

"Cooper," I scolded. "Why is your brother locked in the shed?"

"Because he was trying to shove me in there first."

My sister Caroline breezed in. "Hey, does anyone hear that banging noise?"

"That would be Colton. Apparently he's locked in the shed."

She startled at the information. "And we're okay with that?" she asked, with a raised eyebrow.

"Not necessarily," Dad said. "Cooper, you have thirty seconds to explain before I lock you in there myself."

"He got mad because my clothes were on his side of the room, so he threw them out the window. I made him go get them, but then he tried to shove me in the shed, so I pushed him in instead. The lock was hanging open, so I swung it shut and locked him in."

Cooper seemed to think it was a perfectly legitimate excuse for imprisoning his sibling. Dad's face turned hard. "Get him out now."

"You want me to go out in the rain?" he protested.

Dad gave him the death stare.

"Fine." Cooper stomped off.

We hurried over to the big window facing into the backyard and watched Cooper set his brother free. Colton came out swinging, and the two boys began rolling around in the mud and rain. Dad shook his head, disappointed but resigned, and then calmly walked over and locked them both out of the house.

"You look pretty," Caroline said to me, seemingly unfazed by her brothers' shenanigans. Certainly she was used to them. Caroline was six minutes older than Colton and ten minutes older than Cooper. Yet despite the miniscule age gap, she was more grown up than the two of them combined, although that wasn't saying much as Caroline was hardly the model of maturity. She was a typical impassioned teen with a flair for the dramatic, as evidenced by her repeated use of the words 'basic' and 'squad.'

As Caroline complimented me, she flipped her long brown hair back with the flick of her hand. I soaked in her youthful beauty. It had taken me all day to look presentable, yet she made it seem effortless. Caroline and I shared the same overall features, but that's where our similarities ended. My sister had the confidence of a girl who'd lived her life in the limelight. Being a triplet made her unique. When they were little, the three were like little shining stars. Wherever they went, fanfare followed. Of course everyone in this close-knit community knew our story. My parents had grown up here, and my mother's untimely death had been a blow to the entire town.

"Are you sure I can't come with you? I want to see the studio," Caroline said, as she spruced up my curls with her fingers.

"You can't. I'll be too nervous as it is."

"You better get over it, Kenzie. You're going to be on national television in a few months."

"Don't remind me," I groaned.

"Are you kidding? I'd kill to go on that show."

"Like you could survive a month without your phone."

Caroline made a face, covered her cell with her hands, and whispered, "Shh, you're going to hurt her feelings."

The boys started banging on the back door to be let in, and I took that as my cue to leave. The last thing I wanted was for their filth to rain down upon my outfit. I slipped out the front door and dashed through the downpour to my car. Once in the dry vehicle, I thought about my family. I'd never spent a day away from them, and now, not only would I be gone for nearly two months, but I was also planning to leave them altogether after the show was completed. I wondered if I would have the courage to leave them behind to follow my own path. God, I hoped so.

The interview took about ten minutes. Apparently my life was so boring I couldn't even get my fifteen minutes of fame. I was peppered with questions about the show and the recruiting process, and I happily answered. Slowly I was adjusting to the camera and feeling more comfortable in front of it. At least, until I was hit by a query I hadn't expected. This was supposed to be a lighthearted fluff piece, not an exposé. Yet the reporter began describing my mother's death as if were the most natural thing she could speak of. My stomach clenched in grief, as it always did when someone mentioned her.

"Do you think losing your mother in such a tragic way has conditioned you to seek out adventures in your own life?"

I wanted to laugh in her face. If anything, her loss had driven me inwards and created a more cautious person. What I was doing – competing on *Marooned* – had nothing to do with my mother and everything to do with myself. I'd spent too many years living the life that was supposed to be hers. No more. From now on, my future was mine to make.

CHAPTER THREE

KYLE

Family Matters

Walking up the ramp at LAX, I could hear them before I could see them.

"There he is," Mom sighed in relief.

"Where?" Dad asked in his signature clueless tone.

"Over there!"

"Where? I can't see him."

"Oh, my god, Scott," Mom's irritated voice echoed.
"He's literally right there!"

Dad kept searching the crowd until I magically appeared before him.

"Oh, there you are," he beamed.

Mom rolled her eyes.

A smile spread across my face. *Those two!* "Hi, Mom. Hi, Dad."

"Kyle!" Mom came in for a hug. "Ahh. Look at you! You're taking the scruff to a whole new level, aren't you?"

"Nice to see you too," I grinned.

She pulled on my sorry excuse for a goatee. "What's this thing called?"

"I call it Jim."

Mom laughed. "Well, will 'Jim' be joining us for Mitch's wedding?"

"I don't know. I haven't thought that far ahead."

"Maybe you should start now, since it typically takes you a while to make big decisions," Mom teased.

"Are we really having this discussion?"

"I just want you to look nice for your brother's wedding. That's all."

"No one's going to care if I have whiskers, Mom."

"Yeah, Michelle," Dad grinned. "They'd first have to get past his ugly mug."

I playfully gaped at my parents as if I was offended. "Wow, such heartfelt greetings. Really, guys, you outdid yourselves this time."

Dad swallowed me up in a hug. "I missed you, kid. How's your brother?"

"Doing good. He says hi."

"I called him today, and he totally brushed me off," Mom complained.

"I can't imagine why." I made a face.

"Did he really have a TV appearance today, or was he lying to get me off the phone?"

As far as I knew, Jake didn't have anything going on, but I wasn't about to throw my brother under the bus. "Oh, yeah, he did, actually."

"You're such a bad liar, Kyle."

I laughed. I really was. "Honestly, I have no idea what his schedule is. I stopped looking when it no longer directly impacted me."

"Well, once he gets to Arizona, he won't be able to evade me," Mom jested, using her best crazy stalker-lady voice.

"You keep talking like that and I'll help him hide," Dad countered.

"Yeah, yeah. Come on, Kyle, let's get you home. I need to fatten you up before you get on that show."

"I heard it's better to go into the competition already starving, so you don't crash and burn the first day out there."

"Listen to yourself, Scott. You want to send our son off half-starved onto an unforgiving, deserted island?"

"Well, when you put it that way…" he grinned.

"I think he's trying to kill me, Mom," I pouted, sidling up to my protector.

"No, Kyle, I just know you," Dad said. "And you're definitely the type of person who would blow his chance at a million dollars for a spoonful of peanut butter."

I spent the following two weeks meeting with producers and medical staff and getting briefed on the rules. Because I'd been away on tour, I had some catching up to do in order to be ready to go with the rest of the contestants in three weeks. The producers gave me a little leeway, no doubt because of my connection to Jake.

I had first been approached to do the show by a talent scout after one of my brother's Los Angeles concerts. The guy pretended not to know who I was, saying only that he thought my edgy look would play well with audiences. I wasn't fooled for a second. Of course he knew. I didn't stand out in a crowd. Really, there was very little that distinguished me from any other twenty-something guy on the street. Hell, the only interesting thing about me wasn't me at all... it was Jake.

But dignity had never been high on my list of musthaves. It made no difference to me how I got the gig; it only mattered that I got it. And I jumped at the offer. It's not like I had much else to do. I mean, technically I was 'working,' but it wasn't like the tour couldn't go on without me. I was hardly an integral part of the team. The only one who would miss me was Jake… and even he probably wouldn't miss me all that much.

⸻

"So I gotta know – whose bright idea was it to rent a car and drive to Arizona for the wedding?" I asked, while shoving a piece of bread in my mouth. Mom had been doing an excellent job of fattening me up. I tore into my plate of steak and potatoes as I awaited the answer.

"Yeah, that's what I want to know too," my older brother, Keith, pitched in.

"I thought it would be fun," Mom answered, shrugging.

"You thought it would be *fun*?"

"Yes, Kyle, like old times."

I gaped at my mother. "Clearly you don't remember old times."

"I don't know what you're talking about."

"Um… the motorhome trip?"

Keith laughed. "Oh, god, not the motorhome trip."

"What? I haven't heard this one," Keith's girlfriend, Sam, perked up as she asked.

"It's nothing," Mom said, dismissively waving her hand in front of her. "Kyle's just being dramatic."

"Dramatic? Mom, come on. Dad took the whole side of the house off!"

"It wasn't the whole side of the house," Dad said, in an attempt to downplay the story. "It was just some paneling… and the water spigot."

"Okay, what?" Sam laughed.

"Dad borrowed a neighbor's old motorhome one summer, and we went on a road trip," Keith explained. "But before we even left on the trip, the neighbor was showing Dad how to fill the water tank. So they took a hose, attached it to the spigot in the front of the house, and then forgot about it. Anyway, a few minutes later, the neighbor left, and Dad invited us all in to go on a test run."

"Oh no," Sam gasped. "He didn't take out the hose?"

"Not only did he forget to take the hose out, but he drove off and the spigot and part of the house was trailing behind us for a couple of blocks before someone flagged us down. When we got back to the house, there was water shooting straight up into the air like a geyser."

"Yeah, that was pretty bad," Mom conceded.

"The whole trip was like that. The right blinker didn't work, so at night Dad would make one of us sit in the front seat holding Grace's blinking princess wand out the window when he wanted to change lanes," I recalled.

"Or when the air conditioning stopped working. It was 108 degrees outside, and we were beyond miserable. We complained so much that Dad got pissed, pulled into a 7-11, and bought us all ice blocks," Keith added.

A confused looking Sam asked, "What did you do with the ice blocks?"

"I don't know. We played with them, I guess, stayed cool. Was it you or Jake that got their tongue stuck to the block?"

"Jake," Mom laughed. "I had to pour water over it to unstick him."

"Oh, man. See how fun those trips were?" Dad smiled, reminiscing. Poor guy. He was already in his fifties. What else did he have to look forward to in life?

"No, they weren't fun at all," I teased, although, in reality, I found our family travels pretty hysterical. "It's only funny now because we're not currently living through it. That's why I don't understand the whole road trip to Arizona thing. Why can't we just fly?"

"Because I have gifts for your brother's wedding that I don't want to put in luggage. You will survive, Kyle."

"Geez, you're so whiny," said Dad. "All that luxury has spoiled you, boy."

"I know," Keith agreed. "He's such a pansy-ass."

"Whatever," I huffed. "But the car better have air conditioning and a working blinker."

"I think we can manage that."

The following day, as I climbed into the SUV with my siblings, I considered my father's less than flattering assessment of my spoiled, surly behavior. I had noticed a change in myself lately as well, although I'd been reluctant to acknowledge it. Blaming it all on Jake and his seesawing behavioral swings was the easy way out, but now I was wondering if some of my jaded attitude was actually wearing off on him. Jake had always counted on my upbeat personality to lift him up. Maybe this time away from each other would be good for both of us.

After an argument amongst the five of us over who got to sit where, Keith and Emma pulled rank, choosing the best two seats for themselves. My choice was no legroom in the far back, sitting next to Keith who got the coveted spot closest to the power outlet, or plenty of legroom in the middle seats but having to squeeze in three to a row with my sisters. In the end I picked the middle row since Grace didn't take up much space. I watched in amusement as she crawled right into the crappiest seat without even the slightest protest, as if she'd learned long ago to accept her lot in life as the lowest McKallister on the totem pole.

As I buckled in, I again silently bemoaned the current travel arrangements. I'd become accustomed to a certain standard of travel, and this definitely wasn't it. As Jake's platonic free-loading plus one, I was used to being waited on and catered to right alongside him. If he stayed in nice hotels or flew first class, so did I. We didn't even discuss it. Jake just always bought two of everything, one for him and one for me. Realization dawned on me. *Holy crap.* I was a kept woman. No, worse — I was a skin tag, stuck to my brother like a fleshy little growth! Suddenly this road trip seemed like an exceedingly good idea. I mean, I needed to man up, and quickly. In only a week's time I was going to be wiping my ass with palm fronds.

———

As it turned out, the trip wasn't as bad as expected. In fact, the first two hours were spent joking around, and I was feeling pretty good about my new found self-awareness. If I could survive a car ride in exceedingly close quarters with my siblings so effortlessly, certainly I could endure over a month without deodorant and toothpaste.

However, four hours in, mind-numbing boredom turned my mood sour. As a way to pass the time, I started rating my siblings' grating behaviors. Grace, the youngest at fifteen years old, was on her phone most of the time. Her fingers flew over the keyboard at lightening speed, and aside from the many times she turned the camera for a selfie or a Snapchat, Grace only occasionally looked up from the screen. Clearly she was the least irritating of the bunch, and on a scale from one to annoying, she rested nicely at a one.

My oldest sister had her earplugs in and slept the majority of the trip. A nurse, Emma had just come off a night shift before making the thirty-minute drive from her house in the valley to ours. I actually hadn't seen her since returning home from Europe. Neither one of us could be bothered to make the trip, nor were we particularly enthusiastic to see one another whenever our paths did cross.

Since Emma was zonked out most of the time, she really should have scored low on my informal behavioral graph. However, because she sporadically awakened from her hibernation to growl menacingly at the rest of us, I had no choice but to add points to her overall total.

Keith was chugging right along, being his normal jovial self, and would have scored low on my sibling resentment chart had he not brought the sunflower seeds into play. The suck-crunch-spit combo was bad enough, but once stray bits of slimy seeds that hadn't made it into the narrow spout of the water bottle started landing on the back of my neck, I lost it. Keith had definitely tipped the scale, and not in his favor.

But, as it turned out, the youngest McKallister boy had us all beat. Evidently, sixteen-year-old Quinn was going for gold. On his Spotify app, my little brother had successfully discovered the world's most annoying song: *I Like to Move It*, sung by the Chipmunks. Not only did we get to hear the song in its original glory but we also got to hear Quinn's unbelievably grating rodent version.

I had to admit, it was funny the first time. But not so much after the third. By the sixth time, I was looking for blood. Regrettably, with Quinn sitting in the back row furthest from me, I was too far away to do any real damage.

"Oh, my god," I yelled. "Would somebody please hit him?!"

Without missing a beat, Keith reached out and smacked Quinn.

"Ow!" he screamed, punching back.

"Quinn, if you sing even one more note of that song, I'm dropping you off at the next rest stop!" Dad threatened.

"Keith hit me! Don't you even care?"

"Actually, I do. Thank you, Keith."

"You're welcome, Dad."

I laughed. Over the years our dad had morphed from concerned, doting father to just one of the guys. It was as if seven kids broke the 'dad' right out of him.

"Way to be supportive of my singing abilities," Quinn grumbled to whoever would listen, which happened to be no one. "You wouldn't treat Jake that way."

"Jake doesn't sing like a goddamn chipmunk!"

<hr />

After arriving at the hotel in Arizona, Keith and I decided to make a clandestine beer run. Wandering the aisles of a local grocery store, Keith was acquiring quite a stockpile. Liquor aside, he was throwing chips, candy, and baked goods into the mix.

I flashed him a quizzical look. "You're not planning on getting crossfaded tonight, are you?"

"No, why?"

"I mean, the amount of liquor and munchies you've got here makes me think you might have a secret stash somewhere too."

Keith laughed. "You're shitting me, right? Do you know what Mom would do to me if she found out I brought doobies to Mitch's wedding?"

The thought did actually make me cringe. Mom would definitely not appreciate a stoned Keith. None of us would, really. Keith had a sketchy past when it came to drugs. A few months after Jake's miraculous escape, Keith had decided to add his two cents to the tragedy by going off the deep end himself... and weed was the least of his problems. Two stints in rehab followed before he finally got himself back under control. He'd been clean for about four years now, and when I say *clean*, I mean it in the most liberal of terms. I guess you could say Keith was 'California clean,' in the sense that he, along with a fair portion of the population in this left-leaning state, didn't actually consider pot to be a real drug. Although Keith could occasionally be found toking up or drinking heavily at times, he made a concerted effort to keep that behavior away from our parents, who were not as liberal in their beliefs when it came to Keith's unhealthy pastimes. So when Keith claimed that Mom would not appreciate such conduct, it was no joke. In fact, I suspected if he got caught with weed at Mitch's wedding, we'd probably be planning his funeral soon thereafter.

"Sam's been on a health kick lately, and she won't allow any crap in the house. I haven't had sugar in a month."

"So you plan to eat all this by tomorrow night before she gets here?"

"Yep."

My eyebrows arched in response.

"What?" he asked, sounding genuinely surprised that I cared.

"Dude, grow some balls. I'd never let a chick tell me what I can and can't eat."

"Uh huh, just you wait."

"For what? To be castrated by my girlfriend? No, thanks."

"No – to love someone enough to want to change for them."

"You're not changing!" I exclaimed in a high-pitched voice. "You're literally hiding five pounds of junk food from her."

"Exactly. I love her enough to eat this away from her and never let her know."

At the checkout, Keith pulled a trashy magazine off the rack with Jake's picture on the cover. He shook his head. "What's this bullshit?"

"More of the same, I'm sure."

I watched Keith flip through the magazine until he came to the article featuring Jake. I studied his face for a reaction. First came the clenched jaw, then the furrowed brows and flaring nostrils. When would he learn? Keith had been gripping the sides of the magazine tightly before he slapped it shut and replaced it on the rack.

"Why'd you look in the first place?" I shrugged.

"I don't know. I guess I was hoping it might be a positive article for a change."

I shook my head. I'd learned a long time ago not to take the bait. Nothing that was written about Jake was true, so why bother stooping to their level and reading the lies? "Yeah, it's not gonna happen."

"Does he see this crap?"

"He can't *not* see it."

"How does he react to it?"

"I don't know. He doesn't say."

Keith gave me a curious look. "Ever?"

"You know Jake. He doesn't exactly share his feelings."

My brother shook his head. "You'd think after all this time it would get easier."

"For who? Him? Or us?"

CHAPTER FOUR

KYLE

A Mind Reader

We woke early the next day to eat breakfast with the other half of Mitch's family. Mitch was my half brother and my father's oldest son. We didn't see a lot of him growing up and whenever we got together it was always a little awkward. My dad and Mitch's stepfather, Tony, had never really gotten along. I didn't know the specifics, but the story I'd been told was that Tony had tried to force my father to relinquish his parental rights when Mitch was five. Tony was marrying Mitch's mom and wanted to adopt her son. Dad refused, and a lifelong feud ensued. One thing was for sure: Tony had been more of a father to Mitch than ours, and their close relationship was clear to see.

By the time we arrived at the church for the rehearsal later in the day, my eyes were droopy. Keith and I had stayed up late into the night drinking and eating his junk food. Since nothing of significance was currently happening, I lay down on a pew and closed my eyes. I could not have been relaxing for more than a minute when I sensed an evil entity hovering over me. I opened one eye and then quickly closed it upon seeing who was standing there.

"What are you doing here, Emma? Did someone leave your cage open?"

There was dead silence. Clearly Emma was formulating a comeback but wasn't nearly as quick as me.

"You know, Kyle, I'm jealous of the people who don't know you."

"That's all you've got?" I shook my head. "So disappointing."

"Get up."

"No. Find your own pew."

"I want this one."

"Go away! I'm sleeping."

"We got here two minutes ago. How could you possibly be asleep already?"

"When it comes to relaxing, I'm like an Olympic athlete."

I didn't have to see Emma's face to know she was rolling her eyes at me.

"Can you please leave? You're sucking up all my oxygen," I complained.

Emma huffed and grabbed my legs and swung them off the bench, nearly knocking me to my ass, and took a seat where my feet had been. I was actually forced to perform a backward pushup on the bench to keep from falling to the floor. It was the most exercise I'd gotten all week. I sat up and sneered at my sister.

"What?" Emma shrugged innocently. "I haven't seen you in months. I thought we could chat."

"And you couldn't talk to me yesterday? We were in the car for seven hours together."

"I wanted to talk to you privately."

"Oh, well, why didn't you say that in the first place?" I whispered, like we had some pressing secret between us. "You're finally coming out? Good for you."

She ignored me and stated condescendingly, "I heard you got a job."

"I heard you got a boyfriend," I shot back, and then paused dramatically. "Oh wait…"

A disgusted scowl transformed Emma's smug face. "I'm not looking for a boyfriend."

"Yeah, well, I'm not looking for a job."

Emma and I glared at one another. This had always been our thing. Rarely did a civil word pass between us.

Even as kids, we'd never really gotten along. As far as I could tell, I was the only sibling she disliked. Of course, I'd be the first to admit I probably deserved that distinction. Starting from about five years of age, I'd made it my mission to raise her blood pressure at every opportunity. She was just too easy to annoy. But Emma was no pushover, and she was certainly not above employing tactical warfare to put me in my place. We were two completely opposite human beings. How we'd come from the same parents was a mystery to me. In fact, the only thing we had in common was our undying devotion to Jake.

Interestingly enough, it was probably that same devotion which also drove us apart. Emma had been three years old when Jake was born, and she'd doted on him as if he were her very own real-life baby doll. And then I came along, with my hyperactive antics, and ruined everything.

"Have you talked to him since you left?" Emma asked.

"Yeah. I've been texting him. Why?"

"He's all right?"

"I think so. His knee is flaring up again."

"I figured."

"He promised me he'd get it taken care of after the tour."

Emma nodded, nervously tapping her nails on the bench in front of us. "I talked to him the other day."

"And?" I questioned impatiently.

"He didn't sound great."

My stomach tightened. "Why? What did he say?"

"Nothing alarming. He just seemed drained."

I nodded.

"So you noticed it too?"

"Yeah. He's been moody."

"Like 'moody' moody, or 'we should be worried' moody?"

I cringed, knowing exactly what she meant. Memories of a not-so-distant past still fresh in both our minds. "He's okay. I think."

"You think? That doesn't make me feel better."

"I don't know what to tell you Emma," I shrugged. "I offered to drop out of the show and stay with him, but he insisted I go."

We sat there staring up at a mural of Jesus on the wall, neither of us speaking. I hated the feelings she stirred up in me. An anxious thumping attacked my heart. If something happened... if Jake did anything stupid... I'd never forgive myself. By the look in Emma's eyes, she shared my unease.

"It's been crazy at work, but maybe I can take a week off." Her voice was riddled with uncertainty. "I'll talk to Mom, and we'll work out a schedule while you're gone."

"He'll love that." I frowned. "Not to mention he'll see right through it. You know how much Jake hates it when he thinks we're checking up on him. I mean, he's kind of accepted my constant irritating presence, but you two... oh, yeah, he'll be pissed."

Emma sighed. "I know, but what choice do we have?"

"Well, we could trust him."

"Can we?"

It wasn't an unreasonable question. Jake had given us all a run for our money in the days, months, and years after the kidnapping. Suicide attempts were not an uncommon occurrence in our household. It had taken a comprehensive and proactive effort, on all our parts, to keep him alive.

"He's okay, Emma." I tried reassuring her although I wasn't entirely sure myself. "The tour has been rough on him, that's all."

"I still don't understand why he didn't take more time off between tours."

"Jake's all work and no play," I replied, shrugging.

"That's what I'm worried about."

"What's done is done, Em. Nothing we can do about it now."

"I just don't like him being out there, on the other side of the world, alone."

"Me neither, but he has Lassen. Not to mention he's an adult. We can't babysit him forever."

Emma nodded, grudgingly agreeing with me. "Where is he anyway? He was supposed to be here hours ago."

"I don't know," I replied sarcastically, reverting back to the asshole I usually was with my sister. "I'm not telepathic."

Emma pursed her lips and shook her head in clear disappointment. "I was just asking, jerk!"

Thank god. We were back to being adversaries. Sharing feeling and opinions with Emma was like conceding defeat.

Lost in uncomfortable thought, I didn't see the woman walking up to me until her beauty blocked my view of Jesus. I blinked. Holy hell! Had I just been sent an angel? My eyes zeroed in on her ample rack, which was spilling out from inside her shirt. Nope. This was no angel I'd been sent. How did He know?

Emma kicked the side of my leg, possibly to remind me she was still there. I tore my attention away from my new favorite person long enough to motion, with the flick of an eye, for Emma to get lost. Looking immensely offended, she refused to budge. I gave her a not-so-gentle shove. Emma shot me the look of death before rising off the bench and stomping away indignantly.

"Hi, I'm Sarah," the blonde greeted me, like I was supposed to know who she was.

I stared at her blankly.

"Your partner for the wedding," she added, flashing me an irritated grimace.

"Oh, yeah, hey. I'm Kyle," I replied, standing up and eyeing her greedily. Her legs were long and shapely, and her waist was impossibly tiny. Or maybe it just appeared that way because her breasts were oversized for her thin frame. I lingered on her beauty a moment longer. She looked as if she'd just walked off a beach, her skin shining in a golden hue offset by her glossy blonde hair.

As I was finishing my thorough inspection of the attractive woman before me, I realized she was doing her own assessment of me. I could already tell by the expression in her eyes that she was not nearly as impressed with me as I had been with her. I had to assume, just by the looks of her, that few people met her high standards. My chances of being above that line were iffy at best.

Her eyes flicked over me as if she were deciding whether I was worthy of talking to or not. "So you're Jake's brother, right?"

"I am," I affirmed.

"Well, at least I got a brother," she mumbled under her breath.

"What?" I asked, hearing what she'd said but pretending I hadn't.

"Nothing."

I stuck my hand out to greet her. "It's nice to meet you, Sarah."

"Yeah, you too." She put her hand in mine and stared right through me. "So, um… where is he? He's supposed to be here, right?"

"Who?" I feigned ignorance.

As if she'd just tasted something sour and unpleasant, Sarah's face contorted. "Don't play dumb. You know who."

Damn, girl! She was kind of intimidating. I liked it. "Oh. Yeah, I guess."

"What do you mean, you guess? He's your brother, right?"

"Yeah, but I don't keep him on a leash or anything."

That face again. Geez. This chick didn't play around.

"So we're partnered up then?" I asked, trying to move the topic of conversation off Jake and onto me.

"That's what I was told," she shrugged. "Unless you have other information."

"No one tells me anything."

Sarah's face relaxed a bit and she cracked the tiniest of smiles. It was a nice look on her. "You probably think I'm being rude, don't you?"

"No. I get told off all the time. I'm used to it."

She assessed me more carefully now. "Yeah, you have that whole doormat thing going on."

I laughed.

She sighed heavily. "Look, I'm sorry if I'm being a bitch. I'm just annoyed right now. I was supposed to be partnered with Jake, but then Mitch paired him with someone else. Not cool."

"Yeah, that sucks," I replied sarcastically. "And now you're stuck with me."

"Are you mocking me?"

"Yeah, maybe a little bit."

Furrowed brows let me know she was not happy with my response.

"Oh, come on. It could be worse. You could've been paired with that guy." I pointed to one of Mitch's friends who looked like he'd only recently been forcibly removed from his video consol.

That actually got a laugh from Sarah. "That's very true," she acknowledged, and then looked me up and down. "Yeah, I guess you'll do."

"Wow, I'm flattered."

"Are you a musician, Kyle?"

"No."

"So what do you do, then?"

"Not a whole hell of a lot."

"That's your answer?" she laughed.

"Well, it's the honest answer, and I thought we were being real here."

"Oh, were we?" she replied, with just a hint of flirt.

"You've spent the entire conversation talking about my brother, so yeah."

She smiled again, but this time it was genuine.

Buoyed by a newfound confidence, I added, "And for the sake of transparency, I think you should know that I'm a mind reader."

"A mind reader, huh?" she asked, seemingly fascinated.

"Yep. And I know what you're thinking, Sarah."

"Do you now?"

"Uh-huh, and yes, I will sleep with you."

She giggled as she nodded. "Wow, aren't you the optimistic one!"

"Just psychic is all."

Eyeing me with more interest now, Sarah said, "So what is your sixth sense telling you about me?"

"It's telling me that you're a whole lot of trouble."

"Oh, you have no idea."

"So, Sarah, how can I talk you out of my brother and talk me into you?"

She grinned. "You're smooth."

"I try very, very hard."

Sarah took me in, studying me, and for a moment there, I thought she might actually be contemplating my offer. Would she really swear off Jake for me? There was a first for everything. But then Sarah went the predictable route. "Since we're being real with each other, I'm just letting you know now that there's no talking me out of your brother."

"You and every other girl in the world," I replied, nonchalantly.

That gave Sarah pause. "Yeah, well, I'm not like every other girl."

I scoffed. "You are in his world."

She seemed taken aback by my words.

"Look," I said sighing, "This isn't my first rodeo. I know the whole routine. You're going to hit on my brother. He's going to turn you down. You're going to come running back to me when you realize you've run out of options."

She shot me a dirty look. "Trust me, I never run out of options."

I didn't doubt it. "Well, okay, then, good luck with that," I replied, as I walked away from our conversation.

"What's that supposed to mean?" she called, actually chasing after me.

I turned back to face her. "No offense, Sarah, but you don't stand a chance."

"Oh, really? And how do you know that?"

"Because I know my brother," I replied honestly. Sarah had all the qualities that Jake disliked: shallow, bitchy, over-confident. Although that didn't necessarily disqualify her from a one-night stand, it definitely didn't help her cause. I, on the other hand, wasn't nearly as picky. I could easily overlook her obvious personality flaws for a few minutes of fun.

"You have no idea what I am capable of," she smiled smugly.

"Oh, I have no doubt you're capable of great things," I replied, grinning. "But bagging my brother won't be one of them."

"You underestimate me," she replied indignantly.

I couldn't help but be impressed. She wasn't giving up easily. "All right, then, like I said before, good luck with that."

I walked away from Sarah without another word. I knew that I'd done enough to plant the seed of doubt in her mind. And once Jake shot her down, like I hoped he would, I was going to look a hell of a lot more appealing.

The rehearsal began, bringing Sarah and me back together. Gone was the bitchy, Jake-obsessed groupie. In her place was a flirty, clingy Sarah. She was laying on the charm now, laughing at my jokes and whispering dirty nothings in my ear. At one point she even grabbed my ass, when no one was around to see. I wasn't sure if her little display of playfulness was for my benefit or a way for me to put a good word in for her with Jake... although, come to think of it, that would be a strange way to go about it.

Whatever had created Sarah's change of heart, I was happy for it. She was undeniably smokin'! My dirty mind was conjuring up all kinds of scenarios, and each and every one of them included a naked Sarah.

As soon as the rehearsal was over, she steered me behind the one of the doors in the back of the church and boldly pushed me up against it.

"You're actually sort of hot," she stated, oozing sex appeal.

It wasn't much of a compliment, but I decided to take it anyway.

"Yeah?" I responded stupidly.

"Uh huh."

Sarah's lips grazed my neck and her hand slid down my back. My body shuddered. Light kisses enflamed my craving. When her lips touched mine, I eagerly took her in. Our tongues were a tangled mass. The heat between us was smoldering and intense, so much so that when her hands dipped further down, I fought the urge to find the nearest pew to throw her onto.

In the name of fairness, my hands snaked down her body as well, but Sarah was not as welcoming to me as I'd been to her. Establishing her boundaries, she swatted my hands away immediately.

Not one to be deterred, I took my chances and copped a feel of her ample breast. Sarah didn't have a chance to slap my hand away, for the moment I laid my hand on her chest, I heard a horrified gasp, shocking me from my flesh-filled bliss.

"KYLE!"

Sarah and I whipped our heads in the direction of the wail. Emma was standing there, open mouthed, with a look of incredulousness on her face. I realized my hand was still on Sarah's boob, and I quickly removed it. Emma's own hand was covering Grace's eyes as if she were protecting some innocent toddler from irreparable harm. Grace, in all her teenage swag, grabbed Emma's hand and pried it away. She immediately laughed when she saw me in an uncompromising position.

"You're in a church, dummy! Geez. Use your brain," my sister blasted, before she grabbed Grace's arm and shuffled her off to the bathroom.

"Well, that was awkward," Sarah smirked, not looking the least bit embarrassed. "Your sister's kind of a bitch."

I didn't appreciate her comment. No one got to shit on Emma but me.

"Nah, she's cool," I defended.

Shrugging, Sarah brushed her perfectly straight hair back with her hand. She screamed high maintenance, like the basic white girl who straightened her straight hair with a straightener.

"Well, it's been fun," she said, adjusting her shirt and turning to walk away.

"Seriously? You're leaving now?"

"You heard your sister. Besides, it's probably a sin."

"Somehow I don't think you care about that sort of thing."

"I don't." She grinned. "See you at dinner, Kyle."

"Yeah, okay," I called out. "Maybe we can find a more private spot later."

"Maybe," she answered without turning around. "If you're lucky."

I watched her well-rounded booty sashay its way out of the church. *Yeah. I'd be very lucky.*

CHAPTER FIVE

KYLE

The 'Prodigy' Son Returns

As always, Jake's arrival later that evening was met with shock and awe. He'd been delayed for hours in airports around the world trying to get to the rehearsal on time. By the look on his face when he strode through the restaurant, it had not been a good day. Getting pounced on by a fangirl the minute he came through the door didn't help matters. I could almost feel the stress radiating off him. Jake carried way too much weight on his shoulders for a guy his age. That's where I came in. And Keith and Emma and Mom and Dad. We were Jake's safety net, a place for him to relax and feel normal.

I knew better than anyone that Jake craved that normalcy. People tiptoed around him, always worried about offending or upsetting him, like he was some fragile flower. And at times, he did seem shaky. But there was also a strength to him that defied all logic. What he had endured was beyond what any human should have to endure, yet he was still going… still surviving.

After Jake greeted the family, he and I walked over to Keith and Quinn.

"You look like you've had a good day," Keith sarcastically commented.

A genuine smile formed on Jake's face. He replied with just as snarky a tone. "Do I?"

"Oh, yeah. You're just glowing."

"Uh-huh. Scoot over," he said as he settled into a seat beside Keith. Of course he would pick that one. Jake had always looked up to Keith, and I'd be lying if I said I wasn't jealous at times. Where Jake often had a level of disdain when interacting with me, he always treated Keith like his shit didn't stink. I'd smelled it… it did.

I hadn't always been Jake's right-hand man. When he was just getting popular and I was too young to go on tour, Keith had been the one to travel with him. Yeah, *that* had been a clusterfuck. Keith had only recently come off his first rehab stint, and traveling on a rock and roll tour was just the push he needed to jump right back into the druggie lifestyle. A second rehab followed, and Keith was never invited back.

I took my seat next to Jake, but because his back was to me, I was effectively shut out of the conversation. "Sit back," I complained. "I can't hear."

Jake groaned as if my request was totally unreasonable, but nonetheless he leaned back in his chair to accommodate me. His eyes focused on my face and I saw them squint as he studied me with interest. "Hold up. What happened to your little baby beard?"

"You mean the one that looked like pubic hair growing all over his face?" Keith added, helpfully.

"That would be the one."

"Mom made me shave it off… some bullshit about shaming the family name. I don't know, I wasn't really paying attention."

Jake grinned.

"Why? Do you like it?" I asked, theatrically rubbing my hand over the smooth skin.

"Well, I mean, it doesn't look like you crawled out of a gutter anymore."

"Sweet." I nodded as if his opinion really mattered.

Jake grabbed a chip out of a basket and dipped it in the salsa. "So where's Sammy?" he asked Keith.

"She's flying in tomorrow."

"Wait. Was that allowed?" Jake asked in a raised voice.

"Not for you, it wasn't."

"Well, shit." His eyes narrowed in on our mom as he gave her a dirty look. "It shouldn't be allowed for Sam either, then."

"Do you see a ring on her finger?" Keith asked, smugly.

"No. Do you see a ring on mine?"

"You were born into this family. There's no escape."

Jake stopped his conversation with Keith. "What are you leaning on me for?" he bristled, pushing me off him.

"You keep turning your back. I can't hear," I said, straightening up.

"You're, like, lying on top of me. It's annoying."

"You want to talk annoying? I've watched you double dip not once, not twice, but like fifteen fucking times."

"I wasn't double dipping."

"News flash. When you dip a chip twice, that's double dipping," I challenged.

"If you must know, I took a bite, flipped it, *then* re-dipped it, asshole." Jake's words dripped contempt.

"That's still double dipping," I mumbled under my breath. Jake ignored me and turned his back, shutting me out of the conversation again. My instinct was to smother him in a big, gushy hug to really piss him off, and I would have had we been alone, but since there was a rather large audience, I refrained.

"What took you so long, anyway?" Keith asked.

"Honestly, I have no good explanation. Today just sucked ass. So many damn delays. I'm surprised I even made it."

"Like you had it so bad," I scoffed. "You didn't have to drive seven hours in a car with Quinn."

"Wait," Quinn, sitting on the other side of Keith, objected. "What did I do?"

"Seriously? The chipmunk song?"

"Oh, yeah," he grinned.

"Do I even want to know?" Jake asked.

"Not unless you want him to sing it for you."

"Oh no, I don't want that. Never mind."

"You guys just don't appreciate good music, the way Jake and I do," Quinn joked.

"Do *not* drag me down with you!" Jake exclaimed.

We all laughed. Jake leaned back in his chair, stretching out. I could see the stress lines in his forehead slowly receding. His tight shoulders opened up and gradually relaxed, and the forced smile he had carried since arriving had disappeared completely. This was a good start. Maybe a more pleasant mood would follow.

"Anyway, I have a game for us to play later."

"Shut up, Quinn. No one's talking to you," Keith kidded.

"Seriously. It's fun."

I glanced around. Neither Jake nor Keith looked the least bit interested in Quinn's version of fun, so I took pity on him. "Okay, I'll bite. What's your game?"

"Bean Boozled."

"Oh, god no!" I blurted out, laughing.

Looking confused, Jake asked, "Bean what?"

"Bean Boozled," I answered. "It's that game where you spin the wheel and there are two jellybeans on each stop. One is a good flavor like peach or blueberry, and the other is like vomit or baby wipe. And you don't know what you'll get until you put it in your mouth."

"You're joking, right?" Jake asked, not seeming amused.

"No. Sadly, I'm not. And apparently, the flavors are pretty spot on, too."

Jake had a confused look on his face as he shook his head. "And this is supposed to be fun?"

"That's what the kid says." I shrugged.

"It is," Quinn tried. "It's really funny, I promise."

"No offense, Quinn, but I wouldn't play that game if you put a gun to my head," Jake countered dramatically. Seriously? Did he have to use that reference?

"You guys are fun suckers."

———

Multiple times throughout the dinner, I tried to get Sarah's attention. And, although she smiled at me a few times, her focus was almost entirely on Jake. I knew I shouldn't be surprised, seeing as Sarah had been very candid in her intentions, but after the church encounter, I'd mistakenly believed that she was into me.

Dinner hadn't been over for more than one minute when my church hookup threw herself at my big brother. Unexpected pangs of jealousy crept in through my bones. Even though it was to be expected, Sarah's lack of consideration took me by surprise. Typically I didn't let things like this aggravate me. I wasn't stupid. I knew I didn't bring much to the table in comparison to my brother. I got why women would want him over me. I mean, why settle for the spark when you could have the flame?

I stood off in the distance, pissed, silently praying that Jake would shut her down like I'd predicted he would. I knew it shouldn't bother me… yet this one stung a bit. Who was I to think a woman would be into me for me?

"Nice girl."

Emma was suddenly beside me, motioning toward Sarah.

"Are you here to gloat?" I replied glumly.

"No."

"Yeah, right."

"I'm not. I promise. She was totally leading you on earlier, Kyle. That's a bitch move. You can do so much better than someone like her," Emma said sympathetically, and then added, "And if Jake even thinks about it, we'll do a tag team takedown."

I laughed. That was the nicest thing she'd said to me in, like, forever!

CHAPTER SIX

KYLE
The Tale Of Two Jellybeans

When Jake first told me about Casey after the rehearsal dinner, I was immediately suspicious of her intentions. They'd met in the restaurant moments after Sarah had tried flinging herself on him. Apparently the two were paired together for the wedding party, and Jake had been instantly hooked. I'd never seen him have such an immediate attraction to anyone before, so naturally, I was dubious. I didn't know exactly how she'd drawn him in, but I felt sure that she was playing him. And judging by the spellbound look in his eyes, Jake was buying into her game. What was it about this girl that captivated him?

He'd literally met thousands before her, and not one had ever sparked his interest. Not even his ex-girlfriend, Krista, who had basically wormed her way into his life without Jake even realizing what was happening. If I'd had to hear him complain one more time about not being able to break it off with her, I would have done it for him!

Once Krista was gone for good, there had been no others. Occasionally he had one-night stands, but Jake seemed completely uninterested in another relationship. So his uncharacteristic attraction to Casey blew my mind and made me question her motives. Was she tricking him? Could she be an undercover reporter? I needed to figure out her angle. If this Casey girl thought she was going to mess with Jake, she'd be going through me first.

That evening, I was hanging out with my brothers in the atrium area of the hotel lobby when Jake saw her walking by and pointed her out. Oh, yeah, how convenient. She just magically appeared? I wasn't buying it for a second. This girl was probably a stalker… a goddamn savvy one… but still a stalker. The sooner she was exposed as a fraud, the better. No sense in Jake getting all amped up over this girl if she was just going to crush him.

Much to Jake's horror, I called her over and was all prepared to squash her like the cockroach I assumed her to be when something totally unexpected happened. The girl was legit, and the chemistry between them was off the hook. I immediately saw in Casey what Jake had seen. She had a glow to her that lit up the room. I watched in amazement as the two flirted their way through the conversation.

And Jake? Damn. Keith, Quinn, and I watched in awe as our normally beleaguered brother proved that he actually had some honest-to-god game when it came to women! He matched her wit step for step. Jake interacted with us like this, but never had I seen him charm a girl. Feeling giddy with optimistic fervor, a stupid smile was stamped on my face, and I was seriously contemplating giving Jake a high five for a job well done.

The only time my brother ever came close to the flicker he had with Casey was when he performed on stage. But those were small snippets of light, reserved for his fans who would never get close enough to him to even benefit from the glow. Sometimes during those moments, I'd stand mesmerized at the side of the stage and watch Jake with the same dopey smile I had on my face now and pretend he was still the same electrifying kid he'd once been, before his life was stolen away so cruelly.

At some point during our lively conversation, Quinn's bean game appeared on the table. He sure wasn't giving up easily.

"No way!" Casey squealed. "I love this game!"

"How am I the only person who's never heard of this?" Jake asked.

"Not just you. My ninety-eight-year-old grandma hasn't heard of it either."

Jake grinned. "Well, that explains it, then, since we run in the same circles and all."

"Exactly," Casey beamed. Her pretty oval shaped face lit up when she smiled. I grinned like a fool every time she flashed her deep dimples. She exuded happiness. Casey was the polar opposite of Jake in every way, yet somehow she seemed perfect for him.

"Are we going to play this, or what?" Jake asked, completely reversing his earlier decision. So much for the gun to his head.

Quinn jumped to attention. "Really? Okay."

"So who starts?" Keith asked. "I think it should be youngest to oldest."

"Oh, of course *you* do, grandpa!" I blasted.

"I don't know," Jake teased. "Casey loves this game sooo much. I think it should be ladies first."

Casey grinned. "All right. You're on!"

She spun the wheel, and it landed on two brownish-orange jellybeans. Quinn read the flavors.

"You are either going to eat tutti-fruitti or sweaty sock."

The rest of us burst out laughing.

"Sweaty sock?" Jake questioned. "How would the creators of the game even know what that tastes like?"

"Please, Jake," Casey interrupted. "I need absolute silence. It's incredibly important to be in the zone."

Amusement danced on Jake's face. He was really digging this girl. We all were. Silence ensued as Casey took a deep breath and gamely popped one of the two beans in her mouth. It was clear from the first bite which one she got.

"Tutti-fruitti, bitches!" she declared happily as she high-fived the rest of us. "Now I get to pick."

"Wait, who made you boss?" Jake asked.

"It's the rules."

"According to who?"

"Me," she laughed.

"Does anyone else have a problem with this?"

"No," the rest of us yelled out, knowing that by allowing Casey to choose, Jake would be the next to go.

"Awesome. Okay, so I'm going to choose… oh gosh, who should it be?" Casey asked, with a wicked smile on her face. "I just can't decide…"

"Just give me the damn spinner," Jake replied, as he grabbed the game.

His spin landed on two dark green ones.

"Oh, shit!" Quinn exclaimed, looking sufficiently nervous. Because Jake hadn't been around much when he was growing up, Quinn didn't have the close relationship with him that Keith and I had. As a result, he always seemed to be looking for validation of some sort.

"What? What did I get?"

"Well, yours are juicy pear…"

"Gross, I hate pears," Jake complained.

"Actually, Jake, that's the good flavor." Quinn winced.

"What's the bad flavor?"

"Booger."

"Booger?" Jake asked in astonishment.

"Yeah," Quinn said, apologetically.

"So let me just clarify here. I won't know until I put it in my mouth if I am eating pear or booger?"

"That's the game, dork," Casey pitched in, supportively. "Get on with it."

Jake gave Quinn the stink eye before popping one of the two jellybeans in his mouth. Because he gave nothing away in his expression, it was impossible to know what flavor he was eating. We all waited expectantly. No reaction.

"Oh, my god!" Casey screeched. "The suspense is killing me."

"Well, I'm no expert, but I'm pretty sure I just ate booger."

"Don't sell yourself short, J, I'm sure you've eaten plenty of boogers in your lifetime," I offered helpfully.

Casey rolled with laughter before asking, "Was it sweet?"

"No. Definitely not sweet," Jake grinned.

"Then you ate booger."

Jake put his hand over his mouth like he was going to barf, and then started laughing.

Again, I was taken by complete surprise at Jake's playfulness. Earlier he'd almost had me assassinated for suggesting he might possibly be double dipping a chip, and now he was eating boogers with glee.

"Okay, my turn to choose. Quinn, you're up. And I really hope you get the barf bean, you little jerk! Does anyone have any water?"

"I have whiskey."

"That's even better."

While Jake took a pull of whiskey to get the taste of booger out of his mouth, Quinn spun the wheel. He got the option of rotten egg or buttered popcorn, and wouldn't you know it, he got buttered popcorn.

"Nooo!" Jake whined. "How is that fair?"

"It's the game," Quinn said shrugging, as he finished savoring his tasty bean.

"A rigged game," I grumbled. I had yet to play, and I knew my time in the hot seat was quickly approaching.

"How can I rig jellybeans, Kyle?" Quinn asked, mocking in a snooty, teenage way.

"Yeah, Kyle," Casey added, mimicking Quinn's tone. "How can he rig jellybeans?"

"Jake, will you please keep that girl quiet?" I teased, as I spun the wheel.

"I'm not sure if that's possible."

Casey's nose crinkled when she smiled. I had to admit it was pretty cute.

And as luck would have it, I landed on skunk spray or black licorice. "Of course! Two flavors I totally hate."

"Right," Keith joked. "Because he's tried skunk spray on multiple occasions."

"I'm just saying, no matter what, I lose," I complained.

"Oh right, 'cuz I totally won with my booger bean." Jake rolled his eyes.

I ignored him, cracking my knuckles and popping my neck in preparation. With an overly exaggerated breath, I picked up the jellybean and, plugging my nose, popped it in my mouth. As soon as I started chewing, heat rose up through every bone in my body. My skin tingled. My ears felt like they would burst into flames at any moment.

"Oh, god. Skunk. It's frickin' hot skunk. It burns," I gasped, real fear gripping me. "I'm not kidding, guys. I think my insides have caught fire."

But nobody was listening to my pleas because they were all hysterically laughing at me, no one more so than Quinn, who was literally rolling on the floor. Now I understood why he liked this game.

Jake handed over the whiskey and I took a swig, which only made it burn worse. I grabbed my throat and made dramatic gestures of dying. Again, my torment was only met with laughter.

"Water! Water!" I panted, frantically trying to wipe the taste of butt spray off my tongue with my fingers, but nothing eliminated the burn. Frantic, I dipped my hand into the atrium's koi pond, scooped up some water, and flushed my mouth with soggy fish shit.

Quinn's hysterics hit a fever pitch. I wasn't positive, but I was pretty sure he might actually have peed himself a little bit. Which would have served him right, the little shit.

"You're going to have to get used to that, Kyle," Keith said, after catching his breath. "They're going to make you eat all kinds of crazy crap on the show."

"Nothing… and I mean *nothing* will be that disgusting," I said coughing. "Let's see how funny it is once you spin!"

Keith grabbed the spinner and took his turn. I felt somewhat redeemed when he got the baby wipe flavor. He tried to play it cool like Jake had, but quickly broke down and had to rinse his mouth with whiskey like the rest of us.

"Well, thanks, Quinn. That was awesome," I said, expressionlessly.

"You're just pissed because you ate skunk spray. I found my booger quite pleasing," Jake joked.

"Oh, did you?" I challenged. "How about another round then, J?"

"That's okay. I'll pass."

"Hey, how come you call each other J and K, but Quinn isn't Q and Keith isn't K-squared?" Casey asked.

"They've been doing that since they were seven or eight," Keith shared. "J-K, get it?"

"Huh?" Casey's face was twisted in confusion.

"Just kidding," Jake elaborated. "J. K."

"When we were kids we used to get into all kinds of trouble, so we came up with the tagline J K to ease the punishment," I explained.

"No way!" Casey laughed. "That's ingenious."

"Yeah, it really wasn't," Keith countered. "They tried that shit on me when they destroyed my skateboard, and I still beat them both with what was left of it."

"Oh, yeah, I forgot about your skateboard," Jake laughed. "We set it on fire, right?"

"No. You blew it up." Keith frowned as if he were remembering the day quite clearly.

"How'd you manage that?" Casey asked.

"With a firework," I explained. "We strapped it on, lit it, then sent it down the ramp. It was awesome until it exploded… then it was epic."

"The firework was called the Red, White, and Bomb! What did you expect?" Keith complained.

"Why didn't you use your own skateboards?" Casey asked.

"We didn't want to ruin ours. Geez, Casey. Use your brain," Jake teased.

"Oh, right. Of course. Sorry."

"And they thought their little tagline would save them." Keith shook his head. "So naïve."

"I don't remember any of this," Quinn whined.

"That's because you were still walking around with shit in your diaper," I said.

"I missed out on everything! It sucks that I'm so much younger than you guys."

"Yeah, well, at least you have your whole life ahead of you. We're all old and washed up," Keith said with a dramatic sigh.

"Oh, yeah, a group of hot, young washed-up has-beens," Casey laughed, fanning her hand in front of her face. "If we could all be so lucky."

———

In the elevator, after saying goodbye to Jake and Casey, the three of us stood in the glass box with big, dumb grins on our faces.

"Well, that was unexpected," I offered up.

"Yeah. What the fuck?" Keith replied, looking dazed. "Since when is Jake a player?"

"Since never."

"He was so damn flirty with her, I thought I was in some alternate universe."

I nodded. "I've never seen him act like that around a woman."

"I know. When he was with Krista, he could barely control his boredom."

I shook my head, having trouble grasping the striking change in Jake's demeanor. It had been a long time since I'd seen that side of him. Sure, he laughed and joked around with us, and to an untrained eye, he might seem fine; but Jake was a master at concealing his darkness. Sometimes I wondered if I was the only one who knew it still festered. But tonight... Casey... she'd brought the brightest of lights, and for the first time in what seemed like forever, Jake didn't squint away.

Hope flowed through me. I wanted this for him so much more than I wanted it for myself. His pain was my pain, and as evidenced tonight, so was his happiness. Our lives were entwined in ways no one, not even our parents, understood. Only Jake and I knew what had really happened that day – the sacrifices that had been made. Our whole lives could be traced to that one, terrible moment in time... a moment so cruel that neither one of us had ever dared speak of it since.

"I liked her," Quinn said, interrupting my dark memories. "She was the only one tonight who was nice to me."

"Aw." Keith laughed and wrapped Quinn in a hug, adding a knuckle rub to his head. "We're only mean to you because we love you."

"That's messed up."

"Would you rather be ignored?" I offered.

"Are those my only two options?"

After dropping off Quinn and his moronic bean game, Keith and I went back to my room. We each grabbed a beer and a seat.

THE THEORY OF SECOND BEST

"So seriously, what do you think?" Keith asked.

"I think she's perfect for him. I just hope he doesn't fuck it up."

"You think he will?"

I dropped my head and gaped at Keith to let him know how ridiculously stupid his question was. "This is Jake we're talking about."

Keith nodded. "Yeah, I get that, but he definitely seemed to be able to relax around her. That's huge."

I shrugged. "I mean, it's definitely unusual, I'll give you that. I guess we can always hope."

"Geez, Kyle, way to be optimistic."

And as if on cue, the door flung open and Jake burst through. The happy, glowing guy we'd left at the elevator was not the same one who stormed into the room in a fiery display of conflict and distress. He was now a bundle of electrified energy and was throwing his bolts of lightning in my direction. I was always the most convenient metal rod.

I glanced at Keith. He raised his eyebrows, seemingly impressed with my psychic skills. Yep. I'd definitely called it. Apparently it had taken less than five minutes for Jake to ruin whatever it was he had going with the girl. Optimism was for idiots.

Jake spent the next few minutes tearing into me for inviting Casey to sit with us. I had shaken up his carefully crafted world, and he refused to admit he'd actually liked it. Dark, ominous clouds hovered over Jake. I knew better than to stir up the storm, but I couldn't help myself. He was being an idiot and he needed to hear it.

Only thirty minutes earlier, watching Jake with Casey, I'd dared dream. I knew my brother had it in him, but there was something that held him back, something that refused to allow him to grab life and live it. A ragged frustration gripped me. So much for hope. It had gotten me all excited for nothing.

The next day at the wedding, I noticed Jake was ignoring Casey. I also detected the confused look in her eyes. Evidently, she had done nothing to invite his silence. That whole stormy display last night had been all his doing. I wanted to shake sense into him. How could he not seize what was right in front of him?

"What are you doing?"

Jake flicked his eyes at me and shrugged.

"Did she do something to piss you off last night?"

"No. She didn't do anything."

"Then why?"

Another shrug.

"When was the last time you felt something with a girl?"

"Just drop it, K."

"No. I saw the way you looked at her last night. I just don't get why you're doing this. She likes you, and clearly you like her. So what's the hold up?"

"Why bother?"

"What do you mean? From what I saw last night, Casey seems worth the effort."

Jake sighed. "I said drop it, and I meant it."

I balked at his indifference. Shaking his head, Jake walked away from me.

Oddly enough, at some point during the evening, he had an abrupt change of heart. One minute Jake was sitting stone-faced and miserable at the dinner table, and the next, his hands were halfway up Casey's dress. What the hell? I really didn't know why his flip-flopping behavior surprised me. I'd stopped trying to figure him out long ago. Whatever his hang up had been, it obviously couldn't withstand the onslaught of Casey's undeniable charms.

As the evening wound down, I wandered back over to our table and joined Emma and Quinn, who were laughing at something on his phone.

"What are you watching?"

"Quinn filmed Dad dabbing."

"No way. Let me see."

No man his age should be caught dead, or at least on camera, doing the dabbing dance move. It's just embarrassing for all those involved. But I understood my dad couldn't help being a dork; and really, I never tired of watching him make a fool of himself, so expectantly, I pulled up a chair next to my siblings.

Mesmerized by Quinn's video, I didn't notice Sarah until Emma motioned to my left. I turned to find her standing next to me.

"Can I talk to you for a sec?" she asked.

"I'm kind of busy," I replied coolly. She wasn't fooling me. The only reason she was standing here now was because Jake was off to nail another.

"It'll just take a second. Please," Sarah cooed, running her hand seductively up my arm and across my shoulder.

I opened my mouth to tell her to go to hell, but an instant hard-on gave me away. In a feeble attempt to shield my growing package, my awkward fumbling did nothing but draw more attention to it.

Sarah flicked her eyes downward and her lips tilted into a sly little smile. *Damn my traitor dick!*

She leaned over and whispered in my ear, "I can take care of that if you want."

I jerked my head up in surprise. Sarah grinned. I knew damn well she wasn't interested in me – I wasn't dumb – but she was back anyway, because, presumably, I was the last available male option with the last name McKallister, if you didn't count the underage dweeb sitting beside me. God, how I wanted to put her in her place, punish her for her earlier betrayal; but I was a member of the weaker sex, and as such, was a slave to my nether regions.

Without a word to my siblings, I stood up and left with Sarah. From the corner of my eye I could see Emma shaking her head. *Yeah, yeah. I have no self-respect. Shoot me!*

Away from my family, Sarah sidled up next to me. "How come you didn't come find me tonight?" she whispered seductively in my ear, as her hand brushed past my dick. It jolted to attention.

I knew myself well enough to know I would have no will power against the likes of Sarah. At the same time, I refused to make it too easy on her.

"So how did it go with Jake?" I asked in a friendly, conversational tone.

Sarah rolled her eyes. "I think you know."

I grinned.

"You think it's funny?"

"Sort of, yeah. I did warn you."

"Warn me about what? Jake hasn't had a spare moment to talk to me, so we'll never know."

"Oh, okay."

"What's that supposed to mean?"

"I told you he wouldn't be interested. You're not his type."

"Oh, and the skank is?" Sarah asked in a raised voice.

"Casey?" I questioned in surprise.

"How do you know her name?"

"I met her last night. We hung out. She's a cool girl."

"Jake hung out with her last night?" Sarah's voice was high-pitched and pissed.

"Yeah. We all did."

Her mouth dropped open in shock. "That little…" She caught herself then added, "Well, you don't know her like I do. She's putting on a show for Jake."

With an exaggerated groan, I asked, "Did you invite me over here to talk about Jake again, or are we gonna get it on? Because honestly, Sarah, that's the only reason I am still talking to you."

I took a step back, expecting to get slapped in the face, but instead I was treated to a megawatt smile. Sarah really was so damn beautiful. It made me wonder why she didn't grace the world with that carefree look more often.

"We're gonna get it on," she answered matter-of-factly.

"Yay me!" I raised my arms in victory.

After saying my goodbyes, Sarah and I made our way to her room. Originally she'd wanted to go back to my place, but I had visions of her rummaging through Jake's bag and sniffing his underwear while I used the bathroom, so I ve-toed her request. Reluctantly she agreed to a romp in her room.

"So what's your job, really?"

"I'm a bodyguard."

"*You're* a bodyguard?" she scoffed.

"What? You don't think I can guard bodies?"

"Well, you aren't exactly the threatening type."

"Oh, and what type am I?"

"The stoner type," she laughed.

"Hey!" I exclaimed and nudged her. "What's your job?"

"I'm a model."

Of course. "Are you a working model?"

Sarah gaped at me like I'd asked a ridiculous question. "What do you think?"

"I'm thinking you probably make a very good living."

"And you would be right."

We stopped at her door. As she fumbled with the key card, she asked. "So whose body do you guard?"

"I think you know."

"You travel with him, then?"

Crap. She was back to Jake again. "Yes."

"On tour?"

"Yep."

"That's got to be exciting."

"Um... yeah, it's a nice gig if you can get it."

"Have you ever had to guard his body, like, for real?"

"All the time," I nodded. "Usually just overzealous groupies, though."

"What would happen if someone was really threatening him? Would you throw yourself in front of a bullet for him?"

Without hesitation, I replied, "Yes."

"Really?" She grinned, putting her hands on her hips like she thought I was joking.

I stopped and stared down at her. My jaw cramped as I ground my teeth in irritation. I never joked about Jake's life. Ever. "I would die for him," I replied.

Sarah's expression softened as if she were realizing, for the first time, that I was more than just Jake's stupid sidekick. "Well now *that's* interesting."

I rolled off Sarah. It had taken about five minutes to finish our emotionless tryst. It was fun, don't get me wrong, but there was definitely no spark. Not like I expected one, or even wanted one, for that matter. Sarah was just a hook up… one of many.

Afterward, we made uncomfortable small talk. Really, I just wanted out of there.

"Do you live in LA?"

"Just outside. Why?"

"You know, I'm going to be there in a couple of days for work. Maybe we can hook up again."

"I'm actually leaving for the Cook Islands next week."

"Must be nice. On vacation?"

"No, I'm gonna be on *Marooned*."

"The reality show?" Sarah bolted upright, her attention piqued. "No way!"

"Yes way," I mimicked, grinning.

"Why didn't you tell me that?"

"I just did."

"Kyle, that's so cool."

I shrugged. "Yeah, I guess."

"I've auditioned for a bunch of reality shows but haven't gotten anything yet. When are you leaving for filming?"

"Friday."

"I'm coming to LA on Wednesday. Let's get together. I'm staying in Santa Monica for the shoot."

"I don't know. I'm not sure if I'll have time."

Sarah crawled onto her knees, her hands snaking up my body. I shuddered involuntarily. "Come on. You know you liked it."

Regardless of the fact that I saw right through her new-found interest in me, I couldn't deny that she turned me on, and one more romp in the sack with a smoking hot model wouldn't be the worst thing ever. I could swallow my pride for one more night.

CHAPTER SEVEN

KYLE

Someone For Everyone

The next morning I awoke to "Mom-gate". After Jake had failed to return from his evening with Casey and subsequently missed brunch, Mom went on a rampage. I frantically texted my brother, but he was not answering. Mom's initial irritation quickly turned to worry. A missing Jake was obviously not something our family took lightly. I tried to reassure her that he was fine, but Mom was pacing the floor by the time Jake's text finally came in.

"He's fine," I announced with a heavy sigh of relief. "Just overslept."

"How do you know?" she answered in a frazzled-sounding voice.

I showed her his text. Mom's posture instantly relaxed.

"Thank god. Now that I know he's safe, I'm going to kill him!"

———

Jake sat perched on the edge of the bed, rambling on and on about his night with Casey. He was like a kid at Christmas, his face flushed with excitement.

"And you were gone all night, but you didn't have sex?"

"I told you it wasn't in her rulebook. It didn't matter, though. Last night was so hot. She's just..." Jake didn't finish his sentence. He was looking off somewhere, a slight smile on his face. He often spaced out during conversations, but normally he was remembering something unpleasant and his lips were curved in a frown. Today was the opposite. The memory filling his head clearly made him happy, and he was relaxed, as if a weight had been lifted off him. I felt that treacherous hope rising up inside me once more.

"It's weird," Jake finally continued. "I've only known her a day, but it feels like I've known her forever. Have you ever felt that way?"

"No."

"You're going to think I'm crazy, but I actually think I really like her, and I want to see her again."

I stood there transfixed, just staring at this stranger before me. I couldn't remember the last time Jake had talked to me like this – his voice so full of positivity and excitement. As kids, he and I used to talk non-stop about all kinds of things, but our main topic of discussion as we got older was girls and sex. What I had done. What he had done. What we both wanted to do. But it was all talk. Neither one of us had gotten past first base. Of the two of us, I was the more experienced, having once convinced a girl to touch my dick through my shorts in a game of truth or dare. It had lasted about two seconds before she squealed, "Eew, it's squishy." Yeah, that had done wonders for my self-esteem.

After the kidnapping, we didn't talk about girls and sex anymore. Honestly, we didn't talk about much at all. Jake had been so traumatized by the experience that anything more than a superficial conversation with him was a major victory. In those early years, pushing him beyond his comfort zone was never a good idea. Jake had triggers, and if one of us accidently stumbled onto one of them, he would blow up. We all learned to tread lightly, never knowing exactly what was acceptable to say or do.

Gradually, a revised version of the old Jake returned to us. It was as if he'd decided to accept his fate and move on. But that closeness we'd once shared, the one where we would lie on our beds at night and confess everything to each other... that had never returned.

"So what did you do last night after I left?" he asked.

"Sarah."

It took a second for my response to register with Jake. When it did, he threw his head back and laughed. Damn, he was in a good mood.

"And how did that go?" He grinned knowingly.

"Eh…it was fine."

"Just fine?"

"She pretty much just talked about you the whole time. I had to cover her mouth with my hand while we fucked."

Jake gaped at me before an amused smile took over. "Liar."

"I'm not kidding. It was like, 'Oh, Jake. Oh, yeah. Give it to me'," I panted, in my sexiest female voice.

"Shut up," he laughed, stretching his leg out to kick me. "Why do you go for women like that, anyway?"

"What? You mean women who like me for you?" I asked, shrugging.

"Yes. I'm sure there's a girl out there somewhere who hasn't heard of me and who might not find you butt-ugly."

"Really? You think?" I replied sarcastically.

"I mean, stranger things have happened," he shrugged.

I nodded, slapped on my best 'bewildered' expression, and tapped my chin with my pointer finger.

"But where to find such a girl? I mean, pretty much everyone on the planet has heard of you, so that kind of limits my options."

THE THEORY OF SECOND BEST

"Well, what about a girl from one of those religious cults, who's grown up without running water and television and shit?"

"Ooh, yeah. Good idea. When will the tour be rolling through Pennsylvania next?"

"It might be a while. Or hold up — you know all those freaky science labs? One of them has to be genetically engineering some half breed that would be perfect for you."

"Interesting idea. So basically what you're saying is that to find myself the perfect girl, I either need to travel back in time to the Wild West or visit a futuristic genetic bio lab and find myself a half-lizard, half-human hottie?"

"That's exactly what I'm saying. See, you aren't that stupid... Lizard Lady's going to eat that shit up."

CHAPTER EIGHT

KENZIE

Baby Steps

The force of the acceleration plastered my frame to the back of the seat as I fought to control my breathing. My fingers clutched the armrest with such intensity that my knuckles turned a splotchy white, even whiter than my normal chalky, sun-deprived shade. I couldn't lift my head. Was that normal? My eyeballs swiveled around, the only part of me still able to move. How could the other passengers remain so calm? Did they not feel the shaking? Were their teeth not banging together like mine? And the noise, oh, the noise! It was screeching through my brain, ricocheting back and forth as if inside a pinball machine.

No, this was definitely not normal! Fear like I'd never experienced swept through me. In moments, I'd be flying…
or crashing. Both seemed equally possible outcomes. The
wheels lifted off the runaway and I gasped in shock. The
weightlessness caught in my throat. I snapped my eyes se-
curely shut. Whatever was about to happen, I would not be
seeing it. I preferred my tragedy to go down blind.

The plane soared higher, and my stomach did a somer-
sault. I bravely cracked one eye open to make sure my barf-
bag was just where I'd left it, and then promptly squeezed it
shut again. I remained sightless even after the plane began
to level out. In a matter of minutes I would be further away
from my hometown than I'd ever been in my entire life.
Twenty-four years old, and there was so much I'd never
experienced. Like flying, for example. Actually, that was
one experience I could do without. In some ways I felt like
a newborn baby taking my first shaky steps out into the
world.

I really couldn't remember what had possessed me to
think that competing on a reality show would be the best
way to test my wings. In all honesty, when I'd applied way
back when, I never expected a visit from one of the show's
scouts, much less a spot on the eighteen-member cast. But
here I was, Kenzie Williams, small town girl with no life
experiences, beyond the walls of my sheltered existence,
about to go big or go home… or die in a fiery plane crash.
That was still a very real possibility. Yet somehow I sensed

something big was waiting for me, something life changing. Taking a deep breath, I opened my eyes.

This was something I wanted to see.

CHAPTER NINE

KYLE

Fifteen Minutes of Fame

"How are you feeling about tomorrow?" Mom asked. It was just the two of us in the kitchen.

"I'm good."

"Nervous?"

"A little, I guess. I'm excited."

"That's good," she nodded, although I didn't get the impression she actually thought it was good. Obviously there was more to her questioning than just idle chit-chat.

Mom inhaled slightly, and I saw her splayed fingers tighten on the countertop. I met her eyes with my own. I knew that look well. Mom had never been good at concealing her anxiety.

"What's wrong?"

"Do you know what you're getting yourself into, Kyle?"

"The show?" I asked.

"No – the fame that will come with it."

"I'm not Jake, Mom," I scoffed.

"You underestimate yourself. You're a likeable, funny guy. Pair that with the fact that the producers are going to exploit your connection to Jake… it will be instant celebrity."

"Does that bother you?"

"It worries me."

"Why?"

"Look what it's done to Jake."

"No offense, Mom, but fame did *not* do this to Jake."

Oh, yeah. I went there. Daggers shot from Mom's eyes. We'd never been allowed to openly discuss Jake's issues. It was a sticky subject in our house. Mom preferred to pretend that he was totally fine and completely unaffected by the crime that had shaken our family to its core ten years ago. I understood she did that for Jake's sake, to help him feel normal as he healed, but I'd always resented it.

It's not like my siblings and I had existed in a germ-free bubble of oblivion while all that shit was going down with our brother. We'd had a front row seat to the unraveling of Jake's life… hell, the unraveling of all our lives. Even though so many years had passed, it still irked me that we had to tippy-toe around the subject.

"I'm just saying, put the blame squarely where it belongs," I bravely added.

Mom stared me down for an uncomfortably long time before finally saying, "It's just, I've seen the things they say about Jake, and I don't want that for you."

"If you had concerns, why didn't you say something before?" I asked, annoyance creeping out through my words.

"Would it have made a difference?"

"Probably not. But dumping it on me now when there's nothing I could do about it even if I wanted to... that sucks."

"Sorry. I shouldn't have said anything," she replied chewing on her bottom lip. "I just want to know that you're prepared for what's coming. You seem to not really get it."

"What is there to get? I know what fame is. I live with it everyday."

"I know... it's just... Jake casts a wide shadow, and tomorrow you'll step out from under it in a big way."

The talk with Mom had made me jittery. I wasn't so sure of my decision anymore. Was I actually ready for the media attention? I'd always been the invisible brother. The cameras flashed for Jake, not me. Even what happened last night with Sarah had unnerved me. Maybe Mom was right. Maybe I was being totally naïve. Was I really cut out for the spotlight?

Last night was fun. Don't forget about me on the island.

The text was from Sarah. I'd met up with her at the hotel last night. I was hoping for a quickie so I could get home early, but she had other plans. The minute she opened the door, I knew we would not be staying in. Sarah was dressed to impress, and something told me it wasn't for my sake.

"Where are we going?" I asked.

"I thought we could hang out with some friends of mine tonight."

"Oh. You know I only have a few hours right? I have to be up early."

She grabbed my hand and steered us to the elevator. "Relax. You're not going to turn into a pumpkin at midnight."

It wasn't an evening with friends. It was a big Hollywood-type party at a house overlooking the beach in Malibu. Sarah was well known in these stomping grounds, and, regardless of the fact that she'd arrived with me, men were hitting on her right and left. There was a DJ playing and partygoers doing lines of coke on the kitchen counter. The minute I stepped in the place, I wanted to leave. This was definitely not my scene.

Despite the fact that I spent my life on the road with a rock star, I actually lived a fairly boring and sheltered existence. Having Keith as a glaring example of drug use gone badly, none of the rest of my siblings had chosen the same path. Perhaps if Jake had been more of a partier, I would have followed suit, but since he wasn't, neither was I. Our biggest vice was alcohol, and even that wasn't much.

Because Jake tended to surround himself with people who had a proven record of self-control, gatherings for us on the road were more like backyard barbeque parties than full on ragers. After some particularly bad experiences with drug-addicted employees, Jake now ran his tours like one of America's pot-friendly states. Weed was okay, but you did it at your own peril, meaning if you got caught with it in an inhospitable state or country, no one was coming for your doped-up ass. In fact, the rest of us would pretend we didn't even know the hapless dude, and it'd be up to him to find his way back to the tour. Those guys who were found using hard drugs Jake cut loose immediately.

"Come on. I want to introduce you," Sarah said, grabbing my hand and leading me to a group of five beautiful, leggy women. "Guys, say hi to Kyle."

Two women acknowledged me with friendly smiles, but the other three only managed to look up for a moment to size me up before returning to their conversation.

"Kyle is Jake McKallister's brother."

It was as if the music came to a screeching halt. Heads craned in my direction. The bored women perked up. One unfurled her long legs and got up off the couch. I was instantly surrounded and being peppered with questions about Jake. One woman even tried swiping my phone to call him. Sarah hung all over me. I was now the most interesting person in the room, and she loved it.

As new people wandered over, Sarah began introducing me as Jake's brother, not even bothering to use my actual name anymore. At the start of the evening my blood had been lukewarm, but by the end, it was boiling. My teeth actually hurt from all the grinding they were doing. It was becoming clear that Sarah's motivation for bringing me here was to show me off. And normally that would have been flattering, but not when she was showing me off as Jake's frickin' brother.

I was on edge and ready to leave fifteen minutes after arriving, but Sarah was not ready to go. She was loving the attention my connection to Jake was bringing to the table. Since I had been driven over by Sarah, I was at her mercy.

An hour into the party, I was cornered by a half naked man, clad only in board shorts and a shirt that was open wide. Deeply tanned and obviously lit, his eyes darted back and forth, struggling to focus on mine. This guy was my dad's age, but that's where the similarity ended. Rich, privileged, and used to getting what he wanted, this dude was like a caricature of every drunk, wealthy, obnoxious guy who'd ever appeared on the silver screen.

"Kyle, right?"

"Yes."

"Steve," he said, slurring a second word, which I assumed was his last name. He shook my hand. "This is your lucky day."

"Oh, yeah? How do you figure?"

"I can make you a lot of money. We're talking buttloads. You can buy your very own cocaine castle."

His eyes scurried every which way. *Jesus, dude, pull it together.*

"Uh-huh," I said. "And what would I be required to do to obtain this pot of white gold?"

"What do you know about your brother's kidnapping?"

My heart rate shot up in an instant, and my fists clamped with fury. I seriously considered punching the asshole in his smug, plastic surgery-altered face, but getting arrested for assault was the last thing I needed before leaving for the show. I took a deep breath and then turned and stomped off.

"You're being stupid. You have no idea what I can offer you," he called out to me.

He didn't deserve a response, so I didn't reward him with one. I walked up to Sarah and grabbed her arm.

"I'm leaving."

"What? What happened?"

"Nothing. This isn't my scene. Are you coming, or should I Uber?"

Sarah looked at me in surprise and then glanced around. She was clearly conflicted. Really? Jesus Christ.

What the hell was I doing here? I turned and walked out of the house. Sarah followed, her stiletto heels clacking something fierce on the concrete path.

"Wait up, Kyle, geez."

My jaw was clenched so tightly that it actually ached. When she finally caught up to me, her eyed grew large as she saw the angry expression on my face.

"Did something happen back there?"

"Aside from some guy named Steve offering me money to sell out my brother? Nope, nothing exciting."

Sarah crossed her arms in from of her. "Oh. Sorry."

I shrugged, still pissed and not willing to accept her apology. "Why did you bring me here?"

"I thought it would be fun."

"For who?"

"For you. Most guys would kill to go to a party like this. Those were supermodels in there."

"Yeah, well, I'm not most guys."

Sarah's eyes scanned me, and her features softened. "No, I'm starting to get that." She reached out and grabbed my hand. "I'm sorry. I should have asked you first. Forgive me."

She sidled up to me and started nibbling on my neck. Slowly but surely, my anger and resentment began to recede. Her lips found mine, and I groaned. We stood on the sidewalk making out for a few minutes, and then she took my hand and drove me back to the hotel.

I woke up in my bed the next morning not feeling real good about where my life was currently headed. Jake was right. I needed to stop putting myself through this crap. I was tired of playing the game. I knew it seemed clichéd, but I was actually starting to feel used by these women. Yeah, I was obviously getting something out of the hook ups, but was it really enough? Maybe I was just in a funk. Or maybe I needed to find a girl who actually liked me for me.

I flung the covers off and stretched. Today was the day. A nervous flutter traveled through me. I wasn't sure what I was getting myself into. I picked up my phone, and there was a text from Jake.

Remember I'm expecting a train wreck. Don't disappoint.

I smiled as I ran my hand through my tangled mass of hair.

Don't you worry, I texted back. *Tell Casey I love her.*

He didn't reply. It was probably evening wherever he was in the world, which meant Jake was most likely on stage performing. I felt a pang of guilt. I was going to be gone for forty-five days and completely off the radar. If there were a problem, I wouldn't know about it. I just had to trust he was going to be okay. He had told me yesterday that he'd been talking to Casey via Facetime and that things were going well. He sounded upbeat and encouraged. But what if something happened? What if she broke his heart, and he had no one to talk to?

Frustrated, I got up and walked into the bathroom. I splashed some water on my face and stared at myself in the mirror. Worry lines etched my forehead. Was I making the right choice here? Why was it so hard for me to leave? The face that stared back at me in the mirror had morphed into my twelve-year-old self.

You know why, he said.

Marooned
List of Contestants

East Tribe

1. Fergus: Police Detective

2. Lena: Body builder

3. Carol: Homemaker

4. Eugene: Broadway Singer

5. Marina: Lawyer

6. Randall: Soldier

7. Sandra: Student

8. Amir: Harvard Professor

9. Jenni: Unemployed

West Tribe

1. Gene: Retired Football Coach

2. Aisha: Miss Nevada

3. Carl: Logger

4. Kenzie: Assistant Manager

5. Dale: Computer Technician

6. Marsha: Ranch Owner

7. Kyle: Security

8. Bobby: Actor

9. Summer: Yoga Instructor

Gameplay:

Contestants are stranded in an isolated location, and must provide all essential survival needs for themselves. Contestants compete in challenges for immunity from elimination, and are progressively ejected from the game as they are voted out by their fellow contestants until only one remains and is declared the winner and awarded the prize money.

CHAPTER TEN

KENZIE
First Impressions

My stomach rumbled as the boat bobbed like a cork on the choppy waves. I gripped my knees, trying to look calm and cool in the face of great distress. "One more shot," the producer kept calling. I'd been hearing that for the past hour, and my insides were now rebelling. My clammy hands and tingling skin were signs of the inevitable: I was going to spew. I looked around in a panic, trying to determine the best vomit pose. What would look best on television? Bending over and barfing where I sat seemed easiest, but there was a cameraman directly below me. Maybe I should yack over the side of the boat. Could I even turn my body around in time? And most importantly, would my butt look big on camera?

Oh god, this was like the 'Notorious Zipper Incident' all over again. The memory of that day had been burned into my psyche for eternity. I was thirteen, I knew better than to mess with the Zipper. No carnival ride turned my insides to mush quite like that one. But I gave into peer pressure. Tanner Crowell was there. And he was so cute. "It will be fun," my friends urged. Why hadn't I said no?

My classmates and I filled all the cages, and then the vile ride started flipping and turning and jerking. I didn't last more than 30 seconds before I violently began emptying my stomach, not only all over the unlucky girl sitting beside me but also onto every single cage spinning and twisting and whirling below me. Let's just say by the time it was over, there wasn't a dry eye in the place. I deservingly earned the nickname 'Chunks,' and spent the rest of middle school trying to live it down.

And now I had a horrible feeling that this was about to become Zipper 2.0. Looking to my right, my eyes fell on an unbelievably polished, mocha-skinned beauty. A model? Or was she a pageant queen? In my panicked state, I couldn't remember what she'd said earlier; however, instinctively I understood she would not appreciate my lunch being unceremoniously dumped onto her lap.

I looked to my left. A scruffy, tattooed guy who reminded me of Shaggy from *Scooby Doo* sat blissfully unaware of the fate about to befall him. Perhaps sensing me staring, Shaggy looked over at me with a pleasant smile. His eyes met mine, and I saw the change in them immediately. His face formed into a mask of horror. He was smart enough to realize I wasn't messing around and scrappy enough to try to save himself. Shaggy dove from his spot on the bench just as I tossed my cookies into his vacated seat. Like magic, every single person on my side of the boat disappeared. The vessel listed to one side, challenged by the weight of seventeen cast members desperately attempting to escape my gastric waterfall.

In a display of great courage, a member of the medical team rushed to my side. He held my sweaty hair and rubbed my tense back as I got my body turned in the right direction and dry heaved over the side of the boat. When it was over, and I had successfully concluded my disgusting little sideshow, I glanced down morosely to take in the mess I'd made – only to discover crewmembers had mercifully already cleaned it up. My hopeful eyes continued along the boat until they reached poor Shaggy, who was being treated by medical for a cut on his arm, an injury he'd apparently acquired during his impressive escape. And finally, I remorsefully lifted my eyes to find a row of faces staring back at me in unabashed revulsion. Yep, definitely Zipper 2.0… only, this time, on a national scale. From somewhere on the back of the boat I heard a producer shout, "Cut."

TV Confessional
"So...THAT just happened."
— Kenzie

CHAPTER ELEVEN

KYLE

The Left Coast

I watched the needle poke through my skin. What the hell just happened? One minute everything was fine; and the next, the backs of my legs and shoes were covered in vomit and I was getting three stitches to close up a cut on my arm! I glowered at the offending female, who was looking everywhere but in my direction. She'd appeared so sweet and innocent with those big blue eyes and delicate ivory skin, but that was right before she morphed into Linda Blair from *The Exorcist* and spewed green vomit from her guts.

"Okay, so we're just going to wrap this up and you're good to go. We'll keep an eye on it, and if you start to feel pain or swelling, let us know immediately," the doctor said.

"What about my shoes?" I complained, looking down at my brand new Nikes with chunks of god knows what embedded in the laces. I knew it was petty of me to care, but I did.

"If that's the worst you get on your shoes in 39 days, consider yourself lucky."

Instantly several unpleasant images flashed before my eyes. Was I in over my head here? And then a more agreeable picture popped into my mind: me rolling down some European interstate in a luxury tour bus, kicking back, playing guitar, and eating Cheetos.

"You ready there, Kyle?" another staff member asked.

I nodded.

"We'll just have you sit back down right over there." And he pointed at the spot on the bench next to *her*!

"Um...I'm not sitting back there."

"We cleaned it with bleach. I can assure you it's safe," one of the executive producers promised.

"The seat's not what I'm worried about," I said, and tossed Puke Girl an accusatory look. Her head hung in shame.

"We've already completed the majority of filming, so it'll just take a couple more minutes. If you don't go back to that spot, we'll have to reshoot the entire bit."

Several of the other cast members shot irritated glances in my direction, as if I were being completely unreasonable in my request not to sit in a spot that, only moments earlier, had been covered in a glob of throw up. When did this all become my fault? I was the goddamn victim here, but somehow the offender had all the sympathy.

The producer turned to the young woman and compassionately consoled her. "You all right there, sweetheart? You still feeling nauseous, or did you get it all out now?"

Oh, I'm pretty sure she got it all out!

"I'm better. I'm really sorry," she apologized to the whole lot of us, still refusing eye contact with me. "I'm ready to continue now."

"Kyle?" The man motioned for me to return to my seat. Feeling that I had no other option, I begrudgingly took my place beside my tormentor.

Thankfully, it only took twenty minutes to complete the filming, and then our boat was headed to shore. At one point, the remorseful girl leaned slightly over in my direction. Like a wuss, I flinched away. It would have been nice to remain calm, but I knew what she was capable of and was not about to give her the benefit of the doubt again.

"Relax. You're safe," she said, regret clear in her voice.

Flustered, I could think of no snappy reply so I just said, "Yeah, okay."

She turned away and we didn't speak again.

Marooned Rule #1

The contestants are separated into two teams called 'tribes.' These two tribes live on separate, isolated beaches and will have limited contact with one another.

All eighteen of us were ushered off the boat and onto dry land. Cameramen were everywhere. I glanced around at all the excited faces and wondered how long the euphoria would last. In a matter of days, our numbers would begin to dwindle, as we were picked off the show one by one.

The producers split us up based on geography: East versus West. That meant, of course, that our team consisted of the free spirit (me, apparently), the actor, Miss Nevada, the vegan yoga instructor, the seven-foot-tall red-headed logger, the Silicon Valley tech nerd, the Division One college football coach, one braless lady, and – wait for it – the barfer.

Glancing over at the East coast tribe, who were high-fiving their good fortune, it was easy to see that they had the brawns, what with their soldier, female body-builder, high-powered lawyer, and an assortment of other tough-looking people. Even their Harvard professor and

THE THEORY OF SECOND BEST

male Broadway singer appeared more formidable than our weakest links.

Aside from our very own Paul Bunyan, us left-coasters were like those frou-frou lap dogs that you'd see being carried around in a name-brand purse, while the East coasters were like badass Rottweilers, frothing at the mouth. It wasn't difficult to determine who had the upper hand in this uneven match up.

The two tribes were given maps to separate locations, and one look at the hand-drawn scribbling told me we were about to have a long, sweltering trek through the jungle to get to our beach. The nine of us took off through the labyrinth of tree limbs and dense bush, and in a matter of minutes, I was drenched in sweat, dying of thirst, and frantically swatting away Volkswagen-sized bugs. So far this really sucked! I was already missing my lazy, air-conditioned life.

Almost immediately personalities began to take form, and straightaway, half the people on my tribe started rubbing me the wrong way. Maybe I was just cranky. Usually I had more patience dealing with idiots, but I'd had a rough day and wasn't feeling real charitable. So when yoga lady commented for the twentieth time about the meditation sessions she planned to run on the beach every morning, I thought I might kick her in her perfectly toned shins.

Worse still was the self-absorbed, unemployed actor, Bobby, who peeled off his shirt to reveal sparkling pecs, and then proceeded to outline every single workout he had done to get every single one of those muscles. He'd only traveled about halfway down his body when I glanced at puke girl… the poor, sweaty little thing. She was not taking this hike well. Her breathing was so labored that there was this wheezy whistle emitting from her nose, and her body was hanging dangerously low to the ground. I half expected her to start walking on all fours.

She must have sensed me staring. Her mascara-smeared eyes met mine and she shook her head, obviously embarrassed by her Cro-Magnon man posture. I smiled at her sympathetically. What else could I do? She was a shit show. I couldn't imagine her lasting more than a day out here.

Bobby continued his nauseating monologue on weight lifting and protein powder. The cave dweller lifted her weary head. Somehow she found the strength to flick her eyes in Bobby's direction, roll them dramatically, then put her finger in her mouth and – you guessed it – fake-barf. Surprised that she would go *there* so soon after actually going *there* made me laugh out loud. Who would have predicted that the knuckle dragger who'd blown chunks on me only an hour earlier would end up being the least offensive person on my tribe?

TV Confessional
*"I mean, it's not the first time a girl
has thrown up on me."*
— Kyle

CHAPTER TWELVE

KENZIE

The Island Of Misfit Toys

I could not have felt sicker if I tried. The sticky heat had zapped me of the only energy I had left in my depleted body. Having purged all necessary nutrients in my earlier escapades, I was stumbling through the thick foliage, arms swinging limply in front of me, like a zombie from *The Walking Dead*. And if that weren't bad enough, I'd come under heavy attack from the shivers. The fine little hairs on my arms and legs stood at attention. Sweat drizzled out of every pore in my body; in fact, I was convinced those little suckers had multiplied by the billions just for today. The quivers made my teeth knock together so violently that I feared they would crumble in my mouth. Oh, yeah, that would really complete the whole apocalyptic vibe I had going on.

I purposefully avoided all eye contact with the other tribe members so as not to alert them to the fact that I was in a rapid state of decline. I needed water badly. I needed rest. What I did not need was for Shaggy to observe me doing the zombie shuffle or flash me that pathetic pity smile of his.

I should be the one consoling *him*. Every time I looked in his direction, I felt a tightness in my chest. I wanted to properly apologize, but I wasn't sure if he would allow me to get close enough to do so. And I didn't blame him one bit. He had three stitches in his arm because of me. I'd always had a weak stomach, but Shaggy was its first real casualty.

I heard the rest of the tribe cheering, and I raised my weighty head to discover that I was trekking through the tropical forest alone. Using the carefree sounds the human people were making as a beacon, I gathered my last remaining strength and dragged myself across the finish line, literally collapsing in front of my indifferent teammates.

So for the second time in a day, the medical team was called to my side. While everyone else was busily setting up camp, I was being treated for dehydration and heat exhaustion. The rest of my tribe mates had no doubt already written me off as dead, and really, who could blame them?

My antics, up to this point, had not painted me in the best light. Kicking me out at the first opportunity would seem a no brainer. There was just no coming back from this humiliation.

It took about an hour and a gallon of water, but I was finally starting to feel mortal again. My skin had returned to its natural sickly pale color, and my overactive sweat glands had decided to take a well-deserved rest. Although my stomach still hurt a bit, the helpful doctor assured me that my earlier violent vomiting spell was most likely the cause of that particular ailment. At least my abs had gotten a good workout.

Once the medical team left, I sat in the shade a few minutes longer, gazing longingly out at the clear blue ocean and wondering what color it would turn once I dipped my rank body into it. But there was no time for that now. Somehow I had to turn around the worst first impression in the history of first impressions. I wasn't sure if it was remotely possible, but I had to try. Not only would my embarrassment be complete if I were the first to go, but also I would miss out on a chance at the money. And if there was one thing worth fighting for, it was that.

So I fixed my attention on the other players, trying to figure out the complex dynamics that had been rapidly evolving during the hour I'd been sprawled out in the throes of death. Clearly, the alpha players were already firmly in control of the camp, and I needed to get back on my feet and prove to them I wasn't the puke-spewing death walker they'd all taken me for.

I allowed myself the time to really observe the other eight players on my tribe. It became clear that a strong sub-group of five had already formed, and it had a leader in the form of Gene, a retired Division One football coach. He was boisterous and domineering, and for reasons I could not yet understand, the others had fallen in line behind him. I rubbed my temples as his voice penetrated my weakened immune system. Did no one else hear the man? Was I the only one wishing for a roll of duct tape?

Fingers snapped in front of my face. Startled, I blinked in rapid reply.

"You all right there, girly?"

It was the gray-haired lady with the long pigtails and denim overalls. I remembered my stunned reaction to seeing her for the first time. Her style was unique, to say the least. I'd always held the belief that at a certain age – like ten – pigtails and overalls were a fashion no-no. But then what did I know? I lived in a place where a Walmart twenty miles away was the main clothing source for young and old. Maybe her farmer look was all the rage in the big cities, and I just hadn't gotten the memo. Still, she was the first person to show even the slightest concern for me, and I was grateful.

"Yes, I'm feeling so much better," I said, forcing a healthy, happy smile.

"Oh… well, good for you," she replied, with clear disappointment in her voice. She then patted my shoulder and walked away. Okay. So much for concern!

My eyes caught the giant of a man, Carl. I remembered him quite vividly from the boat ride. He wasn't one of those forgettable types. The man had to be pushing seven feet tall, and his close-cropped ginger hair was offset by thousands of tiny freckles. This was a person who you didn't just glance at if you saw him out in public, you stopped and stared – maybe even took a covert picture as he passed by. And it wasn't just his exceptional height that set him apart but his impossibly broad shoulders. If you slapped some green paint on the guy, he could totally pass for the Hulk.

And what I could tell from first impressions, Carl even had the temperament of the green-hued monster. He was impatient and gruff and seemed exceedingly annoyed with Gene, who had taken to micromanaging the lodging project. I could understand his annoyance. Carl seemed to be the only one who had a clue how to build a shelter, and yet, he was still forced to take direction from a loudmouth who probably hadn't built a thing in his entire life.

Knowing my love for people watching, I could see myself becoming overly invested in Carl. He was just that enjoyable to observe. The guy had that whole Grumpy Cat face going on. I wondered if, much like the cat, there might be a sweet center beneath his cantankerous surface.

I had no such illusions about Gene. He was transparent in his dealings with others. There was no furry little kitty living inside Gene. He ate loser fluff-balls for breakfast. This was the stereotypical man's man who spoke in sports metaphors and called females 'little ladies.' Gene, with his silver hair, blue eyes, and a stunning golden tan, was in his early sixties and in impeccable shape. Certainly he had run circles around me today, and I was forty years younger.

We were informed several times by the man himself how successful he had been in his coaching career. And from what I gathered, Gene really, really liked winning. I mean, I was rather fond of it myself, but it wasn't the main focus of my life. In the few hours I'd spent with Gene, winning was all he'd talked about. So important was that character trait to the man that he diligently began building his team of winners the minute we hit the beach. Carl, of course, was at the top of his list. And Summer came in a close second.

What to say about the yoga instructor? Summer appeared to be in her early forties, but possessed the most rockin' bod on the island. And I knew that because the minute she stepped foot on the beach she stripped down to the barely legal limit, and every male eyeball bulged in admiration. I imagined the editors would have a field day with her screen time. No doubt little black boxes would be blocking out Summer's sensitive bits on television sets across America.

In addition, I felt it would be a travesty not to mention Summer's noteworthy backside. I'd never been one to admire other women's booties, but Summer's was just that spot on! Perky, rounded, and impossibly toned, I'd venture a bet that she didn't carry an ounce of cellulite on that impressive rump.

Although Summer was a little annoying, with her whole Zen movement and healthy eating snippets, I couldn't argue with the obvious results of her obsession with clean living, nutritious foods, and fitness.

Nor could Gene. His eyes followed her everywhere, watching her shimmy by with a mesmerized grin. Although Summer was essentially doing no hard labor, or really anything with any significance in camp, her effervescence and killer body were enough to carry her through and earn a spot on Gene's dream team. Bobby, the muscle obsessed actor and Aisha, the long-legged beauty queen, rounded out the quintet. Certainly their superior looks and rock-hard bodies would deem them winners in Gene's eyes.

And just like that, I was on the outside of a five-four split: me, Shaggy, nerdy computer geek, Dale, and Marsha, the pigtail lady who wished me dead. Not a great start. It might have seemed a little early in the game to be forming this group within the group, but on *Marooned*, it was a strategy that worked. When it came time to vote out members of our tribe, a solid five could pick off the others one by one with ease.

I knew I needed to jump in head first as I'd wasted so much precious time. Taking a deep breath of courage, I bee-lined it straight to the top. Gene saw me coming and backed away.

"If you're sick, little lady, stay back," he said putting his hands in front of him as if to ward off evil.

"No, I'm not sick. I just have a weak stomach when it comes to boats, or any motion rides, really. And that whole thing on the beach, that was just a little dehydration, but I'm..." I stopped babbling since Gene had already grown tired of my thirty-word sentence and had focused his attention elsewhere.

Undeterred, I made my way around the other side. Gene looked up at me and startled. *Really, dude? We were just talking. How could you be surprised that I'd still be here?* I tried to bury my annoyance.

"Hi again," I smiled and, like a dork, even waved at him. "What I was saying was I'm fine now and ready to work. What would you like me to do?"

Gene eyed me with distaste and pointed at the water buckets.

"We'll need water once the fire is started. Take that kid over there."

My eyes followed the coach's and landed right on Shaggy. Instantly my face flushed. *No. Not him. Anyone but him!*

"The one you vomited on," Gene clarified.

"Yeah, I got that."

"You said you wanted a job. Now you've got one," Gene said gruffly, and turned away from me for the second time in only a minute. I wanted to argue but realized how pointless it would be. Gene had already pegged me as one of the undesirables. My opinion carried no weight with him.

Reluctantly I picked up the buckets and made my way over to where Shaggy was standing by himself, holding a bamboo stalk as those around him built the shelter. Gene's five were already a cohesive group and seemed to have forgotten about him.

"Surprise," I said, making my eyes as big and crazy as possible, which wasn't a huge stretch for me after the day I'd had. I figured going the carefree, fun route would seem less intimidating to my hapless victim. Clutching two water cans in my hands, I lifted them up for him to see. "I'm sure I'm the last person you want to be alone with, but Gene wants us to go get water."

Shaggy squinted his eyes as he focused in on me. He seemed to be considering his options as he took his time slowly scanning me from top to bottom. After what I assumed was a thorough inspection, the left side of his mouth curled up in a smirk, and he said, "Nice to see you survived."

There was a playful tone to his voice, which immediately eased my anxiety.

"Yeah, it was touch and go there for a while."

"I could see that," he nodded. "You were looking like one of those 'after' photos of a meth addict."

"Ahh, thank you." I laughed for probably the first time all day. "So what do you say, Shaggy? Are you coming?"

Oh, crap. The nickname just slipped out. I hoped he didn't think I was being disrespectful. But there was clear amusement in his eyes. Something told me very little fazed this guy.

Shaggy crossed his arms in front of him, and a second eye scan commenced. I waited patiently, as I had no leverage in this conversation. "I will go with you on one condition."

"What's that?"

"No more spewing nasty shit in my direction."

"You don't need to worry. I assure you, I have nothing left to spew."

Shaggy laughed at that, and then dropped his bamboo and grabbed both buckets from my hands. "Let's go, then."

On our way out of camp, we passed by Dale and Marsha, who were bent over the fire trying to get something started. The two had been chosen as the fire-makers presumably because they were the only ones who wore glasses – a most useful tool for magnifying the sun's rays.

Shaggy shook his head playfully and gestured in the direction of the unlikely bespectacled duo. "What are the chances we'll have fire today?"

"I think it will be a cold, dark night."

"Yeah, that's what I was thinking," he said, swinging the buckets. How did he find the energy? "But on the plus side, camp will be totally feng shui!"

I grinned. "Well, there's that."

As we walked, a cameraman and sound guy scrambled to stay in front of us. Having people filming our every move would take some getting used to on my part. Normally I hated when people aimed a camera at me. I assumed that particular aversion stemmed from the embarrassing videos my brothers were always taking of me and then sharing with their friends in order, it seemed, just to laugh at me. I glanced over at Shaggy, who appeared blissfully unaware of the crew clambering about. The fact that he seemed exceedingly comfortable with the attention made me wonder about him. Who was this guy?

"How's your arm?" I asked, rubbing my own in the spot his was bandaged. The guilt was eating me up inside. I needed to get the apology out of the way before I could move on with him.

"It's fine," he replied nonchalantly, as if he'd totally forgotten about the injury.

"Are you in pain?"

"Nah, it's nothing. Don't worry about it."

"I mean, if you wanted to slap me or something, I'd totally be okay with that."

To his credit, Shaggy shook his head, smiling. "It's all good."

I was surprised and impressed by the ease with which he was willing to forgive. I'm not sure I would have been so generous.

Meeting his merciful eyes with my own remorseful ones, I said, "For what it's worth, I really am sorry."

He actually paused a moment before replying, "I know."

I nodded, broke the eye contact, and we continued quietly on our trek. Feeling more at ease, I passed him a sideways glance and joked, "And I promise to share half of my worm stew with you for the rest of the show."

His eyes lit up with mock excitement. "Pinky promise?"

My tense shoulders relaxed, and the feeling of dread I'd been carrying around since the boat fiasco began to fade. If this guy could accept me after our rocky beginning, maybe I wasn't totally doomed with the others.

"So, Shaggy from *Scooby Doo*, I'm assuming?" he asked, with a crooked grin.

"Oh, yeah, sorry. I had to make up something since I didn't exactly have time to introduce myself."

Shaggy nodded. "No, I get it. You were preoccupied. I actually have a nickname for you too."

"Oh, I'm sure you do."

He grinned, sparing me the embarrassment of actually verbalizing it. We arrived at the well, and he set the buckets down.

"I'm Kyle, by the way."

"Kenzie Williams," I said, surprised at how easy he was to talk to. "So where are you from, Kyle?"

"California."

"Me too. Which part?"

"The southern part."

"I'm from the northern part."

"Oh," Kyle winced. "I'm sorry."

I couldn't help but smile at his diss. The rivalry between Northern and Southern California had been going for years, although I suspected we northerners made a bigger deal of it than Kyle's people did. Perhaps we had a little inferiority complex going on up north. Sometimes it was hard being the forgotten little sibling to the larger-than-life Hollywood movie star.

Of course, I had no intention of letting Kyle's slight go unanswered – no self-respecting Northern Californian would. "Well, if it weren't for us northerners exporting all our water to you spoiled Southern Californians, you'd have nothing to fill your swimming pools with."

Cringing, he dramatically replied, "No swimming pools? How would we live?"

"Exactly. And not only that, but without our water putting out your daily forest fires, all your princely mansions would be lying in big piles of ash."

He eyed me in amusement. "Damn, Kenzie, let me flick that gigantic chip off your shoulder."

Yeah, maybe I was a little defensive, but it was hard not to be bitter when we were the ones producing the most water and they were the ones consuming it all. I took in Kyle's sun-kissed skin. Yep, I bet his pool was filled full of our damn water.

"So where exactly are you from?" he asked. "The Bay Area?"

"Why do you people think the state ends in San Francisco?"

"Oh, wait." He snickered. "It doesn't?"

"No," I laughed. "Our state is hella long. It actually goes up a few hundred more miles, and that's where I live. Have you ever heard of Humboldt County?"

Kyle gasped as his eyes ignited with wonder. "The pot capital of the world?"

"That would be the place," I nodded in affirmation.

"Very cool," Kyle nodded, impressed. "Is April 20th a holiday up there for you?" 4-20 being the unofficial day that potheads the world over came out to rejoice.

"Oh, yeah. The government buildings close and everything."

I took in Kyle's smug expression. Typical So-Cal boy. "Let me guess – you're a beach bum, surfer dude?"

"Something like that," he grinned. "And I'm assuming you're a Bigfoot enthusiast?"

I stopped in my tracks, coughing out a laugh. I was thoroughly impressed with his comeback. "I like him just fine."

"Hey, so I gotta ask – is it true what they say about mythical creatures with big feet?"

I think I might have snorted in response. Okay, it was official. Kyle was funny.

"Honestly, last time I saw him, I wasn't that impressed."

Kyle laughed at my retort. "You're not one of those psychos that has given an eyewitness account of his existence, are you?"

I crossed my arms over my body. "Are you implying that Bigfoot isn't real?"

"God no. Just because no actual, sane human being has ever seen him doesn't mean he hasn't been clomping through the woods for the past four hundred years."

"He has a museum, Kyle," I replied, my voice high-pitched and condemning.

"Oh, I'm sure he does." His eyes twinkled in delight. "So, Kenzie, be honest – how many times a day do you say 'hella'?"

"Oh, I'd say at least a third less than you say 'like'," I replied, flinging his insult right back at him.

We stared each other down. This was a stand-off I didn't intend to lose.

"Actually, Kyle, you really impress me."

"Do I?"

"Yeah. I can't believe a So Cal boy like yourself can survive an entire month without Starbucks. It's very brave of you."

"Thank you. It's been a rough couple days so far, but I'm enduring. And actually I was thinking the same thing about a nice Nor-Cal girl like yourself and surviving a month away from pot."

I laughed despite myself, wracking my brain for some snappy one-liner, but I had nothing. Kyle was just too quick, and I had a bad feeling that he had an arsenal of comebacks at his disposal. There would be no way to compete with him.

I threw my hands up in defeat. "You win."

"Thank you," he said, grinning and wiping his hands like he'd completed his task.

And just like that, I had the beginnings of a starry-eyed crush on one very cute and very entertaining Southern California beach boy. Before I'm judged too harshly for my insta-infatuation, it might be worth repeating that I've lived in a small town all my life. That, in and of itself, wasn't notable, but the even smaller percentage of qualified men who lived there sure was. And when I said *qualified* I didn't mean rich, handsome, or successful men. I just meant living, breathing ones. At this point, even guys with a spotty dental history weren't off the table.

In fact, the most noteworthy guy I'd been on a date with in the past year had to remove the pizza sign off the roof of his mom's car before coming to pick me up. His idea of a fun date was the .99 Taco Tuesday at Mario's Taco Shack followed by a stimulating game of Mortal Kombat, where

I got to marvel at how well my date beheaded and slaughtered his innocent victims.

It seemed all the men in my rather broad 'eighteen to dead' age range had already gotten married or had beaten their hasty retreat out of town years ago. Quality males in my neck of the woods were as much an endangered species as Bigfoot. So I was to be forgiven for my instalove approach towards Kyle. In my world, he was the shiniest of new toys, and I wanted to play.

It wasn't just the fact that he was breathing and had a full set of teeth that drew me to him. If possible, there was an even more superficial reason for my infatuation. Simply put, Kyle was easy on my pining eyes. The entire way to the watering hole, I stole glances at the man walking beside me. If I had to be honest, it wasn't the first time today he'd caught my eye, and that didn't include the unfortunate incident on the boat, of which I'd decided to never speak of again. In fact, the minute Kyle had come on board the vessel earlier in the day, my interest was piqued. He wasn't over-the-top gorgeous, like Bobby, but he wasn't cocky and off-putting either. Kyle was handsome but not overly polished, edgy but not dangerously so, and sexy in a dorky kind of way. Add his vibrant, forgiving personality into the mix, and you had the ingredients for my ideal man.

Making a real effort not to act like the male-deprived female I was, I kept my budding libido under wraps. This was certainly not the ideal reality show for a love connection. In a matter of days, I would deteriorate into a foul-smelling, stubbly, emotional beatnik. And what made it worse, I just knew the other women had come onto the show prepared for any scenario. I could only imagine the procedures they'd had done to remain attractive for the entirety of the filming. Laser hair removal, waxing, whitening, cosmetic tattooing – you name it, I was sure most of these ladies had done it. I would have too, had my hometown beauty shop offered more than just lip wax services, but as it was, the 'ladies from the eighties' who worked there hadn't even heard of laser hair removal or teeth bleaching. Hell, I'd have even settled for a Brazilian wax and Crest Teeth Whitening Strips, but those appeared to be foreign concepts as well. I sighed. It was time to face the facts: any chance I'd had at impressing Kyle with my homegrown, 'Pot Capital of the World' beauty had surely already passed.

It's not that I considered myself ugly; in fact, people often told me I had a pretty face, although I wasn't sure if that was code for 'That's the only thing you've got going for you.' And it didn't help my cause that my eyes were larger than seemed necessary. They weren't bulging out of my skull or anything, but they were big and expressive, so that I often resembled a deer in the headlights.

On the short side at five foot four, with a solid sporty body, I certainly wasn't the delicate-looking waif that most guys tended to favor. I was a runner and kept myself in

THE THEORY OF SECOND BEST

good shape, despite the fact that my boobs occasionally got in the way of a good workout. I was fairly busty for a girl my height. In the bra-size arena, I considered myself a respectable 32C; however, on a recent visit to Victoria Secret in a neighboring town, a well-meaning yet highly suspect salesgirl tried to convince me, in her itty bitty little voice, that I was actually a 34D. The memory still pissed me off. And every time I shoved my ample boobs into my little bra, I cursed the gall of that woman.

I wondered what type of girl Kyle liked. Selfishly, I hoped it was sweet, homemade girls like myself whose thighs enthusiastically high-fived one another as they met, but something told me that wasn't Kyle. He seemed the type of guy who had his pick of the litter and never chose runts. Still, a girl could dream big, delusional dreams. And with that in mind, I hastily ran my fingers through my mousy brown, shoulder length 'The Rachel' haircut. Where I came from, being fifteen years behind the trends was actually considered stylish. The moment my hand touched my tresses, I knew I was in trouble. Humidity had taken its nasty toll. My normally straight layers had skipped over the frizzy stage and gone directly for the helmet of fuzz. I let out an audible squeak of alarm.

Luckily Kyle was otherwise occupied with some lively story about Pop Tarts and didn't seem to pick up on my obvious distress. Frantically, I attempted to smooth out my wooly mammoth, do. Maybe he hadn't noticed. But when my fingers took a swipe under my eyes for smeared mascara, I was even more horrified to discover black smudges coating my fingertips. *Oh, yeah, he noticed.* How long had I been walking around looking like a furry, wide-eyed raccoon? And why had I thought mascara would be a good idea when I was getting ready this morning? I was going to an island, not a rave.

I'd learned some tricks over the years to diminish the appearance of my honking big blue eyes – left alone, they made me look perpetually flabbergasted. Make-up was a beautiful thing, until it was running down your face in hundred-degree weather.

I continued wiping under my lashes until my fingers came out clean. I didn't know why I even bothered trying to freshen myself up. After all, he'd already seen, and conversed with, my alter ego. The damage had already been done. Regardless, vanity kept me trying to improve my overall appearance just in case the hot guy in question might want to take a second look.

He didn't.

It was then that I accepted that my less-than-dazzling island beauty would never sway Kyle. My chances of getting with a guy like him were about as low as snapping a selfie of me hugging it out with Sasquatch. It just wasn't going to happen. Once I recognized that fact, I became a completely normal human being again. I allowed myself to relax and just enjoy Kyle's company. And my god, was that boy entertaining! Kyle liked talking, and I welcomed it. He seemed to be able to find the fun in everything. The truth was, I'd always been attracted to guys with big personalities. They just never liked me back.

Listening to him talk sent happy flutters dancing through me. It had been a long time since I'd felt the excitement of being around someone as engaging as Kyle. I found myself giggling at everything he said, which just egged him on. The more I laughed, the livelier he got. A guy like this was just the type I needed to pull myself out of my funk. I was a chameleon of sorts. Put me in a room full of dull, dreary people, and I'd morph into Kristen Stewart with ease. But let me mingle with some entertaining, outgoing characters, and I might actually have something clever to say.

So wrapped up was I in my fantasy land that I didn't realize Kyle had asked me a question.

"Sorry, what?"

"I asked if you'd noticed that the popular kids were already pairing up."

"Oh, yeah, I noticed it. Why aren't you part of the clique?"

"I wasn't invited… maybe because I was covered in puke when they were picking the teams."

Shame immediately colored my cheeks. Kyle saw my horrified expression and backtracked. "I was kidding! Is it too soon to make throw up jokes?"

"It will always be too soon," I replied miserably.

"If you're going to hang around me, you'll have to grow a backbone. In my family, you get a twenty-four hour reprieve from mortal embarrassment… after that, you better just own it because it's going to be smeared in your face relentlessly."

"Charming."

"Yep."

"Okay, if that's the rule, then you at least have to give me the twenty-four hours," I bargained.

"I can honor that."

We walked on. I had a smile on my face, and as I glanced over at him, his expression mirrored mine. Dang, he was a cutie.

"Well, if it makes you feel any better," I said. "I would have picked you first."

There was a pleased expression on his face before he scrunched his brows and said, "Liar. You would have picked Carl first, and you know it."

I laughed. He wasn't wrong. "Fine. Guilty. But you would have been a close second."

Kyle studied me for a moment then asked with a sad, dopey look, "You want to be my friend?"

Yes. Yes! You have no idea how much I want that. Easy, girl. Play it cool. He wants to be your buddy, not your voodoo doll boyfriend.

"I don't think we have a choice at this point. There aren't many friendlies left."

"No doubt. Is it just me, or did we already drop to the bottom of the food chain?" he asked.

"No. I noticed. We're just above the plankton."

"And by plankton, you mean Marsha?"

Oh lord. So witty. Breathe, Kenzie. Just breathe. You're here to compete for a million dollars, and Kyle is the competition, pure and simple — cute, witty, funny competition, but competition nonetheless.

<hr />

Kyle and I carried the water buckets back to camp, and as predicted, we had no fire. It obviously wasn't for lack of trying, as both Dale and Marsha were sweaty and covered in black soot.

"How's it going?" I asked, already anticipating the answer.

"We got a small flame, but it died out right away."

"Bummer," Kyle said. "Keep trying. You'll get it."

We were about to walk away when Marsha stood up and blurted out, "Did you guys know that fire is a chemical reaction between oxygen and fuel?"

I looked at Kyle, and we both shook our heads.

"The fuel has to be heated to a high enough temperature for it to ignite. And when it does, you've got combustion." Marsha illustrated her combustion by pretending to blow up.

The two of us actually took a step back as if she were about to burst into flames herself.

"Everyone knows that," Dale countered, as if it were the most common knowledge a person could have.

My eyes swept over Kyle's dumbfounded expression, which undoubtedly reflected my own. I thought maybe Dale was giving us twenty-somethings too much credit.

"Look at that face," Marsha said speaking in baby talk as she puckered her lips and then grasped Kyle's jaw in her fingers and shook it. "He hasn't got a clue."

And she was right. Kyle looked totally confused as to why this strange woman was palming his face, and he was understandably rendered speechless. Dale and I dropped open our mouths in surprise. Certainly it was the last thing any of us expected. I wasn't sure if Marsha was eccentric or psychotic, but her awkward attempt at comedy was a welcome relief from the stress and excitement of the day. The four of us collapsed into a fit of laughter.

Gene heard our merriment, and decided it wasn't allowed in camp. He hurried over to shush us as if we were kids laughing in church.

"I think it's best if you focus more of your collective energy on fire building and less on chit chat. I'm sure you'll all agree that fire is vital for our survival."

"Sorry, Bossman." Marsha saluted him.

"Don't do that," Gene replied harshly, seemingly taken aback by her gesture.

"Just teaching the young'uns here about fire-making. Are you familiar with the process yourself?" Marsha asked, and put her arm around Gene as she steered him away from our group. We could hear her chattering away, and by the looks of it, Gene was not amused. Several times he appeared to be trying to shake her off, but I had a feeling that Marsha was not easily ignored.

"Wow, she's…" I started, but wasn't sure how to finish.

"Yes, she is," Dale solemnly completed my thought.

Marsha's endless ramblings put Gene on the defensive. As it turned out, the woman without a bra seemed to know something about everything, and she wasn't shy about sharing her knowledge. Of course, Gene was the wrong person to pin into an educational corner. It was only a matter of time before he snapped. And when he did, it was spectacular.

"Woman, please!" he bellowed. "Enough already. If I wanted hours of needless chitchat, I'd still be married. Now go make yourself useful."

Instantly the faces of every woman in camp turned hard and unforgiving. Eye daggers were shot at Gene from every direction. If there was one thing that drew women together, it was a demeaning male bully. The only one who didn't appear offended by Gene's insensitive comment was Marsha herself. She seemed blissfully unaware of her role in the drama.

In an attempt to regain some control, Gene called to order our first of many meetings. With the help of Carl's brawny strength, Summer had arranged logs in a triangle formation, and I had to admit, they were rather comfy. Gene's chosen disciples sat on the two front logs, and the four of us squeezed onto the third and furthest away log.

Sitting shoulder-to-shoulder and slicked with sweat, I scanned our row of eclectic characters. Clearly we were the leftovers. The kids picked last at recess; the sad sack band of misfit toys.

My eyes lingered on Kyle sitting to my right, and I was surprised to find him smiling. This whole ridiculous situation seemed to amuse him. I wished I could muster the same carefree approach. I wondered if he truly appreciated the dangerous predicament we were in or if he just didn't care. Was this merely a fun game to him?

The meeting was called to order, and it became clear almost immediately that our tribe was no democracy. Gene was unmistakably in control, and for now, the others were willing to follow. He launched into a long-winded, pointless game day pep talk. To illustrate his points, he gave us all football positions. Although my town had always revolved around our high school football team and I'd been to pretty much every Friday night home game since birth, I still didn't know all that much about football. It had always been more a social thing for me. But although I was no expert, I knew enough to know that Gene had given the power players in the tribe the more desirable positions, like pass rusher, left tackle, and wide receiver. He conveniently claimed quarterback for himself.

Kyle, Marsha, Dale, and I got the crappier positions, like center, nose tackle, and punter. Gene pointed out that although some positions seemed more important and influential than others, a good team needed all players equally in order to win.

About three quarters of the way through the speech, Kyle put his hand up in the air. Gene ignored him and continued on with his rallying cry. Not willing to give up so easily, Kyle waved his arm around, trying to catch the man's attention. He had it, but Gene refused to engage him until he'd completed his pep talk.

"Yes?" Gene finally asked, pointing to Kyle as if he were a student being called on in class.

"Um… yeah," Kyle began with a completely straight face. "I was just wondering, since the positions are all equal, can I be the quarterback?"

I stifled a giggle, and several other tribe members snickered. I glanced over at Kyle, who caught my eye for a split second, mischievously curling his upper lip, before returning his full attention back to Gene. Damn, now I was going to have to add *smartass* to my list of desirable traits.

"Is this funny to you?" Gene asked, irritably.

"No. I just never get to play quarterback."

"That's not surprising. Quarterbacks are leaders, son."

"How do you know I'm not a leader?"

With a beady-eyed glare, Gene asked, "What's your name again?"

"Kyle."

"Well, Kyle, I've been coaching for forty-five years, and I think I know the difference between a winner and a loser."

"Oh, trust me, coach, so do I."

TV Confessional
"I was just happy Gene didn't make me a cheerleader."
— Kenzie

CHAPTER THIRTEEN

KYLE

Sunscreen and Disney Princesses

I knew I shouldn't bite the hand that feeds, but I couldn't help myself. I was a pro at sensing weakness. People like Gene, who thought they had it all figured out, were the easiest to rattle. Most of the time I just left the poor saps alone with their insecurities, but some – like Gene – who put others down to further their own agendas… they were just too fun to pass up.

Of course, now I'd royally screwed myself because the mob boss had it in for me. It had taken me all of four hours to put a giant target on my back. I nodded, impressed with myself. I'd held out longer than I'd imagined I would.

Although I wasn't real happy about being left out on the curb, the plus side was I got to hang with the other weirdos, who were infinitely more interesting than Gene's crew.

After the meeting, computer whiz Dale pulled me aside. "Meet me behind the rock cliff in ten minutes," he whispered, as he looked around all pasty-faced and shifty-eyed. With his straight black bowl cut hairdo and Harry Potter glasses, Dale's appearance screamed nerdy tech guy.

"You don't want to buy me a drink first?" I countered.

Dale gaped at me. His round face blushed a bright red, and his alarmed eyes were magnified through the thick lenses of his spectacles. Dale obviously didn't get that I was joking.

"I… no… that's not at all…. oh, no… you misunderstood me," Dale stammered.

Was this guy for real? I smiled, trying to relax him. "Kidding, Dale. Joke."

"Oh, good lord, okay. I thought you were serious, and I just… I just want you to know that I wasn't suggesting sex of any kind… with you or, you know, with anyone. I'm married. I have kids, so you know that would just be…." Dale stopped talking when he saw me smiling. "You know what, just forget I said anything."

"No," I grinned. "I'll meet you behind the rocks in ten minutes. Just keep your damn hands to yourself."

Dale's face was scrunched in confusion and worry. He was a little ball of tension. I burst into laughter and patted him on the shoulder. "Again. Joke."

Dale forced an uncomfortable laugh before returning to the fire. I saw him give me a sidelong glance filled with uncertainty. I waved. Dale turned another shade of crimson.

Marooned Rule #2
If found, a relic known as an 'immunity idol' may be kept and played during an elimination ceremony. If, after all votes have been cast, a player presents the idol, the votes placed against him or her will not count. Instead, the person with the second most votes will go home.

I met Dale in his secret hiding spot. He was there waiting, darting his head around looking for spies. I felt it was a little early in the game for such antics, but what did I know? Dale seemed a hell of a lot smarter than me, and it couldn't hurt to align myself with him, especially seeing as I didn't really have any other options to speak of.

"So what exactly are we doing?" I asked.

"I have a plan. I need your height."

"Don't you think Carl is more endowed in that area?" I asked, then, knowing how my brothers would take that rather innocent comment and turn it dirty, I figured I should probably clarify my question. "And when I say *endowed*, I mean height, not dick size... you know, just so we're clear."

"No, I... yes... I understood your reference," Dale answered, as if my remark were totally legitimate. "Anyway to answer your question, Carl is not on our side."

"And we're on the same side?"

"Oh... uh... I, uh... I just assumed we were on the same side. I mean, we were squeezed onto the loser log together. Was I being presumptuous?"

"No. You're spot on. I still can't believe he wouldn't let me be quarterback."

Dale nodded, "I know. For what it's worth, I think you would have made a fine quarterback."

"Actually, I would have totally sucked."

"Yeah, I know. I was just being nice."

Was that a sense of humor I was detecting in Dale? If so, we were going to get along nicely. "So, what do you need my height for?" I asked.

"I've made a mental map of all the areas where I think an immunity idol might exist. Starting with this rock formation. If you look up there" – he pointed up. "See that hole in the rock?"

I nodded.

"Can you reach?"

"You think there's an idol in there?" I asked, thoroughly impressed.

"There's a chance. And if we find it, we might survive the first vote."

"Why trust me?"

Dale thought about my question for a moment and then said, "Why not?"

"Can't argue with that logic."

I scaled the rock formation and stuck my hand into the hole.

"There's something," I said, as I grasped the object inside.

Dale lit up with uncharacteristic joy. He actually smacked his hands together as if he were one of those monkey clappers. The sight of him made me chuckle. I pulled out a bird's nest. The clapping stopped, and Dale deflated like a blow-up doll. Returning the nest to its home, I climbed back down.

"All right. No problem," he said, trying to mask his disappointment. "I have another spot we can try tomorrow. Are you in?"

"Hell, yeah."

Dale was just what I needed. He was going to be the smarts behind the entire operation. I planned to ride his coattails as far as they'd take me.

The minute we returned to camp, Marsha approached holding a smoldering patch of brush. "There you are, Dale." Her eyes were glazed over in crazy.

"Oh, yeah, sorry I just went to the bathroom. Everything okay?"

"My bush caught fire," she announced proudly, her braless breasts flopping every which way under her white tank top.

I swallowed back the comment my dirty mind had conjured up and then glanced at Dale, who had turned all shades of embarrassment. Although I had somewhat gotten used to Marsha's whole free boob movement, Dale clearly had not.

"We need to work together. We're close. I can feel it," she said dramatically as she grabbed Dale's arm and walked away. When her bespectacled partner wasn't looking, Marsha turned and winked at me.

My mouth dropped open. Was this lady only pretending to be crazy? Was that her angle? Or was she actually flirting with me? I wasn't sure which option disturbed me more. I winked back.

"Where did you and Dale take off to?" Kenzie asked, surprising me from behind. She'd taken on a determined stance, attempting to project herself as a tough, serious chick when her appearance was anything but. It was difficult to take her she-man persona seriously when she resembled a real-life Disney princess.

I took in her exaggerated features in amusement. Kenzie's petite oval face was framed by messy brown hair, and her delicate skin had a flawless, porcelain sheen to it. I imagined that creamy color frying up nicely in the steamy, tropical heat. Her over-sized light blue eyes pooled like glaciers against the backdrop of her pearly white skin. Pair that with her long, dark lashes and black makeup smudges, which had been circling her eyes earlier, and Kenzie resembled a beaten up Snow White. I hadn't had the heart to point out her makeup malfunction, she'd already had a bad day. The last thing she needed was a stranger telling her she looked like she'd gone four rounds with a heavyweight boxer. Plus, I liked Kenzie. She had a quirky sense of humor and actually seemed to get my jokes. Most girls I met giggled at my sarcastic humor, but I could tell they didn't really understand the joke.

"Just a little nature walk?" I answered.

"Fun," she said in an overly exaggerated cheerful voice. "You find anything interesting?"

"A couple of different bird species but, um… yep, that's all."

"Oh, really? Huh. I never would have guessed you were such an expert."

I nodded. "Very… very big bird watcher."

"That's hella cool, Kyle. What were the names of the species you found?" she asked casually, not letting me off the hook.

"Uh… we saw *pigeonitis* and, um… *pelicaucus.*"

"Wow, those sound like diseases. You wouldn't be making up species, now, would you?"

"Nope."

"Come on, Kyle. I know you were looking for an idol. Let me in on this. We're allies."

I flicked my eyes over Kenzie. "What's in it for me?"

She offered up a skeptical smile. Her teeth were as white as her skin. "What do you want?"

I raised my eyebrows at her question. Normally I'd respond with something totally sexist and inappropriate, but that probably wasn't a good idea, seeing as cameras were filming our every move and my mom would be watching. Besides, this girl was one of my only allies in this game. I needed to control my natural instinct to offend.

Changing the subject, I asked, "Is pasty white your natural skin tone?"

Kenzie glared at me, looking insulted. Oops! I'd already failed in my attempt to be less offensive. "As a matter of fact, it is."

"So, like, you don't tan at all?"

She shrugged. "I just don't see the sun very often."

I must have had a clueless look on my face because Kenzie felt the need to clarify. "If you must know, it rains a lot where I live and I work all day."

"In a sweatshop?"

"No," she laughed. "My dad and I run a rental business. You know, party supplies, tools, equipment, pretty much anything."

"That sounds fun," I replied, trying hard to keep the sarcasm out of my voice.

"It pays the bills. Something tells me you're not a nine-to-five kind of guy."

"Definitely not," I replied. "So, back to your lack of a tan…"

"You're really fascinated by that, aren't you?" She smiled.

"I am. So, okay, just for arguments sake, do you think that if your skin saw the light of day, it might actually turn brown?"

I wasn't asking this to be an ass. I genuinely wanted an answer to my question.

Kenzie sighed when she realized I wasn't going to stop. "I imagine I'd just turn a darker shade of white, or bright red. I guess we'll see by tomorrow."

"Is it weird that I'm excited for tomorrow to come?"

"Yeah, it's weird."

TV Confessional
"With that snowy skin, Kenzie's an SPF100 girl all the way."
— *Kyle*

CHAPTER FOURTEEN

KENZIE
The Sleep Train

The first night on the island was just a matter of surviving. No water. No fire. No food. Minimal shelter. And bugs, at times so thick in numbers it felt as if I were swiping my hand through water. Yes, misery was in full swing in our no-frills camp, and that was before the rain started.

Because there were no blankets or pillows, or any items of comfort at all, it was necessary to use each other for warmth. Gene's Fab Five had the section of the shelter with the sturdiest flooring and the least amount of dripping water. Although certainly not comfortable, they were clearly drier and warmer than the four of us.

As we huddled together to ward off hypothermia, our little group of oddballs bonded. Dale, a married father of three in his mid-forties, was a curious fellow. He seemed in a perpetual state of paranoia, his eyes constantly scanning the area. What he was looking for I wasn't sure, but I wondered how a guy could maneuver his way through life with that amount of anxiety. A self-described computer geek with a love of pop culture, Dale owned a software company. For years he'd been running algorithms on the show, crunching numbers and tallying statistics in an attempt to predict the winners and losers. When the opportunity arose to put his theories to work by competing himself, he reluctantly agreed. Obviously, this was a guy who preferred to live vicariously through others. One look at Dale and you could tell his brilliant mind was always working, always scheming. I realized straightaway that I was lucky to have him on my side. There might be more to the bundle of nerves than met the eye. Dale certainly wasn't the worst ally to have in this game.

And Marsha. What to say about Marsha? She was in her mid-fifties, and without a doubt, the most eccentric person I'd ever met. Although she was in respectable physical shape and seemed strong and fit, I seriously questioned her mental state. Was she one of those contestants that the producers threw in to bring the crazy? And was she *actually* crazy, or was it her way of flying under the radar? Yet everything I'd seen of her smacked of authenticity. She really was certifiable.

What was interesting about Marsha was she seemed to know a little about everything, but her considerable knowledge came out at the most unusual times. It was hard not to react to her antics. Kyle didn't even try. He openly laughed at the odd things she said, and Marsha loved it.

As for my first ally, Kyle had settled himself nicely within the group. Clearly he was the most well-liked. We all fed off his energy. My initial attraction from earlier in the day was only growing, though, and that worried me. Distractions like that could derail my whole game. I had to remember what was important. The money. My family. My future. This was hardly the time or place to become emotionally invested in a guy who had no investment in me.

That pesky self-doubt I'd been struggling with all day again reared its ugly head. Since arriving on the island I'd been studying my tribe mates, trying to figure out what made them tick. And what I had discovered was that everyone here seemed to have some label that set them apart and made them fascinating characters to follow: crazy, beautiful, funny, smart. And then there was me. What was my claim to fame? While all my teammates had legitimate reasons for being here, I was feeling like a pale, frizzy-haired fraud.

At some point late into the evening, with thunder crackling through the night sky and lightning piercing the darkness, we were huddled in a freezing little mass. Moments earlier, we'd taken advantage of the rain dumping down on us. Lying on our backs, our mouths open like baby birds, we accepted every drop that made it into our dehydrated bodies. But it wasn't until Dale came up with the idea to use a rolled leaf to funnel the water that we actually managed to quench our thirst.

Unfortunately, the prolonged time in the rain drenched us, and we were shivering fiercely when Dale came to the rescue once again.

"I think to stay warm we should try a choo-choo train style sleeping position."

"Are you talking about spooning?" Kyle replied conversationally.

"Is that what spooning means?" Dale asked in surprise. "I had no idea."

"I think it's a great idea," Marsha piped up, and then turned her gaze on Kyle. "I call spooning you."

He laughed, only encouraging her further. In the past few hours, the two of them had been trading subtle innuendos back and forth. Clearly Kyle was joking. I wasn't so sure about her.

"So, aside from Marsha, who else wants to do this?" Dale asked.

"I'm in," Kyle quipped. "But I think we should have some boundaries. I mean, it goes without saying that spooning is all backdoor stuff, so we don't need to worry about any dick-to-dick action, but I think it should also be clear that we are talking guy/girl spooning. I'm not sure about you, Dale, but I don't want your dick anywhere near my ass."

Poor Dale. Even in the dark I could tell he was blushing something fierce. The man was exceedingly uncomfortable with sex talk of any kind, and Kyle seemed to have a keen knack of endowing every conversation with something to embarrass Dale.

"Stop," I laughed, poking Kyle. "You're making him uncomfortable. Don't listen to him, Dale. I think it's a good idea. At least we won't freeze to death."

We held off on the sleep train as long as possible, but once the rain started pounding down onto our shelter and seeping through the palm leaf roof, all pride washed away and we assumed the position. We took turns on who got to be in the coveted middle section of our double-stuffed Oreo cookie configuration. Currently it was as follows: Dale, Marsha, Kyle, and me.

"So what are the rules here, Dale?" Kyle asked. "Where do our arms go?"

"Wrap them around the person in front of you, I guess. I don't know," Dale answered. "I thought you were the expert."

"Me? I try to avoid spooning at all costs."

"Why?" I asked, genuinely curious.

"It gives a chick hope that I'll stick around longer than necessary."

"Oh, okay. I get it. You're one of *those* guys," I laughed, pushing on his wet body. "And here I thought you were the strong, sensitive type."

"What in the *world* gave you that impression?" he replied, with an amused chuckle.

I cringed. I'd had no logical reason to come to that conclusion and he knew it. Would he think I'd been giving him more thought than necessary?

"Speaking of chicks, did you know that there are more chickens on earth than people?" Marsha piped in.

"I did not know that. Thank you for that valuable piece of information, Marsha," Kyle answered in mock seriousness, and then added, "You know I wasn't talking about spooning actual chickens, right?"

Marsha cackled in such a way that I wasn't sure what was going through her mind. I nudged Kyle and he turned to me with a wide-eyed look of bewilderment, as if he were saying, *Is this woman for real?*

"We need to get a few hours of shut-eye, people," Dale whispered, like a father to his children. "Or we'll be worthless in the morning."

We lay there in silence for several minutes, trying to heed Dale's sensible advice, but the explosive thunder made it impossible to actually fall asleep.

After one ear-busting blast, Marsha's increasingly grating narrative came out in a tiny squeak, "Lightning strikes are actually more common than you might think. They hit the earth about eight million times a day."

"Oh, goodie," Dale answered cynically. "We only have about 7,988,000 more to go."

"Um, Marsha?" Kyle questioned in a hushed voice.

"Yes?"

"I'm not sure if you're aware, but your hand is on my ass."

"Yes. I'm aware."

Uncontained giggles burst forth from each and every one of us. The misery of our situation had given way to near hysterics.

"Okay, then, well… enjoy."

"I already am," Marsha replied.

The four of us shook with laughter. The more we tried to be quiet, the louder we got. Even Dale had given up on being practical.

"Do you want to hear a joke?" he whispered, tittering.

"Is it a techie joke?" Kyle asked.

"Sort of."

"That's what I was afraid of. Okay, go."

"What is Forrest Gump's computer password?"

"123456," Marsha answered without skipping a beat.

"What?" Dale asked, astonished. "No. It's a joke, Marsha. And, just so you know, that's literally the worst password ever. You realize every hacker in the world tries that one first, right?"

"That's my password for everything."

"Somehow I'm not surprised."

"Dale," I blurted out. "The suspense is killing me. What is Forrest Gump's password?"

"1forrest1."

None of us responded right away, possibly processing the genius of the joke, but then the floodgates opened and we all dissolved into hysterical fits of laughter.

"Would you please be quiet!" Gene blasted over the thunder. "Some of us are trying to sleep."

"That would be the 'some of us' who don't have water dripping on their heads," Dale mumbled, for only us to hear.

"I don't know about you guys, but tomorrow morning I'm going to have some serious words with the roofer," Marsha declared.

When I awoke the next morning, Marsha and I were in the middle of the spoon train. Kyle was sound asleep, his arms wrapped tightly around my body and his head tucked into the crook of my neck. I had to smile at the intimacy as well as the pure innocence of our embrace. Instead of pulling out of his hold, I snuggled a little tighter into him. Why not? He was warm, and honestly, it had been way too long since I'd had strong, masculine arms draped around me.

My last boyfriend had been three long years ago, the son of the couple who owned the one-screen movie theater in town. I'd known him all my life. Four years older than me, Greg and I had only been dating for a few months when he'd asked me to marry him. I was twenty-one and not ready for the life he was offering. And although Greg was a nice guy, we just didn't have the spark needed to maintain a long and successful marriage. We broke up and, six months later, he married the pharmacist's daughter. I'd been single ever since.

As I lay there listening to Kyle's rhythmic breathing, I smiled despite myself. Last night had been hell. The storm that passed through was fierce. Most of the night we'd lain awake as our senses were assaulted by the wrath of Mother Nature. I might have slept a few hours at most. But strangely, I was wide awake now and excited for the game to really begin. It was one whole month, maybe even longer if I played my cards right. One month with no work, no schedules, no day-to-day stress. I breathed in happily. For the first time since this whole adventure began, I was feeling beyond lucky. I'd spent so many years putting others first to the detriment of my own happiness. Somewhere along the line, I'd given up on my own ambitions to boost the dreams of others. I always told myself that someday, when the triplets were older and on their own, it would be my turn. But the older I got, the further away that seemed. This money, if I could manage to win it, could buy me a new future.

Kyle nap-jerked, pulling me back into the present. I was surprised at how relaxed I was with him. Kyle made me laugh, which was something I'd been lacking lately. Life always tended to get in the way of a good time. Kyle shifted as he woke from his slumber, and I waited as he yawned and stretched his long legs.

"Good morning, Sunshine. Was last night as good for you as it was for me?" he asked in a sleepy voice.

"Better," I smiled. "You were amazing."

I could feel Kyle's lips form into a smile on my neck. Oh, lord, he was pretty awesome. He kept his arms around me. I could definitely get used to this sleep position.

"Check it out," he said, pointing toward Marsha and Dale. Her wayward boobs were squished up against his back and her leg was straddling his. I could only imagine Dale's horror when he woke up to that reality. Attempting to stifle a giggle, I failed miserably. My enjoyment was short-lived, though, when I caught sight of a camera guy and a sound tech coming our way.

"Oh, my god," I said burying my head in his arm.

"What?"

"Camera, four o'clock."

"You're on a reality show, Kenzie. Get used to it. They're everywhere."

And just as he said that, another pair of cameramen made their way over.

"We must be the only ones awake."

"I have to look just terrible," I said as I attempted to tame my wild hair.

"You look fine. Don't worry about it."

Ahh…he was such a sweet guy.

"Although you smell like wet dog."

I gasped in surprise and then elbowed him in the chest. "And here I was thinking how sweet you were," I said as I wrestled out of his arms and sat up. Immediately I lifted my arms to smell myself.

"Relax. I was kidding," he replied, and sat up himself. "We all stink. Don't think you're so special."

Oh, right, because smelling like a wet dog qualifies me as ordinary in my new world. Slipping on his shoes, Kyle scooted himself off the platform and onto his feet.

"I've got to take a piss. You want to come?"

Did I want to take a hike in the woods and squat over a dirt hole with a hot guy I'd just met? No, not really. But this was my life for as many days as I lasted, so I'd better get used to the lack of privacy, not to mention the decimation of my vanity.

"Yeah, I'm coming," I huffed.

TV Confessional

*"Last night sucked. But the morning
was quite nice."*
— Kenzie

CHAPTER FIFTEEN

KYLE

The Blue Lagoon

Kenzie was a riot. She was so clearly out of her element but was trying hard to hide it. Trudging through the tropical brush, my spooning buddy walked head on into a spider web. Of course her first instinct was to panic. Hell, that would have been my first reaction too. Then she proceeded to do the whole customary creepy-crawly dance, frantically attempting to remove the sticky substance from her hair and face. Her expression transformed into that of a sour old man as she pawed at her skin. Once Kenzie realized I was watching her entire entertaining spectacle, she forced herself to calm down. Adopting a façade of indifference, she brushed off the remaining web and marched on with determination etched upon her pretty face.

We found our way to the designated bathroom area. It wasn't an actual bathroom, since we were expected to just go wherever the land-or-sea, allowed. But yesterday as a tribe we'd found a spot off the beaten path that was surprisingly private and collectively deemed it 'the poophole.' The thick barrage of tropical foliage separating the area made a perfect, secluded division into a 'his' and 'hers' section.

As we took off for our individual spaces, I called to her, "I'll meet you back here in a few."

"You don't have to wait," she said, looking down at her shoes as she rolled a strand of hair through her fingers.

"I don't mind."

"It might take awhile."

"Oh," I said getting the mental picture. "Geez, Kenzie. Too much info."

She looked up, confused, and then understanding dawned on her. "What? No. I'm not going number two. I just have issues peeing outside."

"You get stage fright?" I said, nodding.

"No, I'm afraid something's going to bite my butt while I'm squatting."

My mind wandered in so many directions at once. "It's times like these I'm happy to be a guy," I replied, feeling quite superior.

"You do realize that it will become an issue for you at some point too, right?"

"Oh yeah, shit. Great, now you have *me* all worried."

"Sorry," she laughed.

"Anyway, I'll wait here. What else do I have to do?"

<hr>

After about five minutes a relieved-looking Kenzie rounded the corner.

"Everything come out okay?" I asked.

She gave me a dirty look.

"And, most importantly, nothing went in that shouldn't have?"

She grinned and smacked me. "You're pushing it, Kyle. If you want a pissing buddy, you'd better keep your mouth shut."

I stopped talking because, honestly, I did want a pissing buddy.

Kenzie took off in the opposite direction from where we'd come.

"Hold up. You're going the wrong way."

"No, I'm not. I'm exploring. You want to come?"

Like an obedient dog following his master, I trotted over to her side. "Oh boy, do I."

She eyed me with amusement. "You don't like being alone, do you?"

Kenzie's words were nothing more than an innocent observation, but she had no idea just how accurately she'd hit the nail on the head. I'd actually been in therapy for that very issue. I'd never really seen it as a problem, but my mom had insisted on bringing it up, and the therapist harped on it over and over. So I liked company? Big deal. There were worse things to stress over.

"I don't need to be alone when I have my very own Dora the Explorer to follow around."

"Oh, right. This is going to be very informative. Are you ready? That right there is a rock. Oh, and over there, that leafy thing – plant."

"Wow," I said wide-eyed, "You sure know your stuff."

"Yep."

"So forgive me if I have pegged you all wrong, Kenzie, but this doesn't seem like your type of a reality show."

"Why's that?"

"I don't know, you seem like more of an inside girl."

Kenzie raised one eyebrow at me. "I could say the same about you."

"That may be true, but I'm not the one who was nearly taken away on a stretcher yesterday."

"Yeah, well, don't let my fainting, barfing, and bug burrowing phobia fool you. I'm actually a really tough chick," she said, as she ducked out of the way of a dive-bombing insect and let out a little scream.

"Well, that's a relief." I grinned as she circled around the back of me for protection.

Kenzie was definitely growing on me. She had an endearing quality to her that I couldn't quite pinpoint. She wasn't like most of the women I met in my day-to-day life. This one was real and humble, sort of like my sister Emma, only a much nicer version.

Kenzie gasped and grabbed my arm, "There, in the tree. Is that fruit?"

My eyes followed her pointing finger until they focused on some purple orbs bundled high up in a tree.

"I don't know. Either that or they're seed pods."

"We should go up there and check it out."

"And by we, you mean me?"

"Wow, it's like we're so in sync." She grinned playfully. "That's exactly what I meant."

"But you're such a tough chick. I can't believe you don't climb trees."

She looked up at me with her big doe eyes and shrugged her shoulders.

"Well, would you let me know when you plan on being tough? I can't wait to witness it."

"You'll be the first to know."

My empty stomach grumbled in protest. At some point during the night. I wished I'd taken my dad's advice and come into the game with a tolerance to hunger because that extra plate of spaghetti my mom had crammed down my throat was definitely not doing me any favors today.

I sighed. Dammit. Now I had to scale the tree. I was no acrobat and didn't particularly like heights, but nothing was going to stop me from ascending to the highest of elevations to secure my breakfast. I was just that damn hungry.

Kenzie had to hoist me up to the first foothold, but once there, I managed to maneuver myself from branch to branch until I was unsteadily perched on a limb jutting out from the sturdy trunk. I reached for the dark object. It had the coloring of a ripe avocado but was shaped more like a pinecone. I broke it off and reached for another.

"Is it edible?" Kenzie called up to me, squinting as she shielded her eyes from the morning sun.

"How would I know?"

"Well, is it hard or soft?"

Oh, man, she was just asking for it with that question. "Let me just be clear – you're talking about the fruit, right?"

Kenzie shook her head, grinning. "Yes, the fruit."

I made a big show of feeling the produce. "Ooh, wow... yes, uh-huh... this little fella is downright *rigid*... so firm and plump. I think you're really going to like this one, Kenzie."

"You're a nutcase," she laughed. "Just pick some and get back down before you fall on your head."

I filled my pockets with as many guacamole fruits as I could reach and then scooted myself back down the tree in a less than elegant fashion, actually tumbling down the final four feet, spilling the fruit out of my pockets. Kenzie scrambled to gather them, entirely indifferent to my unceremonious decent. She was gingerly picking up the crop and dusting off the dirt as I unfurled my crumpled body and sat up.

"I'm okay, in case you were wondering."

Kenzie wasn't paying any attention to me. Focused solely on our breakfast, her face had suddenly taken on a ravenous appearance. "How do you think we eat these?"

I propped myself up against the tree and Kenzie took her place beside me, our precious bounty gathered lovingly between her outstretched legs. I picked up one of the cones closest to me and turned it over, trying to figure out how to eat it. First I tried biting into it, but the skin was too thick. Then I tried sawing it open on the tree, to no avail. Finally, impatient and starving, I went all caveman on its little purple ass and smashed the unforgiving fruit against a rock until the rind split open and revealed its treasures within. Both Kenzie and I cheered our good fortune.

I sniffed the insides and recoiled at the funky smell.

"You should lick it and see," Kenzie offered up helpfully.

"And see what? If I die?"

"No. If it tastes good."

"Smell it. I'm pretty sure it isn't going to taste much better."

She took a sniff and her nose crinkled in protest.

"What do you think?" I asked her. "Should we eat it?"

"I don't know. Was this on our 'Do not eat or you will die a long and painful death' list?"

"Honestly, I didn't even look at that information," I admitted.

"Why?"

"I figured someone else would take care of it." I shrugged.

"What, like a maid or your own personal chef?"

"I just didn't imagine myself playing Tarzan and swinging from trees to get my nourishment."

I looked over at one of the cameramen who was eagerly waiting to record my untimely demise.

"Do you know if these are edible?" I asked him.

The dude shrugged noncommittally from behind the lens. Seriously? I realized they weren't allowed to talk to us, but still, this was sort of a life or death situation.

"I am going to eat this," I articulated each word slowly and clearly. "Do you think I will die?"

The cameraman made another vague motion with his shoulders.

I gaped at him and his obvious lack of concern for my life and then turned my attention back to Kenzie. "Well, you heard him. We're good."

As I raised the fruit to my mouth, her eyes glazed over in uncertainty then grew double in size, and they were already pretty damn big to begin with.

"Stop. You're making me nervous," I protested.

"I can't help it. This feels like the scene from that movie *Blue Lagoon* where the couple eats the poisonous berries."

I'd never seen *Blue Lagoon*, nor had I even heard of it, but all of the sudden, its plot points seemed over-the-top important to me.

"What happened?" I asked with wide, uneasy eyes.

"Honestly, I can't remember."

I lowered the fruit and glowered at her. "Well, that really doesn't help me at all," I grumbled. "You probably could have omitted that particularly unhelpful piece of information."

"Sorry, I shouldn't have prolonged your life any longer than necessary. Continue."

"Your concern for me is really touching," I said. Then, without further hesitation, I sank my teeth into the fruit while glaring defiantly into the camera. If the dickhead was going to film my death I, at least, wanted to look tough on my way out.

I seesawed my way through the firm, fleshy meat and was chewing for an uncomfortably long time before I managed to swallow the first unappetizing mouthful. I gagged a bit. The fruit had an unsavory taste and texture, but it filled my empty stomach and, as my dad always said, 'Beggars can't be choosers.' And today, I was definitely a beggar.

Kenzie had wisely given me ample time to keel over and die before she finally deemed the fruit safe and ate one of her own. We devoured two more each before shoving the rest into our pockets for Dale and Marsha.

As we got up to leave, I turned to the cameraman and said, "Thanks for nothing, asshole."

I swear I saw him smile.

———

That afternoon, while I was gathering wood for a fire we didn't have, Aisha popped up from behind some trees, startling me.

"Whatcha doing?" I asked.

"Nothing," she answered, looking nervous.

I knew that expression. She was searching for the immunity idol. Dammit! Dale and I needed to find it before Gene's crew did, or we would be completely screwed come the first elimination ceremony. I decided then and there to stay by her side to prevent her from continuing her search.

"I'm gathering wood, if you want to help…"

"Yeah, sure," she said quickly, and bent down to collect some of her own.

Aisha and I chatted our way back to the camp. Up to that point she hadn't said a word to me, preferring to hide behind the other members of Gene's group. I found her to be friendly and easy to talk to but also a bit jumpy, as if she were concerned to be seen with me. I could only assume Gene wouldn't take kindly to her fraternizing with the enemy.

Once back at the shelter, I noticed Gene and Carl were not in camp. Aisha did too, and she instantly relaxed.

"I'm boiling hot," she announced, before stripping down to an itty-bitty bikini, and I couldn't help but appreciate her obvious gifts. She was tall and toned, and her face was the perfect mix of soft and hard angles. But it was her eyes that completed the impressive package: light hazel against the backdrop of her darker skin. It was easy to see how she'd won a beauty contest. Aisha was definitely the type of woman I typically intercepted after concerts.

She saw me staring and smiled. "You want to go swimming?"

"Yeah, definitely." I jumped up and followed her down to the water's edge.

As we waded into the gentle waves, she said, "I feel like we've met before."

I looked at her more closely. Shit, maybe she *was* one of the women I'd slept with following a show. Or maybe she just saw a little of Jake in me. We didn't look that much alike, but there was a slight resemblance, and people often gave me that look like Aisha was giving me now.

"No, I definitely would have remembered you."

Aisha appeared uncertain, as if she were searching her mind for a connection. In an effort to deter her from identifying me, I jumped into the water like a dolphin and swam around her feet a few times. When I surfaced, Aisha was wide-eyed with shock.

"What?" I asked, alarmed, and immediately scanned the water for a shark fin.

"How long can you hold your breath? You were down there for a long time."

"My record is just under three minutes, but that was when I was surfing a lot."

"Dang! That will help our tribe in challenges. You need to tell Gene that you're a good swimmer."

"I'm not exactly his favorite person."

"No, probably not. But what did you expect? Starting quarterback, Kyle? Come on. You should at least have asked to play back-up," Aisha teased.

"Nah, I've played back-up all my life. It's time to go big or go home."

"Well, pissing off Gene is definitely going big, that's for sure. And it will probably get you sent home."

I nodded, my face turning serious. "Be honest, Aisha: am I on the chopping block?"

"No. I think everyone's in agreement that Marsha will be the first to go."

"And then me?"

"You, Dale, or Kenzie. I think it will come down to which one of you sucks the most in challenges."

"Well, that could be any one of us."

Aisha winced, looking pained by my words. "Sorry, I don't make the rules."

"But you're following them... why?"

"It's nothing against you guys. Really, I like all of you. I'm just going with the numbers."

"So let's make our own numbers. Join the underdogs. You know everyone likes them best."

Aisha laughed. "I know, but I'm more comfortable with the prom queens and football players."

"Oh, please, you're not buying into Gene's whole game day winner's speech, are you?"

"I'm just trying to stay alive, Kyle. Just like you. If I jumped ship, you really think they'd find worth in Miss Nevada? I'd be one step up from Marsha and her thousands of interesting facts."

Bobby waded out to join us, and placing a protective arm around Aisha, he flashed me the dirtiest look imaginable. Geez, he wasn't even trying to hide his disdain for me. I wasn't sure what I had done to invite his ire, but I knew to watch my back around him.

I couldn't help wonder how Bobby would be perceived by the viewing public. By looks alone, he was sure to become a fan favorite. In fact, both he and Aisha were just the perfect male and female specimens. They needed to have posters made or something.

"What's going on?" he asked, eyeing me suspiciously. "I hope you're not talking strategy without me."

"We're just talking football," I answered.

"Football, huh?" Bobby glanced between us, unconvinced. "In this tribe, that's as good as treason."

Aisha flashed me a nervous glance. Maybe she wasn't as secure in her alliance as she thought she was.

"Relax, Aisha has no interest in joining the bottom feeders. You're safe."

"Exactly. I mean, why would she?" Bobby faced Aisha and issued a clear warning. "There's safety in numbers. You don't want to be on the wrong side of the split."

Aisha nodded obediently. At that moment I was glad to be in my group of four. Maybe I was on the losing side, but at least I wasn't whoring myself out to the power players.

"So I gotta ask, Kyle, what's going on with you and Marsha? Is it serious?"

Marsha had garnered an unhealthy amount of attention from the fab five and none of it was good. But I'd spent two days with the woman, and I couldn't help but like her. Yeah, she was odd, but that's what made life interesting.

"The two of you were getting pretty cozy last night. Has she let you cop a feel of those granny knockers?" Bobby chuckled to himself.

"Don't be an ass," Aisha scoffed. She seemed rattled by Bobby's distrust in her.

I made a mental note to mention it to Dale. If I could convince Aisha to switch sides, she might be our way out of the mess we'd found ourselves in.

A loud splash caught our collective attention. I looked over just as Kenzie was pulling herself off the shallow ocean floor and resurfacing. She was sputtering and coughing, her drenched hair plastered to her face.

"Are you okay?" I rushed to her. Was she seriously drowning in three feet of water? Damn, this girl was a walking disaster.

"Yeah, I tripped on a rock."

"Jesus," Bobby laughed. "Walk much?"

I helped her back to her feet and her eyes caught mine. She looked worried.

"I'm thinking you've had a bit too much sun today," Bobby smirked.

In fact, Kenzie had fried in the scorching sun, just as I'd predicted she would. Her skin was bright red and beyond painful looking.

"You think?" Kenzie replied, contempt for Bobby clear on her face. Pulling strands of hair out of her eyes, she continued to periodically spit up water.

"I think I burned a little too. It's so hot here." Aisha smiled. "If you need help with the sunscreen, just ask."

Kenzie skimmed her eyes over the beauty queen, almost as if she thought Aisha was being facetious.

"Okay, thanks," Kenzie said, as she self-consciously ran her hands over the burned skin. "So, what did I miss?"

"Kyle here was just about to tell us a bit more about his elderly girlfriend."

Kenzie twisted her head towards me in surprise. The fact that I was talking to the enemy made her assume I'd betrayed our four-way alliance. I shook my head.

"Fire! Fire!"

We all turned to the shore and saw Marsha jumping up and down, a roaring fire behind her.

I turned to Bobby. "Looks like my girl just saved us all."

TV Confessional
"Honestly, with that sunburn, Kenzie
looks like an Oompa Loompa...
but don't tell her I said that."
— Kyle

Chapter Sixteen

KENZIE
No Winner

The minute I saw Kyle walk off with Aisha, panic rose through my body. I tried to reason with myself that it was innocent, but two things troubled me about their newfound friendship. First, his loyalty… and second, her beauty. Of the four of us, Kyle would certainly prove to be the most useful in challenges. Although not rippling with muscles, he was strong, quick, and agile. It would make sense to keep him around the longest.

Plus, as much as I hated to admit, Kyle was a misfit by circumstance only. I was certain that in his everyday life, he wasn't some sad sap sitting on the sidelines watching life pass him by. As much as Gene had tried to put him in his place, it was obvious to me that Kyle had the clear makings of a quarterback, and one everyone would follow.

Then it came to my second, more personal, concern... Aisha. She was all that I wasn't: tall, gorgeous, and glamorous. I'd never known what life was like at her status level. When you looked the way she did, the world granted you certain privileges that us mere mortals could only dream of. I realized I was unfairly generalizing, and I understood that there were gorgeous women with big, beautiful hearts. I just didn't want them taking the attention of my island boy. I'd already claimed Kyle as my own on day one, and I didn't want to share him, especially not with the likes of Aisha. A girl like her, who had never gone to a dance without a date or been left off a party list, would win the boy every time.

Aisha's laugh brought me back to the present. My eyes narrowed in on my competition, or more accurately the bikini body of my competition. I couldn't dream of coming close to that level of perfection. More laughter. *Dammit, Kyle! Stop using your charm on her.* I had to get out there and run interference before everything I'd built in the past two days fell apart. Would it be too obvious if I interrupted him now? Would he think I didn't trust him? Would he think I was jealous?

When Bobby waded out there, my insecure girl worries were replaced with ruthless game strategy. No way was I going to allow them to take away my most important ally. I ran down to the beach and, too distracted to remove my shorts, I just trudged in with them still on. Determined and focused, I was totally unprepared for the rock that broke my stride, and I face-planted onto the shallow ocean floor.

———

Kyle sat beside me on the log as we dried ourselves near the raging fire. Dale and Marsha fed the flames, incredibly proud of their offering. Although they were praised all around, I couldn't help but think those same people wouldn't hesitate to cut them down first chance they got.

"I'm going to the bathroom." I stood up and caught Kyle's eye.

"I'll come with you."

We walked in silence until we were clear of camp.

"That was quite an entrance you made earlier."

"Oh, you mean in the water? Yeah, I meant to do that," I grinned.

"Oh, right, of course."

I stared up at him before asking in a serious tone of voice, "Did they get to you?"

"What do you mean?"

"Just be honest, Kyle. Are you with them now?"

"No. Why would I be with them?"

"Because… I have a feeling that's where you belong."

He stopped walking and stared at me. "Belong?"

"Yes. With the winners."

Kyle's eyes widened. He seemed genuinely surprised by my comment. "Really? You think so?"

"I know so."

He shook his head.

"What?"

Kyle was quiet for a moment. He seemed to be searching for the right words. "I'm no winner, Kenzie."

"What do you mean by that?"

Kyle didn't elaborate. We continued on until we came to the entrance of the poophole and then went our separate ways. His admission surprised me. This wasn't Kyle being self-deprecating, no; this was a guy who truly believed he was nothing special. Suddenly I wanted to make it my mission to figure out why.

Fire was our most important resource. If it went out, there was no telling how long it would take to get it started again. Without it, we had no fresh water and no rice. Every member of the tribe realized this, so it was a smart move on Gene's part to assign shifts throughout the night to keep it going.

I pulled a middle of the night shift with, of all people, Carl. He had barely spoken a word to me since the game began. I tried to make small talk with the man, but he didn't have a lot to say. The long minutes of silence were excruciating. How did this man function in his everyday life?

A rustling in the bushes caught our attention.

Carl jerked forward; the look of fear on his face was palpable. I could almost see the little hairs standing up on the nape of his neck.

"What's that?" he whispered, wide-eyed and afraid.

"I'm sure it's nothing," I offered back feebly. I was no hero, but certainly I wasn't as freaked out as this big lug of a man seemed to be.

"If it's a snake, I'm going to scream like a little girl. I'm just warning you."

I laughed until I realized he was actually serious.

"You're afraid of snakes?"

"That's weird to you?" he asked, sounding taken aback by my question.

"Well, you just don't look like the type of person who is afraid of anything." He didn't respond right away, seemingly annoyed by my reaction. In an attempt to ease the tension, I added, "And I read somewhere there are no snakes on the Cook Islands, so you can relax."

"Really? That's wonderful news." He exhaled loudly, and then did the unthinkable: Carl smiled. At first I thought it was just a facial twitch caused by the stress of the situation, but when his lip turned up in the right corner and a row of teeth could be seen peeking out from below, it was unmistakable. "I'm afraid of rodents and spiders too," he confessed.

He was making a joke. *Wow.* This was a major break-through. I laughed before commenting, "Well, damn, Carl, you are an actual human being."

"What species did you think I was?"

"Honestly, I thought they made a whole new category just for you."

He nodded.

"So I have to ask… is it just snakes, rodents, and spiders, or do you have issues with other creatures?"

"I pretty much run the gamut when it comes to things that scurry or slither."

"Like how scared are we talking?"

"The type of scared where I stand on a chair if I see a mouse."

I laughed at the mental picture of this giant of a man teetering on a chair four times too small for him.

"You're married with kids, right?"

"Was. And I have one kid. A daughter."

"Oh, never mind."

"No, what? Why were you asking?"

"Did you make your wife kill the spiders when you were married?"

"I did. I'd be standing in a corner screaming for her to catch it and, at the same time, begging her not to kill it." He shook his head as if remembering something distasteful. "It was just awful. She would ruthlessly smash out his little life like she was some callous killing machine. It really was the beginning of the end."

"You divorced her over a spider?"

"No, that just pissed me off. We divorced because I told her I like men."

I gaped at Carl, not sure if I'd heard him correctly. "Wait. Are you gay?"

"Yes, you heard me right, and I know what you're thinking: I'm the last guy on earth you'd expect would be gay. Blah, blah, blah, I've heard it all before."

My mouth must have been hanging open.

"You might want to close that before a bug flies in," Carl grumbled. "Because then I can't sit with you anymore."

"Oh, sorry," I said, closing my gaping mouth. "Wow, I swear I never would have guessed."

"We gays come in all shapes and sizes."

"Apparently. I think what I find even more surprising than the fact that you're gay is the fact that you're the sensitive type who has a no kill policy for spiders."

"I'm an animal lover." Carl shrugged.

"But you hate snakes and rodents and spiders."

He sighed, as if explaining himself to me was such a giant chore. "Well certainly I don't want to have tea with them, but I don't wish them dead, either."

I shook my head, smiling. "Wow, Carl, I just thought you were one of Gene's boring old, mindless cronies."

"I *am* one of Gene's mindless cronies, only I'm a big, dumb, gay one."

I snorted out a laugh and had to mask it to keep from waking the others.

"Can you do me a favor, Kenzie?"

"Sure," I said, with a newfound fondness for this goliath.

"Don't blab it around."

"That you're gay?"

"No, that I'm afraid of spiders. It would totally ruin my tough guy image."

I giggled my approval. "Your secret is safe with me."

After his shocking moment of levity, Carl reverted back to the introvert he was known to be. I was confused and even more fascinated by this man than I had been before. What was Carl thinking? Shutting people out the way he did was no way to endear yourself to people. If this game were based on just the physical aspects, Carl would obviously excel. But it wasn't. You couldn't survive out here on your own, not for long, anyway. My eyes darted in his direction. Carl caught me staring and I quickly looked away. Man, this guy had a way of making those around him feel uncomfortable.

Finally I couldn't take it anymore. "Okay, what gives?" I asked.

"What do you mean?"

"We were having a nice conversation and then nothing."

"Oh." He seemed perplexed. "I thought we'd finished talking."

I dropped my head as I took in Carl's innocent expression. Good lord, the guy wasn't being rude, he was just *that* socially awkward.

"Don't look at me like that," he said, his attitude turning hostile.

"I'm not making fun of you. I'm just surprised. Are you shy?"

There was an uncomfortable pause, and I noticed his cheeks burning red in embarrassment. Then he nodded.

"So that's why you don't talk to anyone?"

"I talk when it's necessary. When it's not, I don't."

"You understand this might not be the best reality show for you, Carl."

"You don't think I know that?"

"Why are you here, then?"

"Why are *you* here?" he challenged. "I'm pretty sure for the same reason I am."

"So then you don't actually hate everyone?"

"No, I hate everyone," he said with that strange ogre smile. There was a pause and then, as if he were trying not to offend, he added, "present company excluded."

"Well, thank you," I beamed. "But, this is the first conversation we've ever had, and look, we hit it off. Don't you think maybe if you gave the others a chance, you might be surprised?"

Carl considered my words for a moment and then shook his head. "Gene's an anal retentive big mouth. Summer believes in unicorns. Really? I mean, come on, unicorns, Kenzie! Bobby's a candy-ass prick. Aisha," he stopped, looked around nervously, then whispered, "I think she's a Scientologist. And Dale, he does that weird mouth breather thing. Kyle, I'm pretty sure he was a crack baby. And Marsha, she's just bat-shit crazy."

His overly critical assessment of our tribe mates surprised, amused, and concerned me. Is this how we were seen by viewers, or was it just a grumpy guy's ramblings?

"Geez, Carl, tell me how you really feel."

He shrugged his enormous shoulders in response.

"Do I even want to know what you labeled me?" I asked, slightly worried.

Carl caught my eye and I saw a flicker of gaiety before he averted them. "Probably not."

I smiled, and then stood up and stoked the fire. "I hope you realize that you're going to need these people to get to the end."

"Do you think I like being this way?" he groused. As he dipped his head forward, I noticed Carl's body slump under the weight of his own hang-ups. "I can't help it. I've never been good with social interactions. When I was a kid, I got picked on pretty fiercely. I mean, look at me. I was a freak, over six feet tall at the age of nine. I guess I just assume people are making fun of me at all times, so that's why I'm not nice back."

"That's pretty cynical thinking," I said, leaving the fire to sit down next to him on the log. "You stand out, obviously, but that doesn't mean people are making fun of you. They're just fascinated."

"Yeah, well, I never asked to be a seven-foot-two-inch-tall freak."

"And I never asked to be a motherless eight-year-old. We don't always get to choose, Carl."

My very personal admission shut Carl down. He shifted uncomfortably. If I didn't take action now, the two of us would fall back into that painful silence.

"Oh, stop," I smiled.

"Now I feel bad."

"Don't. I wasn't whining; just stating a fact. You know, when I first saw you, I admit, I was mesmerized by your overall appearance. But I wanted to get to know you. *You* were the one that put up the wall."

"I know," he sighed. "I need to be less defensive. I get that."

He seemed so vulnerable. A variety of emotions were swirling around inside my head for this guy. He was like a sweet, wounded man living inside a crotchety giant's body. Suddenly I felt the need to protect him. Reaching out, I touched his massive shoulder, my hand dwarfed in comparison.

"Would you let me help you?" I asked.

"How?"

"With your social game. You won't last long out here without one."

Carl eyed me, a look of disbelief evident on his face. "Why would you do that?"

I understood his skepticism. Why would I help him? He was basically the enemy. If I were really playing the game only to win, I'd let him choke on his own neuroses. His misfortune was my gain, after all. But I'd already grown attached to Carl, and I couldn't just leave him hanging. Tomorrow I'd start playing a ruthless game, but tonight, I was just Kenzie, the girl who put everyone else first.

"I like you. No other reason. Tomorrow we start your cotillion lessons."

Carl and I talked the rest of our shift. He told me about his life as a lumberjack as well as his side career in Hollywood. He played roles in movies that needed exceptionally tall characters. It didn't bring in much money, but it was something, and was also how he'd been discovered for this show. After some prodding, Carl opened up about his divorce, his daughter, and coming out at thirty-five. Not surprisingly, Carl's surly temperament didn't play well in the gay crowd, and he had yet to find love, or even 'like,' for that matter. As far as I could tell, the only good thing he had in his life was his daughter, and he rarely got to see her as his ex-wife had moved with their daughter to another state after the divorce. There was a deep sadness in Carl that touched my heart and made me want to help him. By the end of our two-hour shift, I felt connected to this gentle giant in ways I never would have thought possible. We even hugged it out before he wandered back to his side of the bamboo tracks and I to mine.

Kyle was snoozing soundly when I got to our sleeping quarters. I wanted to curl up into his body the exact way I had woken up this morning, but I knew that wasn't appropriate given our very short and very platonic, relationship. But the memory of his arms wrapped around me sent warmth through my body. If it were raining I'd have an excuse, but as it was now-with clear, warm skies-there was just no justifiable way to get me some cuddling time in without totally freaking the dude out. Bummed, I slipped in between him and Marsha.

As I lay there waiting for sleep to take me, I watched Kyle's peaceful face. He definitely intrigued me. There was more to him than met the eye. I was sure of it. Unable to fall asleep, I lay there and endlessly speculated what his story might be. His comment earlier about not being a winner played over and over in my mind. I thought I'd heard just the slightest hint of sadness in his words. Kyle presented himself to the world as just some funny, goofy guy, but I had to wonder if that smile was there to mask something deeper... a pain that remained unspoken.

TV Confessional
"I'm going to put the jolly in Carl's green giant.
Wait, that didn't sound right, did it?"
— Kenzie

CHAPTER SEVENTEEN

KYLE
Udder's Day

It was day three, and I was sitting by myself on the beach reflecting on the changes I'd noticed since arriving on the island. Inhaling deeply, I marveled at the relaxed sense of calm I was feeling. The anxiety that had gripped me for weeks leading up to the start of the game was miraculously gone. Being cut off from Jake, with no way to contact him, was actually freeing in a way I never would have thought possible. I'd spent the past ten years tethered to my brother, not only because he needed the support but because I did too. Our shared past haunted me in ways that I'd never been able to shake. Of course it affected Jake so much more. I wasn't trying to downplay his suffering, but his was an accepted pain, maybe even an expected one. Jake's nightmare was out there for the world to see and judge. Me? I was just a background player in the story of his tragic life. No one knew or cared what I'd gone through all those years ago. Yeah, it wasn't anything next to the magnitude of what Jake had survived, but to me it was real and terrifying, and the memories still lived on in my head.

For all my bravado, deep down, I was just a scared kid. New experiences terrified me. Being alone without the support of a trusted few filled me with dread. Just the fact that I was out here at all was a major accomplishment.

I hadn't always been this way. There was a time, many years ago, that I was one of those daredevil kids. You know the type – the kid all other kids admired for his fearlessness and the one other parents shook their heads at in disapproval. I'd broken many bones in my attempts to experience all that life had to offer. Whether it was riding my bike off a store rooftop or flipping through the air on my skateboard, I was always up for a new challenge. The old Kyle would have reveled in an adventure like this, but I'd stopped being that kid a long time ago.

Post-tragedy Kyle spent years in therapy. He no longer felt safe in the world around him and would break out in a cold sweat if strangers got too close. He couldn't step foot outside his front door without the security of family or close, dependable friends nearby. Traumatized Kyle stopped being adventurous because he could no longer trust that he'd land on his own two feet. He'd learned the hard way that the world wasn't as simple or safe as he'd once believed. And guilty Kyle understood he didn't deserve a fulfilling life when the reckless decisions he'd made had destroyed someone else's world.

Of course I understood that I was my own harshest critic and that the chains I put on myself were of my own doing, but at the same time, I also knew what I was made of, and it was decidedly unfavorable stuff. So I hid behind my sarcastic humor and well-crafted insults in order to keep others from seeing the insecurities that lurked beneath the surface.

Coming on this show meant leaving behind my carefully structured life. One might expect that traveling for months on end would be chaotic and unpredictable, but Jake was even less adventurous than I was. He kept things unwaveringly routine. Even though the cities changed and the inside of the venues varied, the experiences largely remained the same. And I thrived in that stable environment.

Over the years, my parents had attempted to steer me away from life on the road in an effort to focus my attention toward my own hopes and dreams, but I always resisted their efforts. It wasn't so much that I didn't want my own life and my own unique experiences; I just didn't know where to begin. Of course, my parents thought they knew what was best for me and were always pushing me toward higher education. I really wasn't sure what they were thinking because I'd barely graduated 'lower education.' It had literally come right down to the wire. Would I graduate or not? In the end, I did, but only because the teacher who passed me did it for the sole purpose of never seeing my face again.

No. I was clearly not cut out for the academic lifestyle. I could barely handle the pressure of island life. These past few days had been an adjustment. When things got tough, my instinct had always been to rush back to the safe and comfortable. I'd never allowed myself the chance to adjust to a new situation, but I realized early on that I had no choice in this instance. This show was taking me out of my comfort zone, forcing me to keep my shit together, for no other reason than to avoid embarrassing myself in front of millions of viewers.

Kenzie came wandering up from the water's edge, carrying a bucket. Her nasty sunburn was peeling in places and now there were patches of blotched, angry red burns. Her ruddy nose glowed like Rudolph's.

"Hey there, Shaggy," she greeted me, with a mischievous smile on her face.

"Hey there, 'girl who puked on me'."

Kenzie rolled her eyes dramatically. "Has it been twenty-four hours already?"

"Yep. Your reprieve officially ended two days ago. Now you're playing by my rules."

"Wonderful. Can I sit?"

"Go for it."

She settled down onto the sand beside me. "You wanna see what I found on my treasure hunt?"

"Depends. Is your find gooey, squishy, stinky, slimy, or covered by a shell?"

Kenzie peered into her bucket, taking inventory of its contents. She wrinkled her nose and looked up at me through her long lashes. I had to admit, Kenzie's wide-eyed innocence was somewhat adorable. "All of the above."

"Forget it then."

"Okay, suit yourself. But all this will be in the stew tonight, so you've been warned."

I fake gagged.

"So what are you doing over here by yourself?"

"Pondering life."

"Damn, that's deep, Kyle. I didn't know you had such self awareness."

I extended my arms as if to say, 'Yeah, that's me – deep.'

Kenzie studied me with interest and then smiled warmly and said, "You intrigue me."

"Me?" I laughed. "I can't imagine why."

She continued to size me up with her eyes, and then shrugged as if she'd decided to shelve the issue for now, but I could bet she'd bring it into play later.

"Tell me about your hometown," I asked.

"There's not much to tell. It's a farming town, mostly dairy cows, and it's got these beautiful, historic Victorian buildings. The people are really nice, but there aren't many of them. It has a population of about 1,500 people."

"Holy shit. You said it was small but that's, like, teaspoon-sized."

"Yeah, it's tiny, all right, but rush hour's a bitch."

I smiled at her joke. I realized then that it was rare for me to have a conversation with a woman my age that didn't revolve around Jake. I had to admit it was somewhat refreshing. "Do you know everyone in town?"

"Of course."

"And is everyone sleeping with their cousins?"

"Probably," Kenzie replied, with such indifference that it made me laugh.

"Do you like living there?"

She pondered my question, pausing for an overly long time. Something told me this girl had a few secrets in her past, too. "About as much as my slimy treasures like being trapped in the bucket."

Her honesty surprised me. "That bad?"

"It's a good place to grow up and to grow old, but the in between years… I'm not digging it as much. I just want to see more of the world, you know?"

"So why do you stay? Aren't you like twenty-two or twenty-three?"

"Twenty-four, actually."

"Really? Jesus, you're old."

She pushed against me like she was offended. "Oh, yeah? How old are you?"

"Almost twenty-three."

"Almost?" She laughed. "You say that like a kid. *I'm ten and three quarter years old*," she mimicked in a child's voice.

"You're just jealous because you're one-and-three-quarter years closer to death than I am."

"Death doesn't go on a timetable, Kyle."

I thought about that. Yeah, I was officially an idiot. Maybe my parents were right and a little higher education would do me good. "Yeah, well lucky for you, I like cougars."

"Lucky for me?" she scoffed. "You wish."

I laughed. Yeah, actually I kind of did.

"Besides, I hardly think one-and-three-quarter-years older qualifies me for cougar status," Kenzie derided, attempting to act all put upon when the amusement in her eyes gave her away.

I put my hand up and waved it in her face. "Okay, Grandma, calm down."

She gaped at me, her eyes huge. "Hasn't your mother ever taught you never to make fun of a woman's age or her weight?"

"She might have, but I typically just tune her out."

Kenzie nodded and went back to observing the inside of her bucket. She seemed suddenly reserved. Had I offended her? I was about to apologize when she looked up at me, her blue eyes so bright, and asked, "So… um… do you have a girlfriend?"

Aww… the girlfriend question. I smiled and answered, "No, I have a goldfish. But we're just friends."

"Shut up," she laughed, tossing some sand on my leg. Not giving up, Kenzie took on an air of indifference and tried her question again. "So do you?"

I grinned. She seemed a little overly interested in my love life. "I do not."

"I figured," she said, trying to cover up her embarrassment. Or maybe her face was just bright red from the burn. I really couldn't tell. "You're rather annoying."

I nodded my head in agreement. *That* I definitely was! I reached over and touched my finger to her nose. "It's really burned."

"Thanks for pointing that out, because I'm not already self-conscious enough as it is."

"Oh, yeah, no problem. I didn't realize you were feeling so insecure. Are all the other reindeer laughing and calling you names?"

Kenzie flicked my finger off her nose and smacked me in the arm.

"Jerk," she laughed.

"So you were going to tell me why you haven't moved away," I said, giving the poor girl a break from my reindeer jokes, because, honestly, I could go on all day.

"Oh," Kenzie exhaled, and shifted her body uncomfortably. "That's a long story. It's not just about me. I have responsibilities." She looked out over the ocean then sighed. "Someday, maybe. What about you?"

"Oh, you know, I'm from Southern California, so naturally I live in a giant mansion, surrounded by famous people."

"Oh, right," she laughed, playing along with my joke. Little did she know I wasn't kidding. "So you just have the perfect life, huh?"

"Pretty much, yeah."

Kenzie wiped sand off her arms and gave me a sideways glance. "I don't believe you."

I wasn't sure if she was teasing me or was really that perceptive. Regardless, she was getting a little too close for comfort, so I quickly changed the subject. "Tell me, Kenzie, what do you do for fun in your town of 1,500 people? Obviously there must be square-dancing and pie-making contests."

"Of course… on Udder's Day," Kenzie said casually, as if she hadn't just uttered the word 'udder.' Upon catching my stunned reaction she added, "What? Is that weird?"

I laughed. Kenzie raised an eyebrow and stuck her tongue out at me. "Well, if you must know, Udder's Day is in honor of dairy month."

"Yeah, I kind of figured that. What exactly is done on Udder's Day? Does everyone milk cows?"

"Well, sure, we have milking contests, but there's also a parade, music, baking competitions... oh, and all the grandmas in town judge cow costumes."

It took me a moment to process all the information my brain was collecting. Kenzie looked on in amusement.

"So... I'm... I...wow..." I stammered. "That's just...."

"Yeah, yeah," she interrupted. "It's more fun than it sounds."

"Really? Because it sounds hysterical."

We both laughed.

"So is the parade, like, cow-themed?"

"What do you think, Kyle?" she asked, as if there were no question.

"Honestly, Kenzie..." I shook my head. "I have no idea what to think."

"Yes, there are cows, but businesses also have trucks and floats."

"Floats? Oh, this just keeps getting better. I don't know if you realize, but it's always been a dream of mine to ride on a float and do that princess wave."

I demonstrated my best closed-hand greeting.

"I could see that about you," she giggled. "I tell you what, Kyle – next year, you can come to Udder's Day as my honored guest."

"Nothing would make me happier."

TV Confessional
"I'd milk her cow any day."
— Kyle

CHAPTER EIGHTEEN

KENZIE

Daydream Believer

Marooned Rule #3
Approximately every two days, the East and West tribes meet and compete against each other in a physical challenge, with the losing tribe sending one of their members home.

My wavy-haired surfer boy wasn't messing around when he said he could swim. The first challenge with the East tribe took place in the water. It was a grueling series of obstacle course style tasks that tested not only our swimming skills but also our physical stamina. Although

Gene was initially reluctant to allow Kyle to take the lead in the challenge, as he preferred one of his own, like Bobby, to get the glory, he was forced to relent as the rest of us, having witnessed Kyle's prowess in the water, insisted he was the man for the job. We all had our roles in the challenge, but Kyle's job – diving down to release six bags from underwater – proved invaluable, as he was able to complete the task without coming up for air. We were a full two minutes ahead of the East tribe as we completed the other parts of the course. Our resounding win meant that all of us on the West tribe were safe until the next challenge, and the East Tribe would be the first to send a teammate home.

Our triumph was not without tribulation. Dale acquired his first of many island injuries. A block from the puzzle, the only part of the challenge that happened on land, fell on his toe. Not even trying to be a tough guy, Dale jumped around, wailing in pain. Later at camp his toe swelled up so big it was unable to fit in a shoe, so he ingeniously fashioned a palm leaf shoe and walked around like Fred Flintstone. Chances were it was broken, but there was very little he could do about it until the game was over.

The mood in camp after winning the challenge was nothing short of euphoric. The nine of us celebrated by taking a swim break in the ocean, and for the first time, it felt like we were an actual team. I was totally starting to get Gene's fascination with winning. It felt good.

But as the day ran down, predictable scheming took over, and slowly but surely, we all returned to our own huddled masses. Clearly the Fab Five enjoyed our company, but it was as if they viewed us as having some collective terminal illness, and none of them wanted to get too close because they knew we'd all be dead soon enough.

Despite the cold shoulder, the four of us were feeling pretty damn good about the events of the day. We all understood-even Marsha-that, that there was a short kill list and we were all on it. It didn't matter who was the first to go because after that person was gone, the rest of us would be picked off one by one. With today's decisive win, we had at least bought ourselves another two days.

⸻

Over the next couple of days, Kyle and I continued our beachside chats. He was quickly becoming my obsession, and I found myself keeping tabs on him wherever he went. Instead of focusing on my game play, I spent the majority of my day fantasizing about our life together after the show. I had it so bad. I'd already named our children (Blake and Madison) *and* our dog (Barkley). Yep, I was teetering on creepy girl territory and feared it wouldn't be long before I was snipping locks of his hair for safekeeping.

This particular morning, I was sitting on the beach alone, applying liberal amounts of sunscreen to my peeling, sunburnt skin. It was one of the only luxuries we were allowed out here, and I lathered myself in its store-bought extravagance. I stared at my crimson flesh, wondering if it might ever turn into the beautiful tan Kyle sported. Some patches were actually bronzing up, making me hopeful that eventually everything would even out.

Of course, in a nod to my stalker mentality, my beach bum boy crush was not far away. In fact, I was watching his adorable self on the beach with Summer, Aisha, Bobby, and Marsha, taking part in the morning yoga class. He'd tried to talk me into it, but I had no interest in doing downward-facing dog in front of a nationwide audience. If cameras added ten pounds, I had no doubt every one of them would congregate on my ass.

Kyle smiled at me from his pretzel pose. I waved at him, but as he attempted to return the friendly gesture, he ungracefully tipped over. Even Summer, in her heightened state of Zen, couldn't suppress a smile. I laughed joyfully at his carefree antics. I couldn't ever remember being so lighthearted and happy. All the stresses of the normal world just melted away out here. And I credited Kyle with my newfound sunny disposition. His zest for life was contagious, and so endearing. I loved that he seemed up for anything. *Uugghh. There I go again.* Soon I would be naming our cat.

After the hour was up, Kyle took a dip in the ocean and then came ambling up the beach toward me, looking stiff and uncomfortable, his face contorted in a strange grimace. I felt the fluttering in my chest as he drew near. I imagined him wrapping me in a hug as he lifted me off the sand, spun me around, and kissed me in a display of loving devotion. Instead, my little fantasy zipped to an abrupt end when Kyle halted in front of me and squirted a mouthful of salty ocean water directly in my face.

"Kyle!" I screeched, standing there in complete and utter shock as water slid down my forehead into my eyes, stinging them something fierce.

His laughter was cut short as he caught sight of my murderous expression. I struggled to rub the acid wash sensation from my eyes, all the while attempting to kick and punch him in retaliation. He easily avoided my assault by taking one giant step back, and since I couldn't see a damn thing, he was fairly safe where he stood.

"Grow up," I hissed. "I'm blind, thanks to you."

"Oh, geez, I'm sorry," he said, failing to suppress his smile. Kyle reached out to help me wipe the water off my cheeks, but I slapped his hand away. He'd ruined my romantic daydream, and I wasn't ready to accept his barely-there apology.

"I wasn't aiming for your eyes."

"Oh, really? You just squirted me straight in the face! Where did you think my eyes were?"

"I… somewhere else," he answered feebly.

I pushed him, and he actually laughed.

"Sorry," Kyle said, and then wrapped me in a hug and gave me raspberries on my neck until I giggled my acceptance of his apology. Damn, he was hard to stay mad at! And why, after spending some quality time in his arms, would I have welcomed another mouthful of salt water in my face?

As we headed back up the beach, I offered some helpful advice: "Your yoga skills suck, by the way."

"I'm aware. That shit's actually way harder than it looks. My muscles are killing me."

"Oh, yeah? I wasn't aware you had any." *There you go, Kenzie. Hit him where it hurts.*

"I do. I have one in particular I'd like to show you later," he offered suggestively.

"I'll pass," I said, forcing myself to sound uninterested, when we all knew I'd welcome the show and tell.

"I guess I have to stop making fun of yoga now," he conceded. "It's legit. Maybe I'll become a guru or something."

"I could see that."

"So back on the beach, while I was all folded up like a decorative napkin, I started thinking," he began.

"Uh-oh. That's never a good thing."

"I know, dangerous, right? Anyway, we call the others the Fab Five," Kyle said, flashing me an unimpressed scowl. "I figure we need some catchy tagline too."

"You're right. What do you suggest?"

"I don't know, maybe the Fucked Four."

I laughed. That little tagline, as accurate as it was, was most definitely not going to make it on TV.

"I think we need something a little less in-your-face."

"You think?" he grinned. "I mean, it's got to have some meaning, you know."

"I agree. We are an odd grouping and deserve a grand title."

"What's another word for four?"

"I don't know if there is another word," I said, as my mind searched my brain. "Oh wait, quadruplet... ooh, we could be called The Quad Squad."

"No, that sounds too middle school girl chic."

I nodded my agreement.

"I got it," Kyle burst out, excitement playing out over his face. "The Dork Quad!"

I laughed loudly. It was the perfect name for our perfectly imperfect group.

TV Confessional
"Yeah, I'm really only into yoga for the pants."
— *Kenzie*

CHAPTER NINETEEN

KYLE
Nerd Speak

Dale and I had been relentlessly searching for the idol since the first day of play. It wasn't as easy as pinpointing a location and going to check. In fact, we were spending way more time warding off tails than looking for the damn thing. Just yesterday, we'd almost made it to the tree Dale had deemed a possible hotspot when Bobby peeked out from behind a rock. My eyes flicked toward Dale and he nodded as we continued on our way, never getting the chance to search.

Spending time with Dale was surprisingly fun. He was my very first nerdy friend. We were complete opposites, yet somehow we meshed perfectly. I was just as big an anomaly in his world as he was in mine. He surrounded himself with intelligent, driven people. My lackluster approach to life was difficult for him to comprehend and he took to mentoring me. And when I say mentoring, I mean he felt the need to explain how every little thing in the world worked. I had to admit, sometimes, when he went on and on about smart people stuff, I'd just tune him out. But we did have a nice little give and take. The more time I spent with Dale, the smarter I felt; and the more time he spent with me, the funnier he got. Dale was brimming with geeky humor that was just begging for an audience.

"So have you always wanted to come on this show?" I asked him as we wandered through the woods.

"God, no. This is the last place I ever thought I'd be."

"But you've been analyzing the game for years. How could you not want to put your theories to the test?"

"I've mastered World of Warcraft, too, but that doesn't mean I want to visit Kalimdor and the Eastern Kingdoms."

Dale said a lot of thing I just didn't understand. Sometimes I gaped at him as the words left his mouth, trying to determine if the language he was speaking was even of this world. In the beginning, I'd ask him for clarification, but he would just follow his comment with more mumbo jumbo that I couldn't comprehend, so I stopped trying to figure it out and just chalked it up to nerd speak.

I realized early on in my interactions with Dale that he liked fantasy worlds… like, a lot. He was always talking about some warrior or planet or gryphon, whatever the hell that was. I'd never had the patience, or the attention span, to follow the complex story lines of fantasy-based video games. I didn't need much to have fun in my gaming world. If you just gave me a ball to dribble or a pimp to shoot, I'd be a happy camper.

"Okay, so why did you come on the show, then?" I asked, curiously.

"Honestly, I don't know. I'm the most predictable guy you'd ever meet. I guess I just felt the need for a change."

"A midlife crisis," I nodded, like I had him all figured out. "Next thing you know you'll be driving a sports car and bagging a hot chick in a bikini."

"I said I needed a change, not a fantasy makeover."

"Gotta dream big, my man." I offered up my twenty-something wisdom and slapped his shoulder in a manly gesture of friendship. Dale actually winced from the unexpected harshness of the contact. Jesus, he was such a nerd. I loved it.

"I'm married with children, Kyle. I can't afford to dream big."

"That sucks."

"No, that's what life looks like when you're a forty-something computer programmer who drives a minivan."

"Dale, no! My god. Not a minivan! Have you no self respect?"

"No!" he laughed. "That's what I've been trying to tell you."

"I'm begging you, man, you need to buy that sports car as soon as you get home."

"I hardly think I have the swag to pull off a muscle car," Dale laughed, which as always came out sounding like a hyena's mating call. Every time he did it, he made me chuckle.

"I have a new mission out here, Dale. I'm going to make you cool."

"Oh, yeah? I'd love to see you try."

"I admit, I have limited resources on the island, and I'm putting a lot of pressure on myself, but mark my words, by the time this show is over, I will make you the envy of every middle-aged couch potato in America."

"Ahh, the grandeur of youth."

"I don't understand your prehistoric idioms, Dale, but sure, we can do that too if you want!"

<hr />

Dale and I came up to the pre-designated area and separated. The plan was to split up and hopefully throw off anyone trying to follow us. It was only maybe a minute after breaking off from Dale that I heard the crackling of branches. *Damn.* Another spy. We were never going to get the idol. Knowing I could no longer meet Dale without blowing our cover, I began walking in a big circle around the perimeter. If I was going to be followed, I might as well make it interesting.

After about my fifth trip around I heard a groan. "Good god, Kyle, get somewhere already."

It was Kenzie.

"Are you following me, twinkle toes?"

"Well, I was trying to, but then you went all crop circle on me."

"Hey, I wasn't the one who asked you to follow me. Oh, and by the way, you might want to consider being a bit daintier in your surveillance techniques. You were like a damn rhinoceros clomping through the forest."

"I was not that loud. Why are you and Dale sneaking off all the time?"

"That's on a need-to-know basis."

"Well, I need to know," Kenzie whined. I half expected her to stomp her foot in protest. "It's called the Dork Quad, Kyle, not the Dork Duo."

I chuckled at that. She had a point. Dale and I had already agreed that if we found the idol, it would be used in the first elimination ceremony for whoever of the four of us needed it.

"I know what you're doing," she whispered. "And I can help."

"Fine. If you can keep up," I said, and started running. I was tall, so my strides were long and sprightly. I expected to be leaps and bounds in front of Kenzie, but when I checked on her progress, she was right up there with me. Damn, she was speedy for someone with short little Corgi legs. After a couple of minutes, I came to a stop, exhausted. Kenzie stopped too, barely winded.

"Dang, girl, you've got wheels," I said, panting.

"I jog five miles a day. You're not losing me."

"I wasn't trying to," I said, pointing out Dale.

"Oh," she said, seeming surprised.

I grinned. We walked up to Dale, and in answer to the question in his eyes I said, "Sorry, she scares me."

He scanned Kenzie cynically before raising his shoulders in defeat. "This is a top secret mission, Kenzie."

"I know. You can trust me. We're on the same side, remember?"

Dale leaned in, motioned for Kenzie and me to do the same, and started talking extra quietly. "Okay, so the conditions are sub-optimal and we don't have the bandwidth for more than one search, but I really do believe we're in the right quadrant, so let's make quick work of it."

Kenzie looked more confused than I did. "What did he just say?" she whispered.

"You're asking me? I don't speak nerd."

"That tree, over there," Dale sighed, as if dealing with us idiots was a real chore.

"Couldn't you have just said that in the first place?"

"I did."

I climbed the tree while Kenzie played lookout. Dale was guiding me.

"See that indentation in the wood?"

"Yeah."

"In there."

I put my hand in, and – damn, that dorky little dude called it! I pulled out the wrapped bundle and we all did a silent cheer as I climbed back down. I handed the idol to Dale, who promptly shoved the little lifesaver down the front of his pants.

"Dale, I'm not sure if you have the swag to pull off a package of that size."

"Well, Kyle, I would have given it to you, but I didn't think there would be any room with that sock you've got shoved in there."

My eyes widened in surprise, and I laughed at his somewhat awkward diss. I would have liked more confidence in his delivery, but it was an excellent start to his training. A feeling of intense pride bubbled up inside me, much like, I assumed, parents who watch their baby take his first wobbly steps out into the world. "Well played, sir."

Dale smiled back proudly. I reached out to give him a fist bump, but he totally misread the gesture and, instead, high-fived my closed hand. Kenzie giggled at the uncomfortable moment. Yeah, I still had a ways to go with this guy.

———

The idol couldn't have come at a better time, as Marsha was systematically alienating every member of the tribe. Although our group had been effectively segregated from Gene's team, Marsha was not playing by the rules. She flitted around camp, interrupting strategy sessions, spying on other players, and talking to anyone who'd listen.

"Did you know that the total weight of all the ants in the world is the same as the total weight of all humans?" Marsha informed Gene as he angrily picked the little critters out of his rice bowl.

"I just don't care, Marsha," he replied through gritted teeth.

"Should we rein her in?" Dale asked me.

"Are you kidding? Look at Gene's beety little face. This is better than a movie. I just wish I had some popcorn."

"Ooh, popcorn," Kenzie said with wonder in her eyes. Her head was lying on my stomach as we lounged in the shelter. "Butter or no butter?"

"Woman, are you really asking me that?" My voice rose in surprise. "Of course butter. And Milk Duds and, you know, what the hell, throw in an Icee, a hotdog, and some nachos while you're at it."

"Why not?" Kenzie said, grinning. "It's your food coma fantasy."

"That's right. And then I'd follow it all down with a large meat lover's pizza dripping in extra cheese."

Dale snorted. "Spoken like a guy in the prime of his life who has yet to experience high triglyceride levels, an expanding mid section, and a receding gum line."

"What the hell is a receding gum line?" I asked.

"When the gums deteriorate and expose the upper areas of the teeth."

"Why would you want that?"

"I don't," he threw his hands up, scoffing at my ignorance. "Nobody does, but when you get older, it happens, and then it makes the teeth sensitive to cold. For that reason I stay clear of anything frozen."

"Damn, Dale, it must suck being you."

He laughed. "Just you wait, young buck."

"Luckily I have a long wait. What are you, like, fifty-five? Sixty?" I teased.

"Forty-two."

"Don't listen to him, Dale," Kenzie consoled, and then completely lost her train of thought and jumped right back into our food discussion. "You know what I really want right now? A big, juicy bacon cheeseburger and an ice cream sundae."

"Yeah, good call. Are you a cherry and nuts kind of girl?"

Kenzie opened her eyes and studied me a second, no doubt trying to determine if I was making a sexual innuendo – which of course I was.

"Both. No point in having a lonely cherry when there are willing nuts," she answered mischievously.

"I like your thinking."

She giggled.

"I'm still here," Dale said, pointing out that he was most definitely the third wheel in our little flirt session.

"I'm not sure if you knew this," Marsha was saying to Gene, "but women blink twice as often as men."

"Uh-huh," he mumbled, clearly not listening to a word she was saying.

"Do we really want to use our idol on Marsha?" I asked Dale.

"If we don't and she's voted out, it will be three against five at the following vote. We have no choice."

"Right, but if we save her, she's all ours."

"She already is," Dale said shaking his head.

Marooned Rule #4
The losing tribe is to gather at an expulsion ceremony called The Council. They will discuss strategies with the host of the show and then vote off one member from their

tribe. An immunity idol may be played to protect the bearer from elimination.

———

A couple days later, the West tribe lost our first challenge, and we ended up at our first Council. Although the general assumption among the five people calling the shots on the West tribe was that Marsha was going home, the Dork Quad had other plans. After the votes were cast, Dale pulled the idol out of the front of his pants and handed it to Marsha. All five votes for her, which came from Gene's crew, did not count, and our four votes for Gene were enough to send him packing.

It was a great moment for the four of us, as we'd successfully sacked the quarterback. Our first target had been a matter of great debate. Would it be best to cut the head off the dragon (Gene), or just weaken him by gouging out his heart (Summer)? In the end we chose to go big, and I could almost hear the cheers going up on couches across America as the Dork Quad took on the power players and won.

Dale got his second injury that day: a black eye after running into a pole during the blindfolded portion of the challenge. But it wasn't just the eye and the toe. Dale was a walking disaster. Everywhere he went, injuries followed. An insect bite swelled to epic levels. A stinger on a palm bush caused temporary paralysis of his right calf. An ingrown toenail tore open and bled for days. Rashes, pink eye, split lip – you name it, Dale had it. Kenzie and I gleefully began chronicling all his injuries because, well, we had very little else to do all day long. And really, Dale was my favorite subject. Teasing him had become like my full time job. I loved the dude. He just rolled with everything. It soon became clear that I'd completely underestimated this carpool dad. Dale was cool enough just as he was.

Things changed drastically after Gene exited the game. There was a shifting of power, and Carl, understanding he was on a sinking ship, was the first to switch allegiances. Seemingly overnight, Kenzie, Marsha, Dale, and I were in charge of the game, and we were sitting pretty. The nicer spot in the shelter became ours, and the others were now asking our opinion on everything. It would have been easy to get a big head and treat the others as Gene had treated us, but practical Dale was always there to keep us in check, reminding us that the game was always changing, and that any pompousness we displayed now would come back to bite us in the butts later. Of course, with Dale's luck, he'd be the one with the sore ass.

So instead of going over-the-top cocky, we appointed Dale as our new quarterback, which, in hindsight, probably wasn't the best fit. Yes, he had the smarts, but poor Dale had absolutely no athletic abilities, and it became clear almost immediately that he'd never thrown a football in his life. This was a man more comfortable programming computers than conversing with actual living, breathing human beings.

Although I really couldn't talk, as I'd been the one standing in the shadows, letting everyone else make the big decisions. During that very first discussion over whom to kick out of the game, Dale noticed me acceding to the others. He pulled me aside and encouraged me to speak up, saying if I didn't voice my opinion that the others would view me as weak. It was an eye-opening moment for me. I hadn't even realized I was holding back. Normally Jake did the thinking for the both of us. I just blindly followed along and was happy for it. I'd never thought to question the division of power, as it had been that way our whole lives.

That's not to say I did everything I was told. Sometimes I just liked opposing Jake to piss him off. But when it came down to the big decisions, I always deferred, never feeling smart enough or informed enough to insert my viewpoint. But out here there was no Jake, and I needed to step up and make my voice heard. And so, for the first time in my life, I was standing on my own and was actually surprised by how much I liked it.

The next two weeks saw a thinning of the herd. Summer was the second casualty, although I had to admit I missed her yoga sessions on the beach. Aisha followed Summer out of the game. Kenzie led the charge on that one. Although I would have preferred wiping Bobby off the roster first,

Kenzie was adamant that it be Aisha next and presented enough supporting facts to persuade the rest of us.

Seeing Aisha leave made it all seem very real to me. We were knocking people out that were liked and respected in order to further our own games. It felt dirty, in a thrilling sort of way. Aisha was a genuinely good person and I liked her, but Kenzie had been right – we needed to win challenges in order to stay strong because in only a week's time the East and the West tribes would merge into one. It was crucial to our survival to get rid of the least essential player in challenges, and that was clearly Aisha. She had been our weakest link from the beginning. Her long, thin flamingo legs, although I'm sure were awesome in high heels on a runway, were not exactly beneficial when it came to being stuck in three feet of mud. In the end, Aisha had been right: no one took Miss Nevada seriously.

I clapped my encouragement as Kenzie twirled around, doing some ballerina move on the sand. Aside from a dance class when she was five, Kenzie told me she hadn't worn a tutu since. And it showed. I knew nothing about ballet, and even I could tell she was awful. But that was the point. Kenzie didn't care who saw. She was just having fun, not worrying about appearances. I liked that. After one particularly horrible pirouette, she lost her footing and fell to the ground.

I walked over to her as if I was going to help her up but instead nudged her with my foot and said, encouragingly, "You suck."

Kenzie laughed, as I knew she would. She was fun like that.

"Are you just going to stand there, or are you going to be a gentleman and help me up?"

"I'm just going to stand here."

She stuck her tongue out at me and collapsed onto her back. "Fine. Go for a walk by yourself."

I smiled down at her. Damn, I enjoyed our daily walks. I got bored sitting around the camp. In the real world, I was inherently a lazy person, but at least I had stuff to occupy my time, like music or video games or television. Out on the island, it was just chores and endless talking. And, unfortunately the person doing the majority of the latter was Marsha. Good God, that woman could talk. Sometimes I just needed a break, and Kenzie was my go-to pal for such things. Luckily she didn't mind keeping me company. She was always up for a stroll.

I bent over and extended my hand. She grabbed it, but instead of pulling herself up, she yanked me down. I tumbled onto my knees, straddling her. Her other hand went to my side, tickling me.

"Oh, is that how you're going to play it?" I said, returning the favor.

We tickled each other for a minute before she grabbed my other hand and panted, "Stop, I can't take it anymore."

"That's what they all say," I answered smugly, swinging my leg off her and plopping my ass into the sand. She sat up too.

"Oh, I'm sure. I bet you're quite the player back home."

"What gives you that impression?" I asked.

"This," she said, gesturing to my entire being in general.

"What? I'm offended," I gasped. "If you must know, I'm still a virgin and looking for just the right woman to show me the ropes."

"Oh, my God, please tell me that you've never used that line on anyone."

"Actually, when I was younger I did. You'd be surprised how effective it was."

Kenzie groaned like I disgusted her. "That's the last thing I'd want – having to teach a guy. It's like some exciting toy you've been looking forward to, and then you open it up and it didn't come with batteries."

I laughed out loud. "Wow, I never thought of it that way."

"Because you're a guy. You all want virgins," she said, rolling her eyes.

"So I guess that answers my burning question."

"What question is that?"

"If you're a virgin or not."

She eyeballed me but didn't seem offended. "How much thought have you been giving toward my purity, Kyle?" There was a clear flirty tone to her voice.

"The required amount. I'm a guy, Kenzie. We ponder these things."

"Well, I'm not a virgin, but I'm far from a 'ho'."

"Oh, perfect. Just the way I like them," I joked.

She grinned, looking at me with a strange expression before she hopped back onto her feet and started walking. I watched her sandy, bikinied bottom shimmy away, and like the obedient mutt I was, I jumped to my feet and ran after her.

TV Confessional
"Just so we're clear, I'm not really a virgin."
— Kyle

CHAPTER TWENTY

KENZIE

Taming the Dragon

Carl and I sat on the rock overhang as we worked on his surly temperament.

"So you're telling me I should just ignore her damn comments?" he complained.

"Yes. That's exactly what I'm saying. We're all annoyed by them, but part of being a decent human being is not rubbing people's noses in the shit they create."

"I don't know if I can do it. I mean, yesterday Marsha told me that fact about turtles being able to breathe through their rear ends three times! I'm trying, Kenzie, but a person can only take so much."

"I know." I patted his giant arm. "And I sympathize. Yesterday I heard the one about the slug again."

"Do they really have four noses? I mean, really, do they? How can we even be certain that these 'facts' she's spouting are true? Maybe she's just feeding us lies in hopes that we'll spread them around the world."

Carl was getting more agitated as he spoke. The large vein that ran through his forehead was bulging and his teeth were clenched.

"That's what I'm talking about, Carl. Control the facial expressions. It makes you look mean. Take that deep breath we talked about."

Carl did as I asked, but he still appeared angry and resentful.

"Let's work on your smile again. Think of something that makes you happy, like your daughter, and then keep that in the back of your mind when you talk to people. Yep, right there. Look at you! So handsome," I cooed.

"Yeah, right."

"I'm not kidding. When you smile, it lights up your face. People respond to that. In my personal opinion, I find guys who smile so much cuter."

"Like Kyle," he teased, and I heard just a hint of his inner diva. "Girl's got a crush."

"No, I don't," I lied. Then I caught sight of Carl's raised eyebrow and knowing smile. "Okay, I do. I mean look at him." Kyle was on the beach not far away from us, so I swept my hand in his direction. "I'm only human."

"Meh… I've seen better. I mean facewise, yeah maybe, but he's too skinny. I can't be sure, but I think he might still be going through puberty."

"Stop," I laughed, and then leaned into Carl and swooned. "I think he's perfectly perfect."

"You would. You've got this whole 'save the world' thing going on. First you take pity on the giant and now the runt."

"Hardly."

"Do you think he likes you?" Carl asked. "The two of you are always pretty cozy at night."

"I don't know. He's so flirty, but I think he's like that with everyone. I never really know what he's thinking."

"You give the kid too much credit. I honestly don't think he's got a lot going on upstairs."

"You just have to get the digs in, don't you?" I shook my head and laughed.

"I can't help it."

"Anyway, I seriously doubt I'm his type of girl. I think he goes for the slutty types, and he basically implied earlier today that he thought I was a virgin."

"You're not?"

"Nooo. Why does everyone think that?"

"You just have that sweet, innocent vibe to you, probably because you look like one of those Beanie Babies with the big, soulful eyes."

"I love those things," I gushed.

"I know, right? You want to know a secret? Sometimes I buy them pretending that I'm going to give them to my daughter, and I keep them for myself."

"I love you, Carl," I grinned. "Too bad you're gay."

"Yeah, too bad for you," he teased. "So what are you planning to do about your boy toy?"

"I don't know," I sighed. "I think he's out of my league."

"HA," he barked. "If you ask me, it's the opposite. Any man would be lucky to have you, and if Kyle can't see that, he's not worth wanting."

"Ahhh, will you be my best friend forever?"

Our laughter halted abruptly when Kyle started up the beach, coming straight toward us.

"Speak of the devil," Carl said, his demeanor instantly souring.

"Carl!" I scolded. "Be nice. Actually, you know what? This is the perfect opportunity for you to practice your friendly greeting. Now, remember what I taught you."

Carl grunted. "This just seems pointless."

I furrowed my brows to display my annoyance. Why did he always have to fight me? "Deep breath; then smile and greet. Here he comes."

Carl transformed his mouth into what looked more like a snarl than a smile. Why he could flash one so effortlessly for me but not for the others puzzled me. Kyle had a happy-go-lucky expression on his face as he ambled up the beach, but once he caught sight of Carl's attempt at a smile, he startled and cut a wide circle around us.

"KYLE!" Carl bellowed. "HELLO!"

I swear Kyle jumped, and then froze in place as if he were convinced he was about to be beaten to a bloody pulp.

I groaned. How could this be so difficult? "With less enthusiasm and no aggression, Carl. Geez." And then to Kyle, I said, "Relax. He's trying to be friendly."

"That was friendly?" Kyle replied in shock. "Seriously, I thought I was about to die."

Carl raised his arms in defeat, stood up, and stomped off.

"Carl!" I called out to him.

"This is stupid." He threw the angry words over his shoulder. "I'm never going to learn to be pleasant, so stop trying!"

TV Confessional
"I think that went well."
— Kenzie

CHAPTER TWENTY-ONE

KYLE
Secret's Out

About two weeks into the game, Kenzie learned the
truth about who I am. I hadn't planned on telling her,
but she had been honest, opening up her life to me, and I
felt I owed her the same. That day, I'd been lying awake in
the shelter, waiting for the first bits of light to peek out over
the horizon. I loved this time of day, when everyone was
still asleep.

Some days I'd just lie there and wait for the light to
flood our camp and gradually wake the others around me.
Other days I'd take a walk by myself. The sounds of the
waves gently rolling up the beach and the rustling of the

trees in the morning breeze were so relaxing. I couldn't remember ever feeling so alive. I'd never really been one with nature before, but I was starting to understand its charms.

More often than not, I had Kenzie for company on my morning strolls. We'd grown close in the past couple of weeks. Out here, with nothing but time on our hands, we did a lot of just hanging out and talking. I'd never really had female friends, not close ones anyway, and I was digging having someone to really communicate with.

Talking to women was different than talking to men. It was acceptable to discuss important things with them. They encouraged it and didn't call you a pansy-ass bitch if you got all gushy, like I did with my newfound fascination with nature. Kenzie didn't think it was stupid. In fact, she told me I was evolving as a person, whatever that meant. I didn't know if I would take it that far, but there was definitely a change in me. I was feeling more decisive and in control of my own life.

As much as we talked, though, I held back an important part of who I was from her. Maybe it was the cameras or maybe it was just the knowledge that once my secret was out there, I would no longer just be Kyle. I would again become an extension of my famous sibling… my connection to him seen as my only redeeming quality. Right now Kenzie and Dale and the others believed I was more than that, and I bristled at the thought of losing that feeling of inclusion.

"Kenzie?" I whispered to her sleeping frame. No response. My arms were around her waist, her head rested against my chest. We had become exceedingly comfortable with each other... sometimes too comfortable. More than once we'd woken up to my hard-on poking into her back. Yeah, that was always an awkward conversation. I'd had to explain, at least four times now, that it wasn't her but my overactive sleep time imagination. Strangely enough, she didn't seem too happy with my explanation, maybe because she knew I was lying. My hard-ons had everything to do with her. Kenzie had this way of burrowing herself into me like a prairie dog. Her shapely ass was always wiggling itself closer to me. I was a guy... what did she expect?

"Kenzie?" I spoke a bit more loudly, but this time added a finger to her ear.

She batted it away like an insect. "What do you want, Kyle?" she groaned.

"Are you awake?"

"Do I look awake?"

"Okay, I'll wait."

There was no movement from Kenzie, but I knew her mind was now stirring. No way could she go back to sleep knowing I was waiting on her to wake up. That was the difference between men and women. Women were more concerned about the well-being of others. Had it been me, I would have rolled over and gone back to sleep in an instant, completely oblivious to her need for company.

Just as predicted, I saw one eye open.

"Hi," I grinned, as attractively as I could, given the fact I hadn't showered in weeks.

She smiled despite herself. "Hi."

"Are you awake now?"

"Not really."

"You want to take a walk?"

"Right now?" She yawned. Her eyes were droopy, and she had little creases on her cheek from the bamboo floor. Her hair was matted down on one side. I fluffed it with my fingers.

"I can't sleep."

She smiled her sleepy smile and stretched her arms, doing a little squiggle. "And if you can't sleep, I can't sleep either?" she whispered.

"That's right. Hurry – the sun is about to rise."

She grinned, gazing up at me in her drowsy way, before reaching out her hand and swiping it playfully across my cheek. I'd never had anyone look at me the way she did. She genuinely enjoyed my company. Most girls viewed me as the opening act for the main attraction. They didn't bother getting to know me because I wasn't their final destination. Kenzie wanted to learn everything about me, as evidenced by the endless questions she asked me on a daily basis. Seriously, I had no idea I had that many interesting facts to give her, but damned if she didn't come up with new things to ask me every day.

I gave Kenzie my best 'come out and play' look to entice her out of bed.

"All right, you win."

We slipped on our shoes and walked down the beach. It was still dark. In a few minutes, the sun would rise from behind the sea, and I felt the fluttering of excitement in my chest. I'd never given stuff like this a second thought in the real world, but out here, in this dream existence, something as everyday as the sun making its first appearance of the morning held a sense of wonder in my expanding universe. Maybe I *was* evolving.

I found the rock on the edge of the waterline that Kenzie and I had used many times to hang out. She sat down as I stood beside her admiring the view. Neither of us spoke as we watched the orange sun peek out over the horizon. Slowly the darkness turned to light. I snuck a glance of Kenzie's profile. Eyes closed, she'd dipped her head to the sun and wore the most content expression on her face. Her sun-streaked hair had caught the rays and sparkled in the light. Her long lashes curled upward, and as she smiled, the little crinkles in the corners of her eyes highlighted her sunny disposition. My own eyes did a double take as I realized what I was seeing. Damn, Kenzie was actually pretty damn attractive.

Perhaps sensing my eyes on her, she peaked one open and smiled. "What?"

"Nothing. You look happy."

"I am," she said. Those two words sounded so relaxed. I kept staring at her.

"Stop," she laughed. "What's your problem?"

"Nothing. I'd just never noticed before how pretty you are."

Kenzie straightened herself up, peeking at me out from under her lashes as a flush crept across her cheeks. "Are you messing with me?"

"No. I'm giving you a compliment. Don't get all weird about it."

"I'm not," she said, concentrating intensely on the rock she was sitting on. "And, uh… thank you… for the compliment."

I shook my head, feeling suddenly embarrassed. "Way to make that awkward, Kenzie."

She laughed softly and then shifted her gaze back up at the sky. Without looking in my direction, she asked, "So what's your deal, Kyle? Why are you here?"

"My deal?" I asked, feeling unexpectedly defensive. I deflected the question back at her. "I don't have a deal. What's your deal?"

"I told you already: I need the money."

"Why do you need it so badly?"

"It's not that I need-need it. I just want it."

I laughed. "We all just want it."

"I guess."

"You're really not going to tell me?" I asked, shooing her with my hand to scoot over. Once she moved, I climbed onto the rock next to her.

"You're expecting something earth-shattering. It's not like that. We've just been struggling financially for a long time, and it would be nice not to have to worry for a change, you know what I mean?"

No, actually I didn't really know what she meant. It's not like I was a millionaire, far from it, but I made a better than average paycheck and all my expenses were taken care of, so I was far from struggling. Still, I wasn't that far removed from reality that I didn't understand people weren't as fortunate as I am.

"Who's 'we'?" I asked.

"My dad and siblings."

"Not your mom?"

Kenzie dropped her head a little. Her shoulders slumped. "She died when I was eight."

"Oh, god, I'm sorry." In hindsight, it was a stupid question to ask. With my mom the dominant figure in my family, it just seemed natural to assume the mother was in the picture.

"It was a long time ago."

An uncomfortable silence commenced. I was more than familiar with this awkward quiet. It happened a lot to me when people learned who my brother was. What was it about tragedy that stole people's voices? I refused to put that burden on Kenzie.

"How'd she die? Or is that too personal?"

Kenzie opened her eyes and studied my face a moment. She seemed surprised that I asked. She opened her mouth to speak and then closed it again.

"Never mind. I'm being too pushy. Sorry."

She placed her icy cold hand on mine for a split second and then stole it back.

"You're not. It's just a sad story that I rarely talk about. It still hurts my heart, even after all these years."

"I get it. Believe me, I do."

Kenzie's eyes squinted as she took me in with a concerned expression. "You do?"

I nodded.

An understanding passed between us. Her face softened.

"After I was born, my mom and my dad tried for years to have another baby. They did everything they could to make it happen, but she would get pregnant and then miscarry. I can't even tell you how many times. It was pretty rough on all of us. After repeated failed IVF treatments, she finally she got pregnant with triplets."

"Triplets? Crap. That sucks."

"That was actually the good part of the story, Kyle," she laughed, slapping me on the leg.

"Oh." Triplets sounded pretty damn awful to me. How would you even feed three babies with two hands… and two nipples?

"And the amazing part was that she didn't lose them. We were all so excited when she went into labor. She had managed to carry them for seven months, which was miraculous, considering my mom was having all kinds of complications with the pregnancy. She delivered three tiny but relatively healthy babies, two boys and a girl. She'd had preeclampsia throughout the pregnancy, though. She had it with me too but the complications weren't as severe. During the C-section with the triplets, her condition turned into eclampsia and she started seizing and then went into cardiac arrest. The doctors tried everything to save her, but she died about forty minutes later without ever getting to hold the babies she wanted so badly."

Kenzie shook her head then looked away. Neither of us said anything. I knew she needed a moment. Sometimes memories just required time to filter through without interruption.

"So," she said, gripping her thighs with her hands. "That's my deal."

"Damn," I said, shaking my head. "That really sucks. I'm sorry." I could see in her expression that she was fighting back tears. I felt bad for asking. Now she was upset and it was my fault. I slipped my arm over her shoulder and squeezed. Kenzie's eyes traveled up to meet mine. There was hurt and sadness in them, but there was something else too… it was almost like she wanted me to kiss her. I broke our contact and glanced over at the camera recording us. What was happening here? Was Kenzie falling for me? At that very moment, we weren't playing a game. Shit just got real, and I wasn't sure where my head was. I had feelings for her, but not in the way she might have for me… at least I didn't think I did. With the moment gone, Kenzie scooted out of my embrace. We sat there quietly looking out over the ocean.

"How long ago was that?" I asked.

"It's been sixteen years. I still miss her so much."

"She sounds like a great mom."

Kenzie smiled sadly. "She was."

"So what did you end up doing with the babies?"

"What do you mean, what did we do with the babies?" she asked, looking amused. "We raised them, of course… me and my dad. I basically became a mom at eight years old. I could change three diapers in five minutes flat."

"Nice," I nodded, although I had no idea if that was impressive or not since I'd never changed a diaper in my life.

"I've spent sixteen years taking care of my siblings, and I love them to death, but I want this money so I can make them secure. Then I can go out and live my own life… finally."

Interestingly enough, Kenzie and I had followed a similar path in that we both had taken on a certain amount of responsibility for our siblings. Her commitment was obviously more extensive than mine, but we both felt that pull. The difference was, I'd never desired to go it alone. Maybe I needed to rethink my game plan.

Possibly taking my silence as a judgment, she added, "I know it's selfish."

"That's not what I was thinking. What you've done – raising your siblings – that's the opposite of selfish."

Our eyes met, and she gave me that look again. Just before I started squirming, she forced a smile on her face and said, "Your turn."

"My turn?"

"Yeah, what's your story?"

"I don't have one," I lied.

"Yes, you do. I know you've been holding back on me. You won't even tell me your last name. Why?"

"What does it matter?"

"Come on, Kyle. I showed you mine, now you have to show me yours."

"Oh, you want me to show you mine? Why didn't you say that in the first place?" I asked, pretending to pull down my shorts.

"No," she laughed and grabbed my hand. "Fine. If you don't want to tell me, then I'm going to guess."

I leaned in, very interested in what she'd have to say about me. "Please do. This ought to be fun."

Her eyes scanned over me as she was coming up with a narrative. "Okay, let me give it a go. You're a trust fund kid. Your parents are filthy rich, maybe even famous, and you've spent your life trying to figure out where you fit in. You know there's more to life than just throwing money at a problem, so you volunteer at soup kitchens and try to make a difference in the world. You probably even wanted to join the Peace Corps at some point in your life…anything to shun the trappings of wealth and privilege. Yuck. Barf. Gag me with a silver spoon."

Kenzie's face was twisted up with disgust as if my fictional life was more than she could stomach.

"Wow, that was so totally bitchy of you."

She looked up, shook herself out of her disappointed fantasy world, and laughed. "I know. I must have some real pent-up anger."

"Seriously. I thought you were going to punch me for a minute there."

Kenzie wiped sand off her leg then asked, "So how did I do?"

"Um… let's see." I started going though all the things in my head that she'd labeled me. "You got one thing right, and even that was only partially right."

"Do you have rich parents?"

"No."

"Do you volunteer in soup kitchens?"

"No. But I should."

"Have you ever wanted to join the Peace Corps?"

"No again."

"Then what did I get partially right?"

I hesitated before saying, "I am related to someone famous, but it's not my parents."

Kenzie leaned forward, immediately interested in my admission. "Okay, now we're getting somewhere. How famous are we talking?"

"Like, *famous* famous," I replied.

"Seriously?" she asked, making a face.

"Yep."

"Would I know this person?"

"Well, I don't know. You do live in Humboldt County, so it's possible you've been stoned the past few years…"

Kenzie smacked me. "Shut up," she said, laughing.

"Yeah, you've probably heard of him."

"Are you going to tell me, or do I have to guess?"

"I'll tell you if you promise me you're not going to freak out."

"I promise."

"Seriously, Kenzie. You can't tell anyone else on this island, not even Dale or Marsha."

"I said I promise. Now just tell me."

"My last name is McKallister."

Kenzie sat there a second processing my words, and then her eyebrows rose in surprise and her lips formed into an O and she even said the word. "Oh." Then followed it with, "Shit. Really?"

"Yes, really."

Then her eyes got even wider, and her face took on a cartoonish expression of shock. *Shit, here it goes. Cue the Jake worship.*

"Oh, my god. Kyle. Crap! Crap!"

"You said you wouldn't freak out. Stop yelling *crap*, Kenzie."

"No. *Crab*. Crab going up your pant leg." She jumped up screeching.

"What?" I looked at my shorts and saw nothing. I patted the fabric, and then I felt the pinch. "Ouch!" I jumped up on the rock. We were both screaming. "It's got me."

I pulled the leg of my board shorts up to reveal a colorful crab actually dangling there on my inner thigh. Kenzie was jumping up and down, laughing and squealing.

"Don't just stand there. Help me get it off."

"You want me to stick my hands up your shorts?"

"You want it to pinch my balls?"

We both looked over to the sound guy and cameraman who had big smiles on their faces. Kenzie started giggling again.

I wasn't paying any mind to her or them. The pink-clawed fiddler crap had my full and undivided attention.

I grabbed his shell and yanked, but the pincher didn't detach from the flesh, and I screamed in protest. Kenzie doubled over in laughter, so loud and so hysterical that I realized I was completely alone in this ordeal.

I took hold of the crab with one hand and tried to pry his claw off me with the other. The two of us were playing tug a war, with my skin as the victim. This went on for an uncomfortably long period of time, neither one of us willing to concede defeat. Finally, after a swift, firm yank, my little tormentor mercifully let go. I gasped in surprise at the sharp pain and then threw the offending creature out into the water.

"Fucking crab," I mumbled.

Kenzie was struggling to pull herself together as I rubbed my sore thigh. "Oh, lord… oh, Kyle, that was classic, really just epic," she said wiping tears away. "I mean, if you weren't already the star of this season, that little episode with the crab is pretty much going to seal the deal."

Kenzie and I didn't talk about my admission until we were well away from the beach and the intrusive cameras. I wasn't sure what was going on in her head, but her reaction surprised me. She didn't seem all that impressed and didn't appear to be treating me any differently. Because the camera typically didn't follow us to the poophole, Kenzie and I made a break for it. It wasn't until we were standing in front of our makeshift bathroom that she brought up my relationship with Jake.

"So are you older or younger?"

"Younger."

"Is it just the two of you, or do you have other siblings?"

"I have four brothers and two sisters."

Kenzie's eyes flickered with surprise. "Geez. I hope you had more than one bathroom growing up."

"We had two. Thanks for your concern."

"No problem. Are you two close?"

"Yes. I'm his bodyguard."

She nodded, seemingly considering my job.

I paused, thinking about my little white lie. I always said I was his bodyguard, but in reality, it was a title I'd given myself to justify my place on the tour and in Jake's life. I knew my brother didn't view me that way. No one did. I was just the kid brother who got a paycheck for being lucky enough to share a bloodline with a superstar.

"Actually, I'm not a bodyguard," I blurted out, surprising myself with my honesty. What was it about Kenzie that made me want to dump my secrets in her lap? "I'm really just a mooch."

"No, you're not."

"Yeah, actually, I am."

She shook her head. "I don't believe that. Your brother is lucky to have you."

I scoffed.

Kenzie stopped and searched my face. "You don't think so?"

"It's more like he's stuck with me and I'm fortunate to have a job."

She considered my comment for a moment before saying, "You're a lot more than you give yourself credit for. If I can see that, so can your brother."

Kenzie's words floored me. I'd always considered myself the lucky one to have Jake. Never had I thought that maybe he would feel that way about me.

"Why were you hiding the fact that you're related to Jake?"

"I wasn't hiding it. I just wasn't announcing it to the world."

She eyed me skeptically. "You were hiding it, don't lie."

This girl had me pegged. It was like she knew me better than I knew myself. She was starting to creep me out. "Okay, fine. Telling people who I'm related to puts a giant bull's eye on my back. Obviously I was trying to avoid that."

"No, I get it. I'd probably keep it quiet too if I were you."

"Well, that's what I was trying to do." I protested. "But you kept harassing me."

"Sorry," she smiled. "I have to say, I think it would be cool to have a famous sibling. But at the same time, it would probably suck. I'm sure everyone you meet just wants to talk about him all the time."

How did she know so much about me? My life was anything but an open book, yet she seemed to have been flipping through the pages for a while.

"Well, Jake's a hell of a lot more interesting than I am, that's for sure."

"No offense, but I beg to differ," she said, assuredly. "I think you're very interesting."

"No offense, but I think you're delusional," I scoffed.

"Do you do that a lot?" she asked, concern etched in her pretty features.

"What?"

"Put yourself down?"

"I'm not putting myself down," I replied, defensively.

"Yeah, you are. Since revealing your secret, you're acting like a different person, like you don't have any confidence in yourself. It's weird."

Was I really? I had to scan back through my behavior to see if she had a point, and then I realized: the minute we started talking about Jake, I got passive aggressive and self-deprecating. I'd never noticed that about myself before. I had to wonder if coming on the show was changing me for the better. Relying on myself really wasn't as hard as I'd thought it would be. As much as I loved being part of Jake's crazy rock star life, maybe I didn't love the corner I'd been crammed into. Maybe I was just as trapped in my world as Kenzie was in hers. Did I really want to be someone's sidekick for the rest of my life? Not particularly. But did I deserve a life of my own? That was the question I wasn't sure how to answer.

Kenzie looked up at me with her Disney princess eyes, and then she placed her hand on my arm. "You don't like talking about your life, do you?"

"It's complicated." I shrugged. "I have to be careful what I say. Jake's scrutinized enough without me adding to his woes. Besides, people aren't all that interested in talking to me anyway."

"I don't believe that. You can't tell me you don't have girls knocking down your door, Kyle."

"No, I do – but only if Jake's behind it."

"Liar," she grinned.

"I'm not lying, Kenzie. When Jake's around, I'm background noise."

She shook her head, not entirely buying my story. "Well, if that's the case, maybe you need to venture out more, because I promise you, if you were to show up in my hometown, you would most definitely *not* be background noise."

"Ehh, and drive all the way to Humboldt County? No thanks."

Kenzie laughed, touched my arm, and said, "I hope you know I'm not most girls. I don't care what your last name is. I think you're a great guy. You know that, right?"

"Yeah, sure."

"Wow, such enthusiasm. How could you think otherwise? I didn't know who your brother was until today, and I've still let you spoon me every night this week."

A smile broke out across my face. She was right about that. Even if you didn't count my breakfast boners, Kenzie and I had been getting all kinds of funky on that hard wood flooring. I loved making her blush with my sexually suggestive comments every evening just before assuming the position. "You know you love it."

"As far as skilled spooners go, you aren't bad… a solid six."

"Six? Clearly I need to bring more dick into play. I just didn't think you'd appreciate it."

Kenzie peered up at me with an expression of surprise. "What made you think I wouldn't appreciate it?"

"You always give me that look when I wake up with a boner."

"Because you're always making up some lame excuse, like that time when you said you were dreaming about pizza. Who gets a hard-on from Italian food?"

I raised my hand and smiled sheepishly. We both laughed.

"So why all the excuses?" she asked.

"You're not that type of girl."

"What type of girl?"

"The type who jumps into it with just anyone."

"You're not just anyone, Kyle. I'd jump into it with you in a second."

My eyes caught hers, and, no doubt seeing the confusion in mine, Kenzie turned bright red and broke the contact. Oh, shit. She *was* into me. That look she gave me on the beach... that was exactly what I'd thought it was. Something in the tone of her voice and the sincerity of her words caught me totally off guard. The minute the words left her mouth, I could tell Kenzie regretted them.

Okay, not good. How had I not seen it coming? I mean, sure, we flirted back and forth all the time, but I thought it was just playful fun. She was cute and fun and sweet, but she was the opposite of the practice women I went after. Kenzie was marriage material, and I was nowhere near that stage in my life. In fact, I didn't know if I would ever be there. The lifestyle I led didn't exactly lend itself to long-term commitment.

Kenzie took on a defensive stance, the horror on her face plain to see.

"What are you looking at?" she snapped. "It was a joke!"

"Yeah, okay. I don't know why you're getting mad at me."

"Because you're standing there staring at me with that idiot expression on your face."

"That's my natural resting face," I argued.

"Yeah, well, then I feel sorry for you," Kenzie spat, looking exasperated and oh, so miserable.

She was working herself up into a frenzy. Clearly this was a woman scorned. And I was the dummy who hadn't figured it out until just now. I had nothing to say that would diffuse the situation, so I remained silent.

"Ugh... I was just kidding, so... so... keep your dick away from me," Kenzie demanded, and then stomped off to her bathroom area. Stunned, I slunk off to mine.

TV Confessional
"I didn't actually think the claws
on those crabs worked."
— Kyle

CHAPTER TWENTY-TWO

KENZIE

Charity Case

'*Keep your dick away from me?*' *Oh god, oh Kenzie. Why?* At that moment, I wanted to cut my leg on a jagged rock and fling myself, bleeding, into a shark-infested ocean. Somehow that demise seemed easier to deal with than having to face Kyle again. The dumbfounded expression on his dazed face said it all. Despite his incessant flirting, he clearly did not see us as anything more than platonic friends, nor did he have any clue as to the extent of my infatuation with him. Until now, of course. What in the world was I thinking? And why would I do it now, when he'd just revealed he was Jake McKallister's brother? I mean, talk about shitty timing. I had outdone myself today. It was no wonder I was still single. I had to be one of the stupidest females alive.

After squatting over a patch of ground and cursing the droplets that splashed onto my legs, I used a leaf to wipe away the remnants of pee, although nature's toilet paper was hardly as efficient as the store-bought variety, and I had to spend an extra minute drip-drying. I took that moment to reflect on my complete and utter embarrassment. My face was burning hot, and I actually felt nauseous. As hard as I tried, my mind could not envision any scenario where this humiliation ended favorably. I pulled up my shorts and paced back and forth. When that didn't ease my suffering, I hunched over, hands gripping my knees, and tried to control my breathing. I felt close to hyperventilating. *Think, Kenzie.* How could I hide from my man-crush on a frickin' reality show? Maybe if I stayed here long enough, Kyle would get bored and go. Yeah, that was a good plan. I'd just wander around the smelly poophole wasting time.

Five minutes must have passed before I heard his voice calling out to me, "Are you coming?"

"Just go on without me," I yelled back. "I'm going to be awhile."

"Are you sure? I can wait."

"No, I'm sure. Go back. I'll be there soon."

He didn't respond right away, and then I heard him say, "Okay."

I let out a huge sigh of relief and stood in place, formulating a plan in my head. Once I got back to camp, I would pull Carl aside and talk some strategy with him. Kyle wouldn't dare interrupt a session with Carl, seeing as I was the only one who wasn't afraid of him. And then what? How could I avoid him? Oh, man, this was bad. Really bad! Why hadn't I kept my big, love-spewing mouth shut? Not only might I lose my friend, but also my most important ally in this game. Now I understood why it was never good to mix business with pleasure.

It was time to take a step back. Kyle was clearly not interested in me beyond a good laugh. And why would he be? He spent his days in the company of a famous rock star. He was Jake McKallister's frickin' brother. I mean, please! Had I known, I *never* would have gone for him. Suddenly our differences seemed glaringly obvious. It wasn't just a matter of north versus south, of a small town girl versus a big city boy. No, this was a matter of an ordinary life versus an extraordinary one.

Knowing Kyle's resistance to going anywhere alone, I gave him ample time to clear out before making my way back through the bushes. Scanning the area where we usually met up, I sighed with relief. He wasn't there. At least I'd have the walk back to clear my head. At the sound of a rock hitting the ground, I swung my head toward the ruckus and found Kyle propped up against a tree, his long legs crossed at the ankles. He was chewing on a skinny twig.

Kyle flashed me his adorable smile as if nothing was amiss and then, using the tree for support, he stood up. "You all set?"

"I told you not to stay."

"I know, but I didn't have anything else to do, so I decided to wait." Kyle headed off back toward camp. I did have to hand it to the boy, he was nothing if not reliable. When I didn't immediately follow, he called over his shoulder, "You coming? Don't you have an etiquette class planned for Carl?"

So that was how he was going to play this? Feign ignorance? *Nice, Kyle.* Then I realized it might not be the worst strategy. If he was okay ignoring my declaration of love, then it was in my best interest to just follow his lead. Giving in, I jogged up to him. "As a matter of fact, I do."

"And how's that going? Are you seeing vast improvements with the ogre?"

"We're making progress."

"Honestly, Kenzie, Carl is a lost cause. He hates everyone."

"No one is a lost cause. Carl is really sweet. You just have to get to know him."

"Yeah, well, I don't really have the time."

"The time? What else do you have to do?" I questioned.

Kyle shrugged. "I've got finger painting at noon."

I couldn't help but crack a smile. I really wished Kyle weren't so enjoyable to be around, especially now that I knew where his head was. While I was falling hard, he was standing up straight. Kyle liked me – that much was obvious – but he didn't *like* like me. He'd thoroughly friend-zoned me, and after all the time we'd spent together in the last two weeks, if he didn't see me as anything more than that, chances were he never would. Clearly I didn't have the physical attributes he was looking for in a girlfriend. No wonder he'd had such a kinship with Aisha. She was the type of girl who probably got special treatment by the security guys at concerts. I'd been in those crowds once myself, desperately trying to stand out in a sea of leggy beauties. I'd watched as the pretty ones got called up and let through, as if they were chosen disciples of the rock gods. I plainly remembered desperately trying to make myself look hot enough to get the nod to go in and meet the singer, all the while instinctively knowing I would be left standing on the sidelines.

I should have realized he was far beyond my wooing capabilities. Lineage aside, guys with his looks and the personality to back it up didn't go for nice girls with good, sturdy childbearing hips. They wanted sexpots… and, unfortunately, I had *long-term baby mama written* all over me. Maybe I just needed to give up my dreams of adventure and find myself a nice, boring Bigfoot enthusiast and call it a life.

Frustrated with my current predicament, I contemplated why I always dared to dream bigger. Why hadn't 'good enough' ever been good enough for me? I had to wonder if a wedding photograph of my parents that hung on the wall of my home was the reason why. How many hours had I spent staring at that picture? After Mom died, I sometimes even took it off the wall at night and propped it next to my bed. Their smiles and the way their eyes danced as they stared at each other, as if they were in on a joke no one else was... the affection that radiated off their faces... it really was a thing of beauty.

I suppose the reason I never settled was because I knew what love looked like. And I knew the devastation and heartache that came with it. My father's adoration for my mother was so raw and so deep that the loss of her thoroughly crushed him. That's when you knew you'd really, truly loved. If I was going to devote my heart and soul to someone, it had better damn well be worth it, because if I was going to lose that person someday, I didn't want to settle for anything less than complete devastation. If I were lucky enough to have what my parents had, then I would be lucky enough.

To Kyle's credit, he didn't discuss my earlier admission, nor did he give me that standard brush off: 'It's me, not you.' In fact, he managed to keep the awkwardness in check, and we fell back into our comfortable banter rather quickly. If he was willing to ignore, who was I to argue?

The others were gathered around the fire, the chill of the morning gradually being replaced by the sweltering heat that would bear down on us for the rest of the day.

I plopped down next to Bobby, knowing that Kyle would have to find another spot to sit because, one, there was no more space, and two, he didn't like the guy. Nobody liked Bobby; but we needed him for just a little bit longer, and then we'd cut him loose. Bobby was a dead man walking.

In recent days he'd taken it upon himself to woo me, presumably because he assumed that with my being female, I wouldn't be able to resist his chiseled good looks. I had rebuffed his obvious ploys at persuasion on multiple occasions, although I had to admit that being pursued by a hot guy, no matter how nefarious his intentions, was an ego booster, especially after Kyle had only very recently crushed my fragile self-esteem into a million pieces. And now, when I knew Kyle wasn't interested in more than just being a buddy, what would it hurt to do a little flirting with a smoking hot guy like Bobby?

"Kenzie," he greeted, dipping his head in a sexy way.

"Bobby," I answered back, mimicking his gesture.

"You were gone a while."

"Did you miss me?" I flirted.

"As a matter of fact, I did," he said, flashing me his hottest leading man smile.

"Kenzie had a bad stomach," Kyle blurted out.

My mouth dropped open in shock as I shot daggers in Kyle's direction. His annoyed expression confused me. Why would he care if I did a little innocent bantering with Bobby? "I did *not* have a bad stomach."

"Then what took you so long?" he challenged.

I just glared at him, unable to come up with any plausible excuse that didn't include hanging out my dirty laundry for all to see.

Bobby looked back and forth between us, a smile forming upon his face. Obviously he was smart enough to see a crack in our alliance, and by the expression on his face, he was savvy enough to try to exploit it.

"You want to go swimming with me?" he asked, nudging himself up against me.

Ripping my angry eyes off Kyle, I turned to address Bobby. "I would love to."

Bobby stood up immediately and offered me his hand. Kyle's irritated expression didn't escape me, but it also didn't sway me. I was not about to continue wasting my time pining over some guy I'd never had a shot at in the first place. Of course, I guess I could say the same thing about Bobby. He was so clearly not interested in me. Seduction was a last ditch effort on his part to stay in the game. But what did I care what his motivations were? He was hot, and I was pissed.

I grabbed Bobby's hand, stood up, and allowed him to lead me to the water's edge. Once there, my smoking hot companion stripped down to his boxer trunks, leaving very little to the imagination. Still, I managed to find the inspiration to continue undressing him in my mind. Bobby was eye candy. Of course, that fact hadn't escaped me before, but because I'd been so focused on Kyle and his dorky sex-iness, I hadn't really given the bad boy a second glance. But now? Ooh-la-la. Kyle who? Bobby was my new Man-crush Monday. Or was it Tuesday? I actually had no idea what day of the week it was. I shook my head. I was getting distracted. *Focus, Kenzie. Hot guy, straight ahead.* My eyes flicked over him in admiration, thinking of all the wonderful day-dreams I could have him star in instead of that doofus up at camp, but then, like a bad movie... Bobby opened his mouth.

"You like what you see?" he asked seductively, and he actually ran his hands over his torso in a male-stripper move. I seriously wanted to barf.

So surprised was I by his vain comment and action that I couldn't come up with anything to say, other than to grunt, "Huh?"

"I know you want it," he grinned, just before diving into the gentle waves. As he reappeared, Bobby shook the water out of his hair. I felt like I was watching a shampoo com-mercial. I fought back a giggle. "Come and get it."

Seriously? Did that really work on women? There was no way to continue to hold it back, and I laughed. I remained firmly planted on land. "No, thank you."

"What?" he asked, his brows furrowed in confusion.

"I'll pass, but thanks anyway."

Bobby's expression changed. He stared at me in contempt for a moment before saying, "Whatever. I was just being charitable."

"Ahh. How sweet of you, a 'ten' giving back to the less fortunate."

His eyes rolled over me playfully. "What can I say, I'm a generous guy. But rest assured, I'm no saint. I have a reputation to uphold. I'd never dip down lower than a six."

Instantly a nervous flutter invaded my insides. I didn't want to know what number he'd ranked me.

"Stop giving me that constipated look, Kenzie. You're a solid seven, and I'm not just saying that to be nice."

"Wow, thanks, Bobby. I didn't take it that way," I replied, amused by his flawed attempts at flattery and relieved I wasn't ranked lower. I mean, wasn't a seven like a B-?

"You'd probably rank even higher, like a 7.5, if you had a shower, wore some makeup, and shaved your underarms and, you know…" His eyes diverted to my bikini region. "The crotch spiders."

My mouth dropped open. Irritation swept through me. Again, was it my fault the local salon didn't offer the Brazilian wax? No, I didn't think so. The nerve of this guy!

"What?" he scoffed. "Oh, please, you aren't one of those feminists, are you?"

I actually laughed at his piling on of insensitive comments. He was just digging himself deeper and deeper.

"Honestly, Bobby, I think you'd be hard pressed to find any girl not offended by that comment, feminist or not."

"Look, all I'm saying is, on this reality show, seven is a really good number. Even Aisha only ranked an eight."

I gaped at him. Really? Aisha? Just an eight? Instantly I felt a whole lot better about his chauvinistic ranking system.

"Come on, the water feels great. I promise I won't be a douche."

"Don't make promises you can't keep," I called out to him.

He stared me down, a half-smile on his face. "I don't beg, Kenzie. Ever! Do whatever you want." And with that, Bobby swam further out. I stood there. Well, there went that man crush. Even incredible hotness couldn't make up for a reptilian personality disorder. Still, I was miserably hot standing in the direct, pounding sun, and according to Bobby, I desperately needed an ocean bath, so I shrugged and jumped in after him. Unlike with Kyle, at least I knew where I stood with Bobby. I was a charity case... a stinky, hairy seven.

TV Confessional
*"I would rate Bobby a 'ten' for looks
and a 'two' for tact."*
— Kenzie

CHAPTER TWENTY-THREE

KYLE
Truth Be Told

I watched Kenzie take off with Bobby and was surprised at how much it bothered me. I knew what he was doing – using her to get further in the game – and it pissed me off that Kenzie would fall for his antics. She was smarter than that. Of course, it was possible that she was doing this just to get back at me. I still didn't really get why she was pissed at me. I wasn't the one who'd changed our relationship out of the blue. How was I to know she liked me? Contrary to what I'd told Sarah back at the wedding, I was most definitely not a mind reader.

Dale stood up, grabbed the water buckets, and said, "Let's get some water."

"I don't really want to," I grumbled, glancing back out at the water.

"Yeah, you do. Let's go."

I caught Dale's eye. He wasn't giving me a choice. His hand was out, ready to pass me one of the buckets. I got up, grabbed it, and followed him out of camp.

"Is something going on with you and Kenzie?"

"No, why?" I lied.

Dale flashed me a knowing look. Sometimes he reminded me of one of those TV dads, whose disapproving looks seemed scripted. Still, Dale had a way of pulling out my honesty.

"It's just awkward. She basically told me she liked me. Totally out of the blue. I mean, what am I supposed to say to that? We're on a fucking reality show."

"I'm not surprised," Dale said.

"That she likes me?" I asked. Was I the only one who hadn't gotten the memo?

Dale looked up at me hesitantly before saying, "You flirt with her a lot, Kyle. What's she supposed to think?"

I was annoyed by Dale's assessment. "I flirt like that with all girls."

"Yeah, well, Kenzie's not all girls. She's sheltered. She lives in a town with a population of 1,500 people. Chances are she's never met anyone like you. I mean, honestly, Kyle, you take flirting to a whole new level. Hell, sometimes I think you're hitting on me too."

"I am, Dale. You know I love you," I said, grabbing for him and trying to kiss his cheek. Dale wormed away from me, laughing.

"I'm serious. You need to lay off all the sexy-time talk with her."

"Who says sexy-time? Jesus, Dale, remember that we're trying to make you cool. Besides, I'm just being friendly." Even though I was joking around and trying to portray myself as indifferent, a sudden uneasiness hit my core. Was I really leading her on?

Dale flashed me another one of his canned expressions. "Yesterday she was headed to the beach and asked if you were coming, and you said, 'Not quite, but I'm getting close.'"

I laughed. "That was funny."

"And all your food sex references?"

"I don't know what you're talking about," I countered.

"The two of you had a sexually charged, twenty-minute discussion about ripe fruit yesterday, and I swear Bobby went off to masturbate."

"Hey, that was a serious conversation. I was genuinely curious about kumquats."

"Look, I know you're just being you, and it's hysterical. I mean, you crack me up. And obviously Kenzie loves it too, but it's not hard to see why she might think you're hitting on her. That's all I'm saying."

"So what do you suggest I do – not talk to her at all?" I answered, irrationally.

"Surely you can communicate with women without inserting sexually graphic remarks. I mean, how do you talk to your grandma?"

"We don't talk about kumquats, that's for sure."

Dale laughed.

I inhaled, anxious energy coursing through me. I had a bad feeling that I had just screwed things up badly. "Shit. I messed up, didn't I?"

"That all depends."

"On what?"

"If you like her or not… because if you do, you've got the girl. Good for you. If you don't, you've led her on, and you've got some explaining to do."

Dale and I headed back to camp with our buckets filled with water. The more I thought about what he'd said, the worse I felt. This was all my fault. I was so comfortable with Kenzie that I'd just started talking to her like I would talk to my brothers. She seemed game for anything. It's what I loved about her. I'd never felt as comfortable around a woman as I did with Kenzie, but was it because I saw her as a friend, or did I actually have feelings for her?

Yeah, our spooning sessions had been getting a rise out of me, but I just figured it was because I hadn't had sex in a while, and unlike Bobby, I wasn't disappearing into the woods every hour to rub it out. But this morning, at the beach, I'd felt things for her that I never had before. I cared what happened to Kenzie. She had become part of my life these past weeks, and I knew I'd miss her when the show was over.

Carl and Marsha were sitting by the fire in complete silence when Dale and I arrived back in camp. They never really talked. For whatever reason, Marsha didn't bombard him with her interesting facts as often as she did us. Don't get me wrong, he still got his fair share, but unlike the rest of us, she typically gave Carl his space. He was just not a friendly dude. I didn't know what Kenzie saw in him or why she was trying to help, but clearly her sessions were not having a big effect on his temperament. He was still a miserable dick wad.

Kenzie and Bobby came back from the water laughing and plopped themselves on the logs. Kenzie sat beside Marsha and Bobby took one of his own.

"How was the water?" Marsha asked.

"It felt great," Kenzie replied shaking her hair out. I watched her smile in that dreamy way of hers, and I couldn't take my eyes off her. It was strange. Now that I knew she liked me, I was seeing her differently. Sizing her up. Possibly sensing me staring, Kenzie glanced in my direction, and I quickly looked away.

"Did you know the average depth of the ocean is 2.7 miles?" Marsha asked.

"Ugghh," I heard Bobby groan.

"No, I didn't know that," Kenzie replied. I smiled. Actually, she did know that. Marsha had repeated that fact at least three times already. But Kenzie was just being polite. I didn't know too many women who would be so patient with someone as annoying as Marsha. It was definitely an endearing quality. If I was going to have a girlfriend, that would definitely be a characteristic I'd like her to have. *See, there I go again.*

"Are you cold?" Bobby asked. "You're shivering."

"No, I'm good," she replied.

I watched him get up and squeeze himself onto the log next to her. When his arm wrapped around Kenzie, I felt a jolt of displeasure. Was she really buying into this whole charade? He was just playing her to stay in the game. I hoped she knew that. When he started rubbing her back, I felt my skin crawl. It's not that I was jealous – at least, I didn't think I was – but Bobby? Come on! He was such a slimy dude. I was seconds away from stomping over there and getting my ass kicked in her honor when Kenzie shrugged him off and walked over to Carl's log.

Bobby gave her a dirty look. Dale caught my eye and then went to sit on an empty log, and I slid in beside him.

With all the awkward glances going on, there was a prolonged moment of silence that rocked the camp. Kenzie caught my eye and we stared at each other. I could see her questioning look, so I smiled at her to ease the tension. She returned my gesture, but there was hesitancy to her smile that tore at me. I hated that I was making her feel this way. Dale was right. We needed to talk.

———

But we didn't. I had no idea how to bring up the topic without things getting awkward between us again, so I just ignored it for now. To her credit, Kenzie kept my identity a secret. In fact, it was me, only one day later, who managed to spill the beans to the entire group.

We'd been sitting around the fire when Bobby dared to speak to Carl. "So, I gotta ask, dude, how exactly did you get picked for the show?"

"I was walking through an airport."

"And?"

"That's it."

"You got spotted at an airport, and they asked you to be on the show? Just like that?" Bobby asked, with disbelief etched into his question.

"Just like that," Carl confirmed curtly.

Bobby laughed.

The indifferent look on Carl's face immediately turned to anger. "You got a problem?"

"No. No problem."

Kenzie chewed on her bottom lip as she watched the interaction between the two. She acted personally invested in Carl's peaceful transition into society. Subjectively, I didn't feel he deserved her devotion, although if I wanted to be completely honest, neither did I.

"Do you want to know how I got on the show?" Marsha asked, as she threw some wood in the fire.

We all turned our attention on her. Yes, actually, that was a very interesting question. How in the hell *did* Marsha get a spot?

"Do tell," I grinned at her.

"I sent in a nudie pic."

I barked out a disbelieving laugh. Everyone else remained frozen in shock.

"Seriously?" Dale asked, his eyes huge behind the glasses.

"No." She waved her hand and threw her head back in amusement. "I made a home video driving my tractor through town, and they liked it."

There was an audible exhale from every single one of us, followed by uncontrolled laughter.

When we'd all had our fill, Dale asked, "You weren't by chance wearing the outfit you came in here with, were you?"

"Yes, I was. How did you know?"

"Lucky guess."

"Okay, Marsha, I'm going to address the elephant in the room," Bobby said, boldly going where no man dared to go. I had to hand it to him, he was a ballsy little creature today.

"Why don't I wear a bra?"

Bobby seemed surprised that she'd guessed what he was going to ask; though in reality, what other elephant did she have? "Well… uh… yeah."

"I don't like having the girls constricted."

"That's it?" He laughed. "No big reveal?"

Marsha shrugged, nonchalantly. "I've never worn a bra."

"Ever?" Kenzie asked in surprise.

"Nope."

"Not even when it's nippy outside?" I joked.

"Not even then," she answered confidently. "Anything else?"

"Oh, uh," Bobby stammered. "I guess not. It's just a little weird."

"What's weird about it?"

"I don't know. Sometimes it's hard to concentrate when they're flopping around."

"Why should I be uncomfortable just to make you comfortable?"

Bobby had no answer for her, so he sealed his mouth shut and abruptly ended that awkward line of questioning.

With the mystery of Marsha's boobs solved (sort of) she turned to Kenzie and asked, "What about you, missy girl? How'd you make it on the show."

"Honestly, I played up the whole small town girl thing."

"And it worked?" Bobby asked, his mouth hanging open.

Kenzie laughed. "Well, I'm here."

"Why are you so shocked when you hear of one of us getting on the show by way of our personality?" Dale asked Bobby.

"I'm just surprised that being tall or braless or a sweet, hometown girl would be enough."

"Why?" I asked. "Did you have to sleep with someone to get on?"

"Pretty much." Bobby nodded and the look in his eye made me think he probably had.

"Okay," Kenzie said, looking embarrassed, "I might also have done a little skit on my Cookie Monster eyes."

"You didn't?" I laughed.

She nodded, blushing. "I had the head from a Halloween costume and did the voice and acted out a whole scene from *Sesame Street*. They must have liked it because I got an interview request right away."

"That…" Bobby shook his head, seemingly annoyed by the stories he was hearing. "Well, shit… clearly I went all out."

"What about you, Kyle?" Marsha asked. "How'd you make it on the show?"

I glanced at Kenzie. Her eyes flashed with uneasiness, no doubt wondering how I would answer. I had no idea myself. Searching my mind for a plausible excuse, I still came up blank so, like a toddler, I replied, "I'm not telling."

"You're not telling?" Bobby asked, stunned by my immature reply. "Why? What do you have to hide?"

"I'm not hiding anything. I'm just not telling."

"That makes you look sketchy," Carl said, in a disapproving tone.

"No more sketchy than you," I countered.

"Do you know his secret?" an irritated Carl asked Kenzie.

She looked around at everyone's expectant faces and then squeaked and buried her head in her hands. "I'm not answering that," she said through her hands.

"Wait, you told Kenzie your secret and not me?" Dale whined. "Really?"

"It's not a secret," I complained. This was not going as I'd hoped.

"You want us to trust you in this game, but you lie," Carl said, actually sounding hurt. What the hell was his problem? Geez, what a colossal wuss!

"I agree," Bobby said, no doubt trying to cash in on the friction. "Clearly there are those in the know and those on the outside."

Marsha added. "And to think I told you why I don't wear a bra, and this is how you repay me! So disappointing."

"Seriously?" I laughed, but one look around told me no one else found it as ridiculous as I did. In fact, they all seemed genuinely pissed. Why hadn't I come up with a goddamn lie? I glanced at the disenchantment on Dale's face. Oh no, not the Cosby look again. "Okay, fine. Jake McKallister is my brother! Are you all happy now?"

TV Confessional
"I hardly think my admission is more stunning than Marsha's shocking revelation."
— *Kyle*

CHAPTER TWENTY-FOUR

KENZIE

Bonds That Tie

Well, people were certainly happy. Kyle's admission had quite an effect on the tribe. I'd never seen a conversation turn as quickly. The others were getting their pitchforks ready to skewer him for keeping secrets when his revelation spun the discussion on its head. All animosity was forgotten as Kyle was peppered with questions about his famous brother. I now totally got why he kept his last name to himself. It had to be hard to reveal something as innocent as who your brother was and then be bombarded with a hundred questions. I watched Kyle's face for reactions. He seemed okay when the questions about Jake were superficial, but when they turned personal, there was a clear line drawn, and Kyle's demeanor changed from patient to defensive.

"Wait," Bobby started. "Were you the one with him when he was taken?"

After a moment of silence, he answered, "Yes."

I gaped at him. I knew there was more to him than met the eye, but never could I have predicted such a difficult past. Kyle shifted on his log, suddenly appearing ready to bolt. I wanted to grab his hand and pull him away from the inquisition, but after our newfound awkwardness, I wasn't sure if he'd welcome that.

"Damn, so you know what went down, then?" Bobby asked, in a mixture of awe and excitement, as if he really believed he was about to get the inside scoop.

Kyle nodded his response. I could only imagine the story he had to tell.

"And you know how he got away?"

Dale intervened. "That's private, Bobby."

"I wasn't talking to you, Dale," Bobby replied condescendingly, before turning to Kyle and saying, "I just want to know how he escaped... how he got the knife."

Kyle was struggling to keep it together. With a clenched jaw, he said, "Like I'd talk to you about that."

"Why not me?" Bobby asked, as if he and Kyle hadn't been adversaries from the very beginning.

"Drop it!"

There was a warning in Kyle's demand that halted the conversation completely. A collective silence commenced before Marsha, in her infinite wisdom, broke it with another fact. "Congress made kidnapping a federal crime after the Lindbergh baby was found dead."

"Marsha, not right now," Dale answered.

"It's a fact," she shrugged. "And here's another one. With your brother being a multi-millionaire, I'd say you don't really need to win this show."

"It's my brother's money, not mine."

"Yeah, but it's not like a necessity for you."

"It's not for you either, Marsha," Kyle lambasted. "You inherited a town from your father."

"My money is all tied up. Your brother is beyond rich."

"That doesn't mean anything," Dale stepped in. "Kyle has as much right to play as anyone else. And as much right to win."

"Well, I wouldn't vote for him."

"Me neither," Bobby added.

"I'm right here," Kyle protested, waving his hand around.

Dale could see Kyle's stress as plainly as I, and he stepped in for his friend. "Everyone needs to lay off Kyle right now."

"Okay. But first, I have one thing to say about this," Carl blurted out, unexpectedly. He hadn't said a word since Kyle's big reveal, but now he turned his giant body toward him and said in the giddiest, fangirl voice he could muster, "This is really exciting for me. Music frees me, and your brother's songs… they just speak to my soul."

Kyle's eyes bugged out in surprise. He looked at me questioningly as if to ask, *Is this guy for real?* I shrugged.

"Are you being serious?" he asked Carl. "I can't tell."

"Have you ever known me to joke?"

"Good point," Kyle said, shaking his head. "Wow."

"What? I'm a huge fan." Carl grunted, instantly morphing back to his normal, disengaged self.

"Well, I'll be sure to let him know," Kyle said, and then stood up abruptly. "I need a break."

I watched him walk away and jumped from my seat to follow him. He stopped when he heard me coming. Without turning around he said, "What do you want, Kenzie?"

"Just checking up on you."

"Promise me you'll never become a double agent," he said, turning to face me.

"I wasn't trying to be sneaky. Are you doing okay?"

He fidgeted back and forth several times, and then stated, "Well, shit… that really wasn't fun."

"Sorry. Bobby was being a dick."

"And Marsha too. I've always stood up for her, but she just gleefully chucked me under the bus."

"I know. She's got an evil streak in her. We need to watch our backs."

"So what was that whole thing with you and Bobby yesterday anyway?"

"Nothing. I was pissed at you."

"I got that."

"I thought I could drown out my embarrassment with a double dose of Bobby, but damn, he's just such a tool."

Kyle laughed. "Don't I know!"

Feeling guilty for my part in his last two crappy days, I caught his eye and said, "I'm sorry about yesterday. I shouldn't have dumped that on you. It's just a stupid schoolyard crush. And I know it's one-sided. I promise to keep my mouth shut from now on."

"It's not that, Kenzie. I think you're a great girl. I just… that's not why I came here, you know, to meet anyone. It was the furthest thing from my mind. You just took me by surprise is all."

"I know. I was being stupid. Every guy I know has been in my life forever. I don't meet a lot of fresh meat."

Kyle grinned. "You understand I could go in so many directions with that statement, right?"

"Of course."

"But Dale says my sexual innuendos are leading you on."

"Honestly, Kyle, I'm so deprived of male companionship that you could have entertained me with stories of health insurance and I still probably would have imprinted on you."

He smiled. "So how do you want to handle this? I'll do whatever you want."

"I don't want things to be weird. Can we just forget that yesterday ever happened?"

"Thank God," he said grabbing his chest. "Does that mean I can still make sex jokes?"

"I'd be bummed if you didn't."

"So do you think it's going to hurt me? Revealing that information about Jake?"

"That depends. Do you live in a mansion?"

Kyle didn't immediately respond. At least he had the decency to look embarrassed.

"Seriously?"

"What? My brother bought my parents a house a few years back. Is that my fault?"

"No." I laughed. "But you might want to omit that fact when you're talking to the others."

"You think?" he grumbled. "And I don't live in a mansion very often. Most of the time I'm in hotels, on the tour bus, or with Jake at his place."

"And again, another possible omission."

"You don't approve of my life?" he asked, with an edge to his voice.

"On the contrary, it sounds amazing. Traveling, concerts, rock stars… I only wish I could be you."

"But you think I'm a spoiled brat."

"I didn't say that."

"You didn't have to. Everyone here assumes that. You don't think I know when I'm being judged?"

"Kyle... I..." I reached out to touch him, but he flinched away.

"My life hasn't been picture perfect, Kenzie. I've dealt with some hard shit too."

I was taken aback by the resentment in his voice. "I didn't mean to offend you."

"No one ever does."

Kyle stomped off, leaving me disbelieving in his wake.

Marooned Rule #5
When there are only ten players left, the two tribes merge into one.

The day was just getting started, and already it sucked. With Kyle pissed at me, I wanted nothing more than to make things right; but then we were called out for an immunity challenge. The East Tribe was down to five members, and we still had six. If we could win this contest, they would be down to four, and we'd go into the merge sitting real pretty. With our six players, we could just pick the Easties off one by one.

Of course, things rarely went as planned, and this was no exception. Our task was, as a team, to make our way through a series of ropes and ladders, all while bound together. We could only go as fast as our slowest guy, and that guy was Dale. He was not a nimble man to begin with, but his injuries made him even more of a liability. There were times where we were literally dragging him through the obstacle course. Despite our extensive efforts, we were handed a resounding loss.

Dejected and exhausted, the moment we stumbled back into camp, the scheming began. Someone was going home tonight, and there were varying opinions on who it was going to be. It was as if the six of us had turned into rabid animals. Backed into corners, there was a lot of threatening and snarling going on. Alliances began to crumble. And much to my dismay, Dale's name was the one being thrown out there the most. Marsha, Carl, and Bobby wanted him gone… and they wanted me to turn against him to make it happen. But in order for me to do that, I'd have to betray Kyle, knowing there was no way he would ever vote Dale out. The worst part was, I was actually considering it. The others weren't wrong to want Dale gone. He'd lost that challenge for us. It was only fair that he be the one to take the fall for it.

It should have been an easy decision to make. Dale's game was dragging mine down. I'd sworn to myself before starting the show that I wouldn't let emotion dictate my decisions. Winning meant staying strong and fierce and focused. No one I could meet on the show, I reasoned, could possibly mean more to me than my family. But then, I hadn't been expecting the strong connections I'd made. This game was tough. Winning took so much more than just physical strength. You needed personal connections. And to get close to people, you needed to open yourself up to the possibility of friendship, all the while knowing you would eventually have to betray them.

The bonds I'd made out here were real… and despite what I'd told Kyle, I felt more for him than just a silly crush. I didn't know when or how, but somewhere along the way my heart had been stolen right out from under me. I had completely broken my promise. Not only had I let emotions get the best of me, I was now making decisions based on them. Dale was too important to Kyle. And Kyle was too important to me. The smart decision became the emotional one. Loyalty won out over strength. Bobby would be the next to go.

TV Confessional
"Imprinted? You know, when werewolves find the right person, they imprint on them. Twilight? No? Okay, never mind."
— Kenzie

CHAPTER TWENTY-FIVE

KYLE

Never Have I Ever

After my childish rant at Kenzie, I'd stalked off in search of food. I was hungry and pissed. My so-called allies were all so quick to write me off the minute my family connection came into play. So much for forging my own identity out here. Dale was always talking to me about finding my way, and I had been buying into all his bullshit rhetoric right up until everyone who meant any-thing to me in this game just shit all over me. What was the point of branching out on my own? When this show aired, I wouldn't be introduced as Kyle McKallister. I was going to be Jake McKallister's brother, nothing more and nothing less. I might as well have just stayed on tour.

I came to the tree where Kenzie and I had foraged for fruit on the second day. We'd been back many times since, stripping the branches free of anything edible. But there was still a bundle higher up that I'd not been able to reach. Grabbing a long stalk of bamboo, I attempted to hoist myself up onto the first branch, but without Kenzie giving me a boost, I couldn't reach.

"You want a hand?" Carl asked, sneaking up from behind and nearly causing me to crap my pants in surprise. The guy actually had a 'Don't worry, I'm not going to kill you' look on his face. Oh, now he wanted to be friendly? And it didn't have anything to do with the fact that he had a chubby for my brother?

"I don't know, Carl," I replied in a snooty tone. "I'm just really not in the mood for company. You should understand that."

Carl raised his arms to concede defeat. "Say no more."

I watched him turn and walk away. My stomach growled in protest. My self-preservation outweighed my pride.

"Maybe just a boost," I called out to him. Carl turned his enormous body on a dime and strode back over to me. He cupped his hands and I stepped into the linked palms. He shot me in the air like a frickin' cannon. My starting point was two branches higher than I'd ever been with one of Kenzie's boosts. Carl handed me the bamboo stick, and

I climbed my way up until I was able to poke down a few more fruits from the tree.

Luckily Carl stayed by the trunk, and I got out of the tree with way fewer cuts and bruises than normal. Kenzie always seemed to lose track of my existence the moment those fruit pods started tumbling down. Carl appeared less interested in piggybacking off my effort. He watched as I hoarded my bounty like a cagey, wounded animal. Surprisingly, he didn't try to take any for himself, although with the mood I was in, I probably would have bit off his fucking hand if he'd tried.

"You need my help with anything else?"

I eyed him suspiciously. "Why are you being nice to me all of the sudden?"

"I was hoping you could get me backstage at one of Jake's concerts."

Stunned, I glared up at Carl. That was *never* going to happen. If it were up to me, I'd have him thrown out of the damn venue. What an asshole! Then I realized he was smiling.

"Was that a joke?" I asked, confused at the scene playing out in front of me.

"My attempt at one, anyway. You looked like you were having a bad day. I just wanted to help. I'll leave you be now."

Three long strides already had the dude a half a block away. "Hey," I called out to him.

Carl turned just as I tossed him a fruit. He caught it in one hand, held it up as if to say thanks, and walked away.

He wasn't so bad after all.

⸻

The last of the Fab Five to get the boot was Bobby, and he went out kicking and screaming. Good riddance, if you asked me. The dickwad dumped our rice in the ocean when he realized nothing would save him. And now we hadn't eaten more than crabs, mollusks, and worms in the past thirty-six hours.

The merge with the East couldn't come soon enough. Without carbs, we were bodies without bones. Most of the last two days had been spent in a state of lethargy. Even walking to the poophole was a challenge. When we weren't foraging for food, we were sprawled out in the shelter, trying to escape the sweltering heat or floating listlessly in the warm ocean water.

Kenzie and I had decided not to talk about our spat. It seemed easier to pretend like nothing happened than to deal with the larger issue at hand; and honestly, I had no idea what that was or why we had been arguing in the first place. The fun, flirty side of our conversations returned, but I sensed a level of tension coming from her end. She was more restrained when I got playful with her, removing my hands from places she hadn't minded them being before.

Sometimes when she thought I wasn't looking, I'd catch Kenzie staring at me with that dreamy far-off look in her eyes. Clearly she felt something for me, but for the life of me, I couldn't figure out why. This was a girl who had her shit together. I was the complete opposite: immature, lazy, essentially unemployed, and suffering from serious abandonment issues. I'd never had a relationship last more than six hours.

The quick (and obvious) answer would be that Kenzie liked me for my DNA, but that argument didn't hold true, seeing as she fell for my slacker act well before knowing my connection to Jake. Nope, as far as I could tell, she liked me for me. *What the hell?* If Kenzie were smart, she'd run as fast as possible in the opposite direction. Warning her seemed the responsible thing to do; yet the selfish asshole in me wasn't ready for her to leave. I liked having someone devoted to me for a change. Maybe I was leading her on, like Dale said… or maybe… I wasn't. Could it be that I actually liked this girl? Certainly, I wasn't immune to her earthy charms. Kenzie was a pretty girl, and I'd have been lying if I said some of her flirty antics didn't get a rise out of me. And strangely enough, even though neither one of us was becoming more eye-catching as the show went on, I was inexplicably finding myself more drawn to her every day.

It was midday, and the sun was beating down upon the shelter, trapping us all under a blanket of humidity. We'd been lounging around for over an hour doing nothing more than bemoaning our lack of food and feeling sorry for ourselves, when I saw something scurry through Kenzie's hair.

"Kenz?" I murmured in a low and emotionless tone of voice.

"Yeah?" she answered back, with even less enthusiasm than I'd just managed to muster.

"There's a bug in your hair."

No response.

"There's a bug in your hair," I repeated a little louder.

"I heard you the first time. Could you take it out, please?"

I could, but that would require exerting energy, of which I had very little.

"It's probably just going to scamper away on its own," I offered feebly.

"I swear, Kyle. If you don't take it out, the next time you get stung by a jellyfish, you're peeing on it yourself."

"That was on the back of my leg. I couldn't have reached it and you know it."

"The point is I did it. Now you owe me."

"Uggghh," I huffed. "Fine."

I maneuvered my body up and rested on my elbow as I started picking through her hair for the offending insect. This is what we'd been reduced to… a family of orangutans, lazing around all day, foraging through each other's hair for bugs.

"If Kenzie's hair bug is big and meaty, I call it," Dale announced.

"Dammit," Carl exclaimed. "I wanted it."

"Yeah, well, I called shotgun."

"I thought you didn't kill living things, Carl," Kenzie called him out.

"That was before I was starving to death. Now I'm not ruling out cannibalism."

We all chuckled, but it was a pathetic sound. It was as if our voices couldn't muster the enthusiasm required for a genuine laugh. My eyes followed the bug's path through Kenzie's hair. He was a quick sucker, much quicker than my shaky fingers could catch. I made a quick movement and jabbed Kenzie in the back of the head.

"Ow!" she protested.

"My bad. He's a slippery sucker. Oh, wait." I captured the bug between my thumb and pointer finger. "Got it," I called out proudly, holding up my creepy crawly treasure.

"You got a size or species?" Dale asked, sounding incredibly apathetic.

"I don't know. It looks like a beetle."

"Gross," Kenzie complained.

"It's dime size and impressively plump. Probably got a good greasy meal in Kenzie's hair before I caught it."

Kenzie reached back to smack me, but her hand hit air and she just gave up.

The bug wiggled in my fingers. I tried to hold on but he had other plans and made an impressive escape. "Oh, shit. It jumped. Sorry, Dale."

"Yeah, it's okay. I wasn't all that invested in it anyway."

"Did you know that one in every four animals on earth are beetles?" Marsha piped up.

"Yes," Carl said, barely able to control his frustration. "And do you know why we know, Marsha? Because you've said it over one hundred times."

Once we'd figured out that Marsha's knowledge wasn't limitless, just on a loop, it was tough to have the patience to deal with her repetitiveness.

"Hardly," she answered with a wave of her hand, completely brushing Carl off.

"Here's one for you Marsha," Dale challenged. "Did you know the Rubik's cube can always be solved in twenty moves or less?"

"Of course," she rolled her eyes. "Sometimes you act like I'm two."

"That wasn't my intention."

"Do you know what the world record is?" she parried, an air of superiority in her question.

"Six seconds," Dale answered confidently.

"Wrong. The world record is 5.55 seconds."

"Too bad I don't have the Internet so I can fact check you."

"You don't need it. I'm a walking encyclopedia," Marsha answered smugly.

"Of regurgitated facts," Carl mumbled. "I can't believe there even is a website to fact check stupid shit like that."

"They have videos of cats licking their asses, Carl," I answered helpfully. "Why not geek trivia sites?"

"Really? Cats licking their butts?" Marsha asked, seemingly intrigued. I got a visual of her going home and googling it.

"Well, did you know the Rubik's cube was invented to help explain three dimensional geometry?" Dale said, not ready to give up on his incredibly stimulating conversation.

"Dale, please don't insult my intelligence."

Kenzie, Carl, and I looked at each other in amusement. Dale and Marsha could do this all day if we let them, and sometimes they did. I wondered if when I was old and decrepit like them I'd have as much useless information floating around in my head. Somehow I didn't think I would.

In an attempt to break up their incredibly nerdy pissing contest, I said, "Hey Dale, how is that hill on your leg coming along?"

"It's swollen to twice its size."

"Any whitehead yet?"

"You know there isn't, Kyle," Dale replied, with just enough edge in his voice to make it funny. "You ask me every few hours. When it's ready to pop, you'll be the first to know."

And as sad and pathetic as it was, I genuinely felt that witnessing the eruption of Dale's pus-filled abscess would be one of the highlights of my time on the island. Just the fact that Dale would allow me to share in his special moment made me love him even more.

"Who's up for a little team bonding?" Kenzie asked.

Without bothering to open my eyes, I raised my hand. As hungry and exhausted as I was, if possible I was even more bored. And since Kenzie was willing to put forth the effort to entertain me, I was all for it.

"Good. Kyle. Anyone else?"

"As long as the bonding doesn't require standing up," Carl whined. "I get lightheaded."

"Nothing physical," she agreed. "Dale? Marsha?"

"I guess."

"Whatever."

"Great. I love the enthusiasm. Okay, everyone up and sit in a circle."

Groans went up louder than I would have expected, but then the most vocal of them probably came from me. I had hoped we could bond lying down.

Once we were all in an upright position, Kenzie explained the game. "This is a team bonding exercise called Ten Fingers. Everyone hold up your hands." We all did as instructed except Dale, who had sustained an injury to his pinky finger a few days earlier, and it now appeared to be hanging limply.

"Jesus, Dale." I shook my head. "Is there any part of you that isn't injured?"

"I can't help it. I didn't know I would be required to raise all ten fingers today, or I might have been doing some physical therapy in preparation," he spat back.

"Quiet, boys. I'm trying to explain the rules. So I'm going to say something like 'I've never kissed a dog,' and if you *have* kissed a dog, you put one finger down. In Dale's case… we'll just assume he's kissed a dog."

A low rumble of amusement burst forth from the five of us.

"So this is 'Never have I ever'?" I asked. "The drinking game?"

"Yes, but we'll be playing the kid's version."

"Ooh, I'm in," I said, suddenly getting a new wind. Nothing I wanted more than to dig out a little filth from these people. "How dirty can we get?"

Kenzie glanced at the cameras. "Depends on how much you want your mom to know about you, I guess."

I winced. "So PG-13?"

"That's probably smart. Okay, so I'll start. For Dale's sake, we'll get this one out of the way right now. Never have I ever broken a bone."

Everyone but Kenzie lowered a finger. Dale's limp, pathetic one stayed where it was. She gestured for Dale to go next.

"Never have I ever peed in a public pool."

All fingers went down except Carl's. He wrinkled his nose, flinching away from us. "Really? All of you? That's absolutely repulsive."

"Come on. You can't tell me you haven't peed in the ocean," I pressed, honestly not understanding how someone could go through life without committing such an act.

His head snapped in my direction. "Never. Why? Have you?"

"Of course. Sometimes standing right next to you."

Carl's face turned hard and angry. Clearly he was not finding the fun in the game.

"Carl," Kenzie soothed. "Why don't you go next?"

"Never have I ever strangled someone who peed on me," Carl barked, all the while glowering at me. He then lowered one finger in an attempt to intimidate me. Kenzie grabbed his hand and scolded him with her eyes.

"Okay, Carl. Not helpful. Next."

"I've got one," I offered. "Never have I ever had sex in the back of a cop car."

Marsha lowered a finger. I gaped at her. She never ceased to amaze me.

"Okay, I just want to be clear that you understand the game, Marsha."

"I understand the game, Kyle. You think you're so young and hip, but I was running wild years before you were even born. So close your mouth and move on."

"Actually, it's your turn," Kenzie directed.

Marsha took a moment to think about her contribution to the game, and then, with her eyes fixed on Kenzie, said, "Never have I ever fallen in love with someone who only thinks of me as a friend."

Silence flooded the stale, humid air around us. Kenzie's face dropped in horror. I saw her hands actually shake. Carl seemed to pick up on her distress and he lowered a finger. She caught his eye, and I saw tears in hers.

"This is a stupid game!" she proclaimed, and then scooted out of the shelter and stomped off into the woods.

Marsha's face twisted into a smug leer. "Was it something I said?"

Marooned Rule #6

Once the two tribes merge as one, team play is finished and it becomes an individual game. All challenges are played for individual immunity and the winner will be safe from elimination.

The merge came the following day, and we moved our sorry asses to the other tribe's camp. It was clear the moment we stepped foot on their beach that we were a bunch of losers. Their camp was like a Sandals resort in comparison to ours. They had clotheslines and hammocks and log chairs and blankets, all won in reward challenges. They had even designed their own water system. We walked around admiring their offerings in embarrassment. How had we let things get so bad at our camp? After eliminating Gene and all his rules, we'd become a tribe of slackers. And I had a terrible feeling I was their beloved leader.

Dale, for one, was in heaven at the organization and structure of our new digs. I realized how far he would have had to sink as a productive member of society in order to be content living the life I led on an everyday basis. The other tribe had five energetic, robust go-getters, and Dale was the perfect addition to their group. What would be his motivation to stay with us? I mean, we'd been forced together on day one because we had no other choice. I felt like we'd formed real bonds, but it was still a game, and Dale wanted to win it, for no other reason than that he hated to lose. If he could get ahead with another group, would he dump our lazy butts and move on?

I glanced at Kenzie, who was watching the scene unfold before her. It was obvious she shared my apprehension by the way she was chewing on her bottom lip. Her eyes caught mine but then hastily looked away. Things had gone back to being awkward after her overly emotional reaction to Marsha's game question. Not knowing what to say to her, I just kept my distance. But that was before the Dale issue. I needed her now. If the Easties were trying to tempt Dale into a life of luxury, I needed her help to remind him that he loved our squalor.

In addition to our five, the East tribe had Fergus, Amir, Lena, Carol and Eugene. Although they seemed nice enough, I had no idea who any of them were. Our contact with them had been limited to the challenges. As a peace offering, the production staff presented us with an over-flowing basket of food and drink. The other five seemed more interested in getting to know us than actually eating. Apparently they'd been catching fish the entire time we'd been eating slugs. So as they stood around chatting, we five dropped to our knees and started shoveling food in our mouths like the barbarians we'd become. I could hear them giggling at our animalistic behavior. Dale tried to explain away our manners by detailing how Bobby had dumped our rice before exiting the game, but even *he* had to do that through mouthfuls of chicken legs. I'm pretty sure I grunted my way through my meal. Kenzie even elbowed me in the side at one point when my enjoyment got too aggressively boisterous.

Theoretically, this was the part of the game where we ceased team play and began competing as individuals but the reality was you needed numbers in order to stay in the game. So although we'd merged into one, we were still very much two separate groups of five. The only hope for security at the first individual council was to sway a member of the other side to flip, hence the pressure on Dale.

The minute the meal was over, the niceties were dropped and the game began. Everyone was scrambling for positions and looking for weakness. There were conversations going on all around me. I stood there dumbfounded. Clearly, backstabbing was not my strong suit. I was loyal to a fault and would not hesitate to sacrifice myself for those I cared about. And I cared about every person in the Dork Quad, even Carl, our unofficial member.

I watched as the Easties swooped down on Dale like famished vultures. My mind was screaming, *No, not Dale! They can't have him and his leg volcano!* It was like my whole life was spiraling out of control, and I was frozen in place. Kenzie must have sensed my distress and swooped in.

"Are you all right?" she asked, her concern for me outweighing her unease.

"No. We're screwed. Dale's gone."

"He's not gone. You're being paranoid. Dale's smart and playing both sides."

I was still looking around frantically.

"Kyle." Kenzie placed her fingers on my face. "Look at me. We're fine. The boxer lady, what's her name again, Liza?"

I directed my focus to where she was indicating with her eyes. "Lena, I think."

"Well whatever her name is, she's an outsider in that group, and the only person I think we have a chance of swaying. I need you to go over there and charm the pants off her."

My eyes zeroed in on the target: muscles, tattoos, and a seriously scowling face. She looked like she could break me in half with one karate chop. *Really, Kenzie?* I'd have a better chance with the Mormon lady, Carol. Still, she'd given me an assignment, and that allowed me to redirect my focus.

As my tension eased, I grinned and said, "Are you whoring me out?"

"I am. Now go." She shooed me away. As I was about to leave on my mission, Kenzie whispered just loud enough for me to hear, "And don't come back until she's hot for you."

"You give me *way* too much credit," I threw over my shoulder, as I headed straight for my surly, man-killing mark. I had some hustling to do.

"Lena, right?" I asked as I walked up to her. She straightened her back and crossed her arms in front of herself in a defensive stance. A serpent with sharp claws and jagged teeth glared at me from a colorful tattoo on her forearm.

Her eyes rolled over me, and the excessively disgusted look on her face should have been my first clue that I wouldn't be getting to first base with snake lady.

"Yep."

"I'm Kyle."

"McKallister, I know," she said matter-of-factly. My eyes opened wide. I swallowed my surprise.

"How do you know that?" Obviously someone from my side couldn't wait to blab to the other team about my lineage.

Sensing my confusion as to who ratted me out, Lena clarified by making her hand into a talking puppet: "You've got yourself a little chatterbug in your tribe. Good lord, can that woman talk! How on earth did you put up with her for so long?"

I cringed. *Dammit, Marsha!* Had my brother and I become one of her interesting facts? "And everyone in the tribe knows who I am?"

"They do now. And just so you know, you've been the subject of many a discussion."

"I'm sure I have."

"And if you think anyone in their right mind is going to hand you a million dollars, you've got another thing coming, dude."

Well, shit. This was going even worse than I'd imagined. Every word she spoke to me dripped with condemnation. I had done nothing more than be related to a superstar, but that was apparently enough in her book to be a total bitch to me. But, unluckily for Lena, I was an expert at dealing with prickly personalities. It was really just a matter of figuring out what annoyed her and making sure I did lots of that infuriating behavior.

"Tell me, Lena, how come you aren't over there with the rest of your tribe wooing Dale?"

"I was busy with the fire."

"Uh huh, 'cause they sure don't seem interested in your opinion. Seems to me you weren't invited to eat at the cool kids' table."

Her eyes narrowed into laser beams of hate.

"Don't be embarrassed."

"You think I'm embarrassed?" she scoffed, smashing a bug on her arm and then flicking it in my direction. "If you must know, I had a tribe. We fought many battles together, but then my troops got gunned down one by one. Now I'm the last of my kind... a dying breed."

"Is that an analogy?"

"What? I don't know. You aren't the brightest, are you?"

"No, not really. It helps when people explain things slowly to me."

Lena sighed, and then actually spoke deliberately as she responded. "My alliance was picked off one by one... until they were all gone. Poof. Vanished. Do you get it now, Dumbass?"

Jesus. She went right for the insulting nicknames. I wasn't sure what I'd done to invite such scorn, but I knew I needed to stay one step ahead of her.

"So, then, you're not loyal to them?"

"I didn't say that."

"Why would you want to stick with people who picked your friends off one by one?"

"Because I'd rather play with the enemies I know than take a chance on you morons."

"What would it take for you to flip?"

"Depends," Lena said, looking bored as she picked dirt out of her fingernails. "How loyal are you to Larry Bird, the four-eyed nerd, your little groupie girl, and the braless conversationalist?"

I ignored Lena's dig and answered her question of my loyalty. "They're my troops."

"I figured," she said rolling her eyes. "So predictable. Sounds like we're going to have a stalemate... unless they get to your computer geek."

"Dale."

"Huh?"

"His name is Dale, and they aren't going to get to him."

"That's what you think. See the black guy with the 70's 'stache over there?" she said, flicking her eyes in his direction.

I nodded.

"Homicide detective. Goes by his last name, Fergus. Nice, affable guy, but watch out. He's a piranha. You think he's on your side, and he'll get you to agree to anything. And the worst part about it is he'll make you think you like it. Say goodbye to Dale."

"You think you've got it all figured out, don't you?"

"I do have it all figured out. When you're on the outside, you've got a lot of time to observe the nuances of the game. I'll do what's best for me, and if I think I'll have a better shot with your pathetic group of human anomalies, then I'll let you know."

"That'd be awesome, thanks," I replied sarcastically. "Just keep in mind when you're choosing sides who the power players are. We could barely lift our heads as we shuffled into your camp. We're not exactly intimidating. You look tough. Which group do you think you'll have a better chance of beating, our group of underachieving mutts, or your tribe of champion purebreds?"

Lena threw a wicked smile my way. "You're not as dumb as you look."

I didn't give her the satisfaction of a reply. I got what she was doing – putting me down to knock me off balance. She was good at reading people, but so was I. Only we had different approaches on how to use that information. She employed her razor tongue; I preferred humor.

Lena looked at me with more interest. "You realize I could kick your ass with ease?"

I laughed. "I have no doubt."

"And I could make easy work of the accident victim, Boobs McGee, and the girl with Bambi eyes. Lord, how did those three ever make it this far?"

"They have their strengths," I replied, barely controlling my annoyance. I really didn't like her crapping on my family. Lena saw my momentary lapse of control and smiled, no doubt filing it away somewhere to use it against me later.

"Anyway, think about it," I said.

"I already have."

As I was walking away she called out, "Hey, how attached are you to the Jolly Green Giant?"

"Pretty attached."

She shook her head, clearly disappointed in my answer. "That's what I thought. So predictable."

TV Confessional
"I got more action from the crab."
— Kyle

CHAPTER TWENTY-SIX

KENZIE
A Storm Is Coming

Kyle came back shaking his head.

"Nothing?" I asked.

"I'm lucky she didn't grab me by the balls and swing me around."

I winced. "That bad, huh?"

"Well, she's definitely not the type of woman who's going to be swayed by a little flirting."

"So she's a 'no,' then?"

"Not necessarily. The two of us just aren't going to be having sex anytime soon."

I laughed. That was a good thing if you asked me.

"But there is some good news. She's on the outs, like you thought. Oh, and her name is Lena, by the way. Don't forget, or she might punch you in your Bambi eyes."

"She made fun of my eyes?" I frowned.

"Oh, yeah, she was full of unflattering nicknames. Anyway, she's pretty bitter and clearly hates the others on her tribe. I'm just not sure if she's ready to cross over to the dark side. I played the whole 'weakling' angle with her. Told her she could easily beat us."

"Did she buy that?"

Kyle eyed me, his brows scrunched in surprise. "Kenz, she *can* beat us. She's tough and strong. You've seen her in challenges. I think the only one of us she's afraid of is Carl."

It was no wonder the producers chose the East camp for us all to live in now. Not only was their beach nicer, but they had a natural barrier that protected them from the elements. It seemed they'd had a definite advantage from the start. How we'd come into the merge with equal numbers was a mystery to me. I had to wonder if it wasn't our strong bond that had kept us together.

Dale, Kyle, and I took advantage of some free time to float in the ocean. We'd invited Carl to join us, but he no longer went into the water when Kyle was around, even after he'd promised to keep the piss in his pants. The waves were relaxing as we glided over the gentle waves. It had been a long, eventful day, and we needed to talk. As we were out in the water, the skies darkened and the wind picked up.

"A storm is coming," Dale said ominously.

"If it turns into a hurricane, you think they'd evacuate us?" Kyle asked.

We all went silent, contemplating his words. That's the way we were now – slow. Everything took more time to process.

"No. I think they'd just film us all dying," Dale said. "It would make for great television."

"With your luck, Dale, you'd come apart piece by piece. They'd find your little broken pinky finger in New Zealand."

"You ain't a-kidding."

"I've always wanted a hurricane named after me," I mused.

"Hurricane Kenzie? Talk about a wimpy sounding storm," Kyle scoffed, and then his voice went high pitched. "Hi! I'm Hurricane Kenzie! Would you mind if I ripped your roof off? No? Okay, I'll come back later."

"Hey," I laughed. "I think I've proven my toughness. Besides, I'd go by Mackenzie for something as official as a hurricane."

"Mackenzie? Is that your real name?" Dale asked.

"Yes," I answered, and then caught sight of Kyle's amused face. "All right, give it to me. I'm sure you have some snarky comment."

"I didn't say anything. Why do you always assume the worst of me?"

"Why wouldn't we?" Dale quipped.

"Anyway, Hurricane Mackenzie would be a real bitch," I continued. "It would be a category five monster and would not change direction whether there was land in the way or not. I mean, if you're going to have a hurricane named after you, you want to make it big, right?"

Kyle nodded like my logic made perfect sense to him.

"Well, if there was a Hurricane Dale, it would be a moderate category 2.5, slowing down along the way because it would insist on making landfall on every island along its path."

"Your hurricane would be so incredibly organized," Kyle laughed.

"And boring. Everyone would be all worried, and then I'd show up and they'd be like, 'Oh, it's just Dale.'"

"You're not boring," I said.

"Oh, you don't know me very well. I'm unmemorable. Most people forget my name the second they're introduced to me."

"Well, then, people need to pay better attention," I said. "Besides, after this show, you won't be forgettable anymore."

"I'm only going to be viewed as interesting because of the weirdos I'm keeping company with. No offense," Dale said.

"You don't give yourself enough credit," Kyle said. "You're just as weird as the rest of us."

"So what kind of a hurricane would you be, Kyle?" I asked.

"Hurricane Kyle would be sitting out in the water trying to figure out which direction was west."

Dale and I dissolved into laughter.

Spurned on by our reaction, Kyle continued with his self-deprecating storm. "My hurricane would be so dumb that he wouldn't even be able to find an island to make landfall."

We giggled for a bit more, and then Dale turned all serious. "Talk about not giving yourself credit."

"Huh?" Kyle responded.

"You're a lot smarter than you let on."

"Tell that to my teachers."

"There are different ways to be intelligent, Kyle. I'm around smart people all day, every day, and some of them have no common sense. And not only that, but their smarts don't necessarily translate into a high-paying job or extra happiness. In fact, some of the smartest people I know are the unhappiest. You have a way about you. So do you, Kenzie. You two have great potential. I feel privileged to know you," Dale said, before tearing up.

"Are you crying?" Kyle asked in surprise, and stood up.

"No, I'm just emotional. I love you guys."

"Ahh," I cooed. "We love you too, Dale."

"There's something I haven't told you."

Glancing over at Kyle, I had an uneasy feeling.

"We've got a problem," he said with a solemn look on his face. Reaching down, he pulled up his swimsuit leg to reveal his festering bump, which now appeared to be a seriously infected swelling on his upper thigh. The angry red welt was bulging out from the skin.

"Dude," Kyle remarked, shaking his head. Really, there was no need to say more. It was just that bad.

"How long has it looked like this?" I asked, feeling glum.

"Started last night. Medical checked it out this morning. It's not responding well to the antibiotics. I need to at least make it through this first council to give you guys a chance, but once it's over and we win, it's possible they'll pull me from the game."

Tears filled my eyes. Although I'd been seriously contemplating voting against Dale three days ago, I now felt that my heart was being ripped out.

"Maybe they'll just give you stronger antibiotics," Kyle said hopefully.

"Maybe," Dale nodded, but he did not appear optimistic. "I just didn't want you two blindsided by this. I'm not saying anything to the others because, you know, it's always been the three of us to the end, right."

We nodded. I swear I saw Kyle mist up. He genuinely cared about Dale.

"Does this mean I'm not going to get to see the pus?" Kyle pouted, choosing to replace worry with humor.

"Are you kidding? I made a promise to you that I intend to keep. If you're not there to witness the miracle of its birth with me, I'll take video."

We all laughed.

"Let's just get us through the first vote, and then we'll go from there."

———

The news of Dale's predicament hit Kyle hard. Not only was the thought of his possible departure difficult enough to process, but also the emotional jockeying taking place between the members of both tribes was exhausting. Things were moving so quickly. Scheming, lying, and backstabbing were the name of the game. Gone were the days of acting like lazy monkeys. We weren't just surviving anymore; now we were fighting for control of the game.

Marsha won the first individual immunity, which meant she was safe from elimination. She managed to outsmart all of us in a memory game. It really wasn't that surprising, considering the amount of information she carried around in her head on a daily basis. The haughty smile on her face grated on my nerves. I still hadn't forgiven her calling me out in the Ten Fingers game or blabbing to the other tribe about Kyle. It took everything in my power to keep a civil tone with her. If I didn't need her so badly, I would've kicked her to the curb long ago.

With Dale's possible exit from the game looming, it became even more important to get Lena on our side; but she proved a hard nut to crack, and no amount of jostling or sweet-talking from either Kyle, Dale, or me had any effect on her. In fact, the more we tried to pull her onto our side, the nastier she got, with Kyle getting the brunt of the abuse. She gleefully hurled insults at him every chance she got, and although it killed him not to sling them right back at her, we'd convinced him to hold his tongue for the sake of our alliance.

With no way to reach Lena, things were looking bleak for the Dork Quad until an unlikely friendship formed, changing the course of the game. Carl, with his newfound social skills, somehow used them to sway the unlikeable Lena. Apparently they bonded over their shared hatred for the human race and the divorces that had shaken both their lives. And out of nowhere, Lena shocked us all at the first individual Council by sticking it to her former teammates and knocking off Fergus, one of the biggest physical threats in the game.

Lena jumping ship fluffed our sails, but the victory was bittersweet. After being evaluated by the medical team, Dale's infection was deemed too serious for him to continue in the game.

"I'm disappointed in you, dude. After all the stubbed toes, black eyes, and broken bones, you let a *bug* take you down?" Kyle joked, the achy expression on his face belying the light-hearted conversation.

"I know, embarrassing," Dale said, pain evident in his words. He grabbed Kyle's shirt and said dramatically, "Avenge me!"

"I promise you, Dale, I'll track down that damn bug if it's the last thing I do!"

———

And then Dale was gone. Although I'd never admit it, I was glad he went out the way he did, because with his injuries compounding the way they were, it would have been a battle for him to get to the end. My focus shifted with Dale's exit, and my vision became clearer. There were only eight of us left, and I kept my eye on the prize.

Kyle, on the other had, struggled in his absence. I feared he'd put too much of his game play into Dale's hands. Don't get me wrong – he played hard and was a fierce competitor, winning two individual competitions in the days following – but his strategic game play was all over the place. With Dale not there to keep his focus, Kyle was making friends with the remaining Easties and wavering on the group decisions based off that.

Why he was trying to save players on the other side puzzled me. It was a game. We were all going sooner or later;

but obviously he wasn't looking at the big picture. Kyle felt sorry for the marked players and tried to protect them, like stray dogs left out in the rain. In any other aspect of life, that personality trait would be viewed admirably, but out here, kindness was enough to get you booted.

His wishy-washy behavior had caught the attention of Carl and Lena, and both worried that Kyle was becoming a liability. We were picking off the other tribe one at a time, and with their numbers dwindling, Kyle's position in the alliance was getting more precarious. He was no longer necessary to maintain the numbers. At this point I wasn't even sure I could get the others to keep him in the game longer than Marsha, who had always been the lowest man on our shaky totem pole.

After coming back from another elimination ceremony and kicking out Carol, Kyle's favorite Eastie, he was pissed, and he wasn't being real subtle about it. Kicking a basket across camp, Kyle stomped around like a scorned kindergartener. Lena immediately got in his face, and they volleyed a litany of obscenities at one another. To keep him from getting his ass kicked by a woman, I pulled him aside and we took a walk on the beach.

"What the hell was that?" I asked, not even trying to control my temper. Kyle was making my job so much more difficult, and I didn't appreciate it.

"You could have gotten rid of Eugene. I asked you guys for one thing, one favor... save Carol. But no one listens to me. I thought we had an alliance, Kenzie, but you're always siding with Carl and that" – Kyle growled under his breath –"bitch."

"Carol was a stronger player than Eugene. You know that."

"So my opinion doesn't matter, is that what you're saying? Dale was the only one who cared what I had to say."

"I care," I said.

"No, Kenzie, you don't," he answered bitterly.

His words hit me hard. He had no idea how wrong he was.

"I get that you were friends with Carol and Amir, but you have to understand what a target you put on your back by making friends with the enemy. Why would Carl and Lena want to sit next to you in the final if you have a bunch of people who like you and will vote you the winner?"

Kyle gaped at me as if he had never once considered that scenario. *Come on, dude, that's just common sense.*

"No one is going to vote for me. You said it yourself."

"Look, Kyle, I'm going to be honest with you… the others are starting to question you."

"I did what they wanted!" Kyle said in a raised voice. "I voted her out. What more do you want from me?"

Kyle's jaw was clenched tightly, and his fists balled up in frustration. I grabbed him and gave him a hug. He struggled against me for a moment, but when I didn't let go, I felt his body relax and he hugged me back. "What's going on with you?" I whispered in his ear.

"I don't know," he sighed. "This game is getting to me. I don't like backstabbing people that I like."

"It's a game, and if you don't play it, someone else will be happy to do it for you. And you aren't going to like the results."

"I know. I don't think I'm cut out for this shit."

"You're too nice."

"That's just the thing… I'm not. Back home I'm a sarcastic, jaded asshole. And then I come here and I'm an emotional mess. I swear I need tampons."

I laughed. "Can you do me a huge favor?"

"What?"

"Get your shit together, swallow your pride, and apologize to the bitchy snake lady."

"Ugghh," Kyle gagged. "I'd rather drink bleach."

———

He did end up apologizing, though the sincerity behind the words was severely lacking. And really, who could blame him? Lena's verbal assaults were incredibly personal, as if his taking up space on the island left a sour taste in her mouth. Most of the time, her attacks took place away from Kyle, thank god, because he would not have appreciated her accusations of him of riding on his brother's coattails to get this far in the game. I tried to keep my opinions to myself, but her constant nastiness was taking its toll on me. Kyle was my guy, whether he knew it or not. Every insult she leveled against him was a personal affront to me. The more Lena and I butted heads, the more I worried that my devotion to Kyle might eventually be my undoing.

———————

Marsha went home in a blaze of glory, as well as middle fingers wagging. I wasn't sorry to see her go, since her ouster only came after I uncovered her diabolical plan to break up the Dork Quad by voting out either Kyle or me. And since Kyle won the immunity challenge that day and was safe from elimination, that left me on the chopping block.

With Marsha's exit, and Eugene's directly before hers, that left four: Kyle, Carl, Lena, and me. It was a major feat to have lasted as long in the game as we had, and we celebrated around the fire upon our return. The mood was relaxed and fun, until Lena decided make it personal.

"So what's the deal with you two?" she asked Kyle and me. We exchanged glances. As far as I knew, there was no deal. We'd remained incredibly close even after my dramatic, dick-shaming declaration of love. In fact, I dared say, Kyle might possibly be the best friend I'd ever had. Of course, I said that through gritted teeth, since friendship wasn't really the objective. I had plenty of buddies, but this was the only one I wanted to fornicate with.

"That's none of your business," Kyle replied, glaring at her across the fire.

"I'm just asking. Don't be a dick."

"Then don't be a bitch."

Obscenities started flying. Carl and I sighed. After Lena criticized the way Kyle had scooped his rice from his coconut bowl a couple of days ago, it had become an all-out war between them. And once they got started, the four-letter gender bits dripped off their tongues like acid. Kyle and Lena were like two peas in a very dysfunctional pod.

"It's not an S.A.T. question, dumbshit. Would you bang her or not?"

"Can you please leave me out of this?" I complained. Carl gave me a sympathetic shrug, but the other two were foaming at the mouth and not in the mood to take my feelings into consideration.

"Oh, wait, maybe you don't swing that way." Lena pursed her lips. "I could see that with you."

"I do swing that way, and yeah, I'd bang her," Kyle answered, without even looking my direction. In a pathetic kind of way, I was flattered.

"In her current condition, or after a shower?"

I raised my hand, chancing a quick sniff, as I said, "Um… hello? Right here."

Kyle appeared flustered by Lena's line of questioning. "I… I'd prefer she take a shower first," and then turned to me and said, "No offense."

"None taken," I smiled happily. The important thing was, he'd bang me.

TV Confessional
"I'm no stinkier than anyone else out here."
— Kenzie

CHAPTER TWENTY-SEVEN

KYLE
Night Terrors

I looked into my brother's eyes, his fear reflecting my own. The man's knee was digging in his back as he bound Jake. I shifted my position, catching Ray's attention.

'Didn't I tell you to stay down? Do you want to die? Get back down! Hands over your head. Do it now!' And then he was on me, pulling my arm back. I could hear the snap. Then blinding pain.

'If I have to tell you again, he dies!'

To drive home his point, the man grabbed my hair, slamming my head into the ground. Jake screamed, drawing the attention away from me. Blood dripped into my eyes. I couldn't move my arm. I blinked back my shock. What was happen-

ing? A minute ago we'd been jumping our skateboards down the steps, and now we were lying face down in the parking lot. Where had the guy come from? What did he want?

His mouth covered in tape, Jake had only his eyes to speak, and they were fraught with warning. What are you saying? What do you want me to do?

"Kyle?"

A hand touched my back, shaking me. I bolted upright, sweat rolling down my face. I darted my eyes around in a panic, looking for Jake before landing on Kenzie's worried face. I knew I had to focus and do the breathing. *It's just a nightmare. It's not real… just a nightmare.*

"Are you okay?" she whispered.

"Yeah…" I exhaled, a tremor rumbling through my body. "I'll be… just give me a second."

Kenzie nodded, her eyes were trained on me. Thankfully she didn't say anything. Once I got my wits about me, I glanced around, looking for the camera guys who were never far away, even in the middle of the night. "Did they get that on film?"

"No, I don't think so. I just woke up myself."

I dragged in some oxygen. My heart was still pounding. You'd think, after all this time, I would be used to them. It was always the same general dream, but the outcome changed every time, keeping me guessing and worried for the next one to invade my sleep. In reality, though, they weren't really nightmares at all, but memories revisited. Thankfully, my mind had given me a reprieve for the past few months, making me hopeful that they would be warded off during my stint on the island. And I'd almost made it. Five days left. Really? I inhaled another ragged breath, and realized her hand was still rubbing my back.

"Do you get those often?" she asked.

"No. I was dreaming about being eaten by a shark. No biggie."

She nodded as if appeasing me, but I knew she didn't buy it. To her credit, she didn't push. I lay back down on the hard wood flooring. She copied me.

"Sorry if I woke you," I whispered. I was getting really damn tired of being a slave to these nightmares. Usually after one occurred, it took time for me to recover. Going back to sleep immediately following one of them was the worst thing possible as it almost guaranteed me a journey right back into hell. For that reason, I always got out of bed and went to watch TV or play video games, anything to take my mind away from that day. But here, with cameras all around, I had no choice but to pretend it hadn't happened and force myself to stay put on the bamboo floor. Cold, clammy chills spread through me, and I shivered.

Kenzie reached her hand out and gently touched my face. I lifted my eyes to meet hers, and the kindness and compassion I found staring back at me made me wonder why I wasn't looking at this woman with a more objective eye. She was sweet and determined and beautiful, and for some unknown reason, she saw something in me that she liked. Why was I important to her? What had I done to deserve her loyalty? And why in the hell wasn't I jumping at the chance to be with her?

I traced my finger over her lips, and she blinked back her surprise. We didn't speak as I explored her face. I wasn't even sure what I was doing, but at that moment I guess I just needed her. Kenzie's eyes stayed glued to mine as I leaned in and my lips brushed past hers. Two or three light kisses followed before the familiar sound of footsteps descended upon us and I pulled away. The look on Kenzie's face was one of confusion but also one of joy. Suddenly I felt like the biggest shithead ever. I should never have kissed her if I wasn't willing to back it up. Had I just changed the rules of the game?

With the cameras surrounding us, I flipped over, my back to her, and pretended to be asleep. After a good half hour of trying to downplay the kiss in my head, and then another ten minutes of inner panic, I felt arms wrap around me from behind. Surprised, I glanced over my shoulder.

"You're shivering. I'll warm you up."

"Kenzie…" I started to say. She was way too good for me, especially seeing as I was such a gigantic douche.

"It's okay," she whispered. Her sincere, caring eyes met mine. "Please don't say anything… not tonight."

I turned back around and laid my head down once more. She was giving me a pass for the night, and I couldn't help but be incredibly grateful for those few sleepless hours I'd been gifted in order to get my story straight. I blamed my lack of judgment on the nightmare. There was nothing like a visit from Ray to rattle my bones.

I was far from sleep now, but I stayed quiet for Kenzie's sake. My mind was still reeling from the nightmare, and the kiss and knowledge that Carl and Lena were gunning for me. I needed to pull it all together and get through the last few days. Tomorrow, I told myself, I was going to wake up and be the Kyle that could win this damn game: strong, smart, focused. Basically, I just needed to be the opposite of the guy I was in my everyday life.

I hadn't realized that Kenzie was awake until I heard her yawn. No one was more loyal to me than that woman. I needed to sort out my feelings for her before it was too late.

Feeling warmer and more relaxed, I whispered, "You know, I read somewhere that if someone is really cold, the fastest way to warm them up is skin to skin contact."

"I think that procedure is for people who have nearly frozen to death," she replied, her voice heavy with fatigue.

"I don't think so," I countered playfully, feeling more like myself now.

"I'm not getting naked for you, Kyle," Kenzie giggled. "But nice try."

"Fine," I jokingly huffed. "I'll just freeze to death."

Kenzie grunted but didn't respond. A few minutes later I heard her soft breathing. I smiled. The funny thing was, I knew that if I really were freezing to death, Kenzie would stop at nothing to save me. And then a realization hit me like a brick: I'd do the same for her. Suddenly I knew what I wanted. My body relaxed. With Kenzie's arms snug around me, I fell back to sleep.

TV Confessional
"What relationship? Kenzie and I are just friends."
— *Kyle*

CHAPTER TWENTY-EIGHT

KENZIE

The Betrayal

Marooned Rule #7
All players eliminated <u>after</u> the merge will return for the final Council as members of the jury. The jury will decide which of the remaining three contestants deserves to be the overall winner.

I teetered on the peg, my legs shaking, toes numb. I was holding a plate with ping-pong-sized balls, trying to keep them from falling. Lena was the only competition left, as the boys had fallen out of the challenge minutes ago. If I held on longer than Lena, I was guaranteed to be in the final three, so I concentrated on the balls as reminders of my family flashed through my mind. I would not let them down.

After a resounding win, I was feeling on top of the world and took a victory swim with Kyle. He seemed different after the kiss, more attentive. In the water, he wrapped his arms around me and playfully dropped me into the waves, his body landing on top of mine. I took the opportunity to run my hands over his body, all in the name of our little game – or so he thought. Although I had to say, his hands weren't staying in the safe zone either.

We laughed and flirted, and I was more confused than ever. He was definitely acting like a guy who was interested; or at least, that was how my biased brain interpreted it. At one point our eyes met, and his softened, small creases forming in the corners as he smiled seductively at me. He leaned in close, and I held my breath in anticipation. Hot damn, he was going in for a kiss! I'd assumed the sweet kisses from last night were just a fluke, but there was no mistaking Kyle's lustful gaze now. Just then the scrambling of cameramen caught our attention, and we pulled apart immediately.

"Would you two mind repeating that scene, please?" one of the guys said.

"What scene?" Kyle asked, as he dove into the waves and swam out further into the ocean. I was not nearly the swimmer he was, and understanding that our moment had passed, I walked out of the water in disappointment and headed back to camp. Lena was waiting for me.

"You do realize you need to cut the cord, right?"

"What do you mean?"

"Do you really think you can beat Kyle?"

"No one is going to give him the prize money, not with his brother being a multi-millionaire."

"Well, see, that's where you're wrong. If it's you, Kyle, and Carl left at the end, let's just figure out your odds. Shall we?"

I really didn't care for her condescending tone, but I heard her out anyway.

"Who's going to be on the jury? First, you have Dale and Marsha. Of course they would vote for Kyle. They frickin' *love* him. Then you've got the four from my tribe. They don't like Carl because he's got the personality of a shoe. And you – sorry, Bambi, but people view you as weak. You follow Kyle and Carl. You haven't made any big moves on your own. Who wants to vote for someone with no backbone? And then you have Kyle; good old likeable Kyle. Who did he rub the wrong way besides me? Nobody. And he was getting real friendly with my tribe at the end. Do you think that was by accident? The way I see it, you and Carl cancel each other out, and guess what? Kyle wins."

"I don't know," I mumbled.

"Yes, you do, Kenzie. Use your damn head. Kyle's dangerous and you know it. And that's before he even plays his trump card. If he pulls that out…" Lena shook her head, as if to warn me of the potential devastation.

I looked at her in confusion.

"Oh, lord, Kenzie, do I need to spell it out for you? Kyle's got a hell of a story to tell, and if he decides to share it, you… are… screwed."

I just sat there, crestfallen. She was right. With Kyle in the game, I had no chance to win.

"Now, if you take Kyle out of the equation and you add me instead, now all the sudden you have a three-way fight. My tribe doesn't like any of us. I betrayed them, so getting their vote will be next to impossible. It will come down to you and Carl, and my money is on you – if you can convince them that you're the brains behind the operation. Tell them your big move was knocking out Kyle. I think they'd be impressed, considering how obvious your crush on him is."

"I don't… I… it's not… I don't like him." I stumbled helplessly over my words.

"Oh, please. You're like a grease stain on his shirt. You never go away."

"We're friends. We like hanging out, that's all."

"Okay, whatever you say. Just know that if you need that money, Kyle can't be sitting beside you on that final day."

It should have been an easy decision: vote out Lena and take my chances in the finals. That had been the plan all along, only instead of Carl it should have been Dale. If he were here, he would have known what to do. Would he have turned on Kyle? And more pointedly, would Kyle turn on me? I knew the answer to both those questions. Neither one of them would have betrayed me. I just knew it. But Lena's words played over and over in my mind. This was exactly what I didn't want to happen. I told myself I wouldn't let anyone derail my game, especially not a guy. I knew Kyle liked me, we were friends. Maybe we were more than that, but since he wouldn't talk to me about it, I couldn't be sure. He'd been emotional after the nightmare. Was the kiss just a reaction to that?

I was feeling sick, knowing the decision I had to make. Kyle's fate in the game was in my hands. I could either vote with Carl and Lena and knock him out, or vote with Kyle and bring it to a tie. In that case, the two chosen contestants would compete to see who could build a fire fastest. And Kyle, over the course of the last month, had become quite skilled at starting fires. Chances were he'd win, and I'd be sitting next to him in the finals.

Dammit. If Kyle would just give me some sort of reassurance, so I knew where we were in our relationship, then I could make a more informed decision. As it stood now, if I kept him in the game solely because I was falling for him, there was no guarantee I'd get the outcome I was hoping for. In fact, there was a very real possibility that I would be walking away at the end of this without the guy *or* the money.

As if sensing my apprehension, Carl approached. "It's the right move, and you know it."

"But he's my friend."

"And you're mine – and I wouldn't hesitate to cut you down if it meant winning a million dollars."

"That's comforting."

"It's a game, Kenzie. Take the emotions out of it."

"That's not so easy, and you know it."

Carl was the only one who knew my true feelings for Kyle. "I'm not saying it will be easy, but you know it's your only chance."

I nodded, tears flooding my eyes. "If I did that to him, he'd never forgive me."

"But a million dollars will wipe away countless tears."

I slipped away from the others then, needing to be alone with my thoughts. I especially didn't want the pressure from the others to make the decision for me. I knew what I was facing. If I sent him home, I'd lose the guy. If I kept him, I'd lose the money. There was no scenario where I could have both. My choice was grim: Kyle or my family.

"Hey." Kyle came out from around the tree and startled me. "I've been looking for you."

"Oh, sorry. I wasn't feeling good."

"What's wrong?"

"Nothing exciting. Just cramps."

"Oh, geez, say no more," he grinned. "And I mean it."

I smiled, but, in reality, I was miserable. How could I betray him?

"You seem a little emotional. Is everything okay?"

"I'm fine," I answered, forcing a smile on my face. "You ready?"

Kyle grabbed my hand and squeezed. *Us to the end.* That had always been the plan; and what kind of a person would I be if I turned on Kyle now? Even if I didn't win, I'd still have my dignity and pride… and a possibility with the guy. No, I would stay true to my word. I would stay true to Kyle.

The night was dark and stormy, only magnifying the terrible sinking feeling in the pit of my stomach. Last minute scrambling by Carl and Lena had broken down my resolve, and I was once again questioning my reasoning for keeping Kyle in the game. My wavering went right down to the wire, and when it was my turn to vote, I stood there numb with indecision.

As the rain drenched my hair and sent chills down my spine, I thought about Kyle and his faith in me. In any other situation, he'd be right to trust in my integrity. I was, after all, the girl who put everyone else's well being before her own. I was the girl who was letting the promise of a boy rule my world. But tonight I didn't want to be that meek girl. I wanted to be a strong, determined woman who benefitted from making her own decisions. And so I did. I chose me.

Yet the minute the paper left my trembling hand, there was no feeling of empowerment or vindication. There was just overwhelming dread. In a few minutes, Kyle would know what I'd done, but he wouldn't know why... nor would he care. I'd betrayed him, lied straight to his face. How could I have done such a thing? Kyle wasn't just a boy crush. He was the man I'd fallen in love with. Suddenly I felt dirty, and oh, so sorry.

As I slunk back to where the others were gathered, I passed by the jury, former players who'd earlier been eliminated from the game. The jury members watched each Council, and the information they gathered from it helped them make the final decision of who deserved to win the prize money. Dale was there, having obviously recovered from his illness.

I could feel him staring as I returned to my place on the log. Tilting my head up, I reluctantly met his gaze. Dale's eyes swelled in shock upon seeing the uncertainty and strife in mine. He shook his head as if to say *No, you didn't.* I bowed my head in shame. *Oh, yes, I did.*

In a nod to his exceptional character, Kyle's confidence in me never wavered. Not when I wrote his name down on the sheet. Not when he received the first vote. Not even when he received the second. But when the third vote was pulled from the box and his name was written on it, Kyle knew I'd betrayed him. I covered my face with my hands, refusing to look at him. I knew what I would see if I dared chance a peek. The hurt and confusion would be palpable. So I allowed Kyle to walk out of the game, without even giving him the courtesy of a goodbye.

TV Confessional
"I'm sorry."
— Kenzie

CHAPTER TWENTY-NINE

KYLE
Seething

I was seeing red as I took the walk of shame. What the fuck was that? I was numb with shock. It almost didn't seem real. Kenzie had lied to me, flat-out bald-faced lied to me, and I, like the trusting idiot I was, had believed every minute of it. And then she wouldn't even look at me? What the hell was that? Goddamn coward!

I wandered through the medical evaluations in a daze. The fact that I'd been kicked out still hadn't really registered with me. It wasn't until I arrived at the hotel and saw Dale that shit got real.

J. BENGTSSON

"You okay?" he asked.

"Uh... no."

"You didn't see it coming at all?"

"Nope," I replied angrily. "I got played."

Dale guided me into the hotel and over to the kitchen area. He handed me a menu. "Order something. You need to eat and shower, and then we'll talk."

"I'm done talking. If she thinks she's going to win now, she's got another thing coming."

"What are you planning on doing?"

"I'm going to make sure everyone in here votes for Carl. That's what I'm going to do."

After eating, showering, and shaving, I was actually feeling a whole lot better, but the anger was still there, festering. I'd kissed her last night... and meant it. Hell, I actually had feelings for that traitor. What an idiot I'd been!

There was a knock on the door and, when I opened it, Dale breezed past me without waiting for an invitation.

"I've got something for you," Dale said, eyes gleaming with excitement. He pulled a phone out of his pocket and held it up to me.

I gasped. "No?"

"Yessiree," Dale replied. "One leg volcano eruption for your viewing pleasure."

And truly, Dale's pus was just what I needed to take my mind off Kenzie. I watched his video multiple times, becoming more impressed with the green, oozing goo with each subsequent view. "Wow, Dale, I'm speechless. This was truly special."

Dale laughed. "I knew you'd appreciate it. Are you feeling better now?"

"Surprisingly, I am. Who needs women when you've got disgusting, infected abscesses?

"Exactly," Dale smiled. "And can I just say... you smell lovely."

"Well, thank you," I grinned. "I used a whole bar of soap... most of it on my gooch."

"I don't doubt that." He laughed just before his mood quieted. "Can I just say one more thing?"

"Not if you're going to talk about her."

"She didn't do it to hurt you. I saw her face after the vote. Kenzie seemed so upset and conflicted."

"Ahh, poor thing," I whined. "Sorry but I can't seem to muster any sympathy for her. She's there, and I'm here."

"She knew she couldn't win against you. You two had something..."

"Dale!" I interrupted, unable to harness the irritation. "No offense, but I don't want to talk about Kenzie... like, ever again."

TV Confessional
"Yeah, I'm pissed, but my conscience is clear.
I can't say the same for hers."
— Kyle

CHAPTER THIRTY

KENZIE

Making the Case

After the deed was done, I refused to allow myself to feel. I knew what I'd done had ruined any chance I could've had with him; but in reality, he was never mine to begin with. I'd stayed true to myself and did what was best for me. Or had I? What if what was best for me had just angrily stomped out of my life? *No. No. No. Enough with the self-doubt.* Once this was all over and I had my prize money, I could buy myself a new life and maybe, just maybe, I'd find a guy I liked as much as Kyle. Or maybe not.

Carl, Lena, and I returned to camp. They were jubilant and I tried my best to muster the same enthusiasm, but I couldn't shake the feeling of impending doom. Tomorrow I would face him again. What would I say? Could I really look into his eyes and make him understand?

"You all right, Kenzie?" Carl asked.

"No."

"You did the right thing."

"For who? Me? You? Because it definitely wasn't for Kyle."

"He doesn't need the money."

"How do we know what he needs?"

Carl sighed and wrapped his giant arms around me. I was dwarfed against his body, but I didn't pull away. I felt like a defector. Suddenly I wanted to go home. I was done with this damn game. Tomorrow couldn't come fast enough.

Marooned Rule #8

The final three contestants will face the eliminated players and explain why they should win the game. The jury will then vote for the player they feel is most deserving of the grand prize. The winner will be announced at a live studio taping in Los Angeles several months after filming wraps.

The next day was spent memorizing my speech. I had two minutes to make my case to seven people whom I had a hand in kicking out of the game. Somehow I had to convince them I was deserving of the money. Of course I knew I had to exploit my childhood trauma in order to stand out. I had to talk about losing my mom and raising my siblings. It wasn't something I wanted to do, but then I'd been doing a lot of things I didn't want to do lately. I feared when I returned home, I was going to have to take an acid bath to rid myself of all the nastiness I'd been part of.

I sat nervously as the exited players returned to take their seats in the jury box. One by one they filed in. I tried to make eye contact with every single one, but most were not exactly emotive. In fact, they looked as though they were headed to a funeral. I hoped to god it wouldn't be mine. Kyle was the last of the bunch to take his seat. I almost didn't recognize him. His brown, sun-streaked hair had been cut shorter and was slicked back. He was clean and shaved and, although thin from his time on the island, surprisingly healthy-looking. Wearing tan jeans and a tight white V-neck t-shirt, I couldn't help but gape at him. Kyle was so handsome. For the first time I saw in him a strong resemblance to his famous brother. *You let that go, Kenzie? Idiot. No wonder you're single.*

I stared at Kyle, willing him to look back, but even with my eyes burning holes through him, he steadfastly refused to engage me. And really, why would he? I could only imagine some of those nasty words he'd been exchanging with Lena the past few days were now being directed at me.

Lena was up first. She told a story of the struggles of being a single mom raising two boys. And while that was admirable and important, it seemed to do little to sway the angry-looking jury. She reminded them that she was the last of the East tribe, and for that reason she deserved their respect. A few of her former tribe mates actually scoffed, and I was feeling pretty certain she was not getting any of their votes.

I was next. And I told my story. I tried to explain why I'd made the choices I did in the game and played up some of the big moves I'd made to get me to this point. Kyle stared down at his hands the entire time. If he would just look at me... scream at me... anything but this agonizing silence. I looked around at the other members of the jury – their interest in me seemed lukewarm, but at least it was better than Lena's chilly reception. And then I came to Dale, wonderful Dale. He was smiling at me, and I wanted to burst into tears at his unconditional support.

Carl's moment to shine arrived, and he didn't disappoint. The man who hadn't said more than a few words to most of the jury members now had their full and undivided attention. The gruff, ginger-haired giant spoke of his childhood filled with bullying, his coming out, his father's disownment. He talked about his divorce and his daughter and the struggle he had every day to come up with the money to fly to see her. Every word that came out of his mouth made my chances of winning decrease, and by the time he was done, not only did I have tears in my eyes but I was rooting for him myself.

I knew, at that moment, that I'd lost. It was as if karma had come back to give me a swift kick in the ass. Not only was I not coming home with the money, I wasn't coming home with the guy either. And I was surprised to discover that I was way more devastated about losing Kyle than the million dollars. I realized then that I'd made the biggest mistake of my life.

TV Confessional
"Do I take credit for Carl's newfound social skills? Unfortunately, yes."
— Kenzie

CHAPTER THIRTY-ONE

KYLE

The Decision

Even with a day to stew, I was still pissed when I walked into final vote. I didn't want to see her, but then at the same time I did. Despite everything, I missed her. I'd lain in bed for hours the night before, unable to sleep because she wasn't beside me, and I was mad at myself for wanting her to be there. Taking my spot among the losers, I purposefully kept my eyes averted, knowing they would betray me if contact was made.

First Lena poured out her soiled, blackened heart for all to hear. I wanted nothing more than to call her bluff, but I stayed rigid in my seat. The producers wouldn't take kindly to another screaming match. So I let her finish her story, not buying a second of her bullshit. If there was one thing I knew for sure, it was that Lena was not getting my vote.

When Kenzie spoke of her mom and raising her siblings, I could hear the hesitation and tremble in her voice, and I remembered that morning on the beach when she'd shared her story with me. She'd already had so much responsibility in her young life, raising her siblings and working to keep food on the table. What had I accomplished, other than being a pain in the ass to my rock star brother? No matter how I felt about what she'd done to me, I couldn't shake the feeling that she deserved to win.

But then Carl opened his soul for the jury, and shocked us all by the depth of his character. All this time, he'd sat there stewing, and he had this story to tell. When it was over, all the women, as well as Dale, were crying. I felt for Carl, I really did; but I'd heard sad stories before, ones that were ten times worse than what he had to offer. Hopefully I could be forgiven for not crying him a river of tears.

The confessions ended, and I actually had to console an overly emotional Dale. He had been adamant about voting for Kenzie earlier in the day, but I wondered if Carl's story had changed his mind. Going into the night, I still had no idea what I was going to do. In the height of my anger, I'd sworn to myself that Carl would get my vote, but I felt myself wavering now.

One by one we were each allowed to address the three finalists. Lena fielded the most attacks on her character, but Kenzie got her fair share of hate as well. Several of the ousted players knocked her for riding on my and Dale's coattails, when in reality I'd ridden on hers. They could say what they wanted about her – hell, I could say what I wanted – but I knew the truth. Kenzie was a strong, fierce competitor, and she wasn't sitting up there in the winner's circle because she'd been hiding behind a man hoping for her moment to shine.

When it was my turn to speak, I kept my questions generic. I didn't care what any of them had to say. My decision would not be based on their answers tonight, they would be based on the people I knew them to be. So, despite the fact that Kenzie had betrayed me in the cruelest of ways, I wrote her name down on the paper, voting for her to win.

TV Confessional
"I don't want to talk about it."
— Kyle

CHAPTER THIRTY-TWO

KENZIE

Homecoming

After the voting was complete, Lena, Carl, and I were whisked away for physical checkups and later to a hotel away from the other players. Because the winner wouldn't be announced until the final show aired in December, they didn't want us discussing the vote with the members of the jury. I was thankful that I didn't have to face Kyle one-on-one. His anger hadn't surprised me, but the fact that he couldn't even look at me spoke volumes to the level of hurt he was carrying with him. He viewed his ousting as a personal attack. He felt betrayed. I couldn't say I'd have reacted any differently if I'd been in his shoes.

Once in the privacy of my own hotel room, I finally broke down and cried. I was exhausted both physically and mentally. The verbal beatdown I'd received at the ceremony left me feeling conflicted and dejected. I showered four times that day, yet I still felt dirty. I wanted to explain myself to Kyle, but I knew he wouldn't listen. Obviously any chance I might have had with him romantically had been destroyed, but what I worried about more was losing his friendship. That was going to be a harder pill to swallow.

I didn't see Kyle again until the flight back to Los Angeles. I was already sitting in my seat when he came walking down the center aisle. Our eyes met. His were hard and unforgiving; mine were sad and remorseful. He looked away immediately. I reached for his hand as he passed by, and although he did not recoil, Kyle continued walking until his hand dropped from mine. And that was that. We made the trip home without a word. My island boy was no more.

Once I arrived at LAX, I had to rush to catch my connecting flight to San Francisco. Dale was already there waiting for me at the gate, as we were both headed to the same airport. When I saw him, I broke down. Gallantly, Dale embraced me.

"I'm so sorry. I know you and Kyle hate me. I'm so sorry," I cried on his shoulder.

"I don't hate you, Kenzie. And neither does Kyle. He'll come around. Give him time."

"You didn't see the way he looked at me."

Dale hugged me until the flight attendants announced the last call. They seemed a little hesitant to move me along, obviously feeling compassion for the emotional state I was in, but certainly not willing to hold up a flight because I was being a crybaby.

"This will all blow over. I'll talk to Kyle. I promise."

"Okay." I snorted the snot back up my nose in a less than ladylike fashion. I was a mess and didn't even try to hide it. "Can you give him my phone number?"

Dale took out his phone, and after an overly extended period of time trying to bring up the address book, I took the phone from him and added my information in fifteen seconds flat. I felt better knowing that Dale would go to bat for me. If Kyle would listen to anyone, it would be him.

After landing in San Francisco, I boarded the third and final flight of the day. It was a short jaunt to Eureka. As I descended the stairs and walked across the tarmac and into the terminal, my dad and siblings were there to greet me, and the sadness melted away. This was my family. The reason I'd played the game. No one here cared that I was a lying, backstabbing bitch... well, they probably would care if they knew, but I planned to omit that distasteful piece of information until shortly before the show aired in a few months' time. Honesty was always the best policy, but in this particular instance, I just didn't give a crap. What I needed now was some unconditional love.

My first week home was spent sleeping and eating. Life went on around me, but I needed time to readjust to the real world. One morning I woke to find my dad in the kitchen making his breakfast. He scooped some eggs onto a plate and handed them to me instead.

"Here, you need to put some meat on those bones."

"Thanks, Dad."

He nodded, staring at me for an uncomfortably long time.

"What?" I asked, looking up from my breakfast.

"You seem different."

"I feel different," I agreed, in a low, passive voice.

"Is everything okay? You've been subdued since you got home. Did anything happen that I need to know about?"

"You know I can't talk about it, Dad."

"I know, but I just want to make sure you're okay."

My eyes filled with tears.

"What happened?" he asked, going from sympathetic to 'Who do I kill?' in two seconds flat. That was my father – always jumping to the worst conclusion without any supporting facts.

"It's nothing bad. It's about a guy."

"A guy?" Dad's voice instantly turned hard and condemning. His fists clenched into balls. "What did this... this *guy* do to you?"

"Easy there, Chuck Norris," I said, grabbing his hands and uncurling them.

"If he hurt you, Mackenzie, I swear to God..."

"If you're going to act like this, I'm not going to talk to you," I warned.

My father took a step back and stared at me. He wanted to argue but knew better than to cross me. We had a different relationship than most fathers and daughters in that we were equals in every way. Well, maybe *equals* was the wrong word, since most of the time my father deferred to my judgment. Thank god, because if I'd left it up to my overprotective father, the triplets would have been wimpy little balls of anxiety.

That's not to say that my dad was a bad guy – he meant well, but after losing my mom, he took helicopter parenting to whole new extremes. Everything the triplets did was too dangerous or too messy or too loud. It was my job to remind him that Mom let me do this or that. Maybe he wouldn't listen to me, but he always listened to her. And although I'd only had my mother in my life for a short time, I was very much her daughter. In fact, I basically became her, or what I remembered of her, in order to give my siblings the childhood they deserved. So if I sometimes had to step in and remind my father to act like a grownup, that was a dance we'd been swaying to our whole lives.

His face relaxed. He laid his hand gently on mine and said, "Sorry. Tell me what he did."

"It's not what he did to me, it's…it's what I did to him," I whispered, lowering my head in shame.

"Oh," he replied, still looking flustered. "I'm confused."

"I really liked him, Dad. So much, and…"

"And what? What did you do?"

"I lied to him. I betrayed him."

My father exhaled, looking immensely relieved, as if it made everything better knowing that his daughter was the bully and not the victim.

"And now he hates me and there's no way for me to turn it around."

"Did he feel the same way about you?"

"I… no… I don't know. Maybe. He was hard to read. At the very least we were really close friends."

"But isn't that what the game is all about? Backstabbing people in order to win?" he asked, as if he really didn't see the problem.

"He was my ally. I turned on him, and the worst part is… he never would have done the same to me."

"You don't know that."

"Oh, I do. Kyle's loyal to a fault. He trusted me one hundred percent."

"So if you didn't want to betray him, why did you?"

"For us. For our family."

"For us? Why in the hell would you do that for us?"

"So you wouldn't have to work so hard. So you could find a good woman and have love in your life again. And so Cooper and Colton and Caroline could have a secure future and have money for college. And... and... I did it for myself because..." I stopped myself before I said too much.

"Because what?"

"Nothing."

"It's not nothing. Tell me."

"I need to leave, Dad," I whispered. "I'm moving away. It's time."

He didn't respond right away. Something in his coffee cup seemed to mesmerize him. Finally his voice cracked, and he said, "I don't think I can do this without you."

"You can and you will."

He shook his head. "This last month was really tough while you were gone. They walked all over me."

"But you all survived. The triplets are older and more self-sufficient now. They can drive and cook and do their own homework. You just need to be firm with them."

There was a long silence, and then my father sighed and asked morosely, "When are you leaving?"

"Not until after the final taping in December. Probably January or February."

"Where will you go?"

"South."

Neither of us spoke after that. I saw tears in my father's eyes. He'd relied on me for far too long. It was time he stepped up to the plate. He was their father. And despite spending the last sixteen years playing their mom, I wasn't. I was young and had dreams of my own. For the first time in my life, I wasn't afraid to follow them.

CHAPTER THIRTY-THREE

KYLE
Self Discovery

I stepped off the plane at LAX, relief taking hold of my tired body. Although my experience on the island overall had been incredible, the last days had put a sour taste in my mouth. I just couldn't shake the anger and disappointment over what Kenzie had done. Just looking at her on the plane upset me. It almost felt like she'd cheated on me, and trusting her again seemed impossible. For that reason I'd decided to just end our friendship. Obviously it hadn't meant anything to her in the first place.

My mom and Grace met me at the airport in baggage claim.

"You're so tan," my sister fussed. "And skinny. You look like you've been drifting in the ocean in a rowboat for a month."

"Wow, thank you."

"That means you got far," mom said, her eyes twinkling as she winked at me.

"Maybe, maybe not," I grinned as I hugged my welcoming committee.

"And you know it's going to drive me absolutely insane not knowing."

"Oh, I know. That'll be half the fun."

"How long are you planning on staying?"

"I don't know. Originally I was going to fly back to Europe as soon as I got home, but it appears Jake has not been as lonely as I thought he would be." I arched my eyebrows knowingly.

"No, you got that right," mom agreed.

"He's in love," Grace said, making kissy-faces.

"How do you know that?"

"I asked, and he told me." She shrugged, like it was no big deal. "I've got a direct line, you know."

"Oh, right. I forgot. The two of you are like this," I said entwining my fingers.

"We are," she shot back defensively. "Jake even Snapchats me sometimes, so there."

I held my hands up, conceding defeat. It was no secret Grace adored Jake, and all he had to do was throw her a bone once in a while in the form of a text, Snapchat, or a gift, and that was enough to secure his place in her heart. She was always a little starry-eyed around him, probably because he hadn't lived at home since she was eight, and Grace knew him more as a rock star than as a brother. I'd heard her with her friends acting like the supreme authority on all things Jake when, in reality, she didn't know the first thing about him. In fact, I found her expertise rather ironic, given their rocky past. There had been a time when the two of them couldn't be in the same room together without her throwing a screaming fit.

Growing up, Keith and Jake had always been the nice brothers, with Quinn and I being the pricklier sort. Whether it was playing music together or riding Grace on the front of his skateboard, Jake had always carved out time for her. When he'd disappeared, Grace had been too young to really understand what was happening. During that time, when she'd ask for Jake, the answer was always, 'He'll be home soon,' so it was possible she'd thought he was away on vacation or something. The day he arrived home, after spending nearly a month in the hospital, Grace still had not seen him, nor did she have any clue as to where he'd been or the extent of his injuries. She was just excited to have him home. In retrospect, we should have prepared her better. Obviously she'd been expecting Jake back and not the battered, broken boy Dad pushed through the door in the wheelchair. Grace took one look at him and started screaming. We never really figured out what terrified her so much, but she refused to be alone with him in the same room for a very long time. Needless to say, Jake was not pleased by her reaction, and he made it a point to stay as far away from her as possible. Their relationship had only in the past few years morphed into what it was today.

"Did you know Jake had a girlfriend before you left?" Mom asked me.

"No. I mean, I knew he really liked her after they met at the wedding, but I had no idea she went on tour with him or that they were together."

"I guess it was a good thing you were gone, or it would have been real crowded on that bus," Mom teased.

"Yeah, that would have been awkward, especially with my bunk right up against the bedroom wall."

"Ew... Like I want to hear that," Grace complained.

"Oh, sorry. I thought you already knew, being best friends with him and all."

"Shut up."

"Grace," Mom admonished, shaking her head. "Anyway, it shouldn't be a problem now. Casey is back home for school. Did you know she moved to LA?"

"I talked to Jake yesterday and he filled me in."

"I can't wait to meet her. When Jake comes home, he said he'd bring her by."

I nodded. Little did my mother know I'd been planning to bring my own girl home to meet her... until that girl crapped all over me.

"Wait... I thought you met Casey at the wedding," I said.

"Well, I guess I did, but I don't remember her. I just thought she was another groupie. I don't think I even looked at her," Mom laughed.

It wasn't a joke. She was not subtle when it came to her dislike of the women who hung all over Jake. She took on that judgmental face that screamed, 'You're not good enough for my boy.'

Mom grabbed my arm. "Enough about your brother. I want to hear everything about your adventures."

"Did you shame the family name?" Grace eyed me mischievously.

"Probably," I said pulling her into a hug and then attacking her side with my fingers. "Would you expect any less?"

"From you?" She giggled, squirming away from me. "No way."

I stayed home for a few days, hanging out with the family, but I wasn't planning on staying long. I was itching to get back to the tour and Jake. Returning to a normal routine was what I needed to get my mind off the show. It was all

I could think about. I missed the island and Dale and Carl and hell, even Marsha, but most of all, I missed Kenzie. And that pissed me off. It was easier to hate her than to miss her. I just needed to get away. The fast pace and excitement of touring would take my mind off everything.

The plan was for me to join the tour in Amsterdam, and then the busses would roll into Denmark to begin the Scandinavia portion of the tour. Because Jake had a concert the night I arrived, I was picked up by one of our security guys, Dominic, who'd worked for Jake for years and had become a good friend.

"You're all they could part with?" I insulted, as I walked up lugging my bags.

Dom smiled and opened his arms as if to say, *Yeah, I'm it.*

"I'm hurt. I'm not even worth getting an escort from Vadim?"

"Nope. You're lucky they didn't send Beau to pick your sorry ass up."

"Beau?" I laughed. "Talk about scraping the bottom of the barrel."

"Exactly. So aren't you happy to see me now?"

"I guess. And on the bright side, at least I got the pretty boy of the group," I complimented, although we both knew he was anything but. With body-covering tattoos that climbed up his neck, his shiny bald top, and his near-continuous, badass grimace, Dom was as far from a pretty boy as you could get.

"Yep, I'm trying something new with my hair. You like?"

"Love," I complimented, wrapping my arm around his shoulder in greeting. I'd watched this guy single-handedly handle entire crowds with his dominating roar, but off-duty, Dom had a funny bone that, when tickled, would induce the funniest damn giggle I'd ever heard. Get him going on some joke and I swear the guy would be bent over in hysterics, gasping for breath.

Like the old friends we were, Dom and I chatted the entire length of the drive to the stadium. Fans lined the sidewalks on the street that led to the bus entrance of the arena. As our car was stopped by stadium security, screams erupted from the crowds.

"They think you're Jake," Dom laughed, shaking his head. "Idiots."

I rolled down the window just enough to stick my hand out and wave. The roar that immediately went up was deafening. I continued my greeting until Dom started rolling the window up on my hand.

"Really?" he questioned, eyeing me in amusement.

"What? I was being friendly."

"No. You were lying to hoards of Jake's fans."

"Oh, please. You're always so detail-oriented. You need a vacation."

"Yeah, well, unlike you, I have to work for a living."

His words hit me. I knew how the crew viewed me – hell, we even kidded about it, which was clearly what Dom was doing now – but I wasn't entirely sure I liked that distinction anymore. We sat in silence for a minute. I could feel Dom evaluating me.

"I was only kidding. You know that, right?"

"Yeah, of course," I replied, trying to appear unaffected by his words. Was I just a fucking joke? In an attempt to steer the conversation away from my shitty work ethic, I asked, "So did you meet Casey?"

"Yep. Nice girl. Everyone loved her."

"And Jake seemed happy with her?"

Dom glanced in my direction and then looked away.

"Really? You're going to be a stickler with me?"

"I don't talk about Jake's personal life with anyone – not even you, Kyle."

"Fine, I'll ask him myself," I grumbled.

"You do that," he smiled. "And leave my name out of it."

Dom dropped me off at the bus. The door was locked, so I knocked lightly. After a moment, Lassen opened it.

"Hey," he said hastily, and then scooted his big, old body back into his space up front.

"Nice to see you again," I called after him.

"Yep, I can't talk. I'm watching a soccer game right now."

"Since when do you watch soccer?"

"Since it's the only sport on television in all of Europe."

"Where's Jake?"

"In his room."

Walking to the back of the bus, I dropped my bags and then made my way quietly to the bedroom door. It was ajar, so I nudged it open with my foot. Jake was on his stomach on the bed, sleeping, I assumed. I decided to announce my arrival in the most obtrusive of ways, by jumping on his back.

"What the…" Jake grunted, earphones flying out of his ears as he flipped over and smacked me in the face with a pillow. "Don't do that! Goddammit!"

"Sorry. Sorry," I said waving my hands. I took in Jake's wild, crazy eyes and instantly felt bad.

"Fucking dick," he protested. "You scared the shit out of me. "

I never could control my impulses around him. It was as if I reverted to the annoying little brother role as soon as we were together. I seriously had no idea how he'd put up with me for so damn long. "That was stupid. I'm an idiot. Sorry."

My sincere apology seemed to ease Jake's ire. His body relaxed, and his eyes returned to their normal 'What the fuck is wrong with you?' look.

To ease the tension I'd created, I opened my arms and plastered on a shit-eating grin. "I'm back!!"

Jake exhaled loudly. "Lucky me."

"I know. Now accept my apology and get up. Entertain me."

"I'm trying. Get off me."

I stood back up. "What are you doing sleeping in the middle of the day, anyway?" I grabbed the pillow and struck him with it for good measure.

"You're pushing it, Kyle," he warned. "And I wasn't sleeping, I was texting Casey."

"Oh." I nodded, a knowing smile forming on my face. "You were sexting Casey."

"No," Jake corrected, with the tiniest grin. "I was texting her, like I said."

"Uh-huh, right. If you prefer, I'll just wait out there so you can finish beating off."

"Six seconds, Kyle. That's all it took for you to get on my nerves."

"I was going for four, but I'll take six."

Jake got off the bed and pushed me out of his way.

"What, I don't get a hug?"

"You don't deserve a hug."

"Fine," I pouted.

"How'd the show go?" Jake asked as he walked into the kitchen. I followed after him, as I always did.

"I discovered a lot about myself, actually."

Jake scanned me with his eyes, no doubt trying to determine if I was messing with him or not. "Really? Like what did you discover?"

"I don't like shitting in the woods."

Jake shook his head, smiling. "No one ever does."

"And, on a more wussy note, I like the sunrise."

"Now that *is* noteworthy. That means you woke up before noon at some point during your time away."

"Yep. That's what happens when you sleep on a bamboo stalk in the middle of a jungle."

"Sounds fun. So were there any hotties in the jungle?"

"Oh, yeah, this one, you would have loved her. Long pigtails, overalls, no bra."

"Sounds..." Jake hesitated, confused by my less-than-flattering description. "Interesting, I guess."

"Oh, yeah, and she was smart too. She knew a little about everything and spent hours teaching us all these interesting facts about... well, about fucking nothing."

"I'm getting less interested for every word you speak," he said.

"And she was a cougar... a really old, goddamn cougar. She was always grabbing my ass."

Jake nodded his head in approval. "Well, she sounds amazing, Kyle. Congratulations."

"Thank you. We really are happy together."

"So no island romance, then?"

I hesitated, and Jake picked up on it right away.

"What? Did you meet someone?" Jake's eyes lit up. "Was she from a religious cult?"

"No, but she was from a really small town. So small in fact that they have pie baking competitions and dress up like frickin' dairy cows."

"What type of people did you meet on this show?" Jake asked, appearing not only highly amused but perplexed as well.

"Oh I've only just begun, Jake. Wait until you hear about the seven foot, ginger-haired giant who had a total fat, fangirl boner for you."

"Okay," Jake's said putting his hands up to stop me. "One thing at a time. You are feeding me way too much information at once. Let's shelve the giant – for now – and get back to the cowgirl. Was she hot?"

"Yeah. I mean, she's cute-hot."

Jake raised his eyebrow, questioning my word choice.

"You know, kind of sweet and innocent but still fun to hang with… not like the ladies we'll meet tonight."

"Speak for yourself. I'm not meeting any ladies tonight. Casey wouldn't appreciate that."

"So you guys are exclusive, then?" I asked, surprised. I'd never known Jake to be serious about any woman and was still having trouble wrapping my head around it.

"She's my girlfriend, Kyle. So yeah, very exclusive."

"Geez, first Keith, then Quinn, and now you. Am I the only McKallister boy without a girlfriend?"

"Quinn has a girlfriend?" Jake's voice rose an octave.

"Yep."

"He never told me that."

"Yeah, her name is Lacey, or Lucy… no, maybe it's Lexi."

"Which one is it?"

"I don't know. She came in wearing a crop top and a really shiny belly button ring. She was sixteen and half-naked, so obviously I was trying not to make eye contact."

"Good call. I bet Mom just adores her," Jake said sarcastically.

"You have no idea… it really is heart-warming to see them interact."

"I'm sure," Jake grinned. "Well, way to go, Quinn. I didn't know he was so popular with the girls."

"Are you kidding? Jake, our little brother is quite the stud now. After two rounds of braces, he's grown out of that awkward beaver-tooth stage."

Jake laughed, shaking his head. "You're such a jerk. Okay, so back to that girl. Do you like her?"

"Not anymore."

"Why?"

"'Cause she screwed me."

"Literally?"

"No, figuratively. She kicked me out of the game to have a better chance at winning."

"No?" Jake questioned, in surprise.

"Yes."

"Damn. That's cutthroat."

"Yep. And now I hate her, so that's that."

He eyed me skeptically. "If you say so."

"I do. And I want to get drunk tonight. You in?"

Jake contemplated his decision for longer than seemed necessary. "I'm in."

Before the concert, I passed a few bills off to Beau, the stagehand roadie whom no one wanted to pick them up at the airport, and told him to make a party happen.

"No problem, dude. Are we talking kickback or rager?"

"Whatever that wad of cash buys me," I said, slapping his shoulder. "Don't let me down."

"Have I ever?"

He wasn't the smartest of dudes, but when it came to parties, Beau Beckley was like an idiot savant. No one could outdo a Beau-sponsored soirée. Hand the guy a few hundred bucks and within an hour he'd have a keg and a couple of strippers delivered to the door. He was just that good.

Later that night, I stood on the side of the stage and watched with amazement as my brother played for the sold-out crowd. There was something different about him that I couldn't quite pinpoint. It was almost like he had a renewed purpose in life. We hadn't yet had a chance to talk about Casey, but she'd clearly had a profound effect on him. It seemed I wasn't the only one who'd changed in the past two months. I had an overwhelming feeling that life as I'd known it would never be the same.

After the concert, the band and crew made their way into the underground parking garage. Some local women who'd been invited backstage earlier in the evening were also now at the party. Liquor was freely flowing, and the women were hot. For the first time since the Kenzie take-down, I was feeling no pain. Jake hung with the crowd for a while, but I could tell he wasn't feeling it, and he excused himself soon after. Vadim and Dom escorted him back to the bus. I guess I should have followed, as I normally did, but tonight I wanted to let loose and relax.

After Jake's departure, a beautiful, raven-haired woman named Dunya made her way over to me. My eyes examined her enthusiastically. She'd be the perfect antidote for a backstabbing square dancer. Of course, Dunya was more interested in asking when Jake was coming back than getting to know me. I expertly deflected her questions, but damn if that woman refused to give up. My usual techniques for redirecting the conversation just weren't working. She wasn't falling for any of my bullshit. Maybe I was rusty. Although it also could have been the fact that, in my inebriated state, I kept mispronouncing her name, which caused her mood to sour.

"Dunby?"

"No. Dunya.

"Dunyah?"

"No, Dunya. Ya…can you say 'ya'?" she tried, irritation thick in her accent.

"Yeh. Ya. Yo. Yum," I cackled, really feeling the effects of the alcohol. She swore something in her native tongue.

"Do you like me, Dunby?"

"Dunya. And I like that you're Jake's brother."

"That's it?"

"Well, I might like you better if you weren't making fun of my name."

"I'm not making fun of your name. I just can't pronounce it."

"Yeah, you can. You're just not trying."

She was right. At first I wasn't doing it on purpose. I mean, those five sequential letters in her name were tough to get a handle on. But the more annoyed she got with my mistakes, the more I enjoyed poking the bear.

"So let me ask you this. If I was some random American dude that you met at the concert, would you still want to hang out with me?"

Dundee flashed me a dubious look, and to her credit, actually seemed somewhat apologetic. "I mean, you're not the worst guy here."

That wasn't the compliment I'd been fishing for. Glancing around the room at some of our roadies, I was, at least, comforted by the knowledge that there were shoddier looking guys in here than me. Still, her words bothered me.

"What exactly are you thinking is going to happen here tonight?"

She remained silent for a moment, perhaps contemplating her response. "I'd be willing to do a three-way."

Trying to remain cool in the face of great confoundment, I managed to reply, "And by three-way you're meaning, you, me, and that brunette over there?"

Her eyes followed in the direction I pointed, but then zeroed back in on mine. "I think you know what I mean."

Once the shock wore off, I actually laughed in her face. She didn't care for that, but I couldn't help myself. Just the thought of it cracked me up. I had half a mind to bring her back to the bus just so I could see Jake's horrified reaction.

"Just take me to him, Kale," she sighed, deliberately mispronouncing my name. Clearly she'd had enough of my antics. "I'll take care of the rest."

Maybe it was my newfound self-awareness, or the shock of the offer, or maybe I'd just finally hit my breaking point; whatever it was, that was the moment I decided I no longer wanted to be the means to an end. It had taken surviving on my own to open my eyes to what I'd been allowing to happen for so long. I was not a goddamn runner-up. I didn't blame Jake, or Dunlop, or any of the other women who'd used me as a stepping-stone. I blamed myself. Suddenly it became clear that I was a master at self-sabotage. How could I ever become my own person if I was hiding behind a superstar? And why had I spent so much damn time being okay with this shit?

"You know what, Dunbar, thanks for the enticing offer, but I think I'll pass."

Things changed after that day. I asked Jake for a real job on the security crew. He never asked why, but he immediately turned me over to Vadim, and I was put to work. There were days that being employed really sucked and I would have preferred to go back to the bus and play video games all day long, but I stuck with it because I knew if I wanted to be taken seriously that I needed to stop acting like a teenaged mooch. For the first time in my life, I was actually making an honest day's pay, and with it came a renewed sense of pride.

In addition to the job, I stopped courting the Jake-obsessed ladies. They weren't here for me, and I wasn't playing the game anymore. Just because I *could* have them didn't mean I should. Jake had found a balance with life on the road, even before meeting Casey, and I was determined to have the same self-control.

And finally, I got serious about working out - something I'd always hated. Instead of my usual approach of lifting weights for three minutes and then going off to take a nap, now I worked out with Jake for at least an hour every day. Not only was my body changing and getting stronger, but also Jake and I had a lot of time to talk. We still avoided the heavy issues, but he was more open with me than he'd been in years. I noticed a difference in the way Jake treated me, too. It was definitely with more respect. The fact that I was trying to improve myself was not lost on him. He seemed proud of the changes I'd made, and that, in turn, filled me with a renewed sense of purpose. I liked this new Kyle a whole lot better than the old, and apparently so did Jake.

I thought a lot about the island and my friends, and although I hadn't forgiven Kenzie, I still missed her way more than I wanted to admit. The show would be airing the season premier in the States the week after we arrived home from tour, and I'd have been lying if I said I wasn't worried about how I would be portrayed. A positive edit could make or break a person. Would I be seen as some playboy, leading on the innocent American sweetheart? Grace's words played over and over in my mind. I really hoped I wasn't about to sully the McKallister name, because honestly, I wasn't sure how much more it could take.

CHAPTER THIRTY-FOUR

KENZIE

Tale of the Triplets

"You okay?" Dad asked.

With my head cupped in my hands, I stared out the window as rain hammered the back porch and drained into pools of water on the oversaturated lawn.

"It's such a waste," I moaned.

"What's a waste?"

"The rain. We get so much, and they don't get any in Southern California."

"They don't need it. They just steal ours."

Ah ha! That's where I got my negative attitudes toward our southern brothers. I frowned at my father.

"But is it really stealing if we have so much we can't use it all?"

My dad considered my question for a moment, and then apparently coming up with no good explanation, turned his uncertainty to frustration. "I don't know, Mackenzie, and honestly, I really don't care."

"I once accused Kyle of stealing our water to fill his swimming pool."

My dad gaped at me in surprise. "Why in the hell would you do that?"

"Because he called me a Bigfoot-loving tweaker," I whined.

"Ha!" Colton exclaimed as he sauntered into the kitchen. "That's a good one. I like this guy."

"Kenzie has a guy? Seriously?" Cooper asked, following in after his brother.

"You say that with such shock. Is it so hard to believe?" I asked, slightly offended by the assumption that I couldn't get a guy.

He shrugged. "I mean, sort of."

My brothers both laughed at that. Their personalities were as similar as their looks. Back when Mom was undergoing in vitro, she'd had two embryos implanted. One became Caroline and the other split, creating Colton and Cooper. Now sixteen years old, the boys were filled with blustery confidence and mischievous tendencies. The two had gotten into their fair share of mishaps over the years, but in a county where there was nothing for teenagers to do but get in trouble, it wasn't unusual for teenage boys to be brought home by the local police once in a while. Colton and Cooper were no exception. So far we'd had two visits. Once for cow tipping on the Trayburn farm and another for dumping over garbage cans on trash pick up day. Both offenses required swift retribution. The boys and their friends, were shoveling cow manure for two weeks after the first incident. The second saw the boys picking up every single piece of trash littering the town for a week. I liked to think they'd learned their lesson, but chances were with these two, they hadn't seen their last police car.

Despite the closeness the boys shared, they fought like two male beta fish stuck in a bowl together. It was typically quite a challenge managing their disagreements, which almost always turned physical if a swift resolution could not be brokered. Despite their less than stellar behavior and juvenile delinquent record, they were still my pride and joy. Yes, I was their sister, but my investment in the three of them was more like that of a mother to her children. Their happiness was my most treasured achievement. Leaving them behind to follow my own path was going to be the hardest thing I'd ever do.

"Who called you that, anyway?" Cooper asked.

"This guy I met on the show. You'll see him once it airs."

"Is he cute?" Caroline asked, as she bounced in after her brothers. My sister wormed her way onto my lap and curled herself into my arms.

"Yes." I smiled. "Very."

"If you have his picture," Caroline said, with a lazy smile on her face, "I'll give you his hottie rating."

About a year ago, Caroline had crossed over into boy crazy territory. She and her girlfriends obsessed over the young male actors in the CW channel shows. I could only imagine what her reaction would be when she found out Kyle's lineage. For now, I decided to keep that under wraps, as I didn't have the patience to peel her off the kitchen floor.

"I don't have a picture. And it doesn't matter anyway because we aren't ever going to get together."

Caroline bolted upright, her eyes ablaze with intrigue. "Why not?"

"Because he hates her," Colton informed, as if it were no big deal. My heart clenched in response.

"Colton," Dad scolded.

"How exactly do you know this information?" I asked Colton, but looked to my father in accusation. Another trait I'd obviously inherited from him.

"I overheard you crying to Dad."

"So naturally you eavesdropped?"

"Naturally."

"Just exactly how much did you hear?" I asked, flinching.

Colton actually hesitated a moment, rare emotion flashing through his blue eyes. "Enough to know you're moving away."

"What?" Caroline blurted out. These rapid releases of information were almost too much for her to handle. "Why?"

I laid out my reasoning to the triplets. They were surprised by the suddenness of my decision. Although it had been years in the making for me, this was the first they'd heard of my desire to leave.

After we'd exhausted the conversation about my impending departure, Caroline asked, "Why does that guy hate you?"

"She sold him out," Colton informed, shaking his head in disappointment. "Dick move, Kenz."

"It was more complicated than that," I said, in a feeble attempt to defend myself.

"Oh, great," Cooper huffed. "I've been bragging about you being on the show to everyone, and now they're all going to hate you."

"Yeah, I wouldn't be bragging, Coop. I'm pretty sure by the time this show is over, I'll be as hated as Ariana Grande."

"Ariana Grande *before* or *after* the doughnut-licking scandal?" Cooper asked in alarm.

"After," I admitted, cringing in embarrassment.

"Oh, crap." He got up and ran from the room.

"Where are you going?" I called after him.

"I've got to delete my Twitter page."

I went back to work a week after returning home. My focus was different now. Instead of just going about my day as normal, I was actively preparing for my departure. First on my list was hiring my replacement, and second was getting some new carpeting and windows at our house. Knowing that I had won at least some prize money for coming in the top three on the show, I felt comfortable using what savings I had to pay for home improvements. Left to my father, such repairs would never happen.

I thought about Kyle often during this time, wondering where he was and how he was doing. After giving Dale my number to pass on to him, I had hoped for a call, but as the weeks turned to months, I knew I needed to face the facts. Kyle was gone, and I had to move on for my own good.

A couple weeks after returning home, not only was my earlier television interview aired but also the county paper ran an article about the "Hometown Girl" competing on a popular reality show. In an area where very little changed from year to year, news like this spread quickly and created excitement. Suddenly, I was thrust into the spotlight. Not only was I asked to make appearances at local functions but potential suitors began showing up at my door. Most were the same guys that I'd known forever, but a few were new to me – men from neighboring towns interested in piggybacking on my fifteen minutes of fame. For the briefest moment in time, Mackenzie Williams was the hottest piece of pie in the county, and damned if I wasn't enjoying my newfound celebrity.

Although I went on a few dates during this time, no guy stood out to me. I caught myself comparing them to Kyle, and that was a big mistake because there just was no comparison. It became clear to me that I'd fallen in love during my time on the show, and getting over Kyle was going to take time. Of course, my obsession with all things McKallister probably slowed my progress. Interestingly enough, Kyle had no presence on the Internet. What guy his age didn't at least have a Twitter or Instagram page? So, in hopes of getting some idea of where Kyle was, I took to stalking Jake on social media. I figured out his tour schedule and followed along his route through Europe. I also read everything I could find about Jake and his kidnapping, fixated on any mention of Kyle, no matter how miniscule. I knew it was creepy behavior, but it was the one thing that made me feel closer to him.

Seeing him again for the final taping was the only ray of hope for my broken heart. I went through all the scenarios in my head of how that evening could play out, even writing down and memorizing what I wanted to say to him in hopes that I wouldn't totally choke when we came face to face. In my little fantasy world, Kyle forgave me and we lived happily ever after. The reality, I was sure, would not be as kind.

CHAPTER THIRTY-FIVE

KYLE

A Brother's Bond

We arrived back in Los Angeles the last week of September into the middle of a heat wave. The Santa Ana winds were whipping up fires all over the southland. Typically I stayed at Jake's place during the off months of touring, but he'd made it pretty clear to me that my presence was no longer required, or even wanted for that matter. I got it. He was in love with Casey and wanted time alone with her, but at the same time, I didn't want to move out of my comfortable digs, either. I tried to negotiate an acceptable compromise, but Jake was having none of it. So like the big boy I was, I had my mommy come pick me up and take me home. Damn, I needed to get a place of my own, and soon.

Two days after arriving home, I was packing again, only this time to evacuate. A fire that had been raging for days shifted course and roared over the mountains, coming dangerously close to our place. While my mom and sisters packed the valuables, Dad, Keith, Quinn, and I cut brush around the perimeter of the property and hosed down the roof as the fire barreled toward our neighborhood. Firefighters were hosing down the hills around our house as helicopters were dropping water and retardant. Just as evacuation orders had been issued for our area, the winds shifted suddenly, the fire changed course, and off it went to torment another community. The entire time we were preparing for the worst, I couldn't get Kenzie's accusation out of my head. Her damn water might actually have just saved my mansion.

The first episode of *Marooned* aired the following week, and I went to Jake's to watch. I figured there'd be less of a chance of being heckled and tormented at his place than at home. Of course, I hadn't counted on Casey and her wicked sense of humor. She found something embarrassing to comment on every time I was in the shot. It was a cringe-worthy experience seeing myself on television for the first time and even more appalling to relive my stupid antics. It struck me how much I'd changed as a person since stepping off the boat onto the island. I felt stronger and more mature, and I credited the people I'd been with for my growth.

I re-experienced every minute of my time on the show with Dale as my virtual wingman. Texting back and forth obsessively, we speculated on which scenes would air and marveled at what was happening on the other tribe. That was a part of the story we'd never seen. After each show, Dale would remind me to contact Kenzie, and I would always conveniently ignore him.

"Seriously, Kyle, I can't picture Kenzie betraying you," Jake said.

"Whaaat?" Casey gasped.

"Jake, what part of 'You can't talk about the show' did you not understand?"

"She betrays you?" Casey whispers, her face shrouded in intrigue. "I promise I won't tell."

"No offense, Casey, but you don't look like you can keep a secret."

"Me? Are you kidding? I am the most trustworthy person you'll ever meet. Tell him, Jake," she said, smacking him in the leg.

"She's very trustworthy. Trust me," Jake repeated robotically, then grabbed Casey around the waist and pulled her on top of him. She screamed, laughing as she was jolted back. "Just tell her. She'll never stop. Will you?"

"Never!" she screeched.

I fake-barfed at their playfulness. There was nothing worse than a happy couple when you yourself were miserable. Not that I was necessarily miserable, but I was still angry and resentful. Watching Kenzie on television had brought back memories of the good times we'd shared, and that, in turn, was making it more difficult to stay mad.

I didn't tell Casey why I was pissed at Kenzie until the fifth episode. She saw something in Kenzie's reaction to me that caught her off guard.

"She's in love with you," Casey stated, matter-of-factly.

"What?" I asked, although I'd heard exactly what she'd said.

"What happened to make her betray you? From what I can tell, her feelings for you are genuine."

I spent the next few minutes telling her the story as best as I knew it. I still didn't understand Kenzie's reasoning other than she was doing it to secure her family's future.

"Wow, this is getting good." Jake leaned over, grabbing some popcorn and shoving it in his mouth. "If you want my advice, I think you should forgive her already."

"Well, actually, I didn't ask for your advice, so shut up."

"I'm with Jake," Casey added.

"Shocker."

"I'm serious, Kyle. I like her. She's got spunk, and you two have mad chemistry. Too bad you hate her so much," she said.

"Yeah, too bad," I mumbled.

THE THEORY OF SECOND BEST

"I'm just bummed I'm having surgery right in the middle of this. You have to keep it recorded for me," he informed Casey.

"You know I will. But I think we need to have an intervention before you go under the knife."

"For me?" Jake asked, seemingly confused as to why he'd need one.

"No, your brother and his Kenzie. Kyle, give me her number and I'll set it up."

"Oh right and will you be present at this intervention?"

"Of course. I'll be the mediator and we'll talk it out... like adults. And Jake can be..." she paused, no doubt attempting to invent a role in her little fantasy psychotherapy session for my brother. "You can be the entertainment."

"That's it? Are you saying I have no useful talents other than being amusing?" Jake protested.

"Nothing I can think of, anyway," she said flippantly.

"No?" he flirted. She shook her head, laughing, and once again the two delved into their cutesy shit, verbally sparring for the next five minutes.

I was seconds away from smacking both of them up top the head until Casey came up for air and said, "Seriously, though, Kyle, you need to make up with that girl. She's perfect for you."

And as the season went on, my anger faded. I wanted to see her again. Maybe Casey's mediation wasn't a bad idea. The longer I went without seeing her, the more I couldn't remember why I was mad. I'd decided that as soon as Jake's knee replacement surgery was over, I was going to contact her and work things out, maybe even make a trip to Humboldt County to see her. One of the changes I'd made was trying to be more mature, and that applied to my relationships too. Maybe it was too late for more than just a friendship with her, but I had to try.

Unfortunately, that moment never arrived. Jake suffered some life-threatening complications after surgery, which plunged him into a coma and me into a nightmare of epic proportions. My newfound strength crumbled as the fear of losing him overwhelmed me. Once again my brother was struggling for his life, and I, as always, was standing on the sidelines, powerless to help him.

I wandered through the hospital those first few days, unsure of what to do or how to feel. I was just numb. It seemed as though my life had been a series of circles, always connecting back at the same spot. Three times I had felt this level of terror and dread, and all those instances revolved around Jake. The hell of not knowing, those days after he was taken; the shock of his return and the realization that the hollowed out shell of a person he'd become would be our new norm; and then this damn surgery and the very real possibility that it would end his short and tragic life.

I didn't sleep much during this time. The nightmares had come back full force. I could no longer close my eyes without seeing Jake's own imploring ones. That was always the point in the nightmare where I screamed in my head and forced myself awake. The moment I hated remembering. His eyes. It was the last thing I saw of him before he was ripped from my life. And they spoke to me. I knew what he'd wanted in those desperate moments, what he was pleading for me to do, but I'd struggled to follow his direction. I couldn't leave him. But that look he gave me… it was clear. He wanted me to run. Jake's last act before going to what he could only have assumed would be his grave was saving me.

CHAPTER THIRTY-SIX

KENZIE
The Apology

I watched *Marooned* along with every other person in my hometown. It wasn't that the show was over-the-top popular in our area; it was the fact that one of their own was competing in it. Viewing parties had cropped up all over the county, and my presence was often requested. I'd thought it would be tough to watch myself on television in front of so many people, but the support of my friends, neighbors, and townspeople was overwhelming, even after my very public on-air confession that I was unhappy living here and wanted to move away.

Thankfully the volcano of vomit never made it onto the show, but the zombie shuffle and my meet cute with Kyle on that first day did. Watching us together on TV made me fall in love with him all over again. And our interactions made for entertaining television, as audiences seemed to love our moments together. Kyle and I, and the rest of the Dork Quad, became instant fan favorites. The positive reaction toward me was surprising. I knew people would love Kyle and Dale, but I never imagined I would be part of that goodwill. Although the moment I dreaded – the backstab heard 'round the reality TV world – would surely put an end to all the positive feedback being thrown my way.

My only connection to Kyle now was through Dale. During the airing of the various episodes, Dale would sometimes forward me funny little quotes that Kyle had sent to him. Those few words were the only thing I had to hold onto, so I treasured them. It wasn't until the eleventh episode aired that word leaked out about Jake's serious medical condition. Every day a new report or rumor surfaced, most of them were erroneous claims of his demise. I worried endlessly about Kyle and how he was handling the crisis. But once Jake's medical emergency was revealed, Kyle no longer responded to Dale's texts. It was as if he'd completely fallen off the radar, and there was no way to track him down.

"Whatcha doing?" Caroline came into my room and plopped down on my bed.

"Moping," I answered casually. "What are you doing?"

Caroline crinkled her nose in that way I loved. When she was little I couldn't help but smother her in kisses every time she did it. "You sure do a lot of that lately."

"It's just my thing."

"That's just it – moping is *not* your thing. I mean, if I'd been raised by a moper, do you think I'd be this fabulous?"

She had a point, although her simplistic sixteen-year-old assessment of my very adult predicament did little to lighten my mood.

"You wouldn't understand," I answered.

"I get it, Kenzie. We *all* get it," Caroline emphasized the word *all* in such an overdramatic way. I wasn't *that* annoying, was I? "You did a crappy thing. Kyle's pissed. Now you need to make it right."

"I wish it were that easy. He won't call me. I don't know where he lives. And his brother, the person who means most to him in the whole world, is lying in a hospital close to death. I'm pretty sure I'm the last person he wants to see."

"Or maybe you're just the person he needs to see."

The last few days I'd been thinking the same thing. In my heart and soul, I knew Kyle needed me, whether he wanted to admit it or not. But with no connection to him, and no way to make my support known, I was helpless. Tears rolled down my cheeks.

"What's wrong, Kenzie?" Caroline asked, smoothing my hair. My sister was maddeningly superficial at times, but if there was one thing that could bring her back to reality, it was family and her undying devotion to it. "What are you so afraid of?"

"I'm scared he'll reject me. At least now I can pretend I still have a shot. But if I go and he turns me away, then it'll be over forever. I'm not sure I'm ready to hear that."

"A lot has happened since then," Caroline reasoned, sounding so much more grown up than she was. "Maybe those stupid things that happened on a reality television show don't matter to him as much, now that he has real life things to worry about."

"Yeah, maybe. But what if he won't give me the chance to explain?"

"Don't give him the option."

"It's not that simple."

"Yes. It is. Get in his face and keep getting in his face until he listens. Don't take no for an answer. I wouldn't."

"Oh, I know you wouldn't," I laughed through my tears. "Maybe you can do it for me."

"I wish. He's hot."

Caroline lit a fire under my ass. The trip to Los Angeles for the live finale was scheduled in a matter of days. We'd already decided to leave a few days early, not only because the drive took a good ten hours but also because Dad had promised us all a trip to Universal Studios and Disneyland. If all went as I hoped, I wouldn't be joining my family at the Magic Kingdom; instead I would be with Kyle, forcing him to forgive me and offering him the support he needed.

It wasn't much of a plan, but it was all I had.

———◆———

With my arm hanging in a sling and gauze hastily wrapped around my head, my dad and I entered the hospital emergency room. It was the only way to get into the facility, with all of Jake's fans on the sidewalks being held back by security guards and police officers. The main entrance was being manned, and if you didn't have a close relative in the hospital, you weren't getting in. So it came down to the emergency room and a faked injury. I employed my father in my deception, and he came willingly. He'd been watching me pine for weeks and knew I needed this.

The triage line was long and the emergency room bursting at the seams. We sat for a while just blending in with all the sickies, and then I grabbed my dad's hand and looked him in the eyes.

"Go get him," he said, and kissed my cheek.

"Oh, right." I laughed. "Like it'll be that easy."

One thing I knew for certain, I wasn't going to go down without a fight. Regardless of everything that had happened, our friendship had been real. I owed him an apology, and he owed me the time to give it. Inhaling a deep breath, I stood up with determination. *I got this.* With my head held high, I moved down the hall and just kept walking. No one said a word to me, and if they had, I would have told them I was going to the cafeteria. It wasn't a lie; I planned to sit in there all day and all night. I knew Kyle was in the hospital, and he needed to eat at some point, so I began my vigil at 7:15 a.m., armed with my iPad and wallet full of cash for snacks. Every few hours I'd get up and buy some food, and then move to another table so people wouldn't get suspicious that I didn't belong.

It wasn't until after three in the afternoon that Kyle walked in. My heart leapt in my chest and my body flushed with excitement. Just seeing him again brought back so many emotions. Thankfully I was able to keep everything under control. My feelings right now were irrelevant. The last thing Kyle needed was a lovesick girl throwing herself at his feet when he was struggling with so much.

I watched nervously as he picked out his food. His shoulders were slumped and his head drooped. The magnetic personality that I'd come to love was nowhere in sight. Kyle was worse than I'd imagined. He looked gutted. My eyes misted over, and the lump that had formed in my throat had me worried that I'd be crying before I ever got a word out. I took a few deep breaths and pulled myself back together. I was determined to be the person Kyle needed – strong and supportive, not needy and wounded.

I watched as he dropped heavily into a chair in the back of the cafeteria. He was slow and methodical in his movements. Whatever was happening with Jake was sucking the life out of Kyle.

Standing up on shaking legs, I smoothed down my hair as I took my first tentative steps forward. Kyle didn't see me coming. Lost in thought, his eyes were fixed on his tray of food, yet none of its contents had left the plate. I stopped at his table and Kyle looked up, his blue eyes dulled with grief. They widened in surprise as they fixed on me. We just stared at each other, tears welling up in my eyes.

"Kyle, I…"

He stood up swiftly, the chair hitting the wall behind him. Oh, god, he was leaving. I had to make him hear me.

"Please, Kyle, just give me a chance."

As he came around the table, I expected him to push past me angrily and was prepared to latch onto him and not let go. But instead of trying to evade me, Kyle's arms wrapped around me and squeezed. Shocked, it took me a second to hug him back, but when I did, I held him fiercely. His head dug into my neck as I felt shudders rack through his body. He sighed heavily in my arms. This was a man with the weight of the world on his shoulders. I could feel the sorrow coursing through him. We didn't speak. There was no need. We held on to each other as if our lives depended on it.

Maybe they did.

After a minute, Kyle pulled back slightly, but we were still entangled in an embrace. Dark circles were heavy under his tired eyes. "How did you know I'd be here?"

"You know me and my surveillance techniques."

He nodded, his lip turned up slightly. He couldn't even muster a full smile, and that worried me more than I cared to admit. His family had not released much information about Jake's condition, but by the look on Kyle's face, it wasn't good.

"I've been waiting here all day," I admitted. "Hoping you'd come in."

He nodded, eyes searching mine.

"I want you to know, Kyle, I'm so sorry. What I did was inexcusable."

Kyle hugged me again. "Stop," he whispered in my ear.

"No, you need to understand."

"I do understand. I was just pissed that I got kicked out."

"And you should have been. I betrayed you."

"It was a game. You played it. I'm proud of you. After your less-than-stellar start, I didn't think you'd last a day on the island, and now look at you."

I shook my head. "You and I both know it went beyond the game. I really cared about you… or let me change that to present tense, I care about you. A lot. And the minute I made the decision I made, I knew it was a huge mistake. I wanted to take it back, but I couldn't. And I've spent the last three months just agonizing over it. I would have come sooner to apologize, but I didn't know where to find you."

"I'm not mad at you. Honestly, I just don't have the energy for petty shit like that. I get it. You did what you had to do. Family is the most important thing. Trust me – I know that," Kyle said, morosely. "You were just looking out for them. I would have done the same thing if I were in your position."

"No," I whispered, shamefaced. "I did it for me, because I was selfish."

"I don't care. I accept your apology, and I don't want to talk about it again. Okay?"

I hesitated. Much like when he accepted my apology for vomiting on him, I couldn't fathom how he could be so forgiving.

"Seriously, no more apologies. Promise."

"I promise."

Kyle dropped his head and put his hand on the table to steady himself. He seemed exhausted to the point where he might drop at any moment.

"Are you okay?" I asked, grabbing his arm to support him.

"Yeah. I need to sit down. I haven't eaten in a while," he said as he slid back into his chair.

Sitting down opposite Kyle, I placed my hand over his.

"Sorry," he apologized. "I'm a mess right now."

"Don't be sorry. I wish I could do something to help you."

Kyle lifted his eyes, and the look he gave me was one of pure misery.

I grabbed his hand and squeezed.

"It's so fucked up, Kenzie." His voice faltered.

"Is he...will he..." I stammered, unsure of what I was even asking.

"I can't..." Kyle sighed heavily. "I just... I don't want to talk about it now. I'm just trying to get from one day to the next."

He looked so lost. Instinctively I knew he needed strength and direction. "Well, the first thing you need to do is take care of yourself. You're no good to Jake if you're falling apart yourself. You need to eat. And then you need to shower. Maybe put on some clean clothes. And then we can get some fresh air and just talk. Okay?"

"Yeah. Okay."

He picked up the chicken wrap on his tray and shoved half of it in his mouth. My eyes widened in surprise, wondering how guys did that. My brothers were the same way. They inhaled food. I always thought of them like dogs, swiping and swallowing their food before anyone had a chance to snatch it away from them. Kyle spent the next minute chewing, when he could have taken smaller bites and still been in the same place he was now.

Once he had finished his first wrap and was tearing through a bag of chips, I went back up and bought him a second one, which was also devoured in minutes.

"Damn, Kyle, when was the last time you ate?"

"I don't know. I just snack here and there. I've been eating lots of Jell-O and pudding cups."

"Well, I guess it beats mollusks."

"Oh, god, don't remind me. That was the worst."

"Yeah," I agreed. "But the best too. I had the time of my life on that island, with you and the rest of the Dork Quad."

"Me too. It was a great time, wasn't it?" Kyle said, with a far-off look in his eye. "It was like a fucked-up summer camp."

I laughed. "That it was. Have you been watching?"

"I saw the first few episodes, but then everything happened, and I just couldn't really concentrate."

"So you have no idea how popular you are, then?"

"Really?" Kyle grinned, seeming surprised. "Why? Was it my crab scene?"

"It was everything. People love you, Kyle. You just come across so real and genuine. I was actually looking pretty good too, until… well, you know. And now everyone hates me."

"For kicking me off?"

"Yes."

Kyle actually laughed. "Serves you right."

"Yes, it does," I agreed wholeheartedly. I deserved all the scorn heaped on me. Still, his words soothed me. It felt good to laugh about it. Kyle seemed not to hold a grudge, and that spoke volumes to the type of person he was.

"Dale's been really worried about you. You haven't been returning his texts."

"I know. I haven't been up to talking to anyone. Can you let him know I'm okay?"

"You can tell him yourself on Wednesday."

Kyle looked confused by my words.

"The finale? You're going to the taping, right?"

"Wait – what day is it today?"

"Monday. The taping is in two days. Didn't anyone tell you?"

Kyle exhaled noisily and dropped his head. "Last week they started putting all kinds of pressure on me, so I blocked their calls. I'm just not going to show up."

"Don't you have to be there? It's in the contract."

"Yeah, well, fuck the contract. They can sue me. I'm not going to go in there so they can exploit what happened to Jake and parade me around for the cameras."

Kyle's words dripped resentment. I sympathized with his plight, but the legal ramifications if he bailed would be a nightmare. The look on his face kept me from commenting further. He didn't ask for or want my opinion, so I kept it to myself.

We sat there awkwardly for a moment until he pushed back his chair once more and stood up. The food had done him some good. He looked stronger now. "Let's go. I really need a shower."

"You do." I fanned my hand over my nose. "But lucky for you, I'm used to stinky Kyle."

"You like me au natural."

"I never said I *liked* it," I balked. "Being used to something and liking it are two wildly separate things."

"Well, I'm not showering for you anyway. I'm doing it for my poor mother. She's been begging me for days and has resorted to wearing a surgical mask around her nose and mouth when I'm around."

"You're not that bad."

"You don't know my mom. She has the nose of a bloodhound."

Kyle grabbed his tray, and we walked over to the moving dish receptacle system that sent the dishes back into the kitchen. He stared in fascination as his tray was robotically whisked away. I had to smile. That was the Kyle I knew and loved.

I touched his back. "You ready?"

Kyle nodded and led me out of the cafeteria, taking one last look over his shoulder as his tray disappeared into the kitchen. He strode through the hospital like a man who knew exactly where he was going, and I struggled to keep up with his long legs. We rode elevators and crossed internal bridges between buildings until we came to a door. Kyle opened it with a key card.

"What is this?"

"An apartment. It's like for hospice families. We use it so we can be close to him, just in case…" His voice trailed off.

Just in case. My heart sank. I wanted to ask him what was happening, but I knew it wasn't my place. Suddenly, memories of my mother lying covered with a sheet on a gurney flashed before my eyes. I prayed that wouldn't be Jake's fate. I'd never met him before, but I knew how important he was to Kyle and that made him important to me.

I stepped into the apartment behind him. "Wow."

"What?"

"It's just weird to think this apartment is in a hospital." It was a homey two-bedroom place with a spacious living room and kitchen. "I mean, this is really nice. Is your whole family staying here?"

"Off and on. We go in shifts, so he's never alone. I just got off mine before going for some food."

Just then a pretty young woman with long brown hair walked out of the bathroom, drying her hair with a towel. A sister, maybe? She looked up and startled when she saw us.

"Oh, geez. You scared me. I was starting to worry about you when you didn't come back," she said to Kyle, giving him a quick hug.

"Casey, this is…"

"Kenzie. I know," she smiled, running her hands through her wet hair. "Sorry, I didn't know Kyle was bringing home company, or I would have looked a bit more presentable. At least I have my clothes on, right?"

As I looked on, a knowing glance passed between them, and they smiled at one another. Definitely not a sister. Then it dawned on me. Oh, shit. This was Kyle's girlfriend. It had never occurred to me that he might have one, but several months had passed since the filming, so, of course he did. I felt my walls go up. How stupid could I be? I thought I was here to help him through these rough times, but he already had someone for that.

In a gesture of greeting, Casey came in for a hug. Surprised, I returned it, and took a step back. "I've been watching you and Kyle on the show. I feel like I already know you," she said.

Okay, so she wasn't the jealous type. That was good. Kyle gave me a quizzical look, and then his eyes brightened as if a light bulb had gone off inside his head.

"Casey is Jake's girlfriend," he said to me.

"Oh." My eyebrows danced in surprise. "Oh, I thought…"

"Yeah, I know what you thought," Kyle nodded, teasing me.

Casey's expression showed confusion.

"She thought you were my girlfriend."

They both laughed like it was the stupidest thing they'd ever heard.

"Oh, please, I have better taste than that," she needled Kyle. "I prefer my guys with less stink."

"I'm showering, Jesus. What's with all of you? I really don't smell that bad," he said, as he lifted his arm and took a sniff. I saw his eyes squint in response, but he masked it quickly. "See? Nothing."

"Just go, Kyle. No one can procrastinate like you. I'll keep Kenzie company."

"Fine," he huffed, and disappeared into the bathroom.

Casey motioned to the couch. "Sit. I'll be right back. I'm going to get my makeup so I don't scare you off."

I smiled as she disappeared behind a door. Casey was definitely not the type of girl I'd think would be dating a rock star. There was nothing glamorous or mouth-dropping in her appearance. Certainly she was a pretty woman, but she was also real… just an average, everyday girl, like me. I wondered how long she had been dating Jake. There were so many questions I had swirling around my brain, and so far, not a single answer.

Casey whooshed back in and sat down. She fixed her gaze on me and said with sincerity, "I'm glad you're here."

"Me too. How is he doing, really?"

"Not good. This is the best I've seen him actually. He's been having a rough time. I mean, we all have, but Kyle…" Casey choked up. "Sorry, it's been… hell. And Kyle, he's

just struggling. He's not eating or sleeping or showing emotion. I'm scared for him. How long are you staying?"

"I don't know. As long as he needs me, I guess."

"That might be awhile."

"Then that's how long I'll stay."

Casey smiled, but it was a sad one. "He missed you. He
was just too proud to admit it. You being here will help. I
really feel that."

The fact that this girl cared so much for Kyle's well-being gave us an instant connection. Casey's face tensed and
her forehead wrinkled. Tears filled her eyes. "Sorry."

"Are you doing okay?

"No. But I'm trying to stay strong. It's just not that easy."

"I'm sorry, Casey. I really am."

She nodded. The tears that had earlier pooled in her
eyes were now rolling down her cheeks. She wiped them
away. "I can't control them. I feel like all I do is cry."

I reached out and touched her shoulder. Not knowing
what to say to ease her pain, I simply stayed silent.

Casey shook slightly and sat up straighter. "Anyway, he's
going to wake up," she said with determination. "I feel it
in my bones."

"He will."

"And when he does, he'll be happy to meet you. We
watched the first few episodes together with Kyle. Oh, my
god, Kenzie, you and Kyle were adorable together. We
laughed so hard."

"I can't believe we got so much airtime," I marveled.

"How could they not?"

We chatted about the show until Kyle came out in a towel hanging dangerously low around his midsection. I'm not sure but I think my eyes bulged out more than normal. *Wow. Just wow.* He'd definitely been working out since the last time I'd seen him. If Carl were here now, he wouldn't be calling him a runt anymore. I'd seen Kyle half naked plenty of times and had always considered it a treat, but now? Yikes!

"So shaving is asking too much of you, then?" Casey questioned, not seeming nearly as impressed by his nakedness as I was.

"Are you never happy, woman? I have no idea how Jake puts up with you."

"Watch it, creep. I'm a lovely person. And you need a shave."

"You're sounding more like my mom every day."

"Thank you. Michelle and I are like this," she said and held up her hand with two fingers crossed.

"It wasn't meant as a compliment, Casey, but take it whatever way you want."

She grinned and then cast her uninterested eyes over Kyle. "Can you please get dressed? I'm afraid bits of you might dangle out, and I'd prefer not to see that."

"I'm not doing it for you." Kyle said dismissively then looked over at me and assumed his sexiest man pose. "You like?"

Um, yeah! Do I ever! I fought the urge to tackle him to the ground, but since his brother's girlfriend was in the room, I figured I'd better play it cool. Shrugging, I said, "Eh, I've seen better."

Casey transformed her hand into a gun and pulled the trigger. "Ooh, shot down."

He clutched his chest as if the invisible bullet had punctured it, but his towel slipped and Kyle grabbed for it on its way down. He caught the cloth just before exposing himself, and then turned and ran for the bedroom door. His naked ass was in full view of both of us girls.

"Dammit, Kyle!" Casey complained, covering her eyes. "I told you this would happen. I can't ever *unsee* that."

"You better not tell Jake!" he called from the bedroom.

"Oh, I will, and he's gonna be pissed. In fact, I'm going to go tell him right now. If that doesn't wake him up, I don't know what will," Casey said with an amused look on her face. She turned to me and winked.

Casey finished putting on a little makeup and swept her long brown hair into a ponytail before standing up. "I'm leaving," she called to Kyle.

He opened the door and stepped out dressed in jeans and a t-shirt, flip-flops on his feet. "Okay, give Jake a big, smoochy kiss for me."

"I always do," Casey affirmed, and hugged me. "It was really nice meeting you Kenzie. When Jake wakes up, we'll all hang out."

Just as she turned to leave, I saw the flash of grief in her eyes. I knew that look. It was the same one my father had worn after my mom died. I prayed she would get the happy ending my dad had been deprived of all those years ago.

"You ready?" Kyle asked.

"Where are we going?"

"You said I needed fresh air. I have somewhere I want to take you."

"Are we leaving the hospital?"

"Yes. I need a break."

"Are you sure that's okay?" I questioned. The last thing I wanted was for him to feel obligated to entertain me.

"With who? Jake? I hardly think he'll mind. Besides, we have a family group message. Any changes are reported within seconds." Kyle opened the door. "Let's go. We don't have much time."

"For what?"

"You'll see."

I followed Kyle to the elevators, which we took to the ground floor parking garage. He led me to a white truck and opened the door for me. The entrance was higher than normal, and I contemplated how to get into the damn thing.

"Do you need a boost?"

Tapping one of the tires, I asked, "Are you compensating for something?"

He dipped his head as if he were embarrassed and shrugged. "Probably, but not for the reason you think."

Kyle helped me into the cab, and after exiting the garage, he maneuvered his way through traffic until we merged onto the freeway into a sea of brake lights.

"Damn LA traffic. I guess you don't see this very often?"

"Sometimes I get stuck behind a tractor, but otherwise no."

Kyle didn't react to my joke, as he was busy expertly changing seven lanes of traffic to get his truck into the carpool lane. I gawked at his driving skills. "*That* was impressive."

"You like that?" He grinned.

"You're like a magician."

"Naw. Any Los Angeles driver worth anything can do that."

We drove on the freeway for a short time until Kyle performed his second straight lane change miracle of the day, and within minutes we were sailing along the Pacific Coast Highway, the long sandy beach off to the right. Kyle pulled into a parking spot along the road, and my face lit up. I now understood why we were here.

"The sunset?"

He nodded. "I haven't seen one in a while, and I miss it."

As we walked down the beach, Kyle took my hand in his. I looked at our fingers entwined and wondered what he was thinking. Was it just a friendly gesture?

"It's so warm," I said. "I can't believe it's December."

"I know. It sucks. Is it too much to ask for some seasons? It's frickin' December! It's supposed to be cold."

"Yeah, well, I love it. For me, it's been raining almost non-stop for months. Which explains the ghostly skin tone you love so much."

"Are you mad at me for all my on-air insults? I was only joking. It was like a game, coming up with different ways to describe your skin."

"No, I thought it was funny."

"Over here." Kyle led me to a lifeguard station, and we propped ourselves up against it. There were very few people left on the beach, so it almost felt like we were alone. Kyle gazed out at the horizon, sighing heavily. I wrapped my arm around him and laid my head against his shoulder as we breathed in the ocean air and watched the sun fade to black.

"This reminds me of the island," I whispered wistfully, "I miss it."

"Yeah, me too. It was the calm before the storm."

"I'm sorry about Jake."

"I know."

Kyle leaned into me and our eyes met. He was going to kiss me, and although it was what I'd dreamed about since our last one, I worried that his newfound interest in me was because of the tremendous stress he was under. Was he just looking for a convenient outlet to release his tension? His lips dipped close to mine.

"Kyle?" I said, stopping him with my hand.

"What?" he asked, sounding confused as he leaned away from me.

"You can't kiss me…"

"Why?"

"… because you don't mean it."

"What are you talking about?"

"There are things you don't know."

Kyle immediately tensed up, his face turning hard and defensive.

"On the island, it wasn't just a crush. I actually fell for you… like, really hard. And that day, when I let it slip how much I wanted you… and that look on your face…" I looked away in embarrassment, the memory still raw. "I knew you didn't feel the same way. This whole thing right now, I think there's so much sadness in you that you're confusing the emotions. You're looking for something to ease the pain. And I'd totally do that for you if it weren't for the fact that I won't be able to turn off my feelings, and my heart just can't take anymore."

439

After my speech, Kyle and I sat there quietly staring out at the ocean.

"Are you finished?" he asked.

I'd just poured my soul out to him and was taken aback by the brashness of his response.

"I… yes, I guess."

"Good."

Kyle leaned into me again, and before I could protest, his hands grabbed my face and his lips touched mine. The kiss took me by surprise, and my body reacted by tightening in response. I knew I should fight it, but I couldn't. I wanted this more than I could say, and even though I knew I was going to pay for it later with a big old slice of heartbreak, I gave in to my need and melted into submission.

"Kyle?" I moaned.

He responded by kissing me deeper and with more heat. Okay. Yep. I was done for. Wildly out of control, I threw myself onto him, straddled my island boy. My intensity matched his. His hands went around me and grabbed my butt as he drew me closer into him. I threw my head back and he attacked my neck with kisses. From the distance I heard snickering. We were in public and this was wrong, but Kyle wasn't stopping, so neither was I.

With his hands tangled in my hair, I wrapped my arms around his back and slid my hands up his shirt. Our lips were locked in furious intensity. I had never wanted anyone like I wanted Kyle right now. I rocked into him and he groaned, his hands still cupping my ass.

"Get a room!" a female voice yelled in our direction. Kyle pulled his lips off mine and looked toward the source. It was a woman walking down the beach, and she did not look pleased by our display of unabashed passion. I pulled my arms out from under his shirt and covered my mouth as I giggled in embarrassment.

Kyle laughed out loud before shouting, "Thanks, we will."

The woman shooed us with her hand as if saying 'The hell with you' and marched on her way. Kyle lifted me off him and stood up. His pants were tented in the front. Obviously whatever had just happened between us had excited him as much as it had me. He pulled me to my feet.

"Where are we going?"

"We're getting a room."

I liked his thinking.

The walk back to his truck took longer than expected. Kyle wrapped his arm around my waist and pulled me into him. My dazed eyes met his lust-filled ones, and I couldn't control myself. I was back in his arms and we were putting on another public display of affection. Kyle lifted me off the sand, my legs wrapped around his waist, and carried me a few feet to the public bathrooms.

"Are you serious?" A laugh caught in my throat. We rounded the corner to the women's bathroom. "Kyle!"

He deftly held me up with one hand as he attempted to open the door with the other. It was locked. *Thank God.*

"Well, fuck," Kyle verbalized, clear disappointment and frustration in his tone.

"It's just as well because if you think I was going to do you in a public restroom, then you are more delusional than I thought." I smacked him. "Now put me down and find me a more appropriate room."

"Would a hotdog stand suffice?" he grinned.

"Good lord, Kyle. You're like the bargain basement hookup. Is that all I'm worth to you? You couldn't find a nice steak house bathroom somewhere?"

Kyle dropped me to my feet and reached down to adjust himself. He looked up at me with a sheepish grin, pulled me to him again, and whispered in my ear, "How about my truck?"

"I feel like you have to put in more effort."

"Ugh… I don't know any five star facilities in the area," he protested, but then he stopped and I could almost see him thinking. "Okay, I know a place nearby, but you have to promise me you won't faint when you get there."

"Faint? Why would I do that?"

Kyle's mouth twisted in a funny way. I searched his eyes for an explanation, but he wasn't giving anything away as he grabbed my hand and led me to his truck. Again I had to be helped up, but this time Kyle nearly chucked me into the leather bucket seat. He ran around to the other side and bounded in like an excited puppy dog. I couldn't help but laugh. This was the guy I remembered from the island. All the stress appeared to be gone, and he had the familiar flicker in his eyes that I'd grown to love.

Kyle was right – the place he took me to was close by. It was a gated community with brightly colored beach-chic townhomes. Kyle punched in a code and drove through the gates. There were only about eight townhomes in the entire complex. Kyle drove to the one in the far back and parked on the street.

"Where are we?"

"My brother's place."

"Jake's?" I asked in surprise.

"Yep." Kyle jumped out of the truck and came around to get me. "We have to hurry before a neighbor sees me and comes over to ask questions."

"You're not supposed to be here?" I gasped.

"No, it's not that. They're Jake's neighbors and will want to know how he's doing. I don't have anything good to tell them. Let's go."

Skeptical, I followed Kyle to the front door. I stood behind him as he unlocked it and held it open for me.

"Should I be here?" I asked as I took a tentative step inside, feeling strangely like a burglar. Looking around, I was struck by the place. It was definitely nice but nothing fancy. Certainly nothing to suggest a musician lived here, much less a rich, famous one.

"It feels like we're trespassing," I whispered.

"Relax. I live here… or at least, I did until Jake met Casey. Then he kicked me to the curb. I was actually in the process of finding my own place until Jake's surgery went to hell, and now everything is on hold. My whole life is on hold." Kyle's voice faltered, and he looked away, the tension returning to his body.

"Hey," I said, pulling him to me.

The flirty Kyle was gone and the vulnerable one was back.

"Did you notice that I didn't faint?" I teased, in an attempt to change the mood.

"I did, actually." He nodded. "And I'm impressed. Most girls would have already knocked me over and been rummaging through his drawers to find a memento."

"How often do you bring girls back here?"

"Never." Kyle laughed. "Jake would kill me."

"Kyle?" I admonished him, stepping out of our embrace. My face flushed with unease. I had no business being in Jake's home. "I think we should go."

"In this case, I don't think he'd mind," Kyle said, pulling me close again.

"In what case?"

"You. Jake liked you. We watched the show together until, you know, everything… anyway, he kept telling me I should call you."

"He did? Why would he like me?" I asked, truly stumped. The idea that someone as famous as Jake would even know who I was blew me away.

Our eyes met, and his face relaxed. "He liked you... because you liked me."

Kyle's words warmed me, making me feel, for the first time, that he had given more thought to our relationship than I'd previously given him credit for. "How could he know I liked you?"

Kyle dropped his head to the side, grinning, "Seriously? You were like a lovesick schoolgirl. Your big blue eyes going all mushy... everyone saw it."

I dipped my face into my hands in embarrassment. "Oh, god. I thought I was being so sly."

"Yeah. You weren't."

"You must think I'm such an idiot," I said through my fingers.

Kyle pulled my hands away and lifted my chin.

"I don't. I promise. If you want the truth, I was flattered. Having someone pine for me isn't something I'm used to."

"You said on the island that you felt invisible."

"Yeah. It's weird being related to someone as famous as Jake. When I'm with him in a crowd, people jockey for position, knocking me out of the way to get closer to him. And women – I mean, they'll do anything to get at him. I figured out a way to take advantage of that."

I nodded. I was well aware of his womanizing. He'd been very open about it on the island. Although I wasn't thrilled about his man whoring ways, if it were his past, I could overlook it.

"Don't look at me like that," he said. "I'm not doing that anymore."

"What stopped you?"

Kyle didn't reply for the longest time. I waited patiently because I desperately needed to hear his answer. "I can't really explain it, but I've changed. Remember that time you came and sat with me on the beach, and you had that bucket full of nasties?"

I nodded.

"And you said, 'Someday I'm going to be somebody'?"

"I remember."

"Well, so am I."

I smiled. "I don't doubt it for a second."

He leaned into me and our lips touched. I wrapped my arms around him and pleasured in the feel of him. Kyle began walking me backward.

"Where are we going?" I asked between kisses.

"My room."

Somehow we made it up the stairs, and Kyle pushed the door to his bedroom open with his foot. Our lips never stopped working, our tongues twining in effort. Then we were on his bed, Kyle closing the space between us, and his heat melted the last of my resolve. At that moment I didn't care that we were trespassing in a rock star's house. And it wasn't really trespassing if Kyle lived here, right?

And then he was on top me and our lips crushed together, mouths open, tongues engaged in a war of erotic wills, and I didn't give two shits anymore. My desire for Kyle trumped all rational thought. I'd wanted him for so long. Crazed with desire for this man, I threw myself shamelessly at him. My excitement aroused him further and his hands were under my shirt in a flash, attempting to unbuckle my bra. I could feel his eagerness and also his frustration as the clasp wouldn't give way. Kyle groaned and finally gave up. I fought the urge to giggle.

Not to be deterred, he grabbed at my shirt, pulling it over my head. I tried to get his shirt off too, but we were all hands and tongues and writhing bodies. He broke the kiss long enough to take off his own shirt and unbuckle his jeans. The entire twenty seconds we were apart, my hands were groping him. Kyle's eyes were lust-filled as he sank down on top of me. I ran my nails over his back, shaking with desire. Sliding my hands into his jeans and under his boxers, I grabbed his butt and forced him deeper onto me, and we were grinding into each other.

Kyle pushed himself up and grabbed the waistband of my jeans. I helped him get them off before he easily slid his own down his slim waist. My hands were on him and his on me. We were quickly losing control.

"Condom," I panted but he was already a step ahead and was ripping open the little package. It took him a minute to get it on, but once he did he was hastily back in the game. I opened my legs for him and he sank himself into me with a grunt. I gasped, excitement coursing through me, then grabbed his ass and pushed him in deeper. I'd wanted him for so long and the idea that he was mine, even just for the night, was overwhelming.

He thrust into me as his hand went back to my bra and he cupped the lacy fabric. There was a clear look of disappointment on his face. He had failed to release my breasts once, but he wasn't done trying. Laying all his weight on me, he grasped the cups and lifted the entire bra up and over my head. My ample bosom lifted with the effort and then bounced back in response. This time I did laugh. Kyle was nothing if not persistent.

"What?" He smiled at me with that clueless look that I'd come to love.

"If at first you don't succeed, use force."

Propping himself on one elbow, Kyle thrust deeper into me and I moaned my approval. His other hand had hold of my breasts, and his eyes were wide with wonder.

"Damn, Kenzie," he said, and then went to town, lapping at my nipples.

My hips were working furiously now, pressing into his. I was close. Our grunts changed to whimpering as the moment drew near. His finger found my clit and I lost it, climaxing seconds before him in a display of intense and uncontrolled arousal. Kyle continued pushing until he too was spent.

When we were both satiated, his mouth found mine again and we kissed. His eyes were fixed on mine. "You're beautiful," he whispered.

I'd never considered myself that before, but now with the guy I adored hovering over me with that lustful look in his eyes, I felt beautiful and desired. But I also felt something else… foreboding. I had a strange feeling that this might be our one and only night together. And if that were the case, I planned to make it count.

The next morning we were eating cereal in the kitchen of the townhouse. I was dressed in Kyle's t-shirt. His hand was moving higher up on my thigh. I batted it away.

"Remember on the island how I was so hungry that there were times you thought I might hurt you?"

"Yeah."

"Well, this is one of those times."

Kyle lifted both his hands in surrender and backed away, laughing. I looked around the place and was struck by the paintings on the wall. They were dark and haunting but strangely beautiful. Kyle followed my gaze.

"Jake painted those."

"No, he didn't," I gasped.

He nodded. "I have no idea what they mean."

"They're such soulful paintings."

"You think?" Kyle said, looking surprised. "I don't know anything about art. They look like a bunch of blobs of paint to me."

"He never told you what they meant?"

"Jake's a private person." Kyle shrugged, disappointment clouding his features. "He doesn't talk to me about stuff like that."

"Huh." I tore my eyes away from the paintings and glanced around the room. One thing struck me as peculiar. "You know what's weird? A musician lives here, but I haven't seen one instrument."

Kyle reached his hand out to me. "Come."

I let him pull me to my feet and lead me over to a door, which I assumed led to the other townhome attached to his. But I was wrong. On the other side of the door was a full music studio, chock full of every instrument you could imagine.

"This once belonged to another musician. The townhome was converted into one unit a long time ago so the guy could put the studio in. It's totally soundproof. That's why Jake bought this place."

"Wow. This is hella cool."

Kyle rolled his eyes. "And there's that word again."

"What? *Hella* is a cool word."

"No. I live in the cool part of California, and I can assure you, it isn't."

I stuck out my tongue at him.

"Careful, Kenzie, or I'll take that as an invitation." He sidled up to me and wrapped his hand around me, pulling me up tight against him. I groaned as he leaned in and nibbled at my neck. "Damn," Kyle complained. "I wish we could be together all day, but I've got to get back to the hospital."

"I figured. When do you need to go?"

"Now."

"When can I see you again?"

Kyle winced. "I feel bad, but I probably won't be able to see you again until tomorrow. Jake has a test today and…"

"Hey. Stop," I interrupted. "You don't have to explain yourself."

"You sure?"

"Yes."

"At least you'll be happy to know that I decided to go to the show's final taping."

"You are? That's smart. What changed your mind?"

"You. The Sunset. Sex. Oh… and the fact that I don't want to get sued."

Chapter Thirty-Seven

KYLE

Finale

I paced back and forth as I waited for the driver to pick me up and take me to the studio for the show's finale. The last thing I wanted was to go on television when things were the way they were, but I was contractually obligated, and the legal ramifications were something I didn't want to deal with. Not now.

Wringing my hands in nervous anticipation, I looked around at the empty room. This was supposed to be my night, my debutante ball. Originally everyone had planned to be in the audience to support me, even Jake, if he was healed enough after surgery. But things didn't always go as planned, and now I was alone, as the vigil continued on at the hospital.

A knock on the door shook me from my thoughts. For one fleeting moment I thought maybe someone from my family might be on the other side, but when I opened the door and saw the limo driver, I dipped my head in disappointment and followed him out to the waiting vehicle. My stomach was clenched tightly from the anxiety of the unknown. I was being whisked to a live taping where my family tragedy would, mostly likely, be exploited for ratings and would no doubt dominate my airtime. Once again I was taking a backseat to my own life. The fact that I felt resentment pissed me off and made me feel worse. Of course I didn't blame Jake, I just wished things could have played out differently – not only for him but for myself.

The car took me to a private entrance where I was met by some of the network bigwigs, a lawyer, the show's host, and one of the producers. These were the last people I wanted to be cornered by.

"Where is everyone else?" I asked. If I couldn't have my family here for support, I at least wanted my friends.

"We'll take you to them in a few minutes. We just wanted to talk to you about our expectations for tonight," said a guy I'd never seen before.

Nervous dread rushed through me. What the hell did he mean by that?

"I thought all that was expected of me was to show up, and I did. What more do you want from me?"

"We want to make sure you don't show any animosity towards the show or network," he answered.

"Why would I do that?" I asked, seriously annoyed that they considered me a risk.

"Well, because you've been a little difficult to deal with the last couple weeks."

"Oh, I'm sorry I wasn't more considerate of your feelings," I snapped.

"Kyle, we understand this is a trying time…" the producer began.

"No offense, but it's more than 'trying.'"

"Yes, well, you have our sympathies, but your family issues do not negate the contract, and I'm sure you don't want any legal troubles, especially not now," the lawyer threatened.

"I appreciate your concern for my well-being."

"You're expected to answer questions and be as close to the character you were on television," the first guy said.

"Character? That was me."

"Oh, right, yes. Be like you, then."

"Can I go now?" I asked, trying to escape before I said something I knew I would live to regret.

"Yes, but one more thing," the host said, actually looking remorseful. "The audience is expecting me to ask you about Jake. How you answer is up to you."

The inquisitors left me then, and I was cycled through a series of people to get me ready to appear in front of the cameras. By this point I was cranky and on edge. Definitely not the Kyle they were demanding.

Finally I was brought to the room where the others were waiting. I sighed with relief at the friendly faces that greeted me. My eyes fixed on Kenzie, and I had to blink a few times to take her all in. She was wearing a light pink dress with a little crown hairband. With her sideswept hair and glamorous makeup, Kenzie really did look like a fictional princess. I smiled. She beamed. In a daze, I walked over and kissed her on the cheek. Several other contestants seemed surprised by our affection. It was the common assumption, not only of everyone in this room but also the viewing audience, that I hated Kenzie... which, after the other night, was the furthest thing from the truth. Still, we had both agreed to keep our budding romance a secret for now. With everything that was happening, the last thing I needed was more media attention.

Dale hobbled up to me, his foot in a medical boot. The sheepish grin on his face made me laugh. "No way!" I exclaimed loudly. "What now?"

"Well, if you ever looked at my texts, you would have seen that I crashed into another skier in Lake Tahoe and twisted my ankle."

I shook my disbelieving head. "I swear to god, Dale, you need to wear a helmet and be packed in popcorn at all times."

"I know. I know. I knew you were going to give me shit." He smiled widely before his face took on a more serious expression. "Are you doing okay? I've been worried about you. You stopped responding to me."

"I know. I'm sorry. It's just been…" I had to stop for fear of my emotions getting the better of me.

"Hey, it's okay. We'll talk later. Oh, and my kids really want to meet the guy who did the impossible and made their dad cool, so don't disappear right away after the taping."

"I won't."

"Will I get to meet any of your family?"

"No. It's just me," I answered. "They're with Jake."

"Oh, yeah, of course. We'll be your surrogate family tonight."

"That's what I was counting on."

It was funny – normally I wouldn't know a guy like Dale, much less hang out with him, but his friendship had changed me for the better. He felt like family to me.

I saw the light blue suit before I actually saw the man filling it out. Carl. My eyes scanned him in amusement. He looked like a giant cotton candy as he came in for a quick and impersonal man-slap-hug.

"I'm so sorry about Jake," Carl said, dropping his head and shaking it. Wow, Kenzie's humanization classes had worked wonders on the man. He actually seemed genuinely saddened by Jake's condition.

"Thanks, man, and I promise when he wakes up I'll get you backstage."

Carl nodded and slapped me on the shoulder. Pain radiated through my side and my knees threatened to buckle right out from under me.

Marsha strolled up then, dressed in a classy pantsuit, her signature pigtails gone for the night and her hair instead swept up into a tight bun. She looked like a business executive. Upon seeing the look of surprise on my face, Marsha grinned and hooked her finger into a bra strap on her shoulder.

Theatrically, I covered my hand over my mouth. "Marsha, no?"

"Oh, don't be so dramatic, it's just a bralette." She came in for a hug and, as always, gave my butt cheek a pat. I'd come to accept her unique greetings as a form of endearment.

"Was this outfit your idea?" I asked, as I gestured to her ensemble.

"Do you really think I would let those goons decide for me?"

Marsha's words hit me to the core. No, I didn't suspect she would, but I certainly was letting everyone and their lawyer make decisions for me. At that moment, I wasn't so sure I wanted to force a smile on my face and pretend to be the dopey guy from the show. I was going to be *the me* who sat at my brother's bedside for fifteen hours a day, every day, and if they didn't like it, then too fucking bad.

The activity around us intensified, and cheers from the crowd could be heard. We were taken down the hall and told to huddle by the side of the stage until further notice. I sidled up next to Kenzie and put my arm around her.

"I thought we were keeping this a secret."

"You look incredible," I whispered into her ear. "So beautiful. I just can't keep it to myself."

"Then don't." She smiled happily. "I see Marsha still can't keep her hands off you. I'm going to have to have a talk with her."

"No need to worry about Marsha. We're strictly platonic."

Our conversation was interrupted as we were guided out onto the stage to the overwhelming approval of the crowd. We followed in a line according to our bootlist. Those kicked off first were the first in line, and those of us who'd lasted the longest got the coveted spots in back. I looked out over the audience as I walked with the rest of the cast members towards center stage, and then nearly stopped in my tracks when I saw who was sitting in the first row. As each person came into view, my stoic exterior crumbled and clear emotion crossed over my shocked face.

My parents, Keith, Emma, Sam, Quinn, and Grace had all come. I didn't know why it surprised me so much. We'd talked briefly last week about them coming to the taping, but the look of stress on my mother's face at the prospect of leaving Jake led me to offer her a pass. We never spoke of the show again. I'd just assumed no one was coming, and now I felt bad for the lack of faith I'd shown in them. There were times in my life that I felt sidelined and over-shadowed, but tonight was not one of them.

I caught my mom's eye, and she smiled.

"Thank you," I mouthed.

I saw her eyes fill with tears as she mouthed back, "I love you."

———

The live show started with the reading of the votes for the three finalists. Two were called for Carl, then two for Kenzie, with all the rest coming in for Carl, clinching him the victory. I watched Kenzie for her reaction. Her radiant smile never faltered. She appeared genuinely happy for Carl. It was ironic. Had she not helped him with his social game, he never would have won. But that was the type of person she was, and I was proud of her.

Although she didn't know how the show's votes would pan out, Kenzie had had months to ponder the outcome and had already come to the realization that she was a long shot to win. She'd told me that she was just hoping for a second place finish, which came with its own healthy pay-check; and with Lena not getting a single vote, Kenzie easily clinched that runner-up spot.

Once the winner was announced, Lena, Carl, and Kenzie joined the rest of us in the cast and the questions began. The few inquiries directed my way were lighthearted and fun, and I found myself having a great time reminiscing with the others. Toward the end of the live taping, Kenzie was asked the question we knew was coming.

"You made the decision to vote Kyle out, after admitting to him that you liked him. You seemed pretty torn up by the decision. If you had to do it over, would you make the same decision?"

"It's hard to say. Even before Lena came to me, I already knew Kyle was my biggest competition. I made the choice that was right for me. Really, it was a compliment to Kyle."

"He might disagree," the host grinned, and then turned to me expectantly, waiting for my answer.

"Wow, thanks, Kenzie," I answered, sarcastically.

The audience laughed.

"Honestly, though, there are no hard feelings. At the time, I was just butt hurt. Kenzie played a smart, kick-ass game. More power to her."

"So have the two of you had a chance to talk since the show ended?"

We exchanged knowing glances, and then Kenzie said, "We kissed and made up."

"And then some," I added, grinning.

The audience, as well as the other cast members, went wild at my comment. Lena actually got up and scooted me into her seat so I could be beside Kenzie. I put my arm around her, and she gazed up at me with a surprised but ecstatic smile. So much for keeping it quiet.

Once everyone had settled down after my unexpected comment, the host asked, "So then are you two a couple?"

I placed my hand on her knee and gave the most vague of answers, "It's, you know…."

He waited for me to elaborate, and when I didn't, his demeanor changed, and I knew what was coming. My stomach clenched in anticipation.

"Of course I have to ask you about Jake. There's been such an outpouring of support for him. Has your family drawn strength from that?"

His question surprised me. It was thoughtful and didn't sensationalize the tragedy. I was grateful for his compassion and answered as honestly as possible. "Yeah, you know, on behalf of my family and Jake, I want to thank everyone for their prayers and good wishes. I promise you, they haven't gone unnoticed."

"Has there been any change in his condition?"

"No."

"Well, I think I speak for everyone when I wish you and your family the best."

The conversation moved on to Carl and what he planned to do with his winnings. I had stopped listening. My heart was pounding out of its chest. Kenzie grabbed my hand and squeezed, and I let out a sigh of relief. That hadn't been so bad, and with Kenzie by my side, I was finally breathing a little easier. Now all I needed was Jake back.

CHAPTER THIRTY-EIGHT

KENZIE
Facing the Truth

Losing out on the million dollars was not a surprise. I already knew it was a long shot. Carl had killed it during the final vote. So honest and human, he deserved the money as much as anyone, and I was happy for my friend. I had long ago come to the realization that I'd be playing for second, and when Lena received no votes at all, I knew I'd done it. The prize money for a second-place finish was nothing to sneeze at. I would have enough to give some to my dad and then start up my new life here, in Southern California, near Kyle. I understood that there were no guarantees, but I'd kick myself in the butt if I didn't give it a shot with him. I was young and free and had some cash in my pocket. The future looked bright.

Immediately following the show, the cast members' families crowded the stage. My dad and siblings pushed past the throngs of well-wishers to be by my side. You would have thought I'd won the whole thing by how excited my siblings were for me.

My sister tugged on my arm and whispered, "Is that Kyle's brother?"

I followed her wide, swoony eyes to a teenage boy standing with Kyle. "I have no idea, but he looks like Jake, so probably."

"He's so hot. Take me over there and introduce me."

"Caroline, no. I haven't met his family."

"Kyle's your boyfriend, isn't he?"

"What? No. I don't know. Maybe. No."

"So what is it? Make up your mind."

"I have no idea what we are."

"Then what exactly did he mean by 'and then some'?" Caroline grinned slyly.

"That's none of your business." I poked her in the side. "And don't you dare joke about that in front of Dad," I added in a barely audible voice.

"Oh… he's coming over," my sister gasped, but then her excitement fizzled just as quickly. "Damn, the brother's not."

Kyle strode over to us. He caught my eye and smiled, and I returned the gesture. Caroline looked between us in awe.

"Hi, I'm Caroline, Kenzie's sister. Is that your brother?"

I gaped at her in shocked admiration. Ballsy. That's what she was. How had we come from the same parents?

"Quinn?" Kyle asked, looking surprised. Caroline shrugged and pointed him out for Kyle. He grinned and called over her choice. Quinn bounded up to us, much like I'd seen Kyle do a hundred times on the island. "Quinn, this is Caroline. Caroline is Kenzie's sister."

"Hey." He smiled, eyes bright.

"Hey," she answered back.

"Wow, such stimulating conversation," Kyle whispered in my ear.

I nodded and laughed. Grabbing his arm, I steered him over to my dad and brothers and introduced them. My father hadn't been real thrilled with Kyle's on-air admission, which basically confirmed for the world that we'd had sex. To Dad's credit, however, he played it cool and didn't punch Kyle in the face. My brothers didn't care about any of that, though, as they were starry-eyed upon meeting Kyle for the first time. He had been their favorite player on the show… and that was with me added to the mix.

As the boys chatted for a few minutes, I glanced over to see Caroline and Quinn exchanging numbers. If only it could be that easy for all of us.

Kyle came over to my side.

"Looks like they're hitting it off," I said.

"Yeah. Shocking. It's like Quinn has gone from mega-dork to badass babe magnet overnight."

"He better not give her 'and then some.'"

"Oh, god, I know. Sorry. That was bad. It just slipped out. You know I can't control what comes out of my mouth sometimes."

"Your parents are going to think I'm a slut."

"You're kidding me, right? Their son's a rock star. The women they've seen…" he shook his head playfully. "You're like the Virgin Mary."

"Stop," I laughed. "Where are they, anyway?"

"They left already, and took Grace, Keith, and Sam back to the hospital. It's just Emma and Quinn. Come on, I'll introduce you to my sister."

I glanced at her as we walked up. Emma was beautiful: blonde, high cheek bones, and gorgeous light hazel eyes. Dang. Every one of Kyle's siblings was attractive. What were the chances of having that many kids and not getting at least one stinker in the bunch? I wondered if Kyle's parents high-fived each other every night before going to bed at what gorgeous kids they'd produced.

Bobby was chatting up Emma when we arrived. I had to wonder what *she* would rank on his beauty scale. Kyle and he exchanged handshakes. "Sorry about starving you," he said, smiling.

"That's okay. Sorry for kicking your ass off the island."

"No hard feelings," Bobby said, and turned to Kyle's sister. "Call me."

"Yeah, sure," she nodded. As soon as he sauntered away, she deleted his number from her contacts.

"Not your type?" Kyle asked, grinning.

"Is he anybody's type? You left me stranded, jerk," Emma said, punching Kyle in the arm. "That's eight minutes of my life I can never reclaim."

"Sorry, geez."

"I don't get how you guys put up with him," she said.

"We had Marsha to even things out," Kyle joked. "Emma, this is Kenzie."

"Hi, nice to meet you, and I'm sorry about my brother's stupid comment," she grinned. "He can be an idiot sometimes, but he means well."

I laughed. "It's all good. My father didn't hurt him, so that's positive."

"It really is a wonder Kyle isn't beaten up more often."

"Emma, you're supposed to be making me look good."

"Oh, in that case, this guy's a keeper," she said with a smile.

Emma and I chatted for a few minutes until Dale pulled us away to meet his family. As Kyle hit it off with Dale's kids, I chatted up his wife. She thought it was hysterical how Kyle had hipped up her husband and now he was the most popular carpool dad at the school. We also met Carl's daughter, Trina. She was unmistakably his, with her red curly hair and spattering of freckles. And at only ten years old, she was already taller than me. But physical features aside, Trina differed from her dad in a very important way: she was filled with confidence and happiness. I smiled at Carl as she chattered aimlessly with me. He shrugged his wide shoulders and went back to adoring her.

Once Trina was shooting the breeze with Kyle, Carl pulled me aside and gave me a hug.

"I couldn't have won without you, Kenzie. I owe you so much. If you need any money or anything…"

"No, I'm good. I won a nice little sum myself. I'm happy for you. You deserved it."

"I don't know about that." He shook his head. "Go out there and make a life for yourself. You understand? Don't compromise."

"I won't."

Kyle was leaning into me, almost on my lap, and his hands were roaming my body as our mouths worked furiously. He was with me, but I could tell he wasn't really *with me*. Even this make-out session seemed his way of appeasing me. I'd been here for four days, but aside from our first night together, we'd spent the rest of our time at the hospital. I knew he was trying to squeeze in time with me while still staying devoted to Jake, but the stress of the situation was wearing him down. Instead of my company being a good thing for Kyle, it seemed to just be adding to his anxiety levels. If he was with me, Kyle felt guilty for being away; and if he was with his brother, he was worrying about me sitting alone on a chair outside Jake's hospital room. I tried to reassure him that I didn't need entertaining, but Kyle kept trying to carve out moments like this to spend with me.

Waking up this morning, I knew what needed to be done, for his sake. My family was driving back to northern California today, and I'd be making the trip back with them. I wanted to be there for Kyle, but not like this. It was clear that, at this moment in his life, there was no room for me, and it was selfish to stay if all was I doing was piling more weight onto his shoulders. Kyle's devotion to his brother was absolute, and my presence was a distraction he hadn't asked for.

He pushed me further down until he was on top of me, his hand between my legs. We were on the couch in the apartment, and there was a revolving door of his family members making their way through it at all hours of the day.

"Kyle, stop."

"It's okay. No one will be here for a while."

"You have no way of knowing that," I said, sitting up.

"I know." He groaned and moved off me. "You're right. Maybe we can go to Jake's place later. I can't now, but maybe… I don't know when. Maybe later."

His words only reinforced my decision. Kyle's forehead was creased with strain, and his eyes looked tired and wary. I cupped his jaw and gave him a tender kiss.

"I think I have to leave," I whispered.

"I'm sorry. I know I haven't had much time today. Maybe tomorrow will be better. "

"I meant, go home."

"Oh." Kyle took a deep breath and exhaled loudly. He slumped over, running his hands through his hair and grasping the strands. We sat in silence, neither of us really knowing what to say. Kyle's phone buzzed, and he checked it.

"Is everything okay?"

"Um, yeah. I might have to leave in a few minutes, though. The test results are back. Are you saying we're done?"

"I'm saying you're in no position to start a new relationship."

"I've been trying, Kenzie. I'm doing the best I can."

"I know that, but you're trying too hard, and that's why I have to go. If I could stay here and be a support for you, I would in a heartbeat, but that's not what's happening here and you know it. You need to be there for your family and not worrying about me."

Kyle buried his head in his hands. I wrapped my arms around him.

"I'm not trying to hurt you, Kyle. I'm trying to make this easier on you."

"Why do things always have to be so…" He stopped in the middle of his sentence, struggling to find the words.

I touched his face, running my hands tenderly over the rough patches of whiskers. My lips brushed over his as I dusted them with my affection. "It doesn't have to be a goodbye. We can think of it as a 'to be continued'."

"So when Jake wakes up, we can try again?"

"Yes," I agreed, swallowing the lump in my throat. There was just too much uncertainty in his life to pin my hopes on a future together, and I had a terrible feeling that this was it for us. I stood up. "I'm going to go now," I managed to say before the emotions caught up to me and I gulped back a sob.

"Kenzie." Kyle stood too, grabbing my hand and pulling me into a hug. We held onto each other for a long time. The sadness I'd been struggling to keep in check poured out of me. The reality of our situation weighed heavily on my heart. If the time had been right, we could have been something great, but the fairytale ending I'd imagined with him couldn't overcome the pressures of real life. I pulled out of Kyle's arms.

"I have to go," I sniffled. "My dad is waiting in the parking lot."

"Do you want me to walk you down?"

"No. Go back to Jake. He needs you."

Without another word, we exited the apartment, Kyle heading off in one direction, and I in the other.

"Goodbye," I whispered.

CHAPTER THIRTY-NINE

KYLE

The Awakening

I'd never been good at hiding my emotions and wasn't surprised that Kenzie saw straight through my pathetic façade. She was right to leave me. I would never have room for her in my life as long as Jake lay unresponsive in his. And there was no way for me to explain that to her without divulging the injustice that bound me to my brother in the first place. So I went on with my sad existence, pushing thoughts of her from my mind as I hung on my brother's every tiny flinch. He was in there somewhere, and I wasn't giving up until there was no hope left to hold.

But as the days went on with no change, my family slowly began to deconstruct. Managing tragedy had never been our strong point, and it didn't help that we'd been given more than our fair share of it. Heartbreak had a way of bringing out the worst in all of us. Arguments erupted. Words that could never be taken back were spoken. Feelings were hurt. Apologies attempted. Wash, rinse, and repeat. The McKallister clan was nothing if not consistent in our grieving methods.

Keeping my focus on Jake, I put every last bit of my tattered soul into saving my brother's. Choosing the nightshift to give my overly exhausted parents a break, I kept vigil at Jake's bedside in the dead of night for hours on end. When the medical complications first sent him into the coma, I didn't have one-sided conversations with him like the others did, choosing instead to just sit there impassively, wallowing in my misery, as I obsessively watched him breathe. But after this past week, and Kenzie and the show, something broke open in me, and I couldn't hold back my grief any longer.

That first night after Kenzie left, I just cried – ten years' worth of tears shamelessly poured out of me. Thankfully there was no one to judge me except my comatose brother, who didn't seem to mind my waterworks. Then, in the days that followed, my silent grief found a voice. The thoughts inside my head escaped with such brazen intensity that I wondered how'd they'd all managed to get along up there in my muddled brain. The trivial words came first. Simple stories. Mild observations. Then the deeper layers made their way to the surface: pain, heartbreak, betrayals. From there, the hidden tiers of my psyche pushed their way through the crowds as I recounted every goddamn insecurity I'd ever harbored. Jake was like a slumbering priest and I the disgraced sinner, looking for absolution.

Yet still I held back. That one shameful memory clung to its refuge, refusing to seek amnesty with the others. Whether I kept it safe for my sake or Jake's wasn't clear. In consciousness, Jake had always placed a muzzle on any mention of that day, and my guilt kept me from pushing for answers. But now, with my brother in no condition to protest my insolence, my secret shame crept from the shadows.

"I'm going to start by saying that your objection to this conversation is duly noted. But seeing as you are the asshole who won't wake up, I'm going to dump my shit in your lap and see how you like it."

I realized I was being a total dick, but I couldn't help myself. When I'd first started talking to Jake, my words were kind and quiet and gentle, as if harsh tones might keep him from waking. But as the days went on and he didn't open his eyes, my tone turned sharp and challenging. I was pissed at the world and furious at Jake for remaining in his stupid fucking coma.

"So here it goes. I'm sorry. I'm so damn sorry. I've done way too many dumb things in my life, but that…" My voice faltered, and more tears threatened to burst forth. I had no idea my body could produce so many. "That's one I can't ever take back. If I had just listened to Mom, to you, we wouldn't be here today, and I own that. I'll never forgive myself. And the worst part is, I don't know how you feel about what happened because you never talk about it. Are you mad at me? Do you blame me? Because you should! We were supposed to go the skate park, and you, like the obedient, kiss-ass you were, just mindlessly followed directions. As always, I was the one to lead you astray. I wanted to go to the business park to ride the handrails on the stairs. You said no because we'd gotten in trouble the time before, but it was a Sunday, and no one was there to bust us. I totally played you. All I had to do was insult your skate jumping skills and you were like putty in my hands. Why did you have to be so damn competitive? And why would you even listen to me in the first place? You knew I never made good decisions. Jesus Christ, Jake, how could you have been so stupid?"

I stopped myself. Talk about blaming others for my own shortcomings. Was I seriously pissed at Jake for getting kidnapped when I was the one who'd led him to his doom?

"Okay, sorry, that was a dick move to blame you. Don't be mad. Let me start over. So…" Something caught my eye and I stopped talking. Had his hand just moved? His pointer finger… it moved. Or was I just seeing things? "Jake? Are you awake?" I grabbed his hand. "Squeeze my hand if you can hear me."

I waited. Nothing. Had I just imagined that?

"Jake?" I called to him again, but this time got right up next to his face and blasted his name in his ear. He didn't flinch. I sat back and stared at him for the longest time, willing him to give me a sign that he was in there somewhere.

After several minutes of false hope, I continued my confession. "In my defense, Jake, I didn't know he'd be there. How could I have known that? I mean, he just appeared out of nowhere. I saw him first and panicked. I remember the confusion in your eyes when he grabbed you. You didn't even see him coming. I should have warned you, but it happened too fast. One minute we were fine. The next…" I stopped again, feeling the emotions overwhelm me. "The way he played us against each other, threatening to hurt the other if we didn't obey. It was like he knew we were brothers. How would he know that? I mean, if it was just random, how would he have known?"

That part of the story had never made sense to me. The common assumption was that the kidnapping had been completely indiscriminate, and that Ray had seen us heading toward the business park and had followed us there.

"We were just in the wrong place at the wrong time, that's what they said… the place I brought us to. But if that were true, how would he have known we were brothers? How would he have known we would do anything to protect each other? It certainly wasn't by observing us at the business park because, if you remember, we spent the majority of our time there arguing over who had the better jump off the stairs. I did, by the way."

I stopped and watched his face for a reaction. If he were listening, that last bit would have swayed him to open his eyes. He'd always hated losing to me. But Jake didn't move, so I continued.

"Anyway, I guess it doesn't matter how it happened, just that it did. What I remember most about that day was your eyes. You were talking to me through them and it was like I understood exactly what you were saying. I mean, we didn't speak, but I knew what you wanted. At least I think I did. Maybe I read it all wrong. Maybe you weren't telling me what I thought you were because you never talk about that day. Why? Jake, why did it have to come to this for us to talk about what happened? I have so many questions. Why did you want me to leave you there? Why did you tell me to run? If you knew he was going to take you, why didn't we make a stand and fight? Maybe we could have stopped him together. What did you know that I didn't? Did he say something to you?"

I could feel myself getting heated, and had to pull back and take a few deep breaths. When I thought of that day, it brought up a lot of negative feelings and one of them was anger... toward Jake. His silence had trapped me in a sort of purgatory. I couldn't stay in the past because it was too painful, but I couldn't move forward because of the guilt. If he had just screamed at me, blamed me, beat the living shit out of me… anything would have been preferable to his silence.

"I tried to help you. You know I did. He slammed my head into the concrete. He broke my arm. But you could have run when he was holding me down. Why didn't you? You could have saved yourself too, asshole. Why did you have to put it all on me? Why did you make me run instead?"

The more I talked, the more questions I had, and the more confused I became. He had to have known something I didn't. It was the only explanation. Would I have to go through the rest of my life not knowing? How could I ever let it go if I didn't have the closure I obviously needed? I searched his face for answers. Nothing. He was just blank. Frustrated, I drew his eyelid open with my finger.

"Are you in there?" I asked. "Jake? Wake up. Open your eyes."

Nothing. That's what I always got from Jake. Nothing! Rage bubbled up inside and I let loose. "Wake the fuck up, Jake. You owe me something." I stared angrily into his clear, unfocused eye. "Do you hear me? WAKE UP! Why are you doing this to me?"

Just saying those words made me cringe. My selfishness knew no bounds. I closed his eye and smoothed his hospital gown down.

"Sorry. Sorry, I didn't mean that. You know I didn't. I love you. You didn't do anything wrong. I'm just so tired,

Jake. I guess I just… I guess I thought I'd have more time to get the answers, like our whole lives – but that never works out for us, does it?"

After running out of questions that might never be answered and feeling more exhausted than I had in a long time, I laid my head on his bed.

"I'm sorry," I whispered, my lids heavy with sleep. I didn't remember closing them.

His eyes pleaded with me to go. I shook my head no. I wouldn't leave him. 'Run!' He jerked his head toward the parking lot behind me, desperation clear on his face. 'Run.' So I did. As fast as I could, I ran away from them. I could hear Ray chasing me, threatening to shoot. Then Jake's muffled screaming came from behind the gag. "Run!" The footsteps suddenly reversed, moving away from me. I turned, and Jake had taken off in the opposite direction, forcing Ray to make a decision. Him or me? Ray chose Jake. And I lived.

"Kyle?" My mom woke me at seven in the morning. I opened my groggy eyes. "You look terrible."

"Thanks," I mumbled, rubbing my heavy lids.

"I'm worried about you."

"I know. You tell me everyday."

"And I mean it everyday. Do you want to talk?"

"You know I don't."

Mom sighed. "Kyle. You can't keep going like this. It's not healthy."

"I'm an adult and not your problem anymore."

"I never said you were a problem."

"Not today," I challenged.

"Not ever."

I scoffed. We both knew that wasn't true. Sure, our family was falling apart as Jake lay in a coma, but this was child's play compared to where we'd all collectively fallen that month Jake had gone missing. It had brought out the worst in every one of us. But my mother, in particular, directed her vitriol towards me and made it clear that I was to blame for Jake's kidnapping. Maybe she hadn't said it in so many words, but the implication was unmistakable. My actions caused the hellfire that rained down upon our family. I was twelve.

"I'm going to the apartment."

Mom touched my forearm and our eyes met. Hers were filled with tears and regret. She had a lot of that. I'd heard "I'm sorry" from her mouth more times than I could count, and although I'd long since forgiven her betrayal, I'd never forgotten. In times of stress and anger, her guilt was the weapon I used against her. I pulled away and walked from the room.

———

The text came in at 2:21pm. It had to ding twice before I woke up and fumbled with my phone. I read the words but they didn't immediately register with me. Then, suddenly my brain turned on and I bolted upright, focusing on the text.

He's awake!!!!

A litany of messages followed, each more shocking than the next: *He's alert; trying to communicate; miracle.* Jake was awake! I crazily yanked my legs into my jeans as I tried to get my shoes on at the same time, but I got all tangled up and had to force myself to slow down so I could get myself dressed just enough to make it out the door. With my shirt in hand, I ran the whole way, whizzing by hospital staff, patients, and visitors alike. "Slow down" or "No running" or "Put on some clothes" followed me down every hallway, but I didn't listen; my only goal was getting to him. His hand? I hadn't imagined it. He'd moved it last night! Then a thought gripped me, causing my stomach to twist in regret. If he'd been awake last night, then he'd heard everything. Oh, shit, was he going to be pissed!

By the time I got to his room, several family members were already there, gathered around the bed. Mom was leaning down, smiling as she stroked his hair. Dad looked back when he heard me come in and put his hand out to me, guiding me forward. Suddenly, I was scared. Would he still be Jake? Slowly I stepped forward, and my brother turned his head toward me. Our eyes met, and there was intensity in his. He wanted something. I wormed my way to his side and grabbed his hand.

"Last night, were you awake? Could you hear me? Did you move your hand?"

When Jake nodded his head, I thought I might pass out. His hand gripped mine and he pulled me closer. He mouthed something, but no words came out. Thankfully, I knew a thing or two about Jake's non-verbal communication, and I immediately understood what he was asking for.

"Casey's on her way."

———

When Casey arrived, I saw a calm fall over Jake. He reached for her and she was in his arms in seconds. The moment was so private and so incredibly heartfelt that my parents ushered us out to give them some privacy. As we waited in the hallway, I was forced to watch Grace tell anyone who asked how Jake had awoken on her watch. She acted like she had done something miraculous, yet I was the one who'd spent every night the past week at his side. I was the one who'd poured my soul out to him and hadn't slept more than six hours in a row for nearly a month. And then in waltzes a well-rested Grace who spends twenty minutes chattering on and on about all kinds of worthless nonsense, shows him a picture of Chuck the kitten, and he opens his damn eyes for her. Really, Jake? Come on!

I leaned against the wall, feeling dizzy. After the text came in, my heart had been beating so fast. Add my sprint through the hospital and lack of food to the mix, so by the time I'd finally rested for a minute, my body just shut down. Emma put her hand on my shoulder.

"Are you okay?" she asked. "You look pale."

"I'm okay," I replied, but began sliding down the wall nonetheless.

"Someone get a chair," Emma called out, still gripping my shoulder. Quinn came to my side and kept me from falling to the floor. My dad slipped the chair under me and I sank down into it. Once I was sitting, Emma took my pulse. "It's low. If you don't start feeling better, you're going to have to lie on the floor and put your feet up."

"Just give me a second," I spat at her, throwing my hand up rudely in her face. She blinked her surprise, but instead of insulting me back or stomping off in a huff, Emma ignored my insolence and stayed firmly by my side. Slowly, my head stopped spinning.

She took my pulse again and patted my shoulder. "It's a little better now. Just relax a few more minutes. I think you're a little shocked. Your eyes are all cray-cray," she smiled, teasing me.

I took a couple more deep breaths and said, "Thanks. Sorry for biting your head off."

"It's okay."

Quinn brought a chair over for Emma, and she and I sat next to each other in the hall of the hospital, our heads leaning against the wall, just staring off into space.

"I'm sorry," she whispered.

"For what?"

Silence. I turned to look at my sister. She was staring straight ahead.

"You got a raw deal, Kyle."

"Huh?"

"After the kidnapping... you know what I'm talking about." Emma's voice cracked.

"Oh," I quickly looked away. Why did she have to bring that up now? Hadn't I already done enough sharing with Jake last night?

"I didn't know how to help you... and Mom and Dad, they were, well... you know. I guess I just want you to know I'm sorry, for everything."

"I don't blame you, Em."

She turned her head and our eyes met. The tears in hers told me she didn't quite believe me. I reached over and grabbed her hand. She smiled weakly and then sighed so heavily I wondered how long that breath had been trapped inside her body before making such a dramatic exit.

"We're all screwed up, aren't we?" I asked.

She laughed, but it was a bitter sound. "Oh, Kyle, you have no idea."

I'd meant it in a general way and was surprised at my sister's reaction to the question. She'd always seemed so in control and focused. After the kidnapping, it was Emma who'd basically been forced to take over the parenting duties for Grace and Quinn and to make the dinners and run the household. Holy shit. I'd never really given it a second thought before, but now that I considered it more carefully, that had been a lot of damn responsibility dumped on her shoulders at sixteen years of age. I glanced at Grace, who was a year younger now than Emma had been when it all went down. She seemed so young. I couldn't imagine her taking on the jobs that Emma had. All of a sudden, I saw my sister in a different light. I'd always just assumed she'd escaped the curse that seemed to follow Keith, Jake and me, but now I wasn't so sure. Was her Little Miss Perfect act all a façade? Was Emma just as damaged as the rest of us?

Jake improved hour to hour, and by nightfall his speech was back, although at times he sounded like a drunken soldier. It helped that Casey was there, babbling away. Slow and sluggish at first, Jake rapidly improved, probably because he was forced to keep up with his girlfriend's endless declarations of undying love. The doctors were in and out doing random tests, and they were amazed by the speed of his recovery. He still had a long way to go, especially with his knee, but it was clear that Jake had dodged a very dangerous bullet.

My parents, Casey, and I stayed by Jake's side all night. Every time he'd fall asleep, panic would grip us all. Would he open his eyes again? Was it all a dream? But a few hours later, he'd awaken feeling even better than before. Slowly but surely, the tension eased as we realized that Jake was going to be okay.

Sometime the next afternoon, my parents left to get some food. Jake was feeling good, and he'd convinced Casey to go home and get a good night's sleep before an exam she had the next morning. After she left was the first time we'd been alone.

"You want to talk?" Jake asked.

"About what?"

"I think you know."

"Are you seriously telling me that you heard what I was saying... in a coma?"

"I don't think I was in it anymore. I'm pretty sure I woke up a few days before I actually opened my eyes. I don't know what happened, Kyle. All I can say is that I heard a lot of stuff. Some things I don't remember, other things are fuzzy, but some of it is clear," he said in a knowing way, making me understand that my midnight rant had been one of those things.

"Okay, so in my defense, you need to know I wasn't blaming you. I was just angry and frustrated."

"I know. I'm not mad. Your anger is justified. We should have talked about it," he sighed, shaking his head. "My silence... it was never meant to punish you. I didn't even know you felt that way. There's just too much I'm holding onto, and I have to let it go or I'm never going to have a stable life. I need to go back into therapy, and I think you do too."

"You think?" I blurted out, with a crazy look on my face. We both laughed. Damn, we were a pitiful pair.

"I guess what you need to know is that it wasn't your fault," Jake said.

I looked down at my hands, which instantly began to shake. Were we really going to do this?

"I should have told you sooner. What happened that day… it wasn't random. He'd been following me. If it hadn't happened at the business park, it would have happened on the way home from school or somewhere else."

"You don't know that," I replied, unconvinced.

"Oh, trust me, I know that."

"How?" I asked, desperation clear in my voice. Jake didn't respond right away. *Please. Please. Tell me how you know that.*

"Remember when we went to the mall a couple days before the kidnapping, and Toby took a swim in the fountain?"

I nodded. "I actually pushed him in."

"I know," he grinned. "Anyway, Ray was there. He followed us home, and my fate was sealed. So stop giving yourself so much damn credit. You had nothing to do with it."

"How do you know that?"

"How do you think I know that? He told me."

I wasn't sure how to respond or how to feel about his admission, but if it were true, it would absolve me of so much guilt.

"Did you talk a lot... to him?"

Jake shrugged. "He talked. I listened. I didn't have much of a choice since I was a captive audience."

"Did he ever say anything about me?"

Jake looked away. I waited, hoping his confessions would keep coming. And they did.

"You were never supposed to live. He was furious that you did."

The expression on Jake's face told me that he'd paid the price for my escape.

"Why did you tell me to run?"

"I didn't know if he was trying to terrify me or what, but while he was cuffing me, Ray whispered in my ear that I'd better say goodbye because he was about to blow a hole through the back of your head. I wasn't being brave, Kyle. I wasn't acting the hero and sacrificing my life so you could live. You were seconds away from being shot dead."

I sat there in stunned disbelief. My hands were white from gripping the side rails on his bed.

"Are you okay?" he asked, studying me with concern.

"I... yeah, I guess," I answered then looked up and caught his eye. "Would it have killed you to tell me this years ago?"

Jake shook his head. "I had no idea you cared."

"Shut up. You knew I struggled with it… with the guilt."

"I know. I'm sorry. I guess I was just so focused on my-self I didn't give you much thought. I swear, Kyle, I'm going to be a better brother to you. I've treated you bad for years, but that all ends now. You aren't going to be my punching bag anymore, I promise."

"I actually didn't really mind being your punching bag," I admitted, a smile spreading across my face. "I got lots of free shit."

"That's true. Maybe I'll still throw a few punches here and there if that would make you happy."

"I'd really like that."

Jake laughed. "Come here."

We hugged. The light mood I was feeling instantly changed the minute his arms wrapped around me. Tears rose up in my eyes once more. This emotional shit really sucked.

"You're wrong, you know," I sniffled.

"About what?"

"About being a hero. You saved my life, whether you want to admit it or not."

After my parents returned, I went back to the apartment. I desperately needed a shower and some protein. I'd been snacking on cookies from the nurse's station all day and had one hell of a sugar headache. Alone for the first time since getting the text that changed my life, I sank down onto the sofa and zoned out. Mentally, I was just so exhausted. I dropped my head into my hands and shook with relief and happiness and redemption. It had been a long ten years.

When I'd finally cleared my head, I picked up the phone. There was only one person I wanted to call. I keyed in her number.

"Hello?"

Emotion overwhelmed me again at the sound of her voice. I struggled to get the words out.

"Kyle?" Her voice immediately turned to panic. "Kyle, please tell me you're okay?"

"Kenzie... he woke up."

KENZIE

Six months later

"Can you tell me what these are, exactly? They look like tiny pitchforks," Kyle asked, holding up a few two-pronged skewers. Then, like a kid playing with swords, he actually made swishing and stabbing motions with them.

"They're for roasting marshmallows," I called out, as I continued packing every item I could fit in the plastic container.

"Oh." Kyle studied the skewers, turning them over and over as if his brain just couldn't comprehend the gadgets' very useful function.

"Put them back," I demanded, but I didn't wait for him to comply before ripping them out of his hands and shoving them back in the container. "I don't want to forget them."

"Right, because we can't possibly use a stick to toast a marshmallow."

"Are you going to help me or are you just going to pull things out of my already packed container?"

"We're going camping, Kenzie. What more do you need other than a tent, a sleeping bag, and yours truly?"

He held his arms out for me to admire his wonderfulness. And although I wasn't immune to his bigheaded charms, I had too much left to pack to argue the point with him.

"Look, why don't you go make yourself useful by rewrapping the sleeping bags or something? I need to get this done."

"Fine," he huffed. From the corner of my eye I watched him walk over to the sleeping bags, nudge them with his shoe, and then untie them and actually rewrap the damn things. I was being facetious with him, but he didn't always pick up on the subtleties. I had to keep from bursting out in laughter. Sometimes I didn't know about that guy, but damned if it wasn't what I loved about him.

The beeping of the horn sent me into a frenzy of activity. I shoved the last of the items in, grabbed the meat from the freezer, and packed it in the cooler. I heard Kyle at the door, and then voices flooded the living room. Excitement fluttered through me. We'd been looking forward to this trip for months. I rounded the corner to find Jake and Casey, both dressed for a frickin' blizzard, side-stepping the boxes littering the living room.

"Sorry," I said as I hugged Jake in his big, bulky jacket. "He moved in two months ago and I'm still trying to get Kyle to unpack his crap, but no one can delay like your brother."

"Don't I know." He smiled at me, his eyes flickering in amusement. I had long ago gotten over the awe of being in the same room as a superstar. Over the past few months, he and Casey had become a part of my little world, and I'd grown to love them like family. Sometimes I marveled at my life now. Last year, I'd been bored and lonely, dreaming of adventure and hoping for a new start. When I sent that video of myself into the show, little did I know how much my life would change. I couldn't remember ever feeling so happy and content.

"You know you love my messy ways," Kyle said, grabbing me as I walked by and slapping my ass. He always enjoyed putting on a show for his brother.

"Oh, yeah? You want it? Let's go then, Stud." I teased, turning to the others. "You two don't mind waiting, do you?"

"Yeah. I mean, I don't mind waiting one minute thirty seconds. What about you, Casey?"

"You think it'll take that long?" she replied.

"I hate you both." Kyle grinned as he set me free.

"Hey, Kenzie. I say you give Kyle a timetable, and if he hasn't unpacked by then, call Goodwill," Casey offered helpfully, as she rummaged through one of the open boxes.

"Dammit, Jake," Kyle blasted. "How many times do I have to ask you to control your fiancée? I'm getting tired of her trying to corrupt my girlfriend."

Jake threw his hands up in the air, and we all laughed. He had no more chance of controlling Casey than Kyle did with me. They were both whipped, and they knew it.

"Hey sister," Casey said, stepping over one of Kyle's tattered video chairs to give me a hug. "This should be the first to go," she whispered.

I nodded in agreement. "So what's with the Eskimo outfits?"

"You said it was cold in Northern California."

"Cold, not Arctic."

"Oh, oops," Casey giggled, and I joined in. She had been my first girlfriend after moving to Southern California. Because Kyle and Jake were so close, Casey and I ended up spending a lot of time together and found that we had many similar interests. It wasn't unusual for the two of us to plan excursions together without the boys. And since Kyle had moved in with me, getting some quality girl time to bitch about his annoying habits was just what I needed.

Yes, he could be maddening at times, but I was head over heels for this guy and considered myself very lucky to have found my way back into his life. Even though Kyle and I hadn't become a couple when I left him in December, my plans to move to Southern California never wavered. With some of my windfall, I found a little apartment off the main strip in Venice Beach and got a job at a party rental place. With my fifteen minutes of fame working in my favor, I even got paid to make appearances at Hollywood parties and dance clubs, and I collected occasional checks for social media endorsements as well. Those paychecks more than doubled when Kyle and I started showing up together.

After we separated back in December, I'd kept in touch with Kyle, and we talked regularly after Jake woke up. And when I moved into my apartment, he and his older brother Keith were there to help me carry in the furniture and unpack. They were also there to eat all the groceries I'd stocked in my fridge and drink the entire case of 36 beers I'd bought for the housewarming.

After getting settled in, Kyle began calling me to hang out. Since Jake wasn't working much, neither was he, so Kyle had a lot of time on his hands. We kept it totally platonic at first, but soon he was dropping by unannounced, and it didn't take long until we were having sex in all two rooms of my tiny apartment. From there our relationship progressed to the point where he would no longer leave, even when I asked him to. Things of his started appearing in my apartment. I'm not even sure how it happened, but three months after I moved in, Kyle had become a permanent fixture on my couch. It just seemed natural to take the next step and ask him to move in. Yet when I formally invited him, the doofus just stared back at me with a blank face and said, 'Oh, I thought I already had.'

"So what are we bringing?" Jake questioned me. "Kyle and I can start packing the truck."

"Oh, I'm glad you asked. So, see *everything* in the apartment?" Kyle answered dramatically, sweeping his arms in giant circles. "Yeah, it's all going."

I rolled my eyes over Kyle in amusement, and then, ignoring his over dramatization of my organization skills, addressed Jake personally: "Just the containers and coolers on the kitchen floor and then all the stuff against the wall."

"Just promise me you won't forget the tiny pitchforks, Kenzie," Kyle begged, hands pressed together in prayer.

"Don't you worry. They're all packed up. And I'll be expecting an apology when you are stuffing your face with s'mores tonight."

"Never," he declared bravely.

I smiled knowingly. I'd be getting my apology, or he wouldn't be getting what he was hoping for in the tent tonight.

Speaking of tents, on our way out of town, the boys needed to stop at their parents' house to pick them up. As we pulled through the fence, I felt nerves fluttering in my stomach. Sometimes I still had to pinch myself that I was living this life: hot boyfriend, sun-kissed days on the beach, mansions of the rich and famous. If it weren't for my job keeping me grounded, I'd think I was in another universe at times.

Casey and I had talked a lot about handling the pressures of being part of the McKallister family. There were dynamics in play that neither of us were privy to, and I suspected that this family had many surprises in store for us. Often I looked to Casey for my cues. Although she had come into this life only a few months before me, I wondered if Jake had been more open with her about his childhood than Kyle had been with me. I pondered if that was because he'd been conditioned to keep quiet to protect Jake's privacy, and safeguarding his family from scrutiny had just become his way of life.

We followed the guys into the house and were instantly met by Michelle, who lavished attention on all four of us. I hugged Michelle politely and watched the fun and vibrant Casey chat her up something fierce. Clearly she was loved by the family and just blended in effortlessly. I wondered if I'd ever possess that ease.

"I'm ready." Quinn appeared in boxers and nothing else. His hair was wild from sleep, as if he'd just rolled out of bed to greet us.

"I can see that," Kyle grinned, taking in his little brother's scantily clad body. "What exactly are you ready for?"

"I'm coming with you. I'll hang out with your sister," he said, flicking his head in my direction. "While you guys go camping."

"You and Caroline are still friends?" I asked in surprise.

"Yeah. We've had a Snapchat streak going for ninety-three days," Quinn said, looking quite impressed with himself.

"Wow, a ninety-three day Snapchat streak, huh," Jake said, nodding. "Sounds serious."

"What happened to your girlfriend?" I asked, my motherly instincts kicking in, as I felt a need to protect my little sister from this half-naked teenage player.

"It's over. She cheated on me with the quarterback."

Michelle turned away from her youngest son and mouthed, "Thank god."

"Well, you know," Kyle replied, "you can never trust a sixteen-year-old with a belly button ring."

"Nope, it's a scientific fact," Casey pitched in.

"Sorry, Quinn," Jake said. "But Kenzie and Casey did the packing, so we don't have any room, unless you want to be strapped to the roof."

"That's what I figured," Quinn shrugged. "I can't go anyway. My band has that gig at the fair this weekend. I was just going to see what you said. And, of course, I wasn't invited."

"Geez, am I detecting some poor self esteem? Mom, maybe Quinn needs some therapy," Kyle stated. He and Michelle exchanged a look, and I got the impression she wasn't pleased with his comment. It was times like this that I understood there was a lot more to this family than met the eye.

Jake jumped in to change the subject by addressing Quinn, asking, "You're not playing all cover songs, are you?"

"Pretty much, yeah."

"Not just any cover songs. I'm going to bet they're all your songs," Kyle said to Jake.

"Shut up, Kyle!" Quinn exclaimed.

"Dude," Jake shook his head. "If you want to be taken seriously, you need to play your own stuff."

"Well, funny you mention that, because I have a brother who is this world-renowned singer-songwriter, and he's been promising me for months to help polish up the songs I've written, but he keeps flaking."

"Oh, wait," Jake smirked. "Is he talking about me?"

Casey smacked him and said to Quinn, "I promise I'll make him find a free day as soon as we get back."

"I'll believe it when I see it."

"Where does this go?" Jake asked, holding up a floppy tent pole. "I think it's broken."

"That's the piece that makes the roof, dumbass," Kyle insulted.

"If the roof is three feet tall, dickhead!" Jake spat back.

Casey and I exchanged a look. These boys had no clue what they were doing.

"It's possible we'll be sleeping in the truck tonight," she whispered.

"Honestly, I had higher hopes for Kyle. He survived over a month camping with no provisions, and just look at him. I mean, I'm embarrassed *for* him."

"I don't blame you," Casey shook her head. "Jake I can understand. His idea of camping is a Motel 6 with spotty cable, but Kyle… no, just no excuse."

We both snickered at our superiority. It had taken nine hours of driving to get to the campground, and if the guys didn't get their act together soon, the sun was going to go down, making tent building a hell of a lot more difficult.

"Watch this," Casey said, blocking her voice with her hand so only I could hear. "I love messing with him." Then she called out, "Jake, I think you put that thingy into the other thingy."

Jake reached down and picked up another pole, looking totally confused. "Can you be more specific? What thingy are you talking about?"

"That one. No not that thingy, Jake. The *other* thingy," Casey said, then turned to me with a wicked smile on her face and said, "I can do this all day."

"You're terrible," I giggled.

"Being an awesome woman just has so many advantages," Casey teased.

And she was right. There really was no female I enjoyed hanging out with more than her. I loved the way she kept things light and fun. From what Kyle had related to me, she'd changed Jake for the better, and I could see how. For all the hardships he'd suffered in life, Casey was definitely his shiny, beautiful reward.

Once all the 'thingys' had found their proper places, we were the proud owners of two very shoddy looking tents. Then came the interior decorating phase of the operation. Jake and Casey went all in and decked out their tent like it was an episode of *Pimp My Digs.* Jake had bought two very comfy looking queen-size self-inflating air mattresses with triple layers of awesomeness. The damn things even had inflatable headboards attached. I was happily filling ours with air when Kyle pulled me aside.

"I want us to have the full experience," he'd said. "We're tough, Kenzie. Let's just live off the land… like old times."

Although my preference would have been to use the fancy schmancy mattresses bought by a multi-millionaire, no doubt of excellent quality, I also wanted to make Kyle happy, so I followed his lead. As the others lavishly decorated their home away from home, Kyle and I went the no frills route. It took us no time at all to adorn our tent with two sleeping bags, two pillows, and a pair of flashlights. Because our setup was so quick, we treated ourselves to a beer while we waited for Jake and Casey to finish embellishing their architectural masterpiece.

Kyle and I watched them go back and forth to the truck like it was some sporting event. A battery-powered light, heater, and fan as well as a side table, rug, sheets, pillows, and plush looking blankets.

"What the hell are they doing?" Kyle asked.

"I don't know. Is all that stuff going to fit?" I whispered back.

"God, they're such amateurs," he said and we both laughed with the haughty air of undisputed supremacy.

When they finally joined us, the two looked exhausted by their efforts.

"You sure you got everything?" I teased. "I think you forgot the kitchen sink."

"You laugh, but who's going to be all snug tonight?" Casey asked, clinking her beer bottle against Jake's.

"We are, baby," he answered back.

After dinner, Jake and Kyle brought out their guitars, and we sat around the fire chatting and listening to them play. I'd been awestruck the first time I heard Kyle on the guitar. Although he'd told me that he sucked, it became perfectly clear that he'd grossly underestimated his talent. Not only was he incredibly skilled at the guitar but Kyle also had a beautiful voice. He was reluctant to share it with me at first, but once he understood how much I loved hearing him sing, he let his guard down.

Casey and I finagled ourselves a little mini concert, throwing out requests of songs we wanted to hear. I was impressed to discover Jake knew the words to just about every song we pitched to him. Of course, Casey couldn't help but mess with Jake and conspired with me to request the saddest songs possible for him to sing. After playing *Cat's in the Cradle*, *Tears in Heaven*, and *Without You*, he finally caught on to our little game and refused to play any more of our choices.

It was after ten o'clock and the guys were still quietly strumming their guitars when the light beam of a flashlight made its way into camp.

"Folks, just reminding you it's quiet hour now," the ranger said.

"Okay, thanks, man. We'll be quiet," Jake replied.

"You all sound pretty good. I play a little guitar myself."

"Oh, yeah? That's cool?"

The ranger puffed out his chest and boasted, "I'm actually quite good. Play in a popular band and everything."

"Is that right?" Jake sat up straighter, his interest piqued. "What kind of music?"

"Rock, folk, country, even throw in a little rap now and then."

"Wow, I'm impressed. That's a lot of genres to master," Jake replied, and to his credit, kept a totally straight face. The fact that the ranger didn't know he was talking to an actual 'popular' musician had me assuming it was too dark out or that he'd been living his life under a rock. With this particular dude, either option seemed possible.

"Yeah, well, it's hard work. We're called The Seedlings. If you're from these parts, you've probably heard of us."

I exchanged an amused glance with Casey. If this guy only knew!

"No, I'm from the LA area, but good for you, man."

"Yep, well, you folks have a good night. And keep the music down."

"We will, thanks."

The ranger was striding out of our camp when he turned around and said, "Oh, almost forgot. There was a bear sighting a few sites over, so make sure you put your food in the lockboxes. Looks like it might be a female with her cub. Those mamas can get pretty aggressive, so don't engage with either of them. All right, then, folks. Have a great evening."

If I could have taken a picture of all our faces at that moment, it would have been a Pulitzer Prize-winning photograph. After the initial shock wore off, I took control, barking out orders to my shell-shocked fellow campers. Being from this area, it certainly wasn't my first experience with bears, far from it, but it was the first time I'd ever seen such a strong reaction. It would have been funny if the bears weren't already 'a few sites over.'

After gathering our food and shoving it into the lockboxes, the four of us huddled in our barren tent because Casey and Jake's was so full of luxury items there wasn't room for four bodies to fit inside. With two flashlights between us, we sat in silence, reacting to every broken twig or falling pinecone.

"Guys, relax, it's just a bear. I'm sure they're more afraid of us than we are of them," I said, in an attempt to be the voice of reason.

"No offense, Kenzie," Jake said. "But I can almost guarantee you that's not the case in this particular situation."

"Maybe mama bear is eating another camper right now," Kyle whispered, his voice full of hope.

"Doubtful," Jake answered, his tone rife with foreboding as he shined the flashlight up on his face. "We'd hear the bloodcurdling screams."

"And the ripping of flesh from bone," Casey added, with a disturbing horror movie chuckle.

I glanced at Kyle, who was obviously not finding this as amusing as the rest of us. I hooked my arm in his to show my support. Although we had survived the elements on the island, we'd never encountered a dangerous animal.

"You're not worried?" he asked me.

"Not really. Bears are pretty common around here. If you leave them alone, they'll usually leave you alone."

"Usually?"

"I mean, there have been instances…" I hesitated, recalling a recent bear attack.

"Instances?"

"What do you want her to say, Kyle? It's a bear. Sometimes they eat people," Jake answered, helpfully. "Besides, I don't know what you're worried about. With my luck, if that bear attacks, we all know who'll get ripped to shreds."

"No, Jake, with your luck, you'll be the only one to survive."

"The media would go wild. Jake McKallister, bear-attack survivor," Casey teased.

"Right, because they've got nothing else exciting to write about me."

"Can you guys be any louder? Jesus. You might as well be calling them over for a nice meaty snack," my irritated boyfriend complained.

"So Kyle," Jake asked. "On a scale from one to ten, how much do you want Mom right now?"

A low, rumble of hysteria burst forth from the four of us and we had to hush our laughter so as not to beckon an angry bear.

"Honestly, I'm at, like, a twelve. That furry-assed fear-monger has nothing on our mom."

Our tormentors didn't wait long to amble into our camp. We sat in tense anticipation as the bear and her cub tried to force open the lockbox, and when that didn't work, they ripped open a plastic bag filled with beer bottles. Then, as quickly as they arrived, the bears moved on, hoping to find an even less-prepared group of campers than us.

Once they were long gone, Jake and Casey left for their five-star resort. Kyle had zipped our sleeping bags together and we both climbed inside. He held his arms open for me and I snuggling up to his warm, inviting body.

"I thought they'd never leave," I whispered in his ear, as I nibbled on his tender flesh.

"It's so nice, isn't it?" Kyle reminisced, a happy smile on his face. "Just living off the land like old times?"

"It is," I answered, not really paying attention to his Bear Grylls fascination with the wild. I was only interested in one thing, and that was him. Dropping my hands below the waist, I unbuttoned his jeans. That was all it took to curtail his nature ramblings and get focused on me. And the lustful look in his eye was all I needed to throw myself at him. We were grinding into each other and kissing fervently when a loud vacuum sound emitted from the adjacent tent. Kyle looked at me in confusion. The ruckus went on for at least a minute, disturbing the peaceful quiet that could only be experienced on a night spent in the wilderness.

"What the hell was that?" Kyle called over to his brother.

"Sorry, we were filling our bed with more air," Casey answered.

Kyle rolled his eyes in disgust. "Well, are you done now?"

"Yep. Sooo comfy. Thanks for asking."

I laughed and said, "You guys enjoy your high thread count Egyptian cotton sheets, you hear?"

"Oh, you know we will, Kenzie," Jake answered, in a suggestive tone. "And you be sure to enjoy the cold, hard ground."

Kyle's face took on a wicked grin. "Don't you worry, Princess, we will."

———

Once quiet had returned to the campground, Kyle regained his composure and asked, "Where were we?"

"About here." I smiled back seductively, brushing my hand past his dick.

"Oh, yeah."

We gleefully resumed where we'd left off. Kyle flipped me onto my back and hovered over me as we continued our make-out session. As he laid his arm to my side, he flinched in pain. "Ow!"

"What?"

"A rock or something. Damn, that hurt." He sat up and rubbed the spot, but just then his knee smacked into an embedded tree root. "Ow, shit."

"Let's scoot over," I encouraged, not yet willing to give up on our tent sex. We both moved further into the tent, and then, regaining some of his lustfulness, Kyle lowered himself over me once again. But while I was running my hands up his back, I felt a sharp pain pinch into mine. "Ow… rock… Kyle, get off, there's a rock. It just stabbed into my back."

We both sat up and he pulled my shirt up to reveal a little bloody puncture wound.

"Dammit, where's that first aid kit?" he asked.

"In the truck, I think."

Kyle trudged out to get the kit for me, and by the time I was all patched up, neither one of us was in the mood anymore. We moved the sleeping bags again and found the least offensive spot possible, and even that was incredibly uncomfortable. As we lay awake, staring up through the mesh ceiling at the stars in the sky, Kyle mumbled, "Well, this sucks."

"I know," I giggled. "How did we ever manage to survive over a month in the wilderness?"

"No clue. Honestly, I'm so frickin' jealous of Jake and Casey right now."

"I know. I don't think we're cut out for rustic living."

"No, I think you're right," Kyle agreed. "I just like my housecat lifestyle too much to put up with this shit."

"Promise me tomorrow night we'll get our very own noisy air mattress."

"Only the finest for you, Babe."

KYLE

Driving over the bridge on the way into Kenzie's hometown, it was clear something was up. Flags were festively attached to all the posts.

"What's with all the decorations?" I asked.

"I have no idea," she answered, and abruptly changed the subject. "I'm so excited to see my family."

Her face was alive with joy, and as always when I looked at her nowadays, I quaked a little inside. Every cute little thing she did gave me that strange tingling feeling. Although I'd been slow to recognize what it was, now I understood. I was in love. The only thing left was to tell her. For whatever reason, the time never seemed right. And the longer it went, the more nervous I became. How hard could it be to utter three little words? I loved her; yet I kept it to myself, waiting for something… although I wasn't sure what.

I watched out the window as we drove the long road into town. Flags and ribbons also adorned the countryside. It seemed they were having some event. That would be fun. Maybe it was a fair. Then it hit me. I turned to Kenzie.

"No!" I blurted out dramatically. "Please tell me… oh, god, Kenzie. Could it be?"

The smile on her face was as wide as it could get. Her eyes sparkled as she nodded her head joyfully.

"But you said it was in June."

"I lied." Kenzie grinned.

"Oh, my god!" I screamed, slapping my hands on the ceiling of the truck.

"What is your problem?" Jake asked irritably. "You're going to cause an accident."

"It's Udder's Day!" I sang out. "It's frickin' Udder's Day. Kenzie, you've just made me the happiest man alive."

I seriously could not have been more excited to experience Udder's Day for myself and was feeling like a kid at Christmas. Since Kenzie revealed its existence to me all those months ago, Udder's Day had become a running joke of ours. I swear I knew all the ins and outs of this unique festival.

We pulled into the driveway of her one-story Victorian-style home.

"Ahh, this is cute, Kenz," Casey complimented. "This whole town is so cool, like going back in time."

"Yeah, it's back in time, all right," Kenzie answered, clearly not as impressed as we were. I could hardly blame her. As fun as it was to visit, I wouldn't want to grow up here either. I needed a little more action than this place had to offer. And besides, when I was home from tour, I had a strict rule that wherever I lived needed to be within a seven-mile radius of a Taco Bell.

Kenzie's dad, Bruce, and her siblings came out of the house when we pulled up. Aside from meeting them briefly at the final taping, we hadn't seen each other since Kenzie and I had gotten together. And we certainly hadn't seen each other since I'd moved in with his daughter. I wasn't sure how much her dad would appreciate that little tidbit. Nervously, I stepped out of the car and was all ready to greet her family when I saw where their eyes were focused… on Jake, and they were sufficiently awed.

"Did you not tell them he was coming?" I asked.

"No. I knew they wouldn't be able to keep a secret, and then the whole town would have shown up… and I'm not kidding."

Kenzie jumped out of the truck to facilitate the introductions.

"Guys," she called out. No one turned to her. "Guys!" she shouted a bit louder, shocking them from their trance.

"This is Jake and his fiancée, Casey. Be nice and close your mouths. You all look like Venus fly traps."

"Nice to meet you." Jake stepped forward, extending his hand.

"Oh, geez, sorry, we're being rude," Bruce said, grasping it. "We just, you know, don't have celebrities visiting very often."

"What do you mean, Dad? Kanye was here last week," Colton joked.

We went around doing the introductions before following the Williams into their modest home.

Bruce, still seeming stunned, stammered, "I wasn't expecting four of you, especially not… uh… you," he said, staring again at Jake as if he still couldn't believe his eyes. "We'll, um, figure out sleeping arrangements."

"They're staying at the bed and breakfast," Kenzie said. "It'll just be Kyle and me, as planned."

"Oh, that's good," he sighed, and then caught himself. "I didn't mean you weren't welcome to stay, I'd just… you know, have to clean the toilet…"

Casey giggled.

"Dad, it's okay. Relax. Everything's covered."

I saw her mouth to Bruce, 'You didn't clean the toilet?' and he shrugged his response. Jake, Casey, and I exchanged amused glances. Apparently I wasn't worth a clean toilet, but Jake certainly was. Maybe Kenzie should have thought through her surprise visit.

"Thanks for having us." I stepped up, in an attempt to stem the awkwardness.

"Oh, yeah, yeah. Of course. It's great to see you again, Kyle. I hear you're a fan of Udder's Day?"

"I am, and I hear you own a cow costume."

"I do." He grinned, looking more relaxed. "Just say the word and it's yours."

"Ooh, wow, such a nice offer. Actually, I was thinking Jake could wear it."

Jake whipped his head around. "Wait, what's a cow costume?"

"Pretty much exactly what it sounds like," I answered, and then turned to the others. "Sorry, he doesn't get out much."

I got a good laugh at my brother's expense. Always my favorite kind.

"Why should *I* wear it?" he complained.

"So no one will recognize you."

"I'd actually rather take a thousand pictures with fans than wear a cow costume."

"And so you will," Kenzie patted his shoulder. "It should be a fun day for you."

"As long as we can pull him away from the crowds long enough so I can get a picture of him milking a cow," Casey said.

"Okay, I don't understand how Kyle's special day has suddenly become my nightmare."

Since none of us had showered in two days, Kenzie and Casey went off to clean up first, and something told me my embarrassed girlfriend would be doing a quick toilet scrub while she was at it. Bruce hung around talking to us for a few minutes and then excused himself to go pick up lunch. That left Jake and me to fend for ourselves with the three C's. Caroline talked non-stop and would just randomly snap photos of us and send them off right in the middle of the conversation. Not to be outdone, Cooper and Colton were one-upping each other in an attempt, apparently, to impress us. Moments later the argument started. First came the f-bombs, and then came the fists. The boys tumbled their way through the living room, knocking over a side table in the process. Jake and I watched wide-eyed and entertained as the boys went at it. I'd never seen anything escalate that quickly.

Kenzie, her hair wet and tangled, rounded the corner with an angry look on her face. She got right between the two boys, grabbed their arms, and, without saying a word, marched them to the front door and pushed them both outside. Then she turned around and walked back to the bedroom without even glancing in our direction.

Caroline, who'd been forced to stop talking during her brothers' brawl, continued her conversation the minute Cooper and Colton were safely killing each other outside.

"So do you mind, then?" she asked.

Jake and I exchanged a look.

"Mind what?" I questioned. I couldn't recall her asking us anything before the MMA fight began.

"If my friends come over? They just want to meet you guys."

"Oh, I don't know," I said. "Maybe you should ask your sister first."

"She won't care."

"How about we meet them later at the festival? Your dad's bringing back lunch, and he probably doesn't have enough for everyone," Jake reasoned.

"Oh. I already told them to come."

"Okay, then." Jake looked my way, grinning.

I was trying to come up with another excuse when the knock came at the door and four teenage girls filed in. *Damn, that was fast.* People sure hustled in small towns.

Jake and I spent the next few minutes talking to a bunch of giggly girls and snapping selfies with each and every one of them before Bruce walked through the door followed by the boys, who were sporting grass stains on their identical faces.

"What is going on here?" he bellowed. "Caroline!"

"What?" she asked, feigning innocence.

He shook his head, looking at us apologetically, and then opened the door wider and shooed the girls out.

J. BENGTSSON

"Sorry. Now that Kenzie's gone, they're out of frickin' control."

Yeah, it was clear Bruce was in way over his head. Taking pity on the poor man, Jake and I pretended like nothing had happened, but our alone time with Kenzie's siblings would go down as one of the highlights of our trip.

We wandered through the old Victorian street taking in the sights, sounds, and cow manure smells of Udder's Day. Jake, as always, was quite a draw; but instead of the thousand pictures he'd predicted, only a few dozen people actually stopped him. The same couldn't be said for Kenzie and me. *Marooned* was a popular television show, but certainly being a cast member didn't bring instant recognition in the general public – unless that public lived right here in this little village. We were like veritable celebrities in these parts. It appeared everyone, and his or her cow, had tuned in to watch the hometown girl compete on the show.

To my complete surprise, strangers were coming up to me and quoting lines I'd apparently said on the island. Half the stuff I didn't even remember, but they sure as hell did. So bombarded were we with well-wishers and picture-takers that Jake and Casey slipped away to wander through the general store undisturbed.

Kenzie was welcomed home with open arms. The love and warmth surrounding her gave me a clearer picture of

522

how she'd come to be the woman she was today. It would have been easy for her to fall through the cracks after her mother passed away, but by her own admission, these people had lifted her up. For all my wisecracks about her lifestyle, I finally got the appeal of growing up like she had. I still wouldn't want it for myself – because, you know, of the Taco Bell issue – but I certainly wasn't going to knock those who chose the quieter way of life.

As I watched her interact with the grace and ease I'd come to admire and love, I felt myself turning all mushy again. Kenzie had that effect on me. I needed to just tell her how I was feeling and get it over with. The anticipation was killing me.

She looked up from a little blond-haired admirer and beamed at me, "Are you good? Is it too much?"

"I'm great. It couldn't be more perfect."

She walked over to me and put her hand in mine. Overwhelmed with affection for this woman, I pulled her into my arms. This was my chance. We were in a warm embrace, gazing adoringly into each other's eyes. There could not have been a more perfect time to tell her I loved her.

"What does this smell like to you?" My brother interrupted the most intensely romantic moment of my life to thrust a round, smelly bath balm under my nose.

"What the…?" I whipped around.

"I seriously think there's pot in this thing. They say its hemp seed oil, but I'm not buying it," Jake whispered, conspiratorially.

"We're going to have ourselves a bath tonight," Casey sang out.

"Casey, please, we've talked about your singing," he responded with a straight face.

And just like that the mood was ruined, making me regret inviting those two along in the first place. A woman in a Victorian-style dress and fancy headpiece hurried up to us. "Kenzie, Kyle… Would you follow me? The parade starts in a few minutes, and your float's ready for you."

Casey looked on in amusement. "Damn, this just gets better and better."

"You can't make this stuff up," Jake agreed.

Leaving the others behind, Kenzie and I were led down a few side streets until we came to the row of parade vehicles. For a town this size, I was sufficiently impressed with the number of participants. It seemed there would be no one left on the streets to watch. We passed a wide assortment of vehicles until the swanky hat lady stopped at ours. We'd been given the pimp spot, and it was no wonder. Our float was a goddamn masterpiece. Someone had painstakingly recreated our home away from home. The island was sitting on the back of a flatbed truck. In the center was a replica of the tree I'd climbed so many times. Purple fruits hung from the papier mâché branches.

"Did you know about this?" I asked her in amusement.

"Not this!" she replied, as wide-eyed as I was. "I knew we'd be in the parade, but this goes above and beyond. You're not mad, are you?"

"Are you kidding? I love it. Do we have to strip down?" I asked. "Because I totally will."

She laughed. "I think clothes are preferred on this island."

I helped her onto our private oasis and then gamely followed her up. As the parade began, so did the syrupy music. The strange song blared from the speakers on top of our float... and played on repeat.

"What is this awful song?" I asked, grimacing when it started for the third time.

Kenzie blushed. "It's the theme song from *Blue Lagoon*."

"Of course it is," I shook my head, grinning. "Man these people sure know their reality shows."

"You aren't kidding. I'm embarrassed," Kenzie said. "Sorry."

"Don't be. This is awesome," I yelled over the music. As pathetic as it sounded, I was giddy with excitement as we rolled through the town practicing our princess waves to the enthusiastic crowds below. It was more than just a corny parade to me. Instead it was an opportunity to re-live a slice of my childhood that I'd missed out on. Only twelve when life turned dark, I'd been following a jaded path ever since. Kenzie helped open my eyes to a different way of life, simpler and full of possibilities. It was what had attracted me to this woman standing beside me - the one who was happily blowing kisses into the wind. I grabbed her around the waist and pulled her to me.

Startled she looked up at me. I took her face in my hands and kissed her for all the world to see. Okay, for maybe just a tiny slice of the world, but still the intention was clear. I wanted everyone to know how I felt about this girl, and the crowd roared their approval.

"What was that for?" she replied breathlessly, her eyes sparkling with joy.

"I love you, that's what it's for."

The End

Made in the USA
Middletown, DE
26 September 2023

38943026R00312